SPELLS AND CELLS

A Spellbinder Bay Cozy Paranormal Mystery -
Book Three

SAM SHORT

www.samshortauthor.com

For my family. There are too many members to name here, but I love each and every one of you.

Chapter 1

*M*illie Thorn took a steadying breath and adjusted the strap of the apron which dug into the back of her neck. She didn't enjoy feeling so out of her depth, but that was precisely how she felt. Out. Of. Her. Depth.

She didn't feel out of her depth with life in general. No, life, in general, was pretty good if she were being honest. In fact, life, in general, was perfect for a twenty-four-year-old woman who'd found out less than a year ago that she was a witch. A wealthy witch, at that — which was a pleasant bonus, and a witch who came from a long line of coven witches, whose innate magic kept at bay the evil forces wishing to cross into the world from another dimension known as The Chaos.

Being responsible for ensuring a dimensional gate remained locked, would, Millie imagined, make the average person feel out of their depth. But not her. Not anymore, anyway.

Neither did the fact that her dead mother had visited her from the other side, make her feel out of her depth. Although the news about the identity of Millie's father which had accompanied her mother on the ghostly visit, *had* affected her. Deeply. And it still did. Yet, that unexpected news hadn't contributed to her current out of her depth experience, either.

Yes, the news had confused her. She'd spent her life believing that she'd been conceived during a brief tryst between her mother and a man who had vanished into society before he could be alerted to his impending status as a father. Of course the news had confused her. The fact that a person's mother would lie to them about who their father was would confuse most people, she imagined.

The news about her father had made her angry, too, but Millie had managed to put it out of her mind, to the best of her ability. Not forever, of course — she'd promised herself that she'd confront the dilemma head-on when she'd had time to think it through properly and work out how to approach the man in question — a good man who had no idea that he was her father. Not only would Millie's life be turned on its head when she told her father that she was his daughter, but so would his, and the life of his adopted daughter, who Millie happened to like very much.

Judith was her best friend, after all, so liking her

was pretty much a standard requirement. She would tell the man eventually; she'd promised herself and her familiar as much, but she would choose the time wisely — she had no urgent appetite for turning other people's lives upside down. It could wait. *It would have to wait.*

Although all the things that had happened to her had made Millie question the meaning of life, and whether there was something in the Spellbinder Bay water supply — none of those things could be held accountable for the squirming sensation of self-doubt she felt right at *that* very moment. The sensation which made her mouth dry and her stomach queasy — the unsettling feeling of being entirely out of her depth.

No, the reason for her immediate uneasiness could be put down to her current surroundings, and more to the point, the group of people populating her current surroundings. Some of them, anyway.

She took another deep breath and gazed around the classroom at the expectant faces. Twelve of the faces, their owners dutifully standing behind their shared bench desks, dressed in school uniforms protected with blue aprons emblazoned with the school's coat of arms, belonged to her pupils. The other twenty or so older faces belonged to the children's parents, and it was this more mature audience, who huddled at the rear of the cookery classroom with their backs to the large ornate windows offering sweeping views of the sea, which made Millie feel so uneasy.

Not every child had a parent present at the back of the classroom, waiting to heap praise upon their offspring when he or she displayed their burgeoning culinary skills. Eleven of the children had at least one of their parents standing behind them. Not the thin boy with the deep brown eyes and straw-like hair, though.

He'd repeatedly glanced nervously at the clock when his mother had failed to arrive at the appropriate time, and had nobody present to witness his cooking skills being put into action in a classroom environment.

Aware that Norman, the quiet and unassuming young werewolf, came from a tumultuous home, Millie had felt a heart-wrenching sympathy for him when his mother had failed to arrive. Nonetheless, Norman remained as eager as the other pupils to display his skills to the waiting adults, a resilience demonstrated by the young man which Millie considered highly admirable.

Peeling her eyes from Norman, Millie turned her nervous gaze back to the parents. The fact that cookery lessons had been taken off the school curriculum thirty years previously, following a fatal accident involving magic, a teacher who had developed witch dementia, and an oven, had made Millie realise just how much trust the parents were putting in her.

She was, after all, responsible for their children's safety — in a magical school, and more to the point — in the *exact* room in which a person had perished the last time cookery lessons had been on the curriculum.

Millie was not only charged with teaching the youngsters how to bake a cake or roast potatoes, she was also entrusted with ensuring that none of the children was, through an accident of magic, turned into a soufflé mix and baked to death in an oven. The fact that it had been the teacher, and not a pupil who had met her untimely demise at gas mark seven for eleven minutes, or so the story went, did make Millie wonder if it was her own or the children's safety she should be most concerned with.

She knew she was at no risk, really. The facts about the case of the so-called soufflé death, which Millie had managed to glean from the few people who could barely remember it, all pointed to the fact that the teacher in question had been suffering from witch dementia and shouldn't really have been teaching at all. Especially in such a potentially hazardous environment as a room full of ovens, children, and sharp blades.

The exact circumstances which saw her being transferred to a hot oven after accidentally turning herself into the soufflé mix, were not entirely clear, but with a busy classroom full of children, each making their own soufflé, understandable, at least.

Millie refocused on the small crowd at the rear of

the room and licked her lips. She smiled at the woman with the long nose who seemed to be waiting for her to say something. In fact, everybody seemed to be waiting for her to speak. What had she got herself into? Speaking to a group of children was one thing, but speaking to the parents was another. It was equivalent to public speaking, for heaven's sake. Not something she relished.

Who'd have thought that she, Millie Thorn, would ever have become a teacher? In her defence, when she'd agreed to take the job of part-time cookery teacher in Spellbinder Hall, revitalising the classroom with new ovens and equipment in the process, she hadn't *fully* realised that she'd be agreeing to shoulder all the responsibilities of a *real* teacher.

She'd envisioned herself teaching non-judgmental young teens how to cook, but she had not envisaged herself being involved in a school open day presentation of the cookery skills the youngsters had acquired under her tutelage. The unpleasant sensation of being under the microscope, gazed through by the parents, was not one which Millie much liked, and she licked her dry lips again as she gazed once more at her waiting audience.

Realising with growing anxiety that a few of the adults appeared to be visibly bored, Millie smiled at one of the parents, who, presumably concerned by the blank look which Millie imagined was pasted on her face, looked like she wanted to hug her child's cookery teacher. A pity hug was not something Millie wanted to be one half of, so digging deep and finding a thin sliver of courage, somewhere near her spleen, she took a long breath and opened her mouth to speak.

The word her brain ordered her mouth to speak had supposed to be 'hello,' but instead of a friendly greeting, a strangled gasp of fear left her lips as a towering figure shrouded in long loose black robes emerged from the white painted wall to her left. The shimmering upper body of the apparition flickered in and out of what Millie was struggling to consider as being reality, and passed through a poster advocating the necessity of vigorous hand cleanliness before participation in food preparation, before slinking slowly towards the corner.

Although having come to terms with the presence of the multitude of paranormal species who lived in the coastal town of Spellbinder Bay, Millie was still working on being calm around some of the ghosts that populated the town and school. Especially the ones who didn't speak and insisted on covering their faces. *The scary ones.*

A cold shudder ran up Millie's spine as the new arrival to the classroom stopped moving and stood silently, looming over the living people, its head bowed and its dark robes semi-transparent. A silent observer.

"Is that a new ghost?" said one of the male parents, watching the apparition as it lifted its head, any face it may have had hidden in the shadows cast by the drooping hood it wore.

"It certainly wasn't one of the ghosts I was aware of when I was a pupil here at Spellbinder Hall," said a woman wearing a wide-brimmed hat. "It must be new. The person must have died after I left school." She looked the ghost up and down. "Or hundreds of years ago. They do say that some ghosts take centuries to appear after their body dies. I definitely never saw it when I was a pupil, though."

One of the pupils giggled and turned to face the parents. The short, red-haired boy, who Millie knew to be a vampire, gave another laugh as he addressed the woman who had spoken. "The dinosaurs were still roaming the planet when you were a pupil here, Mum," he said. "You're probably way older than that ghost!"

"You cheeky little thing, William," said the woman, with a deep laugh, accompanied by the laughter of the other pupils and some of the parents. "I'm not that old!"

Another of the boys spoke up. A young male witch named Jeremy, whose quick grasp of everything Millie had taught the class over the past month, was fast propelling him to the position of the star pupil, although Millie would never voice that accolade out loud to the rest of the class. She had to remember to pretend that every pupil was as bright as the next, even if one of the other boys in the class, a stocky werewolf named Harry, had genuinely believed that coconut milk was produced by cows which lived in the tropics. "Oh, you were a pupil here once? You're a vampire born to vampire parents, are you, Mrs Jackson?" he enquired. "You weren't bitten and turned into a vampire? You were actually a vampire child once? That's cool!"

"Jeremy!" warned a tall man, who Millie presumed was the young witch's father. "You know it's rude to ask a vampire how they came into existence! Especially a female vampire!" He gave Mrs Jackson, whose cheeks had taken on a red tinge, an apologetic smile. "I'm so sorry, Francine. He wasn't brought up to be so rude!"

"Oh, that's fine, Raymond! I don't get offended that easily," said Mrs Jackson, with a wave of her hand.

"I'm sorry for asking you personal questions, Mrs Jackson," said Jeremy, wilting under the stern glare of his father.

Mrs Jackson gave the young witch a soft smile and adjusted her hat. "I accept your apology, Jeremy, now let it be forgotten."

"Mrs Jackson?" said Katie, the girl with bouncing brown hair and forest green eyes, standing at the long bench nearest to Millie. "Jeremy's dad just called you Francine… were you known as Frannie when you were a pupil here at Spellbinder Hall? And did you attend cookery classes?"

If the girl's eyes had been brown, Millie suspected that had she been the same age as the younger witch, they'd have been hard to tell apart. Aside from the slight bend in Millie's nose which Katie did not possess, or the very shallow cleft in Millie's chin which was also absent on the younger witch's smiling face, they could easily have been mistaken for being members of the same family.

Wondering whether she should intervene and move the focus back to the reason the children and adults were gathered in a classroom on a Friday afternoon — the children's cooking accomplishments, and away from the group conversation which seemed to be developing, Millie took another look at the sinister ghost which stood silently in the corner. She shuddered. Perhaps she'd allow the conversation between parents and children to continue until she was more comfortable about the fact that a robed and hooded apparition appeared to be gazing in her direction from the shadows of its hood.

Mrs Jackson cocked her head inquisitively as she answered Katie's question. "Yes," she confirmed. "Although nobody has called me by *that* name for years, I *was* known as Frannie during my school years, and yes — I did attend cookery classes. We all did in those days, it wasn't a choice like it was for you guys, every pupil was required to attend cookery classes — until the unfortunate incident which forced the closure of this classroom."

"You mean the unfortunate incident involving the teacher who was cooked in the oven?" said Harry, from his position on the bench nearest the rear of the classroom. "That story is so cool!"

A pear-shaped woman stepped forward from

among the group of adults, her hair a disordered mass of curls. "Harry! It was not cool! I happened to be in this classroom when it happened. It was awful, as I've told you many times before! It's certainly not something we laugh about!" She dropped her eyes, and her shoulders slumped. "Poor Miss Timkins. What an awful way to go — turned into a soufflé mix and then baked in an oven."

"I'm sorry, Mum," said Harry. "I know it's not a laughing matter. I won't mention it again. I promise."

Giving the ghost in the corner a sideways glance, Millie cleared her throat. It was time for her to take back control of her classroom. That much was obvious. "If everybody is ready," she said, surprised at the authority her voice conveyed. "Then I think it's about time we allowed the children to begin their cookery demonstration. They've all been very excited about having the opportunity to show you what they can do, and as an extra show of their skills, they each have one of the old recipe books I found in the cupboard when I revamped this room.

"I thought the old books would bring back a few nice memories for any of you parents who once attended this classroom, and using a recipe they've never seen before, will be a good test of the children's skills — which they all possess in abundance. So much so, that as you'll discover for yourselves when you head outside to the school fete later on, they baked a lot of lovely cakes yesterday which are being sold and raffled off for the benefit of a few local charities. I'm certain that all you parents will be very proud of what your children can do."

"I'm certainly very proud of Emma," said a timid voice from the back of the group of adults. "She's a better cook than I was at her age."

"You were a wonderful cook, Beth," said Francine. "Don't put yourself down. You were one of the best cooks in our class!"

"I don't think so," mumbled Beth, looking at the floor. "Anyway, I just wanted Emma to know how proud I am of her."

"That's lovely to hear," said Millie, smiling at the short woman who blushed deep crimson as she attracted everybody's attention. "And Emma is always very enthusiastic in every lesson. It's been a pleasure to teach her." She cast her eyes over the other parents. "It's been a pleasure to teach *all* the children," she added quickly.

Teaching the children had been a pleasure — that wasn't a lie, but it had been a more fulfilling pleasure to watch Emma, the shy young witch, coming out of her shell and gaining confidence amongst her peers as the term had progressed. Millie had genuinely enjoyed teaching her, and gave her a sly wink as she caught her eye. The girl blushed as bright as her mother had, and Millie felt a tinge of sadness that Emma's mother's apparent nervousness had been passed onto her daughter.

"We're all very proud of the children," said Mrs Jackson, "but before we go any further with the cooking demonstration, I'd like to ask Katie why she asked if I was once known as Frannie. That question came very much out of the blue."

Katie pointed at the open book on the bench before her. "There's graffiti written in my old cookery book, Mrs Jackson," she explained, with a smirk. "Written in red ink. It says, 'I love Frannie,' and it's written inside a heart with an arrow through it."

"Well, I'm sure I don't know who could have written that about me," said Mrs Jackson, appearing to grow an inch or two as she puffed out her ample chest and fluttered her long eyelashes.

"Oh, all the boys fancied you, Francine," said an overweight woman standing next to her. "And you know it!"

"Did they?" said Francine, a smile spreading over her face. "I can't say I ever noticed."

"There's graffiti in my book, too!" said Jeremy. "It says 'Spotty Cecil is as thick as this recipe book!' That's hilarious!"

One of the other boys flipped his book open and ran his eyes over the rear of the front cover. "Somebody has written 'Miss Everest loves Mister Mop,' in my book!"

"There's writing in mine, as well," said one of the quieter girls in the class — another vampire. "It says 'hide the cakes that you bake, or Lardy Liz will eat them all and still have room for more.'" She narrowed her eyes and looked over her shoulder at the parents behind her. "What a nasty thing to say about somebody. I'm glad my generation doesn't write such horrid things inside school books."

"Yes, well, we weren't all like that, sweetheart," said a kindly looking man wearing glasses fitted with thick lenses. "Your mother and I brought you up to be nice and to never bully anybody, but when I was at school it was quite different — some of us were bullied, and some of us were —"

A loud bang, accompanied by vibrations which Millie felt running through the wooden floor, stopped the man in mid-sentence, and he jumped in fright, spinning quickly to face the doorway.

Recognising the noise as the heavy classroom door slamming into the wall, Millie turned to confront whoever it was who had barged it open with such force. Before she could speak to the scruffy man standing in the doorway, a fast-moving shadow approaching from her right forced her to flinch, and she gave a low squeal of fright as the robed ghost sped past her, one black-gloved hand raised before it, heading straight for the new arrival.

"What the heck!" shouted the man in the doorway, holding his arms out defensively as the ghost sped towards him, leaving a trail of black sparks resembling soot in its wake. His raised arms offered no protection from the apparition, and the man gave a strangled gasp as the ghost passed directly through him — the two forms, one dead and one alive, briefly melding into a shimmering mass of black robes and a scruffy denim jacket paired with dirty jeans.

As the apparition passed through him entirely, the newcomer waved his arms frantically, as if swatting at invisible flies. "Get out of here! I felt that! You're not supposed to be able to feel a ghost!" he yelled, as the apparition continued its journey across the darkened corridor outside the classroom and through the wood panelled wall opposite, choosing to make its exit below one of the stuffed owls which resided in glass cases lining the corridor. "Bloody ghosts, they're still as annoying as they were when I was unlucky enough to be a pupil here! They're almost as bad as vampires, and they're *bloody* awful… Pun intended."

The man whose sentence had been rudely interrupted by the door crashing open took a step forward and crossed his arms in what appeared to be a defensive stance. "Trevor Giles," he said, staring at the man in the doorway. "I didn't expect to see the old school bully here today. I wasn't aware you even had any children, Trevor. It seems that for some reason, which I can't quite fathom, women choose not to have children with werewolves who spend most of their time either in a police cell or a pub, so I'm not quite sure what you're doing at an open day for parents whose children attend this fine school."

Trevor chuckled under his breath and smiled menacingly at the man who had confronted him. "Just look at you, little Jimmy. You're still the same annoying little vampire you were when I was forced to go to school with you! You always were the nosy type, weren't you? You want to know why I'm here, Jimmy?

I'm here because little Norman over there in the front row is lucky enough to be able to call me his stepfather. I got married last week, to his lovely mother, Helen, who is now lucky enough to be able to call me her husband." He stepped into the classroom and strode with a swagger towards the young boy in the front row, whose face had turned white. "Isn't that right, Norman?"

Chapter 2

*H*er class having been so rudely interrupted, and with one of her pupils looking decidedly nervous as an overtly aggressive man approached him, Millie stepped forward, fully prepared to use her magic if the situation demanded it.

Although spells preventing the accidental use of magic by pupils were cast over the hall, no spells were preventing the use of magic by witches who happened to be part-time cookery teachers. Especially if their school parent's day presentation had been disrupted in such a rude fashion, by such a brash man.

Placing herself between the long bench desk which Norman stood behind, and Trevor, Millie stood as tall as she could in her flat shoes — a lot shorter than Trevor, who she estimated to be a couple of inches over six-foot. She squared her shoulders and looked the man in the eyes. "Excuse me," she said, raising a hand. "Would you mind waiting right there while I speak to Norman, please? Barging into my classroom like that was highly inappropriate. You've made the children nervous."

"You even scared that ghost away!" said Francine. "I don't think I've ever seen a ghost move so quickly. You managed to frighten the dead, that's how loud you banged that door, Trevor Giles! You should show more respect. Although respect is something you never really did understand. Or possess."

"Oh, give me a break," said Trevor, a sneer on his unshaven face. "We're not pupils here anymore, Frannie. I don't care what you think, and it's not like you can go running to the teacher telling tales on me anymore, is it?"

"She doesn't need to tell tales to a teacher, Mister Giles," said Millie. "I'm the teacher in this classroom, and I happen to think your behaviour is highly inappropriate. And I'd say that about a child, let alone a grown man."

Displaying his disinterest with a roll of his yellowed eyes, Trevor gave Millie a thin smile. "I'm just here to support Norman. His mother doesn't care about him. She drank too much gin and fell asleep on the sofa. I couldn't wake her up, so I came instead of her. One of us needs to be here to show that we care about little Norman."

"Okay!" said Millie, extending an arm and corralling Trevor forcefully towards the door, her voice a low hiss which she hoped only Trevor could hear. "That's not the sort of conversation anybody should be having in front of an audience of children. Especially in front of Norman! That's his mother you're talking about. I'd like you to leave, please, Mister Giles. Immediately."

Possibly sensing the anger brewing deep within her, or, more likely, responding to the menacing expression which tightened the muscles around Millie's eyes and mouth, Trevor allowed himself to be guided towards the door. "I'll see you when you get home tonight, Norman," he said, glancing over his shoulder. "I didn't really want to watch a bunch of kids cooking anyway. I was only here for the cheap bar I've heard is going to be available in one of the tents at the stupid little fete that's been set up in the school grounds."

"The fete is to celebrate the end of the school term, and to say goodbye to the older pupils who are moving on from Spellbinder Hall," said Millie. "It's a special day for some people, and a well earned treat for the kids — to mark the end of the school year. There's nothing stupid about it, and I won't allow you to disrupt it. There'll be no visiting the bar for you. You don't seem like the sort of man who should be drinking around children, anyway."

Trevor looked Millie up and down, his top lip curling into a cruel sneer. "And you're going to stop me, are you, little witch? You know you have no real authority here at the school. Only Henry Pinkerton and the headmaster have authority here, and Norman told me that they're both currently away on important magical business, and can't be contacted even in the case of an emergency."

It was true that Henry Pinkerton, the human manifestation of the magic which surged through Spellbinder Hall, was on an important trip with the headmaster, Mister Dickinson, but Millie was confident that the person left in charge of the school in their absence would take no nonsense from somebody like Trevor Giles. Fredrick, the vampire responsible for saving the life of Millie's so-called boyfriend, George, by biting him after a German bayonet disembowelled him during World War One, took no nonsense from anybody.

Although Millie held no love for Fredrick, and the vampire often openly showed his disdain towards Millie, especially making evident his dislike of the troubled relationship she had with his protege, George, Millie couldn't imagine him taking any nonsense from an angry werewolf such as Mister Giles. Guiding Trevor through the door, Millie nodded towards the end of the corridor. "Let's go and ask Fredrick what he thinks about you barging into my classroom and being so nasty in front of the children."

Clicking his tongue, Trevor glowered at Millie. "There's no need," he muttered. "I don't really want to be here anyway." Looking over the top of Millie's head, he pointed a finger into the classroom. "I'll see you tonight, Norman! But first, I'm going to go home to tell your mother what a huge waste of my valuable time this little trip to support her son turned out to be."

"Go on," said Millie, her words cold. "I think you'd better leave, Mister Giles."

As Trevor gave Millie one last scowl, turning his back on her and striding along the corridor, a small voice rose above the concerned murmurings of the parents in the classroom. "Miss Thorn?"

Millie gazed at the young boy who'd joined her in the dimly lit corridor, his complexion still an ashen mask of anxiety. "Norman," she said, placing a hand on the boy's shoulder. "Are you okay?"

"Please let him stay, Miss," said Norman. "Otherwise he'll be angry with Mum and me."

Fresh anger churned in Millie's gut, but she kept it from her voice and face, smiling gently at the frightened young werewolf. "Does he hurt you and your mother, Norman?" she asked.

Norman shook his head vigorously and bit his bottom lip. He dropped his eyes. "No, Miss," he said. "He doesn't hurt us, but he gets so angry. He turns into his wolf whenever he gets mad, and that scares us. He's a big wolf when he transforms, Miss. Especially compared to my wolf and my mother's wolf. Please let him stay. If he goes home in that mood, he'll take it out on Mum. I wouldn't like that. I just want things to be happy at home. I want my mum to be happy."

Millie gave a soft sigh. She looked the young boy

in his troubled eyes and spoke quietly. "I don't think I should do that, Norman. I can't allow him to disrupt the cooking presentation for everybody else."

"Please, Miss," begged Norman. "Please. Let me speak to him. He's not all bad. Sometimes he takes me fishing on the beach, and sometimes he plays football with me. Mum says he has anger issues because of something that happened in his past. If I tell him he can stay if he's nice to people, he'll be good. I promise he will. Mum says he just wants to be liked, and if people gave him a chance they might see that he's not so bad."

"Let him stay," said a voice, accompanied by the clicking of high heels on wood. "We couldn't help overhearing Norman talking to you, and none of the parents wants Trevor taking out his anger on Norman or his mother. We think it would be best if he were allowed to remain."

"Please, Miss," said Norman. "And I promise I'll make sure he behaves when we take the parents on a tour of the rest of our classrooms when we've finished cooking. And I'll make sure he doesn't disrupt the fete, afterwards. He won't be any bother, Miss. I swear."

"Okay," said Millie, frowning. "He can stay, Norman, but you must promise to let me know if he ever hurts you or your mother, okay?"

"I will, Miss, I promise," confirmed Norman, walking after his stepfather. "Trevor!" he called. "Miss Thorn said you can stay and watch me cook… if you want to."

Trevor stopped walking, and turned on the spot, his sneer illuminated by the cone of muddy yellow cast by one of the old ceiling lights. "Of course I want to stay and watch you cook, Norman!" he said, changing direction and marching along the corridor. "Nothing would make me happier." Brushing past Millie as he followed Norman into the classroom, he grinned at his stepson's teacher. "This should be fun," he said.

"The children certainly hope so," replied Millie, quietly. "So please bear that in mind."

Making his way towards the back of the classroom, Trevor paused as he passed one of the benches. He gave a low laugh as he reached for one of the old cookery books in front of the children. "These books bring back some memories," he said. He flicked the book open and gave a loud laugh as he studied the front page. "I don't believe it!" he snorted. "I wrote this, all those years ago… 'if somebody stuck a pin in Lardy Liz, there'd be custard all over the walls!' I even drew a little picture of Lardy Liz exploding after I stuck a pin in her! I bet if I went through the rest of the books I'd find loads more of my little messages!"

"Trevor!" said Francine. "That's really not appropriate! Have some decency, would you?"

"Yes," said another parent, a short and stocky man. "There really is no need to laugh about how cruel you used to be. It wasn't funny then, and it definitely isn't funny now… especially considering who's present here today."

"Ah, yes," said Trevor, slamming the book closed and tossing it onto the desk. "We can't offend the children, can we? Bless their delicate little hearts."

Pushing away the angry urge to throw Trevor out of the classroom, Millie considered her options. She knew that allowing Trevor to remain had been the wrong decision. A bully should never be allowed to get his or her way using threats, but the thought of Norman going home to arguments between his mother and stepfather filled Millie with a cold sadness. She closed her eyes. Sometimes you were forced to act opposite to the way your morals insisted you act. She cleared her throat. "If you could join the parents at the back of the classroom, please, Mr Giles, then the children can begin their demonstration."

Trevor rubbed his hands together in what was quite obviously faux glee. "This is going to be fun," he said, hoisting himself into a seating position on one of the worktops beneath the windows.

"I'm sure it will be fun, Trevor," said Jeremy's father.

"Okay," said Millie, addressing the children. "As you can see, there are a few bowls of ingredients on the countertop near the stoves. Working in pairs, and using the ingredients provided, I'd like you to prepare what you find on page forty-six of the recipe books in front of you. It's a recipe I doubt any of you have seen before."

"Welsh cakes?" said one of the children, amid the sound of pages being turned. "What are they, Miss?"

Millie smiled. "They're delicious, is what they are," she said. "As the name suggests, it's a Welsh recipe. They're simple to make, as well as being absolutely divine to eat, especially with a little butter spread on top of them."

"But we don't have time to make a cake, Miss!" said Jeremy. "Cakes take ages to make! We spent all day yesterday making them for the stall at the fete. They have to go into the oven for a long time!"

"Not these cakes," said Millie. "These cakes will only take a few minutes to cook after you've prepared the mixture, and you don't even need to open the oven — it's all done in a frying pan." She pointed to the clock on the wall. "Okay, you've got fifteen minutes — show your parents what you can do!"

Chatting excitedly to one another, and remembering to wash their hands before creating tiny mushroom clouds of flour as they tossed ingredients into large mixing bowls, the children got on with the task at hand, smiling at their parents as they worked.

Joining the adults at the back of the room, Millie became awkwardly aware of the obvious space between the main group of adults, and Trevor Giles, who remained seated on a worktop, picking at his fingernails. Presumably unaware anybody was watching him, the cocksure expression that had been plastered all over his face had melted away, replaced with what Millie read to be an expression of sadness. No, it was more than that, she decided — the way Trevor's eyelids drooped, and his Adam's apple repeatedly bobbed in his throat, his mouth slightly open, spoke of far more than mere sadness. It spoke of misery. Deep misery.

Remembering that Norman had suggested that something might have happened in Trevor's past that had shaped him into who he was today, Millie was happy to feel pity tugging at her heart. She'd rather experience pity for a fellow human being, than anger. Anger was a waste of time and energy, while pity ensured that good deeds were done and problems were solved.

Trevor raised his head as another group of parents and children passed the open door of the classroom, laughing and chatting with one another as they toured the school. Catching Millie watching him, the mask of misery left his face, instantly swapped for one of disdain. "What are you looking at?" he demanded.

"Nothing," said Millie, offering the man a smile. "I was thinking, that's all."

Making a huffing sound, Trevor turned his attention to the children as gas hobs were lit, and the rich scent of frying butter filled the room, the other parents casting sidelong looks in his direction as the children worked.

Glancing out of the window at the colourful tents and the bouncy castle arranged on one of the large, well-kept lawns below, Millie sighed as she watched a large man helping one of the teachers set up a coconut shy alongside the paddling pool, in which the hook-a-duck game was to be played. The man, his broad smile visible even from Millie's second-floor vantage point, wore his police uniform — his shiny boots reflecting sun rays, and his hat balanced on one of the wooden stakes reserved for a coconut.

Sighing again, Millie looked away, a tear poised to fall — wiped away quickly by her finger. She took one last look outside as the acrid stench of burning smothered the sweet aroma of browning flour and eggs.

There he was. Still smiling, the magical town's only policeman. Sergeant David Spencer. The kindly man who was unaware he had a daughter named Millie.

Chapter 3

*P*ushing open one of the windows, the ancient hinges squealing in protest, Millie used her hands to persuade as much of the black smoke as she could to leave through the small gap.

She joined the parents in a round of applause as the children stood proudly alongside the line of stoves, displaying their Welsh cakes on white plates which they held before them.

"Very well done," said Millie, tasting burning in the air. "You all managed to follow a recipe you'd never seen before, to the letter. You should be proud of yourselves, and I'm sure your parents will enjoy helping you eat your cakes when you get home tonight!"

"Not me!" said Trevor, approaching Norman. "Look at the cakes Norman and Emma have made! Everybody else's are golden brown, you pair have made a plate of charcoal discs!"

"You can still eat them, Trevor," said Norman, his cheeks red. "You can scrape the burnt bits off — like you do with your toast!"

"I don't think so, Norman," said Trevor. "I'm sure your mother will eat one or two, though. She'll always pretend you've done well when you haven't!"

"Oh, that's right, Trevor," said Francine. "That's how you install confidence into a child." She smiled at Norman and Emma. "Your cakes look lovely, don't listen to him."

Emma's mother stepped forward, her hands entwined at waist height and her eyes darting nervously around the room. "I can't wait to try your cakes," she said, giving the two children a kind smile. "I'm sure they'll be delicious."

Trevor gave a loud laugh, tilting his head backwards in cruel emphasis. He looked Emma's mother up and down, his teeth bared in a wicked grin. "Oh, I'm sure *you'll* eat them," he said. "Of that, I have no doubt! Anyway, it was Emma that burnt them, not Norman — I was watching!"

"Don't listen to him, Beth," said Francine, placing a hand on the blushing woman's shoulder, who seemed to be wilting under Trevor's harsh words. "Once a bully, always a bully."

"I'm just having a laugh," said Trevor. "Some of you need to get a sense of humour."

"And one of you needs to get some tact," said Millie, arching an eyebrow at Trevor. She gave each of the children a reassuring smile. "You've all done wonderfully well! I'm very proud of you. Now, being sure to split them equally between the pairs you cooked them in, place your cakes into one of the paper bags at the back of the classroom and get ready to take your parents on a quick tour of the rest of the school.

"I'll probably see a lot of you at the fete later on, but I'd like to take this opportunity to thank you all for being such wonderful pupils. As you all know, you volunteered to attend my class as guinea pigs, to find out whether cookery lessons could be a valid addition to the curriculum." She smiled. "I think it's safe to say that the answer will be yes. You've all impressed Mister Pinkerton and the headmaster, so I would imagine that cookery lessons will become available for every pupil in the school next term, and not just you brave volunteers. Thank you all, and I hope you enjoy your time off before the next school term begins."

Her cheeks warming as the pupils and adults gave her a polite round of applause, Millie gave a small sigh of relief. She'd survived her first term as a teacher, and she'd enjoyed it, much to her surprise. She'd also developed a deep fondness for her pupils, and watched with a heavy heart as Norman smiled up at Trevor, clutching his paper bag of burned cakes, his stepfather barely acknowledging him as he made his way towards the door.

Millie shook her head. There was nothing she could do for Norman, and probably nothing she should do for the boy. If Trevor was hurting him physically, that would be a different story, but she couldn't intervene in the boy's life on the basis that his stepfather was a rude man. It wasn't her job. *She had to remember that*.

She shook such depressing thoughts from her mind and smiled as the children joined their parents, excited at the prospect of showing the adults around the school.

"Come on, Mum!" said William, taking Francine by the hand. "I'll take you to see the gym first, you always said it was your favourite place when you were in school! I bet it's changed loads since you last saw it!"

"I'll take you to the spell room, Dad," said Jeremy, smiling at his father. "It's the best room in the school!" He stuck his tongue out at Harry. "And it's only for witches!"

"Well, I'm taking my mum and dad to see the changing rooms," said Harry. "And they're only for werewolves!"

"Good!" countered Jeremy. "I wouldn't want to go in them anyway. Who *would* want to go into rooms in which smelly kids turn into even smellier wolves! I bet those rooms stink of disgusting fur and dog breath."

"You wouldn't dare come in when we're learning how to change safely into wolves," laughed Harry. "You'd be too scared! Witches are cowards who hide behind magic! That's what my mum says." He looked up at his mother. "Isn't that right, Mum?"

"Not exactly, Harry," said his mother, her cheeks

flushed. "That's not what I said." She glanced at Jeremy's father, guilt evident in her eyes. "I am sorry," she said. "He does tend to get things wrong sometimes."

Jeremy's father laughed. "Don't be silly! There's no need to apologise. Friendly rivalry between paranormals is normal, especially at their age. It's all just healthy banter."

"Where do you want to go, Trevor?" asked Norman. "Is there somewhere you'd like me to show you? Somewhere that was special to you when you were a pupil?"

Francine gave a low laugh. "You were fond of the headmaster's office, as I remember things, Trevor," she said.

"I don't think I can take you there," said Norman. "The headmaster and Mister Pinkerton are away on business, and their offices are probably locked."

"She's trying to make a joke, Norman," said Trevor. "Ignore her, she always was an attention seeker. Instead of showing me around the school, how about you take me outside to the fete and show me the tent that says 'refreshments' above the door? I bet you'd love a nice cold cola?"

The boy's face dropped. "Okay, Trevor," he said.

"I'll take you to the chemistry lab, Mum," said Emma, quietly, taking Beth by the hand. "You'll enjoy looking around in there, and Mister Huggins is such a lovely teacher. He's so funny."

"Yes," said Beth. "Let's go, Emma." She gave

Trevor a sideways glance. "I'd like to put some space between myself and a certain person."

Trevor looked Beth up and down and gave a cruel smile. "There's *plenty* of space between us. *Plenty*."

"Don't talk to my mother like that!" snapped Emma.

"It's okay, darling," said Beth. "It doesn't bother me. Come on, show me the chemistry lab, I used to enjoy chemistry when I was in school. Let's get out of here."

One of the other mothers narrowed her eyes and glared at Trevor. "I think a lot of us feel the same. I'd like to leave, too."

"Listen to yourselves," said Trevor. "So, I went to school with some of you, and had a laugh with you. So what? It was a long time ago. Was I really so popular that I had that much of an effect on you all? I must say, I feel quite proud that you all remember me so well."

"Bullies tend to leave an imprint on the minds of their victims," said Francine. "That's nothing to be proud of." She put a hand on her son's back and pushed him gently towards the door. "Go on, William. It's time to leave."

"It's time for everyone to leave," said Millie, inter-rupting Trevor as he opened his mouth to speak. "The other teachers will remain in their classrooms for another hour and will be happy to show any parents around."

As the parents and children filed through the

doorway, shouting from the corridor startled Millie. "Burning!" came a worried male voice. "Burning! I must stop it!"

The appearance of a bald elderly man in the doorway took Millie by surprise, and impervious to the fact that he was blocking the doorway and preventing people from leaving the room, the man shouted again. "Burning! Stop it from burning!"

Unfortunately for the man, the person whose path he'd stepped directly into was Trevor Giles's, and Trevor seemed to have as much respect for the elderly as he did for children. "Get out of my way, old man," he snapped. "A couple of stupid kids burned some stupid cakes. That's what you can smell."

The man stood still for a moment, and then lifted his face, studying Trevor with old eyes. His expression hardened, and his eyes widened. "You!" he said, his voice a booming ill fit for such a frail body. He lifted a hand and placed a thin finger on Trevor's chest. "You! You evil child!" he shouted. "You're like a snake without cunning, a bird without boots! You are the devil himself! You evil, evil child!"

Pushing the elderly man's hand away, Trevor laughed. "What are you talking about… a bird without boots? What does that even mean? Get out of my way, you daft old sod! Some of us have got better things to do than listen to the demented ramblings of an old codger! There's a bar stocked with real ale waiting for me."

"Evil!" shouted the old man. "Like a shirt without cufflinks!"

"If you don't move out of my way," threatened Trevor, narrowing the gap between himself and the man. "I'll move you."

"Dad!" came a woman's anxious voice from the corridor. "There you are! I've been looking all over the school for you!"

The lady who appeared in the doorway, wearing a smart white summer dress and a straw hat, took the old man by the elbow and smiled an apology as she moved him aside. "I'm sorry if my father offended anybody," she said. "He doesn't know what he's saying most of the time."

Pushing through the doorway, Trevor sneered at the woman. "Keep your father under control, love," he said. "Otherwise he just might say the wrong thing to the wrong person… if you get my drift."

"Erm, yes, I think I understand," stammered the woman, pulling her father towards her, and away from Trevor. "I'm sorry if he was rude to you."

The old man lifted a shaky arm and pointed at Trevor. "As evil as a fox without gloves! That's what he is!"

"Dad!" said his daughter, her eyes avoiding Trevor's. "Please stop saying things like that, or I'll have to take you home. This is a school, remember? There are children here — you don't want to scare a child, do you? You like the children, don't you?"

The old man let out a long breath, his face and

bald head reddening as he leaned against his daughter. "I need to sit down, Julia," he said.

"He can sit down in here," offered Millie, approaching the father and daughter, smiling her thanks at the concerned parents and children who let her pass. "I'll make him a cup of tea. He looks like he could do with one."

Chapter 4

*R*eassuring the parents that their help wasn't required, Millie closed the door when the last of the children and adults had left her classroom, and hurried to the corner counter, flicking on the electric kettle which stood next to the traditional teapot decorated with hand-painted roses. "Is he okay?" she asked, dropping a teabag into a mug.

Seating her father on the comfy chair behind Millie's desk, the woman nodded. "He'll be fine," she said. "He's just a little confused. He used to be a teacher here, and every now and then he likes to come to the school fete and open day when they have one. He really wanted to come this time. He said he wanted to take a look at his old classroom. Anyway, he wandered off as I was speaking to one of the teachers, and with him not being well, I became a little worried. I could hear him in the distance yelling something about burning, so I followed his voice here. I'm so sorry."

"Please don't apologise," said Millie, adding a splash of milk to the mug. "There's absolutely no need to say sorry."

"That's right," said the old man. "If you keep saying sorry, you'll sound like a whistle without a pea, or a donkey without a clock."

"Dad," said the woman, her voice soft. "Those don't really make sense." She smiled at Millie. "Don't take what he says too seriously. He suffers from metaphorettes."

"I'm sorry?" said Millie, crossing the room. "He suffers from what?"

The woman laughed. "We're so used to calling it by that name in our family that we sometimes forget other people won't know what we're talking about!"

Placing the mug of tea and a bowl of sugar in front of the man, and pulling up a seat each for herself and the woman, Millie smiled. "What is it?" she asked. "This... metaphorettes."

"It's nothing! It doesn't exist!" said the man, spooning sugar into his tea. He gave Millie a smile and a wink. "Between you and me, young lady, my family imagines that I say things which I most certainly do not say. The things they imagine I say would not be very appropriate coming from an English literature teacher, would they?"

Not wishing to offend the man, Millie agreed, not

actually knowing what it was she was agreeing to. "I suppose not," she said.

The man extended a frail hand in greeting, the skin papery thin and cold as Millie shook it. "I'm Mister Cuthbert Campion, teacher of both English literature and chemistry at Spellbinder Hall."

"I'm Millie Thorn," replied Millie. "Cookery teacher at Spellbinder Hall."

"Cookery teacher? Are you sure?" asked Cuthbert. He shook his head and gave an embarrassed grin. "Of course you're sure!" He jerked a thumb at the lady next to him. "The young woman with me is my daughter, Julia Campion." He lowered his voice and gave Millie a knowing nod. "Not married, you see. And not so young, really. She's forty if I remember correctly, and between you and I, I think she'll be carrying my surname for the remainder of her days." He lowered his voice even further, almost to a raspy whisper, and moved his face closer to Millie's. "It's the attitude, I think. What man is going to want a woman with such an awful attitude? No man is!"

"I can hear you, Dad," said Julia. "I'm literally right next to you. And yes, I'm forty, and as I keep reminding you, you're no longer a teacher. You retired a long time ago… when you became… poorly."

"Natter, natter, natter," said Cuthbert, his eyes flitting around the classroom. "You're always nattering. You sound like a show jumper who has forgotten her socks!"

Julia gave Millie a smile tinged with sadness. "*That's* metaphorettes," she said. "We invented the name using the words metaphor, and Tourette's. Dad can't help blurting out senseless comments which he thinks are metaphors or analogies... I don't know which. My brother and I just used the word metaphor — so we could give his illness a fun nickname. It makes it seem less scary. Less serious. You know what Tourette's is, I presume?"

Millie nodded. "A condition which causes the sufferer to display physical and verbal ticks. They shout things out. Sometimes inappropriately."

"You look like a horse which ate too many burgers, young lady!" shouted Cuthbert, staring at Millie.

"*Often* inappropriately, in my father's case," said Julia. She put a hand on her father's shoulder. "That was very rude, Dad," she said.

Expelling a grunt, Cuthbert sipped his tea. His eyes widened as he stared at the ovens lining one wall. "Burning!" he yelled. "Get it out of the oven!"

"It's okay," said Millie, placing a hand on the old man's wrist. "Nothing's burning. The smell of smoke is from some cakes that a couple of the children burned, but everything's okay now. All the ovens are cold. Nothing is burning."

Cuthbert relaxed in his seat, smiling at Millie. "That's good news," he said. He glanced towards the windows, his eyes brightening. "There's a lovely view from those windows, isn't there? I remember it well. This school is built on a cliff, and you can look out to sea from those windows. I was a teacher. Did you know that? I spent most of my lunch breaks in this room, enjoying the wonderful views, and the most wonderful conversations." His face dropped, and sadness tainted his eyes. "But those days are over, aren't they?"

"I can't promise the conversation will be as wonderful as you remember," said Millie, "but I can vouch for the view. It's still beautiful. Why don't you take a look?"

"I'd like that," said Cuthbert, stumbling a little as he got to his feet. "I'd really like that."

"Are you okay, Dad?" said Julia getting to her feet, too, and gently grasping her father's elbow.

Cuthbert shook his daughter's hand away and made his way towards the windows, gazing around the room as he walked. "I'm fine," he said. "You worry too much, Julia. You're like a fish which has lost its momentum."

Julia looked at Millie and gave her head a gentle shake. "See?" she said, with a grin. "Metaphorettes. Utter nonsense."

Millie watched the old man as he came to a stop at the tall windows and put a hand on the glass. "I wouldn't say it was utter nonsense," she said. "I mean a fish which had lost its momentum *would* be a little concerned. Worried, even."

Julia gave a snorting laugh. "You're right! I'm so used to Dad saying silly things that I hardly listen to what he says anymore. Perhaps I should try a little harder, perhaps there is meaning behind some of the things he says."

"This view is beautiful," murmured Cuthbert Campion. "Like egg whites and tartar."

"Or maybe not," said Julia, smiling as she used a tissue taken from her bag to wipe up some tea her father had spilt. She paused what she was doing and looked Millie in the eyes. "He was a brilliant man once. He still is, of course. But you know what I mean... his mind was razor sharp. Until the accident that gave him metaphorettes."

"An accident?" asked Millie, taking the wet tissue from Julia and dropping it in the bin beside her desk.

"People don't just develop metaphorettes," said Julia, smiling. "It's not even a real illness."

"I thought he'd naturally developed some sort of dementia," explained Millie. "Which you'd given a nickname."

Julia shook her head. "No. It was an accident. And if the accident hadn't occurred, I think Dad would still be as bright as he ever was, and possibly still a teacher. An old one, but I'd bet he'd be sharper than most of the young ones who teach here." She gave an embarrassed laugh. "Not you, of course! You seem *very* sharp."

Millie disregarded Julia's comment with a wave of her hand. "Oh, I'm not that sharp," she said with a smile. She indicated Julia's father with a nod of her head. "What sort of accident was it? What happened to him?" She instantly gave an apologetic smile. "If you don't mind me asking."

"Of course I don't mind," said Julia. Her face softened as she looked at her father. "As he said, he was a chemistry teacher as well as an English teacher, and as you know — being a teacher here at the hall, alongside normal non-paranormal chemistry, pupils in this school are also taught paranormal chemistry."

"Yes," said Millie. "How the moon-pool works, how potions work… that sort of thing."

Julia nodded. "Dad was a dab hand at potions. Even though he's a halfling, but that didn't matter, some potions don't even require magic, and anybody can teach kids how to make basic potions…. the magic can be added by a full witch at a later date, when the potion is needed." She took her eyes from her father's back and looked at Millie. "I'm led to believe that the current chemistry teacher here at the school has no magic either… he's a werewolf, isn't he?"

Millie nodded. "That's right. His name's Timothy Huggins, and the children love him." She leaned forward across the desk. "What did you say your father is?" she asked. "A halfling? I don't think I've ever heard that word."

"I'm not surprised," said Julia. "They're not very common. I don't think a halfling has been born in Spellbinder Bay for over fifty years."

"What are they?" asked Millie. "What is a halfling?"

"A halfling is a person born to a witch and a werewolf, it doesn't matter which parent is which," said Julia. "A very uncommon occurrence indeed. These days, at least."

"Why is it so uncommon?" asked Millie.

"Because of what happens to the child," said Julia. "It seems that witch blood and werewolf blood just don't play well together. Pick any other species for a witch or a werewolf to have a child with, and everything is fine. In the case of a child born to a vampire and a werewolf, for instance, the child will either be a vampire *or* a werewolf… he or she will display the qualities of the parent whose genes were the strongest. It's a little like a child having blonde hair like its mother or black hair like its father."

"What happens to a child born to a witch and werewolf?" asked Millie.

"Conflict happens," said Julia, her brow furrowed. "Within the child. The child will be neither a witch or a werewolf. The wolf part of the child will fight for dominance, but so will the witch side, and that isn't good for the child, as you can imagine. The wolf grows angry within him or her, never able to be freed, and the magic passed down by the witch bubbles away like boiling water in an airtight pot. It's a toxic combination which often leads to problems."

"What sort of problems?" asked Millie.

"The sort of problems my father experienced. Sometimes when he got frustrated or angry, his wolf would try and emerge. His eyes would yellow for a brief instance, or hairs would sprout on the backs of his hands. It was an unpleasant experience for him. It scared him every time it happened, and it scared the people around him. He was never able to mingle with non-paranormal people — as he had no control over it. He couldn't trust himself. It was much the same for the witch part of him as it was for his werewolf side."

"In what way?" asked Millie.

"He'd accidentally cast spells," said Julia. "Especially when he was younger. It happened mostly when he was tired or poorly, and as he got older, he learned to control it with good sleeping habits and a healthy lifestyle. It was the same with his wolf, and by the time he was an adult and met my mother, he had it mostly under control. Especially by the time I was born. I witnessed a few incidents, but they were infrequent. Which was why his accident came as such a shock to us all. The accident not only caused him to develop metaphorettes, it also calmed the beast and the magic within him. Since the day of his accident, he's not grown so much as one hair on the backs of his hands or cast even the weakest of accidental spells. The accident was a blessing and a curse, some might say."

"What sort of accident has that sort of effect on somebody?" said Millie.

"It was a long time ago. Nobody really knows what happened," admitted Julia. "What is known is that he had just taught an English lesson focusing on metaphors, similes and analogies, before going to the chemistry lab to teach a potion making lesson. The children who were in the chemistry class at the time said the potion he taught them in that lesson was a simple one, designed to cure headaches.

"The kids said that my father was fine when they left the classroom, and it's thought that after the lesson was over my father may have used a little of the potion on himself. Teaching is a stressful job, as you know… perhaps he had a headache. And he did suffer from them sometimes, as a consequence of the wolf and witch fighting within him."

"You think a headache potion affected him so badly that he developed his… condition?" asked Millie.

"No," said Julia, smiling at her father as he stepped away from the window and turned to face them. "It's thought that some of his halfling witch magic was accidentally released as he mixed the potion. Who knows what the magic did to that concoction? It seems to have muddled his brain… or crossed a few wires. Imagine taking a headache potion infused with who knows what sort of magic, just an hour after teaching a lesson on metaphors. It seems something got stuck, and he's never been the same since. I was ten when it happened. He went to work that morning a bright, clever man, and came home a confused man who told my mother over dinner that she resembled a Doberman dog which had got its life together. It isn't just the metaphors and analogies either, he gets very confused, too, as you've already witnessed."

"How sad," said Millie.

"Very sad," agreed Julia, "and I think Dad's illness led indirectly to my mother's death. The stress got to her, and she passed a few years later. Myself and my brother have been caring for him ever since."

"I'm sorry about your mother," said Millie. She watched Cuthbert staring blankly around the room as if he wasn't certain of where he was. "And your father."

"Thank you," said Julia. She gave a smile and her eyes brightened. "Anyway — that's why halflings are so rare. Because most witches and werewolves who fall in love with one another refuse to have children together."

Leaving his position at the window, Cuthbert hurried unsteadily across the classroom, prompting Julia to stand up and approach him. "Slow down, Dad," she said. "You'll fall."

Cuthbert looked around at his surroundings. "I know this room!" he said. He smiled at Millie. "And who are you, young lady? Are you new here? I'm Cuthbert Campion, English Literature and chemistry teacher, here at Spellbinder Hall. It's a pleasure to make your acquaintance."

"Oh, Dad," said Julia, taking her father by his arm. "You've already met her. Come on, we've taken up enough of her time already. Let's go outside into the sunshine and have a look round the fete. You'll like that."

As the father and daughter left the room, a cold

breeze blew across Millie's face, and she gave a quiet cry of surprise as the tall black-robed ghost appeared before her, heading for the door, flickering in and out of existence as if it were a hologram projected by a machine with a faulty circuit.

She shuddered as the apparition slid through the doorway, appearing too weak to hold its form as it faded and vanished before it could reach the corridor.

Millie's spine tingled as she glanced at the clock on the wall. "Ghosts, parents, and an abusive bully," she whispered to the empty room. "I do believe that after today, wine o'clock has come early."

Chapter 5

"How was it?" asked Judith, her sparkling blue eyes matching the stone in the necklace she wore. "I told you you'd be fine. Did you feel out of your depth like you *thought* you would, or did you manage it like a pro, like I *knew* you would?"

Millie sipped her drink, her stress levels dropping immediately as the cold liquid hit her stomach and the alcohol reached her brain. "Thanks to the interruptions of a tall ghost dressed in black, an old school bully, and a confused elderly man, the attention was not really on me at all." She gave Judith a smile and placed her wine glass on the little round wooden table between them. "I did fine. You were right, speaking to a room full of adults wasn't much different than speaking to a class of children. In fact, I'd say that some of the kids came across as being more mature than some of the adults."

"Just look around you," said Judith, her hair

shining gold in the sunlight. "Adults are just big kids at heart."

The table which Millie and her best friend sat at, situated outside the refreshments tent, afforded Millie the perfect position from which to observe people enjoying the school fete.

Judith was correct, Millie realised, smiling as two men tossed their shoes aside and joined the laughing children already having fun on the large red and yellow bouncy castle. Adults *were* just big kids at heart.

She watched on as another man performed a victorious air-punch, proud that the little wooden ball he'd thrown had knocked a coconut from its perch. Choosing a stuffed toy pig as a reward for his marks-manship skills, the man handed the prize to his young daughter, who gazed up at him with admiration evident on her face.

Millie took another sip of her drink. It was nice to see so many smiling faces enjoying the sunlight and the community feeling that events like the school fete were designed to foster.

She gazed out over the clifftop which Spellbinder Hall and its grounds occupied, and allowed her eyes to wander across the calm sea, smiling as she made out the white walls of her cottage in the distance, cradled by golden sand dunes on the opposite side of the horseshoe-shaped bay.

How her life had changed in the last year. Gone were the days of not being able to pay the rent on a hovel of a flat in London, exchanged for carefree days, a beautiful seafront cottage with a magical cavern below it, an inherited financial fortune, and the surprising knowledge that she was a witch and a member of a sizeable paranormal community.

Add in the almost miraculous fact that she'd been able to magic the ghost of her dead mother into existence, then found out that she had a father, and she considered herself very fortunate indeed.

She glanced over at the stall which had been set up to sell the cakes which the pupils in her class had baked, happy that three of her pupils were mature and eager enough to be trusted with running the stall, freeing up Millie's time to enjoy a few glasses of sparkling white wine with her best friend.

Her best friend who just happened to be the adopted daughter of the man who was Millie's real father, she reminded herself, aware of the sickly fear that twisted her stomach whenever she dared think about *that* particular subject.

She drank more wine, this time a gulp rather than a sip. Now was not the time for focusing on stressful issues. Now was the time to enjoy a drink, and watch a middle-aged woman being unceremoniously thrown from the mechanical bucking bronco, which had been set up next to a stall displaying the raffle draw prizes — a few of which were some of the more impressive cakes baked by Millie and her pupils.

The woman climbed to her feet, giggling uncontrollably as she placed her glasses back on her face and joined her husband and son, the small family laughing together as they walked hand in hand towards the coconut shy.

The fete wasn't a grand affair by any stretch of the imagination, but it was doing its job. It was bringing paranormal people together as they celebrated the end of the school year and the achievements of the children who attended Spellbinder Hall.

Remembering that Judith was seated opposite her, no doubt expecting a conversation to occur between the two friends, Millie brought herself back into the moment, sniffing at the air as the universally tempting aroma of fried onions teased her nostrils.

She smiled at Judith, and was just about to suggest that the two of them head back to her cottage after the fete had finished, to polish off more wine, when urgent shouting from within the tent behind her demanded her full attention. "You evil thing! You evil child!" came the distressed voice of a man.

Recognising the voice as Cuthbert Campion's, Millie leapt to her feet, almost spilling the contents of her glass over Judith in the process, who also got to her feet and rushed inside the striped tent alongside Millie.

The spacious refreshments tent, housing a small makeshift bar in the corner, was nearly empty, with most people preferring to enjoy their cold drinks outside in the sunshine, than within the warm musty confines of a canvas tent.

The few people who were inside the tent had gathered together in a huddle near the bar, surrounding Cuthbert Campion and the man he was shouting at. It was no surprise to Millie that Cuthbert's adversary happened to be Trevor Giles. She'd watched from her classroom window as he'd entered the tent with Norman almost half an hour before.

Norman had emerged a few minutes later, clutching a styrofoam cup with a straw protruding from the lid, and set off to join his friends in exploring what the small fete had to offer. Trevor hadn't emerged after his stepson, and Millie had rightly, it seemed, suspected he wouldn't until he'd drank his fair share of some of the real ales lovingly crafted by the local microbrewery and donated to the school fete.

Not great parenting on Trevor's behalf, but Norman was in a safe place. The fete was under the *extremely* beady eyes of several nosy teachers, and under the protection of all manner of spells emitted by Spellbinder Hall. The old hall, which acted as a beacon of magic, continuously transmitted magical energy, such as the concealment spell which kept the paranormal properties of Spellbinder Bay, and a large chunk of its inhabitants, hidden in plain sight from non-paranormal folk.

Amongst the other spells beamed from the hall, was a spell which negated the need for a fence alongside the clifftop, providing an invisible forcefield which would prevent any unfortunate accidents from occurring.

Worried that Cuthbert Campion might require an

invisible forcefield to protect him from Trevor Giles, if he continued hurling abuse at the younger man, Millie hurried across the bouncy grass carpet of the tent. She pushed her way past the few spectators, and stepped between the two men, a hand on each of their chests. "Okay! That's enough!" she ordered.

"You're lucky she's here," growled Trevor, glaring past Millie. "I was just about to teach you some manners, old man."

"Evil!" shouted Cuthbert, his wrinkled face a mask of frightened confusion. "You're evil! Why do they allow you to be here? You're a mountain in a dish, a headache without a cure!"

"What the heck are you waffling about?" said Trevor. He suddenly lifted his arm, making Millie jump, and held a threatening fist an inch away from Cuthbert's face. "You're mental, mate! That's what you are. Somebody needs to get you out of here before you get hurt!"

"I said, that's enough!" said Millie, as Trevor dropped his arm. "Both of you!" She took Cuthbert's hand in hers and gave him a reassuring smile, alarmed at how unwell he appeared. "Where's Julia, Cuthbert? Where's your daughter?"

"I'm here!" came Julia's concerned voice as she hurried inside the tent, veering past Judith and reaching for her father. "What's happening, Dad? I could hear you shouting from halfway across the field. I only went to the cake stall... why didn't you wait for me? I told you to wait. I *asked* you to wait." She placed the paper bag she was carrying on the bar and glared at Trevor. "You again," she said.

Trevor pointed an accusatory finger at Cuthbert's face. "*Him* again," he said. "I was enjoying a beer until *he* came in here and ruined *my* peace. What has he got against me anyway? That's twice today that he's verbally assaulted me! He needs locking up."

"He's poorly," said Julia. "He doesn't mean it. He fixates on things and people, and today he seems to have fixated on you. Maybe you could cut him some slack? He's double your age — what's the point of retaliating?"

"I always retaliate," growled Trevor. "That's just how it is."

"Why don't you bring your father outside?" suggested Judith, offering Julia a kind smile. "Let him sit down in the sun for a while, he looks a little shaken. I'll get him a cup of tea."

Julia gave her head a determined shake. "No. Thank you anyway, but no. I need to get him home. He's getting tired."

"But I'd like a cup of tea," protested Cuthbert.

Julia gestured at the brown paper bag she'd placed on the bar. "I bought us some cakes, Dad, from the cake stall. Let's go home and have one. I believe it was Millie and the pupils in her cookery class who baked them. I bet they taste lovely."

Cuthbert gave Millie a searching look. "You're a cookery teacher? I once knew a cookery teacher. I'm a teacher, too, you see? Are you a halfling?"

"No, Cuthbert," said Millie, giving her head a gentle shake. "I'm not a halfling, but yes, I am a cookery teacher."

"There's not many of us, is there?" said Cuthbert. "We're a rare breed, us halflings. We have to stick together." His eyes widened suddenly, and he pointed at Trevor, whose hand was emerging from the bag of cakes, clutching a chocolate brownie. "Those cakes aren't yours!" he protested. "Put that back!"

"Too late," teased Trevor, taking a bite of the brownie, his lips muddy with chocolate. He gave Millie an approving nod. "Very nice. If you teach Norman how to bake cakes this good, I might reconsider my decision to make him give up cookery lessons next term and study a more manly subject, like mechanics. I hear there are a few old cars around the back of the school which the *normal* boys are learning to restore. I don't know why his mother ever let him attend cookery classes… he's not some apron-wearing prancing male witch, he's supposed to be a werewolf! He's *supposed* to be a young man! And to think he *chose* to take cookery lessons! He wasn't even forced to like I was when I went to school here!"

"That's not a very nice attitude," said Millie. She narrowed her eyes and shrugged. "But from what I've learned about you today, I'm really not surprised that you hold opinions like that."

Trevor took another bite of the brownie and spoke as he chewed. "I don't really care what you think."

"Those aren't your cakes!" repeated Cuthbert, reaching for the bag and getting the tips of his fingers inside before Trevor snatched it away. "They belong to my daughter!"

"Let him keep them, Dad," said Julia, taking her father by the arm, tugging him gently towards the doorway. "I'll buy us some more, I wouldn't want them now. Not after *his* hands have been all over them."

"Yeah, that's right," said Trevor, cake crumbs tumbling from his mouth. "Take your father home." He washed the brownie down with a long swig of beer, gave a belch, and smiled as Julia and Cuthbert left the tent.

"Perhaps *you* should leave now," said the man standing behind the bar. "This wasn't supposed to be the type of bar that people get drunk in. It was meant to be here so that responsible adults could have a drink or two while their children enjoyed the fete."

Trevor gave the diminutive man a cold smile. "You're a vampire, aren't you? And a teacher here at the school?"

"That's right," said the man. "I teach history."

"Well, mate," drawled Trevor. "I'm too old to care what teachers have to say, and I've never much liked vampires, so I'm afraid I won't be taking your advice. I'm staying right here, drinking beer and minding my own business, just like I was until that mad old man wandered into the tent and began abusing me. Anyway, I bought a few tickets for the raffle. I'm not going anywhere until that's been drawn. I've got my eyes on the bottle of champagne and the case of beer. I'm feeling lucky today."

Deciding that allowing Trevor to remain was a better choice than causing any further commotion, Millie gave a frustrated sigh and turned to the vampire behind the bar. "Perhaps it would be better if he stayed?" she suggested. "The raffle is being drawn soon, and the fete will be winding down in an hour or so."

"At which point, I shall be gone," said Trevor, sliding his empty glass across the bar. He smiled at the vampire. "You have my word. Another one, please, bartend."

Shaking his head, the vampire refilled Trevor's glass and slammed it onto the bar. "There you go, sir," he said, his words wrapped liberally in sarcasm. "I'd like to say that I hope you choke on it, but that would be rude, so instead, I'll say I hope you enjoy it."

"I'm sure I will," said Trevor. He slipped his hand inside the paper bag of cakes. "And I'm sure it will go down beautifully with another of those delectable chocolate brownies that the woman with the mad father was kind enough to gift me. All this good beer makes a werewolf hungry." Peering into the bag, he gave a groan. "She only bought one chocolate brownie? The rest of these cakes are no good to me. They're all cream cakes, and I don't much care for cream."

Just as Millie was considering grabbing a cake

from the bag and using it to erase the smug expression from Trevor's face, Norman hurried into the tent, out of breath, his face the shade of red a child's face turns when he or she has been having fun.

His school trousers green at the knees with grass stains, he came to a halt next to his stepfather. "Can I have another drink, please, Trevor?" he said. "I'm playing rugby with a few of the other boys! I'm thirsty!"

Trevor smiled at Millie. "See! That's what a boy should be doing! Playing men's games, not cooking." He grinned at Norman, and slipped his wallet from his back pocket, handing the boy a five-pound note. "Of course you can have a drink, Norman, but first, run along to the cake stall like a good little boy and pick me up a few cakes. No cream ones, mind you."

Taking the money from Trevor, Norman gave an eager nod. "Okay!" he said. "I'll do that for you, Trevor!" He dropped his eyes momentarily and spoke in an uncertain voice. "What did you mean when you said I should be playing men's games and not cooking?"

Trevor sucked a long breath in and stared down at his stepson. "Norman," he drawled. "Real men don't wear aprons and make fancy cakes. Real men drink beer and do man stuff. If you were my *real* son, you wouldn't even know what it feels like to wear an apron, let alone know how to turn on an oven. Watching you and those other *boys* prancing about in the cookery classroom made my heart hurt,

Norman." He took a gulp of beer and smiled. "Does that answer your question?"

Seeming to lose an inch in height, and his already small chest and shoulders deflating, Norman licked his lips. "I suppose so," he said, emotion evident in his voice.

"Good," said Trevor. "Now, off you go. I'm hungry. Go and fetch me some cakes."

"Wait," said Millie, as the young boy turned his back and shuffled towards the door. "I'll accompany you, Norman, I should check and see if the children are still happy serving on the stall, or if they'd like to go and have some fun. Perhaps I'll take over from them."

Judith looked Trevor up and down. "I'll come with you," she said, speaking to Millie. "For some reason, I don't much like being in this tent."

"I don't much want to be near *you*, either," said Trevor, a sneer curling his top lip. "Look at you... little Miss Pompous, daughter of the local idiot policeman."

"What did you call my father?" said Judith.

"An idiot," replied Trevor. "You know what I think of you and your father, and I know what you think of me. I'll say it again. Your father is an idiot."

Ignoring the tense atmosphere building in the tent, Millie's mind still somehow managed to latch on to the fact that there were two of Sergeant Spencer's daughters in the tent, one adopted and one biological.

The sad truth was, though, that only one of them was aware that the other girl was a sister to her.

Perplexed at her brain's inability to adhere to the demand that the issue of her father be ignored for the time being, Millie shook the imposing thoughts away and allowed Judith to defend Sergeant Spencer, ignoring the instinctive urge to fight for her father's honour.

Judith laughed and tossed her head as she glared at Trevor Giles. "You wouldn't dare be rude to my father's face," she said. "You're scared of him. I've seen you when he's around."

Trevor's face darkened. "Don't mix up my necessary fear of his uniform, with me being fearful of him as a man. I'm not scared of *him*. I'm a werewolf, and he's not even paranormal. He doesn't scare me! What does make me respectful of him, is the fact that he's under the protection of Henry Pinkerton, and the fact that he has the power to lock me up in that dingy cell of his for no reason at all." He licked beer foam from his top lip and stared down at Judith. "Remove Henry's protection of him, and take him out of that uniform, and I wouldn't even notice him when he walked into a room, let alone be on my best behaviour around him."

Judith sighed. "Whatever the reasons are, Trevor, you're still scared of him, and I wouldn't say he locks you up for *no* reason. Last weekend he locked you up because you lost your temper in a pub full of non-paranormal people, started a fight, and almost turned into your wolf."

"I wouldn't transform into my wolf in front of non-paranormals," said Trevor. "I'm not that stupid. I might not be scared of your father, but the thought of the punishment that Henry would dole out if I ever did that, makes my blood run cold. Henry has real power, you see. Not the fake power a uniform and a badge afford a man."

From almost the first day she'd arrived in Spellbinder Bay, Millie had been made aware that the punishment bestowed upon members of the paranormal community, for crimes deemed severe enough, was very harsh. Very harsh indeed.

Being banished to another dimension may not have sounded so awful to a person who didn't know what manner of creatures resided there, but Millie knew — she'd looked into the gateway to The Chaos. Locked in a cave in one of the passageways deep in the cliff below Spellbinder Hall, the circular gate of energy remained locked — managing to keep most demons from entering the dimension that Millie liked to call home, but not preventing people from peering into the hell which lay beyond the circle of light.

Demons did manage to sneak through the gate occasionally, and when Millie had looked into the gate, she'd seen one in all its terrifying glory. She certainly wouldn't like to be banished to The Chaos, and she was equally sure that speaking about such punishments in front of Norman was not very responsible of the adults inside the tent.

She gestured towards the young werewolf with a nod of her head. "Now's not the time for arguments," she said.

Trevor nodded. "I agree. Now is the time for beer." He looked at Norman. "But I need something else to eat before I drink too much more. Go on, lad. Go with your teacher and get me those cakes. There'll be a cola waiting for you when you get back."

Chapter 6

*W*alking alongside Norman through the maze of tents and the crowds of happy people, Millie's heart dropped as she approached the cake stall. The cake stall selling the cakes *she* and her pupils had baked. The cake stall that *she* should have been standing behind, doing *her* bit for charity.

"Oh!" said Judith. "You managed to get Beth to serve on the stall!" She glanced at Norman and spoke quietly to Millie. "She's not very well," she half-whispered. "She suffers from some sort of anxiety, or depression. It's lovely to see her joining in like that! She doesn't normally get involved with the community. Well done, Millie!"

"I didn't get her involved," explained Millie. "I left three young girls in charge. Beth's daughter and two other girls! They begged me to let them run the stall. I'm not sure why poor Beth has been dragged into doing it."

"The girls probably got bored after about three and a half minutes," said Judith, laughing. "That's why. That's precisely how teenagers operate."

"Beth!" said Millie, hurrying towards the stall. "I'm so sorry! How did you get dragged into doing this?"

Beth smiled. "Don't worry," she said, taking money from a customer and handing over a paper bag bulging with cakes. "Emma's friends wanted to go and bounce on the inflatable castle, they couldn't find you, so I said I'd help out. It's no problem."

"I am sorry!" said Millie. "You should be enjoying the fete with Emma, not standing here on your own behind a wallpaper pasting table, selling cakes!"

"Oh, don't worry about that," said Beth, "I'm not one for socialising... crowds of people make me very nervous. It's nice just to interact with people for the short time it takes to serve them. It alleviates the need for long conversations. Anyway, I'm not alone. Emma's helping me, she stayed here when the other two girls left. She asked me to help her. She'll be back in a moment, she's just popped off to buy a few raffle tickets." She looked over at the table on which the prizes were piled. "The prizes are very nice, I must say. I think Emma wants to win the television. I don't allow her to have one in her bedroom, you see, and I think that she believes that if she wins one, and I don't have to pay for it, I'll allow her to have it in her room." She smiled at Millie. "Between you and me, I was going to give in and buy her one anyway."

"I won't tell her," smiled Millie. "And I'll be crossing all my fingers for her when Fredrick draws the winning raffle tickets."

"Here she comes now," said Judith, pointing to the young girl running towards them. She smiled at Beth. "Your daughter is a lovely girl," she said. "It's been a pleasure to teach her some magic during the last term, she especially loves lunar magic and anything to do with water. You've brought her up to be wonderfully polite. I'm sure she'll make a very responsible witch when she's older."

Casting her eyes downwards in the way people not fond of compliments tended to, Beth smiled sheepishly. "Thank you," she mumbled.

"Miss Thorn!" gushed Emma, taking the attention away from Beth, who appeared relieved at her daughter's intervention. "You should see how many cakes Mum and I have sold for charity! Somebody even told me that they'd never tasted coconut slices quite like the ones they bought! The man ate one in front of me, and you could see from his face how much he loved it!" She gave a proud smile and stood a little taller. "I made the coconut slices, yesterday! When we baked all the cakes for today!"

"Well done!" said Millie. "That's wonderful. You should be proud of yourself."

"Yes," agreed Judith. "Well done! Perhaps I'll buy some to take home. I'm quite partial to coconut cakes."

"I'm quite good at serving customers, too, aren't I,

Mum?" said Emma. "I think I might like to work in a shop when I'm older." She gazed into space, her eyes narrowed. "*Or* become a brain surgeon. I'm not quite sure yet."

"Well," said Millie. "I can't allow you to practice the skills you'd need to be a brain surgeon, but why don't you show me your customer service skills?" She nodded in Norman's direction. "Norman wants to buy some cakes."

Emma peered around Millie and smiled at Norman. "Oh! Hi, Norman," she said, slight colour rising in her cheeks. "I didn't see you there. The scones you made yesterday have been selling really well. I sold four to the same lady!"

"Oh, good," said Norman, kicking at a tuft of grass and looking at his feet. "I'm glad about that."

"Good," said Emma, fiddling with her hair. "I'm glad that you're glad."

Sensing the awkwardness between the two young teens, Millie laughed inwardly. She'd guessed there was a mutual attraction between the pair when they'd been in the classroom, but seeing them out of the classroom cemented the notion in her head. They fancied each other.

Remembering just how stomach-churning interactions with the opposite sex could be at the age of thirteen, Millie intervened, giving Emma an encouraging smile. "Go on then, show us how you serve."

"Oh, yes!" said Emma, hurrying behind the table

and standing beside her mother. She gave Norman an awkward smile. "Can I help you?"

Norman gave a shy nod of his head and stared at the cakes before him. "I'm not sure what to buy," he said. "They're for my stepfather, and I don't want to buy him the wrong ones."

At the mention of Norman's stepfather, Beth crossed her arms over her ample bosom, her eyes darting quickly from left to right. "Trevor's still here is he, Norman?" she asked quietly. "I thought he'd gone home."

"He's drinking beer in the tent over there," explained Norman, pointing in the direction he'd come from. "He's hungry, and he wants some cakes, but I don't want to get him any that he doesn't like. I want to make him happy." He looked at the floor. "He's never happy."

Placing a hand on Norman's shoulder, Millie glanced at Judith, whose eyes shimmered with tears. "He doesn't like cream cakes," she offered. "And he really seemed to enjoy the chocolate brownie he... found on the bar. So maybe he likes chocolate cakes with no cream."

Emma nodded. "Chocolate *does* make people feel happy," she said, taking her mother's hand in hers. "It makes you happy, doesn't it, Mum? When you feel sad."

Blushing, and giving a self-deprecating grin, Beth glanced down at herself. "Perhaps I eat a little *too* much chocolate," she said.

"I think we all do," said Millie, cheerily, offering Beth a smile she hoped would not be read as patronising. Although Millie occasionally struggled with her weight, her issues were evidently not on the same scale as Beth's. She gave Emma an encouraging smile. "So... can you recommend any chocolate cakes that Norman's stepfather might like?"

The young witch ran her eyes over the selection of cakes on the table and pointed at a plate laden with tiny chocolate chip muffins. "I think he'll love those bite-sized muffins," she said. "Everybody likes muffins, but you don't feel guilty eating five bite-sized ones like you would if you ate five real sized ones! There's no cream in them, either, and they're *bursting* with chocolate. You should buy him some of those, Norman. They'll cheer him up!" She winked at her classmate. "I promise!"

"Okay!" said Norman, attempting to perform a wink of his own, but instead managing to blink for what seemed to be at least four uncomfortable seconds. "I'll take some of those, please... Emma."

"Give him the ones in the plastic box on the other table," said Beth, indicating the smaller table behind them heaped with paper bags, Tupperware boxes, and a cash tray. "They're fresher. The ones on the plate have been out for a little too long. They're beginning to go hard."

"But those are yours, Mum. I baked them especially for you yesterday and then paid for them and put them in that box," said Emma. "I put them aside just for *you* to take home. There *were* ten, but the nice police sergeant helped me pick up all the coins from the grass when I knocked the cash tray over, so I gave him two as a thank you." She smiled at Judith. "Your father loved them, Miss Spencer! He licked the chocolate off his fingers like he was a toddler!"

"I bet he did," said Judith, with a grin. "He's a chocoholic!"

Beth nudged Emma, and spoke in hushed tones. "I know those cakes were for me, but we want Norman's stepfather to get the best ones, *don't we?*" she said, indicating Norman with an urgent jerk of her head as he looked the other way. "We don't want him to get annoyed because his cakes are too hard, *do we?*"

Realisation dawning on Emma's face, her eyes widened slightly. "Oh, yes. You're right, Mum. Norman's stepfather *should* get the fresh ones. You can take some hard ones from the table, and anyway, I can always make you some more." She smiled at Millie. "Now I know how to bake them."

"Yes," said Beth, "give those to Norman for his stepfather, and I'll take a few of the hard ones home with me. You know me, Emma. I'm not a fussy eater."

"That's very kind of you, Miss Taylor," said Norman, passing his five-pound note to Emma. "But are you sure? Trevor is quite drunk, so I don't think he'd care if his cakes are hard. You can have the freshest ones if you like."

Smiling kindly, Beth gave a quick shake of her

head. "I don't want to speak badly about your stepfather, Norman, but we all heard how he spoke to you today. I'm sure he can be very nice sometimes, but I'd rather he didn't have *any* excuse to be nasty to you again."

"He used to be nasty to you, didn't he, Mum?" said Emma. "When you were in school with him. That's why you don't like him, isn't it?"

"He was nasty to me, yes," said Beth, "but that doesn't really matter anymore. It was a long time ago. I shouldn't have told you."

With sudden anger displayed on his face, Norman grabbed the bag of muffins from Emma's hand. "Sometimes I wish he'd just go away and leave Mum and me alone!" he snapped. "Why won't he just go away? For good!"

"I'm sure things will work out for you, Norman," said Beth, softly. "I'm sure of it."

"Me too," said Millie, placing a reassuring hand on the boy's back. "Come on, let's get those cakes to your stepfather before he starts wondering where you've got to. Miss Spencer and I will come with you."

"Of course we will," said Judith.

Looking at the floor, Norman passed the bag of cakes from hand to hand. "Thank you, Miss Thorn and Miss Spencer," he said. "I wish everybody could be as kind as you two."

Leaving Trevor drinking beer and stuffing his mouth with tiny muffins, Judith and Millie escorted Norman back to his rugby game before reclaiming their seats at the small table outside the refreshments tent.

"Poor lad," said Judith, refilling the two wine glasses.

"Yes," agreed Millie. "Seeing the toxicity in other people's lives makes you realise how lucky you are to have nice people in your life, doesn't it?"

Taking a sip of her drink, Judith stared intently at Millie over the rim of her glass, curiosity in her eyes. "By nice people, do you mean George? Are you two an item again like last week, or not an item, like the week before?" she enquired, her tone genuine but teasing.

"Ha ha," said Millie. She sunk in her seat and sighed. "It must seem like that to everybody else. We're like a couple of kids, aren't we?"

"Truthfully?" asked Judith. She nodded, not waiting for Millie to answer. "Yes, you are, although George comes across as the biggest kid. I mean, why doesn't he just tell you who the mysterious woman is? We know he's not involved romantically with her... or at least you *believe* he's not." She looked down at the table. "Although I'm not sure *why* you believe him. He's been spending most of his time with a buxom blonde who has a liking for mini skirts, and you simply believe him when he says there's nothing going on?"

Rotating her glass on the table, Millie looked at

Judith with lowered eyes. "It's not that I *just* believe him," she said. She licked her lips and looked up. "I... I read his mind."

"Millie!" said Judith. "You said you'd never —"

"I know what I said," replied Millie. "I said being able to read people's minds isn't a pleasant power to possess. Accessing people's thoughts makes me anxious, sad, and angry — all rolled into one awful ball of emotions. I said I wouldn't do it again unless it was absolutely necessary, and I told you that I *especially* wouldn't do it to people I care for." She looked away from her friend. "Like George."

Judith gave Millie a reassuring smile. "I think I'd have done the same if I was in your position," she said. "I think I'd have read his mind, too. He was expecting you to accept too much, purely on the basis of his word."

Millie nodded. Judith was right. It had been months since George's relationship with the mystery woman had first come to Millie's attention, and since that day, George had expected Millie to accept the fact that he would be spending a considerable chunk of his time with the woman in question.

Seeing her boyfriend buzz past on his motorbike, with a pretty blonde riding pillion, had not been easy on the first occasion, but as the rides had become more frequent, they had become even more difficult for Millie to accept.

When George had announced matter of factly that the woman would be moving into his large country home with him, Millie's patience had finally been depleted, tempting her into using her mind reading abilities on her boyfriend.

She hadn't delved deep into George's mind. Not deep enough to find out who the woman was — she'd simply asked George one final time if the relationship he was having with the woman was anything that should concern her, and then used her power to discern if his answer was truthful or not. She had compared it more to a lie detector test than actually reading his mind. That may not have been technically true, but it had made Millie feel a little better about betraying George's trust.

Looking back, Millie knew that she'd not *really* needed to read his mind to know that he was telling the truth. The way he'd put his drink down, leaned across the pub table, taken both of her hands in his and whispered his answer as he looked her directly in the eyes, his gaze not dropping for a moment, had persuaded her he was telling the truth.

She could still remember the sincerity he'd projected when he'd spoken. "Millie, I promise you with every fibre of my being that I am *not* romantically involved with her," he'd said. "I realise how hard it is for you, and I wish I could let you in, but it's complicated, and it's not my decision to tell you. I need her permission. I'm sorry. But please know that I don't want to hurt you."

George's vampiric mind had been easy to read, and Millie had only needed a few seconds to completely verify that he was being honest. She hadn't asked George about the other woman since that day, but her relationship with him had suffered as a consequence of the secret, leading to the pair splitting up on numerous occasions, the current occasion being the fourth or fifth time in two months.

Judith broke into Millie's thoughts by pouring her another drink and passing a hand across her face. "Earth to Millie," she said. "Are you in there?"

Millie blinked. "Sorry," she said. "I was lost in thought."

"That's quite alright," said Judith, leaning back in her seat. "But you still haven't answered my question. Are you and George an item this week, or not?"

"Not really," said Millie. "I told him I needed space again, and he's kept his distance. He's got his mystery friend to keep him company, and I've got Reuben to keep me company."

The cheeky cockatiel might not have been the politest of witch's familiars in the world, but Reuben had proved himself to be a loyal and understanding companion. In fact, the spell which Millie had cast which had enabled her to speak to her dead mother, had been Reuben's idea, and the little bird was actively working on a way to bring her back again after Millie's mother had explained that the visit did not have to be a one off occurrence.

A smile teasing her lips, Judith looked past Millie and spoke into her hand. "Speaking of company, your not so secret admirer is approaching from your six o'clock," she warned, laughter in her eyes. "And he's straightening the knot in his tie. He must mean business."

Bracing herself for the inevitable flirting of Timothy Huggins, chemistry teacher and werewolf, Millie took a gulp of wine as footsteps crunched through the grass behind her.

"Millie," came the familiar effeminate voice. "Are you okay? I rushed here as soon as I heard."

Millie looked up at the man whose appearance was an enigma. Much like his voice, Timothy Huggins was a mixture of fully mature man and pubescent teenager. She knew he was in his mid to late twenties, and the lines beginning to show under his eyes proved that, but the outbreak of acne on his cheeks and the wispy attempt at what Millie supposed was an attempt at a beard, tricked the mind into perceiving him as a much younger man. A boy, even.

On the flip-side, when Timothy transformed into his wolf, there was no confusion about his maturity. His wolf was the largest and most powerful in Spellbinder Bay. Other wolves were fearful of Timothy, and it was well known that although his human form was less than intimidating, his wolf form was to be respected.

Learning that the size of a werewolf's animal form was based on the amount of courage in the person's heart, and not the size of their body, had made a lot of sense to Millie, especially where Timothy was concerned. It seemed that Timothy's courageousness knew no bounds when it came to speaking his mind, and he certainly wasn't timid when it came to approaching the woman he'd taken a liking to. Millie just wished that the woman in question wasn't her.

She gave Timothy a polite smile. She liked him, just not in the way he wanted her to like him. "You rushed here when you heard what?" she asked.

Kneeling down next to her seat, Timothy gazed up at Millie. "I rushed here when I heard you were an unclaimed treasure once more. I rushed here to make my feelings known, and to invite you to a meal, tonight." He licked his lips. "It's Friday today, Millie. That means that tonight is steak night at The Embarrassed Lobster."

"Unclaimed treasure?" said Millie, trying not to giggle. "Whatever does that mean?"

Timothy smiled. "You're a treasure which no man has claimed, Millie," he said. "When I heard that you and George were no longer involved romantically, I rushed here to lay down my claim to you. Respectfully, of course. I don't actually think I own you, it's just a saying, but I do think you're a treasure, Millie Thorn… a spectacular treasure which gleams among other less beautiful treasures. Like the barmaid at The Fur and Fangs." He frowned. "Or the woman from the pie shop."

"That's a lovely compliment, Timothy," said Millie. "I think. But may I ask how you heard that George and I aren't together anymore? I'm not sure where you got that information from. I haven't told anybody. Has somebody been talking about me?"

"I heard you tell Judith yourself. Just now," said Timothy. "I was over there, in the process of hooking a duck, when I heard you utter the words I've longed to hear. I rushed over here right away, Millie, and I still had three attempts left to hook a duck with a sticker beneath it which would indicate that I'd won a prize from the top shelf. This was more important, though, although I *was* going to choose a large teddy bear as my prize." He smiled and shifted closer to Millie. "Which I was going to gift to you."

"You were listening in to our conversation?" said Judith, coming to Millie's rescue. "That's rude, Timothy!"

"I wasn't eavesdropping," said the chemistry teacher. "I just can't help hearing things, sometimes! Because my wolf is so powerful, my human senses are very powerful, too. My hearing is exceptional, as is my sense of smell." He pushed his glasses up his nose. "It's just my peepers which need a little help, but I think my new glasses bring out the grey in my eyes. Wouldn't you two lovely witches agree?"

"Your glasses *do* suit you, but you know full well that you were listening to us, Timothy!" said Judith. "Tell the truth!"

Timothy stood up. "Okay. Guilty as charged," he admitted. "But I wasn't trying to listen to you two, honestly. I was listening out for Trevor Giles. I heard about the disruption he caused in your classroom,

Millie, and then about the argument he had in the beer tent. I know Trevor Giles, and I know he has a tendency to turn into his wolf when he loses his temper. I wanted to be certain I was nearby, in case my wolf was required to subdue his." He smiled at Millie. "I just happened to overhear your conversation as I was listening, and decided to make my move." He knelt down again and placed his hand on the arm of Millie's seat. "What *will* your answer be, Millie Thorn? Will you join me tonight for a meal at The Embarrassed Lobster? Will you allow me to claim *you* as *my* treasure?"

Millie smiled at the short man, not wanting to hurt his feelings. He *had* been very nice to her. "I'm afraid I can't, Timothy," she said gently. "I'm sorry. It's just that me and George —"

Timothy stood up quickly and rolled his eyes. "I don't need your life story, Millie," he said. "A simple yes or no is adequate, which you've now given me." He gazed down at Judith and winked. "How about you, Jude... do you like steak?"

"My name is not Jude!" said Judith. "Nobody calls me that! It's Judith!" She glared at Timothy. "And yes, I do like steak, but no, I don't want to attend steak night at The Embarrassed Lobster with you. Thank you very much."

Timothy shrugged. "Oh well," he said. "A man can try." He cocked his head to the side, like an inquisitive dog, as a voice announcing the raffle draw crackled over the tannoy system. "Ah! The moment

I've been waiting for! I've got my heart set on winning the two tickets for a day of pampering at the Golden Sands Spa and Restaurant. You get one full treatment and either lunch or afternoon tea. I'll probably opt for the full body-waxing followed by the afternoon tea option if I win, but I won't rule out lunch completely. I'd have to see a menu before I made a final decision."

Judith swallowed the last of the wine in her glass and got to her feet. "Come on, Millie," she said. "Lets go and watch the draw. I bought ten tickets. Five for me and five for you." She handed five of the little yellow tickets to Millie, and gave Timothy a thin smile. "It's not only you who wants to win the spa tickets."

Chapter 7

*F*inding a spot at the front of the large crowd which had gathered to watch Fredrick draw the winning raffle tickets, Millie and Judith reluctantly made space for Timothy, who pushed his way between them.

He looked at the two witches in turn and narrowed his eyes playfully. "I'll be watching to make sure neither of you cast a spell which will help you win," he warned.

"I wish my magic was that far evolved," replied Millie. "But even if it was, I'm quite certain that the prize draw is protected from magical cheating methods. And anyway, I'd never cheat."

"It was a joke," said Timothy. "Chill out." He stood up straighter and put a finger to his lips, nodding towards the tall man approaching the prize table. "Shush, it's Fredrick."

Fredrick made his way slowly towards the microphone standing alongside the raffle ticket drum, his stiff walk and the sharp angles of his pale face reminiscent of a vulture approaching a corpse on an African plain.

It seemed that Millie wasn't the only person who held a fearful respect for the vampire teacher — a blanket of silence had fallen over the whole crowd as Fredrick picked up the microphone, an unaware child who continued to talk urged into silence by his anxious father.

Fredrick tapped the microphone with a long fingernail, the amplified clicking sounds scaring the seagulls from their perches among the many chimneys of the old hall behind him. He peered through half-closed eyes at the people before him and attempted a smile. "Thank you all for attending the Spellbinder Hall end of year open day," he said. "I'm pleased to see so many people taking an interest in their children's education, and it's nice to witness the paranormal community coming together to enjoy the fete. I'd like to extend a huge thank you to the teachers and volunteers who set up the tents and stalls… entirely without the use of magic… or so I'm told."

Millie joined in with the round of applause and nervous peals of laughter from the audience, noticing Trevor Giles meandering towards the crowd from the direction of the refreshments tent, swaying unsteadily as he approached.

As the clapping subsided, Fredrick continued. "Before I draw the winning raffle tickets, I'd like to extend the congratulations of the headmaster and Mister Pinkerton, neither of whom could be here today, to all the pupils of the school. You've all worked very hard over the last term, and I think I speak for all the teachers when I say it was a pleasure to teach each and every one of you."

As more applause rose above the crowd, Trevor Giles swaggered closer to the prize table, a look of bemusement on his face. "Get on with the raffle draw!" he shouted, attracting angry looks from the people around him. "Nobody cares about listening to you talking!"

Fredrick remained silent for a few moments, and Millie gave a little gasp as his eyes flashed black, his mouth springing open to reveal two long thin fangs, the muscles in his neck tightening as he transformed into his vampiric form.

He regained his composure quickly, his eyes human again and no sign of elongated teeth as he spoke. "Mister Trevor Giles," he said. "I had heard that you were present here today, no doubt taking advantage of the fact that Mister Pinkerton is absent."

"I'd still be here if Henry was here!" yelled Trevor. "I'm not scared of him!"

Fredrick's lips curled slowly, and he gave Trevor a long searching stare. "We all know that's not true. You're emboldened by alcohol, Mister Giles," he said. He paused, before grasping the handle of the old raffle ticket drum on the table next to him. He gave it a single turn, the small wooden barrel creaking as it spun.

He put his mouth close to the microphone and spoke again, a hiss in his voice. "There are children present here today, Mister Giles, so luckily for you, I will ignore you for the time being, and continue with the raffle draw."

"Whatever," replied Trevor. "But you don't scare me, vampire!"

His nostrils flaring, and his lips set tight together, Fredrick opened the small door built into the raffle drum, and reached inside, withdrawing a single ticket. He glanced at it and looked up. "I'll be drawing the tickets in order of the top prize first, so this ticket is for the television set." He looked out over the audience. "And the number on the ticket is… one-hundred and twenty-four."

Despite having enough money in her bank account to purchase all the televisions she would ever require, Millie still gave a little squeal of joy as she waved one of her tickets above her head. "That's me!" she shouted.

"We have a winner!" said Frederick, clearly warming to the role of entertainer. He peered at the front row of the audience, searching for the lucky person, his eyes narrowing when they found Millie. "Oh," he said, his voice flat. "It's you, Miss Thorn. Well, congratulations. I suppose. You can collect your prize when I've finished drawing the other nineteen tickets."

"Has he still got a problem with you?" asked Judith, moving her face closer to Millie's.

"He's had a problem with me ever since I started dating George," replied Millie. "It's frustrating. And *very* rude of him."

Judith nodded. "That's how they are. Vampires, I mean. They're very protective of the vampires that they brought into existence with a bite — they're worse than parents in some cases."

"And Fredrick seems to be one of those cases," said Millie. "I suppose he'll be happy when he finds out that George and I have split up again."

"You may have lost a boyfriend," said Judith, "but at least you've gained a TV!"

Millie ran her eyes over the crowd, finding the hunched shape of Beth, her daughter standing along-side her, appearing crestfallen as she studied the strip of raffle tickets in her hand. "I don't need another television," she said. "But I know a girl who wants one."

"Three down, seventeen prizes to go," commented Timothy, watching Fredrick take a fourth ticket from the drum and announce the winner. "I'm still in the running for the spa treatment."

"As am I," remarked Judith. "And everybody else who bought a ticket. Don't get your hopes up, Timo-thy. You'll only be disappointed when you don't win."

Leaving Timothy and Judith teasing one another as Fredrick's amplified voice boomed across the clifftop, Millie pushed a route through the crowd towards Beth and Emma, noting that Trevor Giles had moved even closer to the prize table, and was obviously very drunk.

Giving a broad smile as she reached Emma and her mother, Millie winked at the young witch. "I hear that you had your heart set on winning the television, Emma?" she said.

Emma gave a quick nod, managing to turn her glum frown into a forced smile. "Yes," she said, "but I'm thrilled that you won it!"

Millie unfolded the winning ticket and held it out. "I don't need a TV, Emma," she said. "I want you to have it."

Emma's hand darted towards the ticket but stopped at the last moment. She looked pleadingly at her mother as the crowd applauded another winner. "Can I have it?" she asked.

Beth gave Millie a searching look. "Are you sure?" she asked. "You won it, are you certain you don't want to keep it?"

Millie laughed. "I live in a small cottage, and I've already got a TV in my living room, and another in my bedroom. I've got nowhere to put a third one, and anyway, you and Emma deserve it for taking over serving duties on the cake stall after my three child labourers deserted me."

"Can I have it, Mum?" asked Emma, her eyes sparkling with joy. "Please may I have it? In my bedroom?"

Beth gave a quick nod accompanied by a smile,

and Millie giggled as Emma wrapped her arms around her in a fierce hug. "Thank you, Miss Thorn! Thank you so much!"

"I hope you enjoy it," said Millie, returning the young witch's hug.

"I will, Miss!" said Emma. "And I'll look after it. I promise I will."

Leaving Emma chattering excitedly to her mother, Millie made her way back towards Judith and Timothy, frowning as she noticed Trevor Giles standing in front of Fredrick, a look of rage on his face. "Fix!" he shouted. "I should have won the beer and champagne!"

Fredrick spoke slowly into the microphone. "I think it's a good thing that you didn't win," he said. "I think you've drunk quite enough alcohol." Looking away from Trevor, he gave the drum another spin and reached inside for a ticket. "This ticket is for the spa treatment," he said, "and the lucky number is forty-seven!"

Smiling to herself as both Judith and Timothy's faces dropped in unison, Millie turned her head as a familiar deep voice gave a loud shout. "That's me! Although I don't think I need any spa treatments. I'm beautiful enough as it is."

"That's debatable, Sergeant Spencer," said Fredrick, humour briefly wiping away the stern expression which normally shaped his features. "But congratulations. Enjoy your prize."

"I *wonder* who's going to get those tickets," said

Timothy, nudging Judith playfully. "I *wonder* who a man like Sergeant Spencer will give his winning tickets for a spa treatment to."

"Hmmm," said Judith. She stuck her tongue out and smiled. "I don't know. I *wonder* who he'll give them to."

"Oh well," said Timothy. "It wasn't to be. If I want a spa treatment, I'll have to pay for a spa treatment. But it's not the same is it? There's something nice about being a winner, isn't there?"

Ignoring Timothy, Judith pointed towards the prize table. "Look out," she said, "Trevor Giles looks like he's about to cause some trouble."

Millie followed Judith's troubled gaze. She was right, Trevor Giles seemed intent on disrupting the prize draw. He staggered towards the table, and with no regard for the people he pushed past or the prizes he knocked from the table top, he reached for the case of beer and the large bottle of champagne. "I'm taking these!" he stated. "And nobody is going to stop me."

Wondering where Norman was, Millie scoured the crowd, relieved to see that Francine had taken the boy under her wing, turning him away from the scene his stepfather was causing and leading him towards the car park. "Poor boy," she said, under her breath.

Fredrick's voice boomed out over the tannoy system, this time making no effort to hide the disdain he held for the drunken werewolf. "Put those prizes down," he ordered. "Put them down immediately."

"Who's going to make me?" shouted Trevor, spinning to face Fredrick. "You?"

Moving quickly, his eyes darkening, Fredrick strode towards Trevor. "Put those down!" he said. "I won't tell you again."

Dropping the case of beer, and the champagne, the bottle saved from destruction by the soft grass, Trevor's body visibly tensed. "You think a vampire can hurt me?" he roared.

Suddenly, and with shredded clothes falling to the ground around him, Trevor was no longer human. In his place was a werewolf, slightly hunched as it balanced on its muscular hind legs, its eyes yellow and its teeth bared in a vicious snarl. It moved menacingly towards Fredrick, a roar building in its long throat.

Millie took an instinctive step backwards, a pressure wave moving the air beside her. She quickly looked to her left, stunned to witness Timothy adding at least three feet to his height and a few hundred pounds of muscle to his frame. His clothes shredded as quickly as Trevor's had, and coarse hairs swiftly carpeted his body. He opened his mouth in an angry roar, long thick teeth shining white against the vivid red of his gums.

Propelling himself forward with strong hind legs, he launched himself towards Trevor, skilfully avoiding the few people in his path. He slammed into the other wolf with a crunching thud, forcing the creature to the ground, leaning over it, his face centimetres from his opponent's snapping teeth, thick drool dripping from his mouth.

The smaller wolf writhed helplessly on the floor, snapping at Timothy's face with sharp teeth, and slashing at empty air with long claws on its hind legs. Timothy's wolf retaliated by placing strong jaws over the throat of the smaller animal, his growl reverberating across the clifftops as he shifted his weight and pinned the other wolf 's flailing limbs to the ground.

As the crowd moved away from the battling werewolves, parents turning children's heads away from the vicious spectacle, the weaker wolf suddenly transformed — no longer a terrifying animal, but a semi-naked man screaming in pain beneath the weight of a monstrous creature. As swiftly as Trevor had changed, Timothy transformed, too. Now much smaller than the man he straddled, he stepped away from his defeated adversary, hiding his modesty beneath a long coat handed to him by a helpful bystander.

"You shouldn't have done that!" shouted Fredrick, approaching Trevor, "that was unacceptable! Wait until Henry hears about this, I'm putting you into the dungeons below Spellbinder Hall until he returns from his trip. Then we'll see what he wishes to do with you."

The alcohol obviously still fuelling his bravado, Trevor appeared remorseless. "You don't have the power to lock me up, Fredrick. Only Henry has the right to put a member of the paranormal community in the dungeons."

The muscles around his mouth twitching, and his eyes still black, Fredrick leaned over Trevor. "You're right," he hissed. "I don't have the power to lock you up, and until Henry returns, there's nothing I can do." He stood up, his features reverting to human. "However, I know a man who does have the power to lock you up." He smiled at Sergeant Spencer. "I think Mr Giles may be guilty of disrupting the peace," he said.

Taking his handcuffs from his belt, Sergeant Spencer nodded. "And he's drunk and disorderly," he said. "Put your hands behind your back, Trevor," he commanded.

Remaining on the floor, Trevor reluctantly turned onto his front and allowed the policeman to cuff him. "Look at you," he said, twisting his neck to look over his shoulder at Sergeant Spencer. "The local bobby on the beat. You think you're so important, don't you? You can lock me up tonight, *Sergeant*, and you might think you have authority over me, but one of these days I'll get you back for all the times you've locked me in that cell of yours."

"You're nothing but trouble," said Sergeant Spencer, pulling Trevor to his feet as a man draped a coat over him. "And if I have my way, you'll be in a cell for longer than one night. In fact, if I had my way — you'd never leave my cell and you'd never trouble this town again."

"Thank you, Sergeant Spencer," said Fredrick. "Please take him away."

Taking Trevor Giles firmly by the arm, the big policeman dragged him towards the car park where his patrol car stood waiting. "It will be my pleasure," he said.

"You can lock me up," yelled Trevor, "but that doesn't bother me! I'll be out again in the morning and free to do what I want."

"We'll see about that," replied Sergeant Spencer.

"What does that mean? Are you threatening me?" yelled Trevor. "Are you saying I'll never leave my cell? I suppose I'll have an *accident*, won't I?"

"Quiet!" said Sergeant Spencer, forcefully guiding Trevor towards his car. "Nobody wants to hear what you have to say."

"What if he changes into his wolf again?" Millie asked Timothy, as Sergeant Spencer pushed his prisoner into the back seat of the car. "A human won't be able to deal with a werewolf. Will you be going to the police station in case you're needed again?"

"I'm not needed. He won't change again today," said Timothy, pulling the coat tighter around him. "He *can't* change again today. He's a weak wolf, I could smell it on him when I fought him. He needs moonlight to recharge his powers, and the moon won't be in the correct position to provide that sort of energy until just after nine o'clock tonight. He'll be safely locked in a police cell at that time, and even a werewolf doesn't have the strength required to rip open a steel cell door."

Millie nodded and looked Timothy up and down.

"Are you okay?" she asked. "Did he hurt you? That was very brave of you."

"It was," agreed Judith. "Very brave."

"It would take more than a wolf as weak as Trevor Giles to hurt or scare me," said Timothy. He smiled, placing his hands on his hips, the coat he was wearing falling open at the front, forcing Millie to avert her eyes. "But, yes — I suppose it was brave of me, and I would imagine that both of you young ladies would like to date me after my display of hero-ism?" He looked between Millie and Judith, scrutin-ising the witches in turn. "I'm afraid I can only date one of you, though," he said. "And I pick Millie to share a steak with me tonight at The Embarrassed Lobster. Congratulations, Millie, you've won twice today." He gave Judith a sideward glance and winked. "No offence, Jude."

Pointing at the portion of Timothy's anatomy which hid in the shadow of his naked stomach, Judith laughed. "I'd have taken more offence if you'd been fully dressed and not displaying your… thingamajig." She shook her head and gave a dry laugh. "I would imagine that Millie is honoured that you requested her company tonight. I bet she can hardly contain her joy."

Trying her hardest not to blast out the belly laugh which rose quickly within her, Millie gave a polite smile instead. "I'm sorry, Timothy," she said. "I'm really not in the mood for steak night at The Embar-rassed Lobster."

"There's no need to be sorry," replied Timothy. "I understand. It must be daunting to be asked out by the strongest wolf in town, but believe me, I do have a gentle side. I'm not all testosterone and masculinity."

Raising an eyebrow as she dropped her eyes to the lower portion of Timothy's body, Millie nodded slowly. "I know, Timothy," she said. "I know."

Chapter 8

illie parked her damson red Triumph Spitfire alongside Windy-dune Cottage, being sure to put the small car's roof up before she locked it and stepped into her home. Bathed in the amber glow emitted by the standing lamp next to the tall stone fireplace, the open plan living room and kitchen was as welcoming as always.

She took a minute to appreciate the view through the French doors in the kitchen, marvelling at how perfectly the sea reflected the oranges and crimsons of the sky and the last rays of the sun, the latter dropping below the distant horizon as the moon took its place in the sky.

Tossing her coat over the back of the large sofa, and slipping her shoes off, replacing them with her comfiest slippers — the tartan pair with the worn faux fur lining, Millie looked around for her familiar. He wasn't perched at his favourite spot on the kitchen table eating leftover pizza, neither was he sitting on the arm of the sofa watching trash TV.

Considering that Reuben only stretched his wings in the great outdoors when forced into exercising by Millie, and doubting very much that he was in one of the two bedrooms or the bathroom, there was only one place he could be. The same place he'd been every night for the last few weeks, pouring over ancient books about magic, looking for a spell which would allow Millie's dead mother to visit once more.

His dedication to finding a spell which would help her had comforted Millie. It was nice to know that he had her back, and he was certainly earning his keep by performing the duties of a witch's familiar.

During her last visit, Millie's mother had explained that the spell Millie had cast, which had allowed Josephine to cross between the realm of the dead into that of the living, had built a permanent bridge between the dimensions — a gate which Millie's mother could use again and again. Since that first visit, though, she hadn't reappeared, and with no logical explanation as to why her mother would not visit again if she could, Reuben and Millie had surmised that the reason for her absence had to be the fault of magic.

Magic, Millie had realised after almost a year of practising it, was not as straightforward as it was made out to be by the more experienced witches in the paranormal community. In fact, it could be down-right frustrating to get a spell to work correctly, and

Millie had no problem in believing that a magical glitch was preventing her mother from visiting again. A glitch which Reuben was adamant he could solve with the aid of the stacks of books in the coven cavern beneath the cottage.

Millie stepped towards the little wooden door built into the stone wall alongside the fireplace. It stood slightly ajar, a faint green glow leaking from around it, and the relaxing scent of ground herbs and old paper managing to seep past it and into the living room.

The entrance to the magical cavern below the cottage had not always been such a prominent fixture in the living room. It had been hidden from view when Millie had first moved into her home, only revealing itself to her when the energy within the cottage had confirmed that Millie had made the decision to stay in Spellbinder Bay, and not move away as she had intended to when things had become difficult.

Recalling how shocked she'd been when the door had first appeared, Millie smiled to herself as she pushed it open and stared down the stone steps hewn out of solid rock. "Reuben! Are you down there?" she called. *No answer.* She called again, her eyes adjusting to the calming green light which crept up the steps, illuminating the rough walls. "Reuben?"

"I'm here," came a squawking reply. "On my own. With nobody to keep me company."

"Well, I'm here now," said Millie, rolling her eyes. *Her familiar really was an attention seeker.* Reaching the bottom of the steps, Millie peered around the cavern, searching for the bird on the book heavy shelves carved from rock, and then on the brooms in the old iron stand, the handles of which Reuben liked to perch on. She smiled when she saw the cockatiel — standing on the rickety table next to the potion cupboard, his back to her, his head lowered as he studied an open book. "Hello, Reuben," she said.

"Where have you been?" said Reuben, his back still turned. "It's past nine! It's very late! I've been on my own all day!"

"It's only a couple of minutes past nine, and you *know* I've been at the school open day and fete," replied Millie, gazing into the waist-high ring of stones in the centre of the cavern. The contents of the cauldron mesmerising her as they always did, she dragged her eyes away from the green liquid which shimmered and swirled, and looked at the cockatiel. "I did invite you, Reuben, but you said, and I quote, 'I'd rather be force-fed sunflower seeds and cuttlefish bones than attend an open day at a school and be forced to share the same space as a herd of children for a whole day.'" She smiled and lifted her eyebrows. "Or words to that effect."

"Words which I stand by!" squawked the bird, spinning to face her, the crest on his head standing proudly upright. "But that still doesn't explain where you've been until *this* hour! Gallivanting, I expect!"

"I had a few glasses of wine with Judith," said Millie. "And time ran away with us. That's all. Nothing exciting."

Reuben cocked his head to the side and fixed one small coal black eye on his witch. "I heard the sound of your car engine! You drove home after drinking alcohol? Well, I never! I would never have imagined you to be the sort of person who would take such an irresponsible risk, Millie Thorn! I'm disappointed in you. Very disappointed!"

"Calm down," said Millie. "Timothy Huggins was kind enough to make a sobering potion for Judith when her dad phoned and asked her to come to the police station. She needed to drive, and instead of leaving my car at the hall and getting a taxi home, I decided to take some of the potion, too. So, don't worry, Reuben. I'm as sober as I was when I woke up this morning."

The bird gave an almost imperceptible nod of his head. "Good for Timothy Huggins. He's a splendid chap," he noted. "A chemistry teacher, a magnificent wolf, and a gentleman. I have a lot of respect for him. A lot of respect indeed." He fluttered the short space between the table and Millie's shoulder, landing with a light touch of his wing tip on her cheek. "Now that you and that awful bloodsucker are no longer an item, perhaps you'd think about... taking Timothy as your *man friend*? I think he likes you!"

"He makes no secret of the fact that he likes me," said Millie, rolling her eyes. "Which you know very well. But I'm afraid he's just not my type."

Reuben leapt from Millie's shoulder and flew in fast circles around the cavern. "Oh, come on!" he screeched. "Don't be so coy! You've had a bit of fang, now try a bit of fur! You might find you like it!" He swooped low, and landed on the top of Millie's head, his claws twisting into her hair.

"As romantic and appealing as you make it sound, I'm not in the market for fur, fangs, or any other embellishment belonging to any manner of paranormal, or non-paranormal person, thank you very much," said Millie. "George and I haven't split up, anyway — we're simply on a temporary break — the necessity of which has been mutually confirmed by us both."

"Jeepers," said Reuben, untangling a foot from Millie's hair. "It was just a suggestion. There was no need for such a *fancy* reply. Nobody uses words like *embellishment* anymore." He gave a whistle, and then a laugh. "Come down here, Millie. Come and spend some time with the commoners. We might not talk fancy like you, but we're good folk. You might like us."

"Ha ha," said Millie, wincing as Reuben pulled at her hair. "Ow! That hurts!"

Reuben gave one last tug and freed his foot. He flew to one of the shelves in the cave wall and perched alongside an unmarked bottle with a cork stopper pushed into the neck, keeping the contents safely inside. "So… what did he want? Why did he phone her?"

"Pardon?" said Millie, straightening her hair.

"Sergeant Spencer. What did he want? You said

Judith had to go to the police station because her father had phoned her. Sergeant Spencer usually closes the station at night time. Has something happened?" he gazed at Millie, the red circle on his cheek as bright as the contents of the bottle next to him. "Oh no! Not *another* murder? That will be the third this year! What is it with this town and murders?"

"Don't worry," smiled Millie. "Nobody has been murdered. Sergeant Spencer had to arrest somebody for being drunk and disorderly at the school fete. He has to stay at the police station all night to look after the prisoner, so he phoned Judith to ask her to bring him some cakes from the fete. He was hungry, that's all. You can rest easy. There have been no violent deaths."

"He asked for some of the cakes which you and your class of tiny people made yesterday?" asked Reuben. "The same ones you brought samples of home with you last night?"

"Yes, the cakes that my pupils and I made, Reuben," said Millie. "The ones I brought a few of home. The ones which we made to sell at the fete."

Reuben nodded. "Oh. You gave him the cakes for free?"

"Erm, no," said Millie. "Judith paid for them. Sergeant Spencer told her he'd give her the money back. It's all for charity, you see?"

Reuben blinked, his head askew. "He said he'd give you money for them? And he actually wanted them for the purpose of *eating*? To enjoy the taste of, and to provide himself with nutrition and energy?"

"Yes, Reuben," said Millie. "That's what most people do with cakes, and he'd already tried a few earlier in the day. He loved them, and he wanted more, you know how he likes his food."

"The fact that he likes good food is what's got me baffled about this cake situation," said Reuben. He studied Millie for a few seconds, his eyes half closed, and then gave a shrill whistle. "You told him, didn't you? You told him he was your father! What did he say, Millie? I bet he was amazed! I'm so happy for you! Do you feel complete?"

"No, Reuben," said Millie. "I haven't told him. I told you I was going to wait for the right moment. It's still only you, me, and Henry who know the truth. And my dead mother, of course." She paused and gave the bird a look of suspicion. "What makes you think I've told him that he's my father?"

"That's the sort of thing a father would do, isn't it?" said Reuben.

"What is?" asked Millie, perplexed.

"Eat his offspring's awful cooking and then pretend he liked it," said Reuben. "It makes no sense that he'd ask for some of the cakes otherwise." He tilted his head to the opposite side. "Hmmm. Perhaps he just wanted to make you feel good. Perhaps he's an even nicer man than I gave him credit for, and I already had him ranked very highly on the scale of niceness."

Scowling, Millie folded her arms and bent at her waist, looking her familiar directly in one eye, her irritated reflection staring back at her. "People like my cakes, Reuben. I'm good at baking. That's why I was asked to teach cookery at Spellbinder Hall. The fact that you have a fussy palate, does not mean that my cakes do not taste nice."

Stretching his wings, Reuben yawned. "I've tried nicer cakes, that's all I'm saying. Your chocolate cakes are acceptable, but anything can be made to taste nice with enough chocolate in the recipe. It's when you try and get clever that your cakes take a wrong turn. Your lemon fancies, for example… how can you possibly make something which looks so delightful, taste so absolutely awful? The only thing fancy about those vile creations is the sound they make when they hit the bottom of the bin."

As Millie was about to explain to Reuben, that with manners like his, he could forget about pizza and kebab for at least a week, and become acquainted with bird seed and broccoli, her phone buzzed in her pocket. "It's Judith," she said, as she lifted it to her ear. "We'll continue the conversation about my cakes in a moment."

"Good," said Reuben. "I'm glad it's finally all out in the open. I've been meaning to have a discussion with you about those *things* which you call Viennese whirls."

Millie stopped paying attention to her familiar as the panicked voice of Judith burst from her phone.

She listened intently, her stomach lurching and the hairs on her arms standing on end. "I'll be there as quickly as I can. Calm down," she promised, before ending the call.

"What is it?" said Reuben. "You've gone white. What's happened, Millie? Is Judith okay?"

Trying to make sense of what she'd just been told, Millie slid her phone back into her pocket and put a hand on the stone cauldron to steady herself. She looked at Reuben. "The third murder this year you were worried about," she said. "Has just been committed, and Sergeant Spenc – my father, is the prime suspect."

Chapter 9

*P*arking in the clinical white glow of one of the wrought iron street lamps which lined the majority of streets in the town centre, Millie slammed the car door shut and bounced up the three steps which led to the police station entrance. Barging the heavy door open with her shoulder, she rushed into the reception area, her face dropping when she saw the glazed look in the eyes of Sergeant Spencer, his anxiety amplified by the dull fluorescent lighting.

Ordinarily jovial, whatever the circumstances, the policeman's face showed overt anxiety and fear, which unnerved Millie. Sitting behind the high reception desk, Sergeant Spencer's demeanour was light years away from his customary happy self, and his voice was laced with uncertainty as he looked up and spoke to Millie. "Thanks for coming," he said. "Judith's in the cell with the body." He looked down at his hands, which were clasped together on the desktop, both sets of knuckles white. "*With Trevor*, I should say. The man did have a name, after all."

"What happened?" said Millie, approaching the desk, her training shoes squeaking on the tiled floor. "Judith didn't make much sense on the phone, but she said something about Trevor being murdered with poison." She considered reaching for one of the big man's hands, but decided against it, giving him a kind smile instead, longing for the day on which it would be acceptable to show him physical affection. "She also said that you've classed yourself as the main suspect in his murder. I don't understand."

"I gave him the poison that killed him," he said, his voice flat.

"What?" said Millie. "You poisoned Trevor? Why are you saying that?"

"I didn't give it to him on purpose, and I'm not quite sure *what* happened yet, but it's the only logical explanation," said Sergeant Spencer. He hesitated and shook his head. "It's better that Judith explains everything to you. I *must* be treated as a suspect, and this isn't the sort of conversation I should be having with you if we're to follow correct investigative procedure. After all, I did make both you and Judith acting police officers after you helped me solve Albert Salmon's murder."

And since that murder, which had occurred on her first day in Spellbinder Bay, she had helped solve one additional murder, Millie recalled with regret. The townsfolk were used to seeing her and Judith working with Sergeant Spencer, and with the help of the concealment spell — transmitted from Spellbinder Hall and enveloping the whole town, the community never asked any questions concerning the validity of the two young women who helped the town's only policeman.

Its strong magic working on the perceptions of non-paranormal people, the concealment spell had the effect of making mysterious occurrences quickly fade from the mind and memory of the human observer. The mysterious incidents in question spanned a broad spectrum — including almost imperceptible occurrences, such as the quick flash of black in an angry vampire's eyes when he argued with a human, and culminating in events as spectacular as a group of five werewolves chasing a frightened fox along High Street and out of town.

The fox had never returned to scatter the contents of any more rubbish bins across the street, and the concealment spell had managed to wipe the memories of the twenty or so people who had witnessed the werewolf stampede, some of them passing out from the effects of fear and requiring medical attention before the spell had finally calmed their minds.

With a concealment spell *that* powerful shielding the paranormal community from discovery, it had been easy to convince the town that she and Judith were legitimate police officers.

She nodded at Sergeant Spencer. "Okay," she said, beginning to realise that the policeman was serious about being treated as a suspect, but also aware that his years of experience would prove invaluable in finding out what had really happened to Trevor. "You say Trevor was poisoned. Will you come and look at the body? You might notice something that Judith and I might miss."

"I shouldn't go near the body," said the sergeant, with an adamant shake of his head. "I can't risk contaminating the evidence any further — I checked Trevor's throat for obstructions and tried to revive him when he died, so traces of me are already all over him and the food and drink I gave him. You and Judith will have to work without me until you've done your due diligence and cleared my name."

"But we know you wouldn't do anything to harm him," said Millie. "And *you* certainly know you didn't kill Trevor. Why are you so insistent on being a suspect?"

"You saw what happened back at the school fete," said the sergeant. "I wasn't exactly pleasant to Trevor when I arrested him, was I? I said some quite nasty things to him, and I specifically remember telling him that if I had my way, he'd never leave that cell. That could be classed as a threat, and there were plenty of witnesses present who heard me."

"Everybody knows you wouldn't do something like that!" said Millie. "Everybody in this town respects you!"

"You're not that naïve, Millie," said Sergeant Spencer. "You know that's not the case. Plenty of people dislike me, especially from the paranormal community. I've arrested a lot of them during my time in the town, and a lot of them don't like the fact that a non-paranormal such as me has so much influence over their community. Add to that the fact that Trevor was a werewolf, and I think you'll find that a lot of the paranormal community will begin showing a loyalty to Trevor that they never showed him while he was alive. They'll want to find the culprit quickly, and they won't like the fact that the man who gave Trevor the meal which killed him is investigating his murder. They'll consider it to be some sort of cover-up." He looked at the desk again. "I can't be part of the investigation until my innocence has been proved."

"Okay," said Millie, relenting. Although painfully aware that Sergeant Spencer was more emotionally vulnerable than she'd ever seen him, she was equally aware that Judith was still alone in a police cell with a dead body. She probably required Millie's support more than the policeman did. "What do you advise we do first?" she asked.

"I think you'd better start by examining the body and trying to work out exactly what happened to him," replied Sergeant Spencer.

"Me and Judith examine the body? Surely a pathologist should do that?" said Millie, unable to hide the concern in her voice.

Sergeant Spencer sighed. "There'll be no pathologist," he said. "A member of the paranormal community has been killed. Trevor's murder is not a matter for the police or the non-paranormal community in general. That's just how things work in Spellbinder Bay. I'm sure you and Judith will be able to find answers, and I'm sure you'll be able to ask for help from people you trust. *Paranormal* people you trust, you mustn't involve anybody outside the paranormal community."

Millie shook her head, still trying to understand what she was being told. "Okay," she said. "*That* makes sense, but what doesn't make sense is the fact that you're so adamant that people will think you had something to do with Trevor's death. Why do you want to be a suspect so badly?"

"I don't *want* to be," answered Sergeant Spencer. "I *have* to be." He frowned, the furrows around his eyes deepening. "It was probably me who gave Trevor the poison, Millie. That's all we know at this stage. Trevor asked for a drink and something to eat, and I gave him something. Of course I did. He may be —" He hesitated, his eyelids drooping. "He *may have been* one of the most unsavoury people in town, but he still deserved to be treated with respect. So, I took him some food and a cup of tea, and by the time I'd locked the cell door behind myself and got a few steps down the corridor, Trevor was coughing and shouting for help. By the time I got the key back in the keyhole, he was making loud choking sounds, and by the time I opened the door, he was dead on the floor with his hands clasped around his throat."

"Maybe he choked?" asked Millie. She shook her head. "No, you already said you'd checked his airway. But why are you assuming he was poisoned? Maybe something else killed him? Something less... murderous."

"You'll understand when you see his body," said Sergeant Spencer. He ran his eyes over Millie's face, suddenly appearing concerned. "If you want to see it of course. Nobody is forcing you to help. It's just that you've been such a great aid in the past; I think Judith assumed that you were the person she had to call, and I agreed. She trusts you. I trust you, and you have to remember that I'm Judith's father. It's probably not easy for a young woman to hear her father telling her that he's to be treated as a murder suspect. She'll need your support."

"No," said Millie, wondering, with a lump in her throat, who would support her. Wishing she could trust herself to hug him without blurting out the truth about their relationship, she gave Sergeant Spencer a thin smile, painfully aware of the similarities between the shape of her mouth and that of his. "I'm sure it's not easy for her. I'm sure any daughter would find that difficult. I'll be there for her, though."

Sergeant Spencer gave a slow nod. "You're a special young lady, Millie. Judith couldn't have asked for a better friend, and I couldn't have wished for a better person to *be* her friend. You two are so close. You're almost like sisters."

"Yes," said Millie, turning her back on the desk

and facing the entrance to the cells, not sure whether the tear which tracked down her cheek was as a result of Sergeant Spencer's words, or the fact that she was about to view a dead body. "Yes," she repeated, rubber squeaking on tiles as she walked slowly across the room. "We're just like sisters."

MILLIE HEARD JUDITH BEFORE SHE SAW HER. THE sound of heavy breathing interspersed with frightened mutterings came from the cell's open doorway, and as Millie peered around the door frame, it was hard to decide which of the two people on the cell floor appeared to be the deadest.

Both of their faces were as pale as the handkerchief which Judith clasped in her hand, and both of them were still, but that was where the similarity between life and death ended. The fact that Trevor's eyes had glazed over and were staring aimlessly at the dull white ceiling, and the fact that a shimmering river of sparkling blue foam trickled from between his grey lips, placed him firmly as the winner of the deadest person on the cell floor contest.

Hunched over Trevor's body, Judith took a deep sobbing breath and looked up as Millie entered the cell. "Millie! Thank goodness you're here! I really need you right now."

Staring in morbid astonishment at the glowing foam which continued to trickle from Trevor's mouth, realising now why Sergeant Spencer had told her that she'd understand why poisoning was the probable cause of Trevor's death when she saw his body, Millie knelt on the floor next to Judith, placing a comforting hand on her friend's shoulder. "What is it?" she said quietly, watching the bubbling river of bright foam forming a small pool on the floor next to the dead man's cheek, before evaporating in tiny multi-coloured sparks, which flickered, flashed, and vanished after rising a few feet in the air. "Is that the poison?"

"It must be," said Judith. "It hasn't stopped coming out of his mouth since I got here. It all just turns into sparks and evaporates, though."

"Is it magic?" asked Millie. "Was Trevor killed by a magical potion?"

"I don't know," said Judith. "But I do know what Dad gave him to eat and drink just before he dropped dead." She pointed at the floor beneath the small window, its brick-thick frosted glass blocks backlit by the moon.

Millie gasped. "Cakes!" she said, staring at the spot where a plastic tray had spilt its contents. "The cakes the children and I made!"

Judith nodded. "Dad didn't know that Trevor didn't like cream, and call me cruel if you like, but I didn't tell him when I saw him selecting the cakes for Trevor. That's why the French horn and the eclair are on the floor, but the mini-muffin has been eaten."

"The poison was in the muffin?" asked Millie, her mouth dry. "The muffin the children and I made?"

"I don't know," said Judith. She nodded towards the brown puddle, pooled next to a steel mug. "Maybe it was in the tea. We won't know if he drank any without finding out what's inside his stomach."

Suddenly feeling faint, Millie choked on the acrid bile which burned her throat. "Oh no!" she said. "If the poison was in one of the cakes I made, what about all the other people who ate one?" Her eyes widened. "Has somebody poisoned the cakes the children and I made? Will other people die?"

Judith shook her head vigorously. "No!" she said. "Those cakes on the floor are the ones that I brought from the fete for Dad. I ate one on the way over here, and Dad ate two when I got here, and we're both fine. If the cake was poisoned, I find it highly unlikely that it was poisoned before I brought the cakes to the police station."

"So, what happened?" said Millie, staring into Trevor's glassy eyes. "Did somebody sneak into the police station and poison Trevor's meal?"

"No," said Judith, getting to her feet. "That would have been impossible. When I got here with the cakes, Dad made a pot of tea… I helped him. He's a traditionalist like that, he always makes a pot when he can. We both sat at the front desk and had a cup each, and Dad ate two cakes. I was still here when Trevor started shouting that he was hungry, and I watched Dad pour a cup of tea for him from the same pot we'd drank from, and put some cakes on a tray.

"I said goodbye to Dad at about nine o'clock, and left the station as he was taking the tray to Trevor. I'd only driven as far as the end of the street when my phone rang. It couldn't have been more than three minutes since I'd left the station. It was Dad telling me that Trevor had died." She stared at Millie, her face white. "Nobody could have sneaked into the police station, and that tea and those cakes weren't poisoned before I left."

"The poison was added to his meal in the three minutes after you left?" asked Millie, understanding what that meant and beginning to fear that Sergeant Spencer *would* be treated as a suspect by other people in the town.

Judith gave a sombre nod. "It must have been. Dad said Trevor started shouting for help almost as soon as he'd closed the cell door behind himself after he'd given him the tray. He obviously went straight for the mini-muffin and not the cream cakes, and maybe he took a sip of tea before he died." She took a long breath as she gazed at the body at her feet. "So, unless Trevor poisoned himself, or Mister Invisible was in the cell with him, then the cake or the tea was poisoned after I'd left, and during the time it took Dad to walk the few steps from the reception desk to the cell."

"Maybe the poison *was* in the cake when you brought it here," suggested Millie. "How can you be so sure it wasn't?"

"Because I'm still alive," said Judith.

"What does that mean?" asked Millie, puzzled.

"I feel so childish telling you," confessed Judith. "And I know it's stupid, but I *really* don't like Trevor Giles. When Dad locked him up last weekend for fighting in a pub, he was very nasty to me, and to Dad. And after seeing him being so nasty to that poor old man in the refreshment tent today, I really didn't think he deserved nice fresh cakes to eat. I told Dad to give Trevor a limp ham sandwich when he started shouting for food, but you know Dad."

"He's too kind," said Millie.

"Yes," agreed Judith. "So that's why I didn't tell Dad that Trevor didn't like cream when he put two cream cakes on the plate." She looked down. "And why I snapped half of his mini-muffin off while Dad was looking the other way, and pushed the rest of it against the French horn to make it look whole again."

"Really?" said Millie. "You did something that a six year old would do to their brother or sister's cake when they were looking the other way?"

"Yes, really," said Judith. "I did that. I knew he wouldn't eat the cream cakes, and I didn't want him to have a whole chocolate muffin. I wanted him to suffer."

Millie raised an eyebrow. "It was a bite-sized muffin," she said. "It's not like it was very large in the first place."

"I know," said Judith. "And I know it was imma-ture of me, but it proves that the poison wasn't in the muffin when I snapped a piece off, because I ate it, and I feel fine."

Digesting the information, Millie stared at the contents of the tray on the floor. If the poison had been in the meal, it had to have been in the tea or the muffin. The muffin that wasn't poisoned when Judith had eaten a piece, and the same tea that both Judith and her father had drank, with no side effects obvious in either of them.

That meant only one thing. If the meal had been poisoned, it must have been poisoned after Judith had left the police station. Blowing out slowly, Millie pushed herself to her feet and stared at Judith. "That's why your father wants to be considered a suspect," she said.

Screwing her face into an expression of anguish, Judith massaged her temples with a finger and thumb. "Yes," she said, "because at the moment he's the only *logical* suspect, and unless we find out what really did happen to Trevor, then everybody is going to believe that he *actually* did it."

Thoughts crowding her mind, Millie concentrated on what needed to be done next. Watching as another dribble of florescent foam bubbled from Trevor's mouth, she slid her phone from her pocket. "We need help," she said, tapping at her phone's screen. "At this stage, we don't even know with absolute certainty that he was poisoned." Putting the phone to her ear, she looked around the cell.

Partially consumed meal on the floor? *Check*. Dead

man on the aforementioned floor, his dead hands clutching his dead throat? *Check*. Mysterious glowing foam which turns into sparks and evaporates, spewing from aforementioned dead man's mouth? *Check*.

She sighed. Of course he'd been poisoned, but they still needed to identify the poison used. They needed the help of somebody with a knowledge of chemistry, potions, and as a helpful bonus — werewolf physiology.

"Who are you ringing?" asked Judith, looking away from Trevor, the handkerchief held to her mouth.

"The only person I can think of right now," replied Millie.

Chapter 10

imothy Huggins answered his phone with a satisfied edge to his voice. "What a pleasure it was to see your name flash up on my screen," he said. "Although it wasn't completely unexpected."

"Timothy!" said Millie. "Stop speaking! I need your —"

"I know *exactly* what you need," said Timothy, speaking over Millie, hardly pausing to breathe as his voice rose in volume. "I knew you'd come to your senses when Judith wasn't around to put a downer on things. She's jealous of you, Millie... jealous that you were asked out by the biggest, strongest wolf in town, and not her."

"Timothy! Please listen to me!" urged Millie, certain she'd heard the pop of a champagne bottle being opened on the other end of the phone. "I need you!"

"I know, Millie," said Timothy. "And it just so happens that I'm available to supply whatever it is that you need. You know where I live, Millie, get yourself over here, pronto. I've just opened some bubbly and I'm about to light the log fire. There's a sheepskin rug in front of it large enough for two… if you know what I mean?"

Scrunching her eyes tightly closed, Millie took a deep breath. "I know *exactly* what you mean, Timothy," she said. "But that's never going to happen! I need your help! We need your help… Judith and me. We —"

"Woah!" said Timothy. "Stop right there! That's an interesting proposition, and I'm very flattered, but I'm not sure that I have the stamina to entertain the two of you. It's been a long day."

"Trevor has been murdered!" Millie yelled, startling Judith, who took a step backwards, almost tripping over Trevor's body. "We need your help as a chemistry teacher and a werewolf! We think he's been poisoned!"

"Trevor Giles? Murdered?" said Timothy, the cockiness in his voice replaced with what sounded like genuine concern. "Where are you?"

"The police station," said Millie. "And please hurry. I'd like to move Trevor's body. He should be somewhere which offers more dignity than the floor of a police cell."

"I'll be there as soon as I can," promised Timothy, ending the call.

Timothy peered over the rims of his glasses, the point of his yellow tie scraping the floor as he kneeled over Trevor Giles, inspecting the foam which still trickled from the dead man's mouth. Reduced from a river to a thin stream, the foam appeared to be drying up, the last of it dissipating in a shower of tiny bright lights which drifted upwards, vanishing into nothingness before they reached the ceiling.

"What is it?" asked Judith. "Is it poison?"

Timothy sniffed at the air, shutting his eyes in apparent concentration. "There's poison involved, alright," he said, opening his eyes again. "It's fading quickly, but I can smell *something* suspicious." He sniffed again, and looked at the two witches. "I can smell a strong scent of cacao, which is presumably from the cakes he ate."

Millie nodded. "We used good quality cacao when the kids and I baked them. That's not suspicious, though, is it?"

Taking long considered breaths through his nostrils, Timothy closed his eyes again. "It's what's in the background which strikes me as unusual," he said. "I'm picking up the scent of a few herbs which wouldn't normally be associated with cakes." He looked up. "In my limited experience of cake baking," he added.

"What sort of herbs?" asked Millie.

"There's lavender," said Timothy, sniffing the air

above Trevor's mouth. "There's valerian root, too." He took a series of short sniffs, his nose twitching as he concentrated. "There's some kava, and a little ginko leaf, I think."

"I haven't heard of those last two," said Millie. "Are they dangerous? Are they poisonous?"

Timothy shook his head. "No," he said. "I have extracts of them all in my chemistry lab, there're perfectly safe on their own, but I'd have to do some testing to find out if they're poisonous when combined. I don't think so, but I'd need to check. There are so many possible herb combinations that it's impossible to memorise the effect they all have when mixed with other herbs."

"Can you smell anything else?" asked Judith.

Smelling again, Timothy used his hand to waft the air above Trevor's face towards his nose. He sniffed. "Yes," he said, after a long moment. "My, my. Now that might be interesting."

"What is it?" said Mille, sniffing the air herself but only getting a nostril full of Timothy's lemony after-shave. "What's so interesting?"

"I can smell Saint John's wort," said Timothy. "Which can be dangerous to werewolves in large enough doses. It's not so dangerous that I have to keep werewolf children away from it in my lab, but they are aware that they shouldn't ingest too much of it when testing the potions they've made. It shouldn't kill a werewolf, though — just make them a little unwell for a short period of time." He frowned. "But as I say… who knows what concoction was made by mixing a few herbs? Maybe somebody found a way of making these herbs fatal when mixed with one another. I'll need to run some experiments."

"What about the cakes and tea on the floor?" observed Judith. "Do they smell of the same herbs?"

Timothy moved towards the two cream cakes and the puddle of tea. "Let's see," he said, lowering his nose towards the floor. He murmured something to himself before looking up at Millie and Judith. "No," he said. "There's no smell. The tea and the cakes smell normal."

"If he was poisoned, the poison must have been in the mini-muffin he ate," stated Judith. "And the muffin I had a bite of."

"You ate some of the same muffin that Trevor ate?" asked Timothy.

"Yes," said Judith, "Just a bite. Before I left Dad here alone, and I feel fine, so that proves that the poison wasn't in the muffin when I left."

"Or it proves that if there was poison in the muffin, it was designed to target werewolves and not witches," noted Timothy. "And it must have been a very fast working poison. Sergeant Spencer says that Trevor began making sounds the moment he'd locked the door behind him. Trevor would only have had the time to quickly chew and swallow his muffin before the poison affected him."

"And before Dad had opened the door, the poison was already a blue foam which was bubbling from Trevor's mouth. I'd say it was very fast working poison indeed," noted Judith.

"No," stated Timothy. "That's not right. The foam you saw wasn't poison."

"It wasn't?" asked Millie. "Then what was it?" She looked upwards, her eyes following a final blue spark as it rose heavenward. "Oh!" she gasped. "Was it his soul?"

"In a manner of speaking," said Timothy. "It *was* his soul. That of his wolf, anyway." He replaced the blanket, which Millie had taken from the cell bed, over Trevor's body and stood up.

"The soul of his wolf?" said Judith. "How awful!"

"It's awful, yes," said Timothy. "But it wasn't really his soul, so to speak. It had no consciousness. It was energy. The magical energy which gave Trevor the gift of being a werewolf. The sparks it created when it evaporated was simply energy rejoining the ether — where it will remain until called upon one day when another werewolf baby is born. It's actually quite a beautiful thing... the energy which once made Trevor who he was, for good or for bad, will one day be within another wolf."

"Is that what happens to every werewolf when they... pass?" asked Millie. "That... foam? Those sparks?"

"No. Absolutely not," said Timothy. "The reason that it happened to Trevor is because somebody must have possessed the knowledge to mix those herbs I smelt into a very cruel poison. A poison which severed the human part of Trevor from the wolf portion of his identity. When a werewolf dies of natural causes, his wolf and human parts die simultaneously... the human soul, or energy, whatever people like to call it — going wherever it is that human energy goes. The wolf energy leaves the body at the same time — invisible, simply melting into the ether. The foam you witnessed is the result of Trevor's human portion dying suddenly — with no warning. His wolf energy found suddenly itself with no host and was forced to expel itself from Trevor's body. The glowing foam and the sparks *were* that energy."

"What sort of poison could do that to a werewolf?" said Millie. "And what sort of person would do such a thing?" She opened her eyes wide as a horrifying thought crossed her mind. "What if all my cakes *were* poisoned? And what if the poison only affects werewolves? What if other wolves eat my cakes and die? We must do something! We must find every single one of my cakes which hasn't been eaten and destroy them!"

Timothy shook his head. "If it was in the cake he ate, which we won't know until we've had a look inside him, then I don't believe anybody else is in danger. I've been eating the cakes you made all day, Millie. As have other wolves." He removed his glasses and rubbed his eyes. "I believe whatever poison Trevor ingested was meant for him, and only him. I don't believe anybody else is in danger. Somebody with a grudge against Trevor administered the poison to him, and him alone, and now it's our job to discover who that person is."

"And how do we do that?" asked Judith. "Where do we begin?"

"One of the first things we should do is go and put your father's mind at rest, Judith," said Timothy. "He looked distraught when I arrived, and he told me that he believed he'd poisoned Trevor."

"That's what he *really* believes," said Judith.

"And to be honest," said Millie, reluctantly, "that's how it might look to somebody who doesn't know him. To a person who doesn't know that Sergeant Spencer is the type of man who wakes up every morning with the intention of helping people and not harming them. To a person who doesn't know what a deeply kind man he is."

"You speak very highly of him," noted Timothy.

"Yes," said Judith, touching Millie's arm. "You do. And it's nice to hear. I suppose my judgement about him could be clouded because I'm his daughter, but hearing you… somebody outside the family, speaking of him in such a lovely way, completely confirms that I'm not wrong."

"Of course you're not wrong," said Timothy. "Sergeant Spencer is heroic, honest, hard-working, decent, and every other quality that helps make up a fine human being." He paused, and then lowered his voice, looking towards the cell door, as if suddenly remembering that the subject of his conversation was less than twenty feet away. "But that's what might turn out to be a problem for him if we don't find out what happened to Trevor," he said.

"I don't get it," said Millie. "How will the fact that he's a nice man be a problem for him?"

Loosening his tie, Timothy frowned. "Not the fact that he's a nice man. I'm talking about the fact that he's a *man*, full stop. He's a human being… he's non-paranormal, and when the paranormal community discover that one of their own has been murdered — a rarity in itself, they'll want to find out who did it. And quickly." He looked towards the door again, lowering his voice once more. "And when certain segments of the community find out that the only suspect is a human, they'll want justice even more so than if the suspect was another member of the para-normal community."

"Why?" asked Millie. "That doesn't sound right. That sounds…" She hesitated. *What did it sound like?*

"Intolerant," spat Judith. "Bigoted. Unfair." Anger flashed in her eyes. "There are plenty more words for that sort of attitude. Take your pick — they all lead to the same conclusion. Some people will treat Dad unfairly just because he's different from them."

"I understand how you feel," said Timothy. "I do, really…"

"But?" said Millie, prompting him. "Go on."

Timothy gave a nod. "*But* it's understandable in some ways. The human race devastated the para-

127

normal community in ages gone by. They burned witches, they hunted werewolves, they put stakes through the hearts of vampires, and their wild stories turned ghosts from the peaceful wandering souls of the dead people that they are, into hideous creatures that should be feared and exorcised. There's a precedent for the paranormal community to fear even a single attack by a human against one of their own... they fear it could lead to worse. Much worse. As their history has proved is viable."

"Yes," said Millie. "But that was history, as you said. Even if people did know of... *our* existence, I think they've evolved past that sort of violent reactionary thinking. I truly believe they'd be more understanding of us than they used to be. More accepting of us."

"Really?" said Timothy, raising an eyebrow. "There are still cultures in the world who hunt and kill vampires... the awful thing is that most of the people they kill are not actually vampires. They're innocent people. There are people who hunt with guns for Bigfoot, Yeti, Sasquatch... whatever name they give the creature, which, incidentally, all stem from werewolf sightings. There are cultures in which it's acceptable to kill a rare animal and use its bones or horns to make potions from. Can you imagine what they'd do with a vampire's fangs or a mermaid's tail?"

Millie thought of Lillieth, the beautiful mermaid who had gifted her a magical dress which allowed

Millie to grow a fin and breathe underwater. The peaceful mermaid was kind and gentle, and the thought of her having her tail hacked off for use as an ingredient in a potion that allegedly increased fertility, or cured an illness, turned her stomach. She looked at Timothy. "I think I understand," she said. "But not all humans would wish us harm."

"That goes without saying," said Timothy. "But as sad as it may be, some of the paranormal community don't fully trust *any* humans." He placed a hand on his chest and looked between himself and the two witches. "Not all of us, of course, but enough of us to make it unsafe for Sergeant Spencer if word got out that he was the man who'd served a werewolf the poison-laced meal which killed him." His eyes darkened. "Even more so because Trevor was a werewolf."

"Why?" asked Millie.

"Let's just say that although rational beings, us werewolves are very tribal and remarkably quick to anger. I'm ashamed to say it, but werewolves are probably the least tolerant of all paranormal folk," said Timothy. "It's imperative that we discover what happened to Trevor before bad rumours begin spreading about the good sergeant. If the wrong sort of werewolf hears those sorts of rumours about Sergeant Spencer, certain wolves within my community will be banging down doors to get at him."

"Especially after he was seen arresting Trevor," said Judith, her expression that of worry. "*And* was heard saying the things he did to him. Things such as the fact that he hoped he'd never leave his cell."

"Empty words," said Timothy. "To us — the people who know your father on a personal level, but imagine how it would look and sound to a wolf who Sergeant Spencer has locked up in the past — a wolf with a grudge against him, and let me promise you, with wolves being as quick-tempered as they are, there are plenty of those in Spellbinder Bay."

"Then we need to find out what happened to Trevor, quickly," said Judith, her voice urgent. "But where do we start?"

"I'll call Fredrick," said Timothy, taking his phone from his pocket and tapping at the screen. "He's running Spellbinder Hall during Henry's absence. I'll tell him what's happened and arrange for Trevor's body to be taken to the hall. We can have a proper look at him there — all the facilities required to find out what killed Trevor are present."

Millie looked up at the high corners of the cell. A tiny red light blinked on the camera that gazed down at them. "We should check the CCTV footage from throughout the station," she said. "Even though it's probably a waste of time."

"It *will* be a waste of time," said Judith. "Those cameras don't record anything. What would be the point? The concealment spell won't allow any para-normal occurrences to be committed to film or digital software; otherwise sites like YouTube would be full of mobile phone videos which would expose the paranormal world to the rest of the globe."

"I'm sure we'll get to the bottom of whatever happened to Trevor without the aid of modern technology," said Timothy, the phone still at his ear as he waited for Fredrick to answer. He cast a final glance at the blanket covered corpse at his feet, before turning to face the cell door. "Before we do anything else, I think we should begin by making poor Sergeant Spencer feel a little better. He's sitting out there on his own, convinced that he's killed a man. That can't be nice for him." He turned away as Fredrick answered his call, speaking quickly into his phone.

As Timothy explained the situation to Fredrick, Millie took one last look around the cell, hoping that they'd missed something, some vital clue which would scream the answer to the riddle of Trevor's death at her.

Finding nothing of significance, she scanned the scene once more. There were no further answers forthcoming. The small glass block window couldn't be opened from inside or out, and the thick metal cell door had only been opened briefly when Sergeant Spencer had served Trevor the meal which lay strewn across the floor. Nobody could have sneaked into the cell and administered a fatal poison to Trevor, and Judith and her father were both certain that there had been nobody else in the police station. It seemed that all available evidence pointed to the distasteful fact that Sergeant Spencer had indeed served Trevor Giles the meal which had killed him.

Following Timothy from the room as he finished his phone call, a dark uneasiness settled in Millie's stomach, sending icy cold tendrils along her limbs. She had a disheartening feeling that this puzzle was going to be hard to solve, and she had an even stronger feeling that things were going to be difficult for Sergeant Spencer in the following days.

Chapter 11

*S*till seated behind the reception desk, his hand moving quickly as he scribbled notes on a piece of paper, Sergeant Spencer looked up as Timothy and the two witches approached the desk. "So," he said. "Did you discover anything of significance?" He shook his head. "No. I shouldn't be asking that. I shouldn't be involved until you've proved my innocence."

"Sergeant Spencer," said Timothy. "I hope you won't take offence at what I'm about to say, but there is absolutely *no* way that I'm going to honour your request to be treated as a suspect. I'll happily help Millie and Judith clear your name if anybody is ignorant enough to believe it was you who harmed Trevor Giles, but I shall not continue with the charade of you being thought of as a suspect."

"Me neither," said Millie. "It's not right."

"You can add my name to the list," said Judith,

approaching the desk and reaching for her father's hand. "Obviously."

His shoulders lifting, as if being hoisted by invisible strings, Sergeant Spencer allowed himself to smile, confidence reigniting in his eyes. Appearing as if he was going to speak, he remained silent, the quick nod he gave conveying his thanks instead. His shoulders rising further, and his chest swelling beneath his crisp white shirt, he got to his feet. "Okay," he said. "I understand." He hesitated briefly before taking a deep breath. "So, did you find anything?"

"We believe the muffin Trevor ate may have been poisoned," said Judith. "We can't be sure until further checks have been done, so Timothy phoned Fredrick. He's coming to collect Trevor's body."

"We can perform a full autopsy at Spellbinder Hall," explained Timothy. "We have all the facilities required, although they're rarely used. We'll know more when we have the results."

"But you agree Trevor was poisoned?" asked Sergeant Spencer. "All that blue stuff coming from his mouth... what sort of poison is that?"

"That wasn't poison," said Millie.

"It was his wolf energy leaving his body, Dad," said Judith. "But Timothy suspects that Trevor was poisoned. He smelled something suspicious coming from him."

Sergeant Spencer looked at Timothy. "You did? What sort of smell?"

Timothy sat down on one of the chairs in the

waiting area, the cheap metal frame creaking as he settled into it. "A strange scent," he said. "Coming from his mouth. A mixture of herbs. I'm not certain exactly how it worked, if the mixture was responsible for Trevor's death, but I'm sure we'll get to the bottom of it when we... look inside him."

"Let's hope so," said Sergeant Spencer. He indicated the piece of paper he'd been writing on. "I've been mulling over everything that happened, and I can't work it out. Judith and I had eaten the same cakes and drank the same tea that I gave to Trevor. It doesn't make sense. If Trevor *was* poisoned, when was the poison added to the meal I served him? There was nobody else here. I would have seen them!"

"There was no poison in the tea, and none in the two cream cakes," explained Millie. "So the poison must have been in the muffin. We'll find the answers. We always do. But don't worry. Nobody thinks you had anything to do with Trevor's death."

"Nobody in this room thinks I did anything," said Sergeant Spencer, "but Trevor was in my care, and I'm sure Timothy won't mind me saying that the werewolf community can be a little..."

"Rash, headstrong, hot-headed," said Timothy. "I take no offence, and I've already warned the girls about the dangers you may face if word gets out that you..." His words trailed off, and he looked at the floor, his face flushed.

"Killed Trevor?" finished Sergeant Spencer.

Timothy shook his head. "No! If word gets out

that you inadvertently served him a meal which *may* have killed him," he said, correcting the policeman. "There's a huge difference between that and purposefully poisoning a man."

"A difference which will be wasted on certain people," said Sergeant Spencer. "I've locked a lot of werewolves up during my time in this town, and that's been thirty years. I can only imagine how many wolves I've put in a cell."

"Yes," said Millie. "Thirty years *is* a long time. Imagine how many friends you've made during that period, too. Imagine how many people there are in this town who won't hear a bad word said about you! There will be a lot more wolves who respect you, than wolves who think you'd be capable of murder."

"You'd be surprised how quickly people can turn," said Sergeant Spencer, drumming his fingers on the desk. "Especially in a community as family orientated as the werewolf community is. Blood is thicker than water, Millie. Family comes first."

"He's right," said Timothy. "Werewolves all belong to large families. Clans, if you will. It's not how it used to be in the old days when clan members lived together like tribes, and fought with rival clans. These days most clan members don't even acknowledge other members of the same clan. Think of a clan as an extended family who only meet up at weddings and funerals." He gave a sigh, blowing his cheeks out. "But when one of the clan is wronged..."

"Family comes first," said Millie, glancing at Sergeant Spencer. "I get it."

Timothy nodded. "Yes, and some of the really hot-headed wolves will begin treating Trevor as a son or a brother, even though they never cared for him while he was alive. Trevor was a loner in life, but he'll have a clan behind him in death. Especially if his clan think he was murdered." He removed his glasses and polished the lenses on his shirt sleeve. "Which is why I think this whole thing should be kept quiet until we have an answer. We'll tell nobody in the wider community that Trevor is dead. Apart from his wife and stepson of course, although I don't think that Helen Giles will shed many tears for Trevor. The rumour is that Helen had never really wanted to marry Trevor in the first place."

"Then why did she?" asked Millie.

"Out of the very real fear of being a social pariah," explained Timothy, scratching his cheek. "When Helen's first husband — Norman's father, upped and left her for what he considered would be a better life in America, Helen was left as a single middle-aged woman with a child. In the werewolf community, that sort of situation can sometimes be considered as..." He hesitated, searching for the correct terminology, Millie presumed. "As wrong," he continued. "As socially unacceptable."

"Really?" said Millie. "That's not nice."

"It's not," agreed Timothy. "But that's the way it is. Werewolves consider the presence of both a mother and a father to be of great importance," he said. "Not all werewolves think that way, but generally, the werewolf community could be considered as being very conservative. They like things to be done in the same way they were done in the old days." He looked up. "And that includes a child having a mother *and* a father. Some of the older wolves, Helen's parents included, I'm told, look down on single mothers. They don't believe that a mother should bring up a child on her own, they believe a father should always be involved."

Millie bristled. "There's nothing wrong with being brought up without a father," she snapped, avoiding looking at Sergeant Spencer. She swallowed her anger, saving it for a better target than the three kind people in the room with her. There was no point in her getting angry over the past. Would her life have been vastly different if Sergeant Spencer had been a part of it from the beginning?

She sneaked a sideways look at him, wondering what sort of father he would have been to her when she was growing up. She'd never know, but that wasn't the point, the point was... that up until her death, her mother had been a perfect parent, and Millie had never wanted for anything. Had her mother made mistakes? Oh yes, the biggest being hiding the fact that she knew who Millie's father was but had chosen to lie instead. Did that make her mother a bad parent? No. Misguided, maybe, but not bad. She was never bad, and had done the job of both a mother and a father to the best of her ability.

She sighed. Maybe having both a mother and a father *would* be preferable to having just one parent, but Millie didn't like the idea that some people tried to sell. The idea that a child was worse off with a single parent. She smiled at Timothy. "I just think that it's a terrible attitude to have, that's all."

Timothy stood up, placing his glasses back on his face. "I agree with you, Millie," he said. "As do a lot of the wolf community. All I'm saying is that I don't believe Helen Giles really wanted to marry Trevor. She settled for him so that she wouldn't be judged for being a single mother. I don't believe she'll shed many tears over his death. In fact..." He stopped speaking and shook his head. "No, I shouldn't say things like that. It's wrong of me. I hardly know Helen. I only know what I've been told."

"Things like what?" said Sergeant Spencer. "What things shouldn't you say?"

Timothy frowned. "It's just that now Trevor is dead, Helen won't be judged so harshly. Like she was when her first husband left her. Quite the opposite will be true... she'll be treated with respect and helped by the rest of the community." He shook his head, his expression remorseful. "It's a sad reflection on my community, but it's acceptable for a woman to be a widow, but not acceptable for her to be an estranged wife. It's sad to say, but she'll be in a better position than she was when Trevor was alive. Not that I'm saying she'd want to hurt him, of course."

"Of course not," said Judith, her eyes darting towards her father.

Not wanting to say what *she* was thinking, having never met Helen Giles, and not wishing to cast aspersions upon people, Millie suddenly realised just how many people may have wanted to harm Trevor Giles — and she was only considering the people she'd seen him arguing with since he'd arrived in her classroom earlier that day. It seemed that Trevor was the sort of man who invited conflict into his life with an open door and a welcome mat.

Trevor had offended most of the other parents who'd attended the children's cooking demonstration, as well as being awfully rude to Cuthbert Campion and his daughter. He'd been aggressive towards Fredrick and he'd fought with Timothy, not to mention annoying the whole of the audience who'd been watching the raffle draw. Heck, even the ghost wearing black robes had been startled at his abrupt entrance into Millie's classroom, so much so that it had rushed at Trevor.

If Trevor's mysterious poisoning was a puzzle, it would have been a jigsaw that had long ago lost its box, and with no reference picture to work from, a puzzle that would prove hard to solve. Impossible, maybe.

Her mind beginning to rummage through the

scattered puzzle pieces, Millie gave her head a slow shake. "It's all just assumptions," she said.

"What is?" asked Timothy, giving her a quizzical look.

"Everything to do with Trevor's death," she said. "*You* assumed that Trevor's wife won't be too upset about her husband's death, Sergeant Spencer is assuming that he gave Trevor the meal which killed him, and we're *all* assuming that Trevor was killed by that meal. We're even assuming that Trevor actually was poisoned. Until somebody has a look at Trevor and finds out exactly what happened to him, it's all wild speculation on our behalf."

"I agree," said Timothy. "We can begin thinking more clearly when we have further information about what actually happened to Trevor." He glanced at the main exit door, his head tilted to the side. "Fredrick will be here in a moment to take the body away. I can hear an engine. He's driving his Range Rover."

"I don't hear anything," said Judith, looking towards the door.

Timothy tapped the lobe of his right ear. "Werewolf ears," he said, with a grin.

Almost as soon as Timothy had finished speaking, Millie heard the roar of a powerful engine outside, followed quickly by the screeching of tyres and a car door being slammed shut.

"Told you," said Timothy, looking up as the police station door swung open.

His eyes flitting quickly from person to person,

darkening briefly as they fell on Millie, Fredrick strode quickly across the room, stopping in front of the reception desk. He stared at Sergeant Spencer, his voice cold as he spoke in accusatory tones. "Henry Pinkerton leaves me in charge, and you have a death in custody, Sergeant? And not just any death... the death of a member of the paranormal community! Do you know how complicated that could get? What happened here? What did you do? Timothy told me on the telephone that you poisoned Trevor Giles!"

"Actually," said Timothy. "I told you that Sergeant Spencer *assumed* he'd poisoned Trevor. Nobody knows what actually happened, yet."

Fredrick sucked in a long slow breath and gave a considered nod. "That may have sounded harsher than I intended it to," he admitted. "I'll begin again. Timothy told me that you locked Trevor in a cell, served him some food and drink, and then almost immediately after shutting the cell door behind yourself, heard him choking. Timothy tells me you opened the cell door and found Trevor dead with his hands clasping his throat and a blue substance bubbling from his mouth. Timothy also tells me that he's never seen anything like it before. He tells me that the way in which Trevor's wolf energy left the body, along with a strange smell emanating from Trevor's mouth, makes him certain that there was poison involved." He turned his glare onto Timothy. "That sums up what you told me, doesn't it?"

Timothy gave a meek nod. "Yes," he said.

Turning back to face Sergeant Spencer, Fredrick nodded. "We don't know what happened yet, Sergeant Spencer, but I've known you for a long time. It goes without saying that I don't believe you purposefully killed a man... however awful that man happened to be."

"Of course he didn't!" said Judith. "And I won't hear anybody saying he did!"

"Calm down," said Fredrick, lifting a leather gloved hand. "We have to judge things as we see them, Judith. However fond we all are of Sergeant Spencer, we must accept the facts as they arrive, however unpalatable. The facts at this moment in time, as I can gather, point to the fact that a man died in a police cell, most probably poisoned, immediately after eating a meal served by the man charged with his safety while in custody."

Judith's face reddened. "That sounds so—"

"Correct," interrupted Sergeant Spencer. "It sounds correct. That's exactly what happened here tonight, Judith."

"Thank you, Sergeant," said Fredrick. "I appreciate your professionalism in this matter." He looked towards the corridor leading to the cell. "We should move Trevor to Spellbinder Hall immediately. I have a witch waiting who is going to examine him as soon as possible." He looked at Timothy. "I'd appreciate your help in carrying him to my vehicle."

Chapter 12

*H*aving stowed Trevor's body in the vehicle, both Fredrick and Timothy appeared a little uneasy as they re-entered the police station, the door swinging slowly closed behind them.

"That felt a little too much like being in a mafia movie," said Timothy, trying to make light of events. "I never thought when I woke up this morning that I'd be stuffing a body wrapped in a sheet into the back of a luxury SUV with black tinted windows."

"Me neither, Timothy," said Fredrick, his black leather gloves and dark clothing making Timothy's reference to the mafia a little too well observed. "However, we cannot change what has happened."

"What now?" asked Timothy.

Fredrick gazed around the room, peeling his gloves from his hands. He spoke to everybody. "Timothy informed me that he thinks it would be better to keep this little… incident under wraps for the time being, and I agree with him. We will of course inform Mrs Giles of her husband's unfortunate demise, but I agree with Timothy that until we are sure of what happened here tonight, Trevor's death should not become common knowledge." He paused, his eyes falling on Sergeant Spencer. "Especially considering the circumstances surrounding his death. People will come to conclusions very quickly if the story were to emerge."

"And they'd conclude that I wanted to hurt Trevor," stated Sergeant Spencer.

"Indeed," murmured Fredrick, "and that could turn out nasty for you, Sergeant. Not all of us in our community have always appreciated the efforts of a human policeman in keeping our little town safe."

"I understand," said Sergeant Spencer.

Fredrick nodded. "Then you'll understand that it would be inappropriate for you to have any part in investigating this crime, Sergeant?" he said, plucking at a piece of fluff on the sleeve of his suit jacket. "Until we understand what happened to Trevor."

"So you can eliminate me from your enquiries," said Sergeant Spencer.

"I wouldn't have put it quite like that," said Fredrick.

The policeman forced a smile. "Don't worry. I understand. There *should* be doubt on your behalf until you've established what happened. I wouldn't have it any other way."

"You're a stickler for procedure, as always, Sergeant," noted Fredrick. "I respect that." He turned to face the doorway, slipping his gloves into his pocket. "I should be getting poor Trevor back to Spellbinder Hall. I'd like the autopsy to be done as soon as possible. You'll follow along, Timothy? A werewolf with a knowledge of chemistry may come in handy at the autopsy of a fellow wolf murdered by what we believe to be poison."

Timothy nodded. "Yes, I'll be present."

"I'll come, too," said Judith. "I'd like to be there."

"No," said Fredrick, with a shake of his head. "It's an autopsy, not a public freak show."

Judith took a step towards the vampire, a flash of anger in her eyes. "This is about my father, as well as Trevor. I want to make sure everything is done properly. I want to make sure that nothing is missed."

"Are you insinuating that the autopsy wouldn't be above board if you weren't present, Miss Spencer?" asked Fredrick, a shadow in his eyes.

"That's not what she means," said Millie, interjecting on her friend's behalf. She knew exactly how Judith felt. Narrowing her eyes, she locked Fredrick in a stare. "She's worried. She wants to find out what happened to Trevor so not even a shadow of suspicion is laid at Sergeant Spencer's feet. Sergeant

Spencer is her father. Judith loves him, and even though we all know he's not capable of murdering a man, her father is still being spoken about in words which suggest he might have had something to do with what happened to Trevor." She stood straighter, keeping her eyes on the vampire's. "You said yourself that Sergeant Spencer shouldn't be involved in the investigation until we've cleared him of any wrong doing."

Fredrick put a hand up. "I didn't mean —"

"I haven't finished," snapped Millie, an angry rush of blood in her ears, no longer arguing just for Judith's right to be at an autopsy, but for the honour of the man who was unaware he was her father. "Sergeant Spencer has served this town for longer than I've been alive. I've been in Spellbinder Bay for just less than a year, but already I've seen what this town means to him — how much he cares about the paranormal community *and* the non-paranormal community. I've seen how much he cares about everyone in this town, and I've seen how much he's done for this town. Can you imagine how it sounds to his daughter to hear you even saying in passing that her father's name needs to be cleared before he's permitted to investigate a murder?"

"I —" mumbled Fredrick.

Millie cut him off quickly, bleeding her pent-up emotions, knowing she wasn't being fair to the vampire, but needing to vent, nonetheless. "I'll tell you how it probably sounds," she said. "It sounds disrespectful, it sounds rude, it sounds uncaring, it sounds callous, it —" She hesitated, her words caught in her throat. What did it feel like? She took a steadying breath, grounding herself once more. "It probably sounds terrifying to Judith, Fredrick. The thought of her father being accused of a crime probably feels scary and out of her control. It probably makes her afraid of what could happen to him."

"Thank you, Millie," came the soft voice of Judith beside her, accompanied by a hand on her arm. "That's precisely how it feels."

"Those were some nice things you said about me, Millie," said Sergeant Spencer. "And I appreciate them. I really do, but never let emotions rule your thought process when it concerns a criminal investigation." He glanced at his adopted daughter. "Or you, Judith. Due process must always be followed, and if that involves hurting some feelings, then so be it. Fredrick is only doing what he thinks is right, and I'd hoped we were all in agreement."

Aware that all eyes were on her, Millie shifted her weight between both feet, already conscious of the stifling guilt that always followed a loss of temper. No, not guilt. Shame. Shame that burned in her face, and shame that would linger within her for days. She dropped her eyes from Fredrick's face. "I didn't mean to be so angry," she said, in way of an apology. "It's been a long day."

"That's fine," said Fredrick, his expression indecipherable. He looked towards Judith. "Of course you may attend the autopsy. Millie may, too, if she desires. We all wish to find out what happened to Trevor." He turned his head towards Sergeant Spencer and gave the policeman a dry smile. "We all share the opinion that your father isn't capable of murder, Judith, but we must gather the proof to present to the small-minded people who might believe otherwise when the news about what happened becomes common knowledge. It would be unwise to involve your father in that process. I hope you understand, Judith."

Judith nodded. "I understand. I just want to get on with finding out what happened to Trevor."

"You won't find anything out standing around here," noted Sergeant Spencer. "You'd all better go. Get the autopsy done. I'll lock up and go home. The police station is a murder scene now, anyway, and I think it's best that I remove myself from duty for the time being."

"You're a good man, Sergeant," said Timothy, thrusting a chubby hand towards the policeman. "And you'll be back at work in no time at all, when we find out what really happened here tonight!"

Smiling, Sergeant Spencer took Timothy's hand in his, shaking it vigorously. "Thank you, Timothy," he said. "I have every confidence in each of you to discover how Trevor Giles ended up dead on the floor of my cell."

"Rest assured, we'll have an answer about what exactly happened to Trevor soon enough," said Timothy, releasing Sergeant Spencer's hand and pushing his glasses along his nose. His face suddenly changed and he sniffed the air, his eyes narrowing. "Hmmm, peculiar," he said, putting his hand to his nose and smelling his fingers.

"What's peculiar?" asked Judith.

Timothy sniffed his hand again, looking at Sergeant Spencer as he did so. "There's a smell on my hand," he said. "The same smell I picked up on Trevor's body... the scent of herbs. Only this time it's stronger."

"The smell which you thought might be poison?" asked Fredrick, his face darkening.

"Yes," murmured Timothy. "The smell coming from Trevor's mouth, but strangely, the scent on my hand is even stronger than it was on Trevor."

"Did you pick it up from Trevor?" asked Judith.

"I hardly touched his body," said Timothy, "and the smell was emanating from Trevor's mouth... rising from his stomach. The smell on my hand is stronger, more potent. As if I'd touched the source of the smell."

"So where did it come from?" asked Judith.

Timothy gave Sergeant Spencer a searching look. "May I smell your right hand, please?" he asked. "In fact, may I smell both of your hands?"

Chapter 13

"hat's wrong?" said Judith. "Why do you want to smell my father's hands, Timothy?"

Judith may not have understood, but Millie did, and she also understood why Timothy had suddenly become rigid, the muscles beneath the plump folds of his neck visibly tense. He was suspicious. Suspicious of Sergeant Spencer. *Suspicious of her father.*

Politely ignoring Judith, Timothy took a step closer to the policeman. "Would you mind, Sergeant?" he asked.

"What's going on?" demanded Judith. She paused, her mouth suddenly opening in a gasp. "You think my dad has the poison... or whatever it is, on his hands, don't you?"

Holding up his right hand, Sergeant Spencer smiled at Judith. "If I have got traces of whatever it is that killed Trevor on my hands, then I'd like to know."

He smiled at Timothy, holding his hand higher. "Smell away, Timothy, but if you have traces of a poison that killed another werewolf on your hand, shouldn't you be worried?"

"If it is poison, I'd be dead already if it could kill through contact with the skin, and I don't intend on putting my hands anywhere near my mouth until they've been thoroughly washed," said Timothy, moving his face toward Sergeant Spencer's raised hand, his nostrils flared.

As Timothy sniffed, Sergeant Spencer turned his hand slowly, allowing Timothy to smell his fingers and palm. "Well?" he said, as Timothy drew away from him.

Timothy turned to face Fredrick, confusion on his face. "The scent is very strong on the sergeant's hand," he said. "I believe that if it is the scent of a poison which killed Trevor, then Sergeant Spencer definitely had some form of contact with it."

"What are you saying?" said Judith. "What are you insinuating?"

"I'm not insinuating anything," promised Timothy. "I'm just stating facts. I can smell the same mixture of herbs that emanated from Trevor's mouth, on Sergeant Spencer's hands."

"Can you explain this turn of events Sergeant Spencer?" asked Fredrick, the skin around his mouth taut. "Maybe there is a logical explanation."

Sergeant Spencer looked at his hands. "I did put my fingers in Trevor's throat when I found him on the cell floor. I thought he'd choked on some food, so I looked for an obstruction. Maybe the smell got on my hands then? I washed them afterwards, but maybe it's one of those scents that washing doesn't remove? Other than that possibility, I have no idea how it got there."

An expression of contemplation on his face, Fredrick nodded. "Okay, Sergeant," he said. "That would make sense." He gave Timothy an enquiring look. "What do you think, Timothy? Does that explanation make sense to you?"

"I suppose so," said Timothy, his eyes flitting from Fredrick to Sergeant Spencer. "There's no other logical explanation. At the moment."

"What about me?" said Judith, thrusting her hand towards Timothy's face. "Have I got the scent on my skin? I handled the cakes as well. I even ate some of the muffin."

"You did?" said Sergeant Spencer.

"Yes," said Judith, as Timothy sniffed her fingers. "When you weren't looking. I didn't tell you, because I didn't think Trevor deserved a plate of cakes — but he didn't like cream cakes, so I knew he'd only eat the muffin. So, I took a bite, just to be... childish, I suppose."

Sergeant Spencer hurried toward his daughter, his eyes frightened. "Do you feel okay? You think that muffin had poison in it, and you've taken a bite of it!"

"I'm fine, Dad," said Judith. "Timothy thinks the

poison could have been designed purely to target werewolves."

"But I don't think Judith need worry anyway," said Timothy. "There's no scent of any herbs on her hands, and the smell was so potent I'd smell it on her breath when she spoke if she'd ingested any. I don't think the muffin had any poison in it when Judith took a bite."

Sergeant Spencer looked at his hands. "Then if the muffin *was* poisoned, the poison was added after Judith had left the police station, and the scent of whatever it was is on my hands." He looked up. "I don't understand."

"You didn't see Judith take a bite of the muffin," said Millie, "so it goes to say that maybe you wouldn't have seen somebody sneak into the police station and poison the cake."

"I don't see how," said Sergeant Spencer. "There were only a few minutes between Judith leaving and me giving the cakes to Trevor. Nobody could have sneaked into the police station and poisoned the muffin in such a short space of time. I didn't leave the plate unattended, anyway." He shook his head. "It's impossible."

"Impossible for a human," suggested Millie. "But not for somebody with paranormal qualities. Think about it… a vampire can move very quickly and very quietly, and some witches are very good at invisibility spells."

"Not to mention ghosts," added Judith.

"It's worth considering the fact that a vampire or witch may have sneaked into the building," admitted Timothy. "But it would take a ghost with tremendous willpower to carry off such a feat. Ghosts can manipulate solid objects if they try hard enough, but to transport a vial of poison would be an almost impossible feat for most ghosts. Any apparition attempting to transport an object would need to be highly motivated. It's very difficult for a spirit to make itself felt in our dimension — either through touch, or manipulation of objects."

"But anything is worth considering at the moment," said Millie. "However fanciful it may sound."

"I agree," said Frederick. "We must consider all possibilities." He cast a surreptitious glance in Sergeant Spencer's direction, unseen by Judith or her father, but spotted by Millie. "Although I think it would be foolish to stray too far from logic."

"None of what has happened sounds logical to me," protested Judith. "There has to be an explanation which *isn't* logical."

"Might I suggest we save conversations such as this for after an autopsy has been performed on Mister Giles," said Fredrick, sliding a hand into a glove. "We are speculating, without understanding what it is we are speculating about." He looked towards the door. "I have the body of a man in my vehicle. I think it's about time I got it back to Spellbinder Hall."

STEPPING OUT OF THE POLICE STATION, MILLIE GAVE an involuntary shiver. She'd rushed from her cottage without a coat when Judith had phoned her, and with no cloud cover to trap the warmth of the day, the night air had a crisp edge as sharp as a knife.

As Timothy stepped onto the pavement, he gazed up at the moon and rolled his shoulders. He took a deep breath, expelling it slowly. "That's a feeling none of you will ever experience," he said, his words making smoky shapes in the cool air and his glasses magnifying the sparkle in his eyes. "The feeling of standing beneath a bright moon after being trapped under fluorescent lighting for so long. It really gets the blood pumping... and the wolf roaring."

"No roaring please, Timothy," said Fredrick, striding towards the Range Rover parked in front of Millie's car, dwarfing the little Triumph. "This is a residential area."

"I didn't mean it literally," retorted Timothy. "As you well know, Fredrick."

The thud of the police station door being slammed shut and the jangle of keys as Sergeant Spencer locked it echoed along the quiet street, drawing the attention of a nearby black cat which hurried into the shadows of an alleyway between two shops. The policeman pocketed the large bunch of keys. "It feels good to be locking the door and knowing I've got some time off from work, while you good folk do my job for me!" he said, his voice edged again with the humour that had been absent for most of the night. He looked at his watch. "Anybody fancy a nightcap back at mine?" he asked, cheerfully. "Judith has a few bottles of wine in the fridge, and I've got plenty of beers under the stairs for us men — or women, if they so wish. I'm not a sexist!"

"Dad," said Judith, looking uncomfortable. "We're just about to take a dead body to have an autopsy performed on it. I don't think going home for a nightcap is very appropriate."

"Nonsense!" said Sergeant Spencer. "A nightcap is always appropriate! I don't know about anybody else, but I'm feeling highly optimistic about life, and I'd like to celebrate with a few beers and some good music!"

"Dad!" said Judith. "What's wrong with you?"

"Nothing," remarked Sergeant Spencer. "In fact, everything is just perfect."

"Sergeant Spencer," said Fredrick, standing alongside his vehicle. "What on earth has got into you?"

Hopping down the three steps below the police station door, Sergeant Spencer stood alongside Timothy on the pavement, a wide grin on his face. He nudged Timothy playfully in his ribs with an elbow. "What about you, wolf-man? Do you fancy a beer?"

"Dad!" said Judith. "A man has died! What *is* wrong with you?"

Sergeant Spencer stared at his daughter, his brow furrowed in confusion. He took a step backwards, almost stumbling, but regaining his balance before he fell. He put a hand to his head. "I— I'm not sure what just happened to me. I'm so sorry," he said, putting his face in his hands. "I don't feel so good."

"Shock," mouthed Timothy, to Judith and Millie. He put a hand on Sergeant Spencer's shoulder. "Come on," he said. "I think we should get you home and make you a nice cup of tea." He looked at Fredrick. "You go ahead with Trevor's body. I'll help Judith and Millie take the sergeant home. He's had a long night."

Giving Sergeant Spencer a puzzled look, Fredrick nodded. "I won't wait for you. I'll order the autopsy to be performed as soon as I get the body to the hall."

Timothy nodded. "We won't be long."

"Dad?" said Judith, as the Range Rover engine roared to life behind her. "Are you okay?"

Leaning against the wall of the station, Sergeant Spencer nodded, his head in his hands. "I don't know what happened," he admitted. "I've seen far worse sights than Trevor's body during my time as a police-man." He gave a sheepish grin. "But I can promise you that the last thing on my mind is having a knees-up."

"A lot has happened today, Dad," said Judith. "You've never lost one of your prisoners before. Espe-cially in the circumstances under which Trevor… died. Stepping out of the police station and into the fresh air must have sent you into some sort of delayed shock."

"I agree," said Millie, her heart aching for the

man who was normally so unshakeable. She'd never expected a man as stoic as he was to seem so... unnerved, but everybody had a breaking point at which stoicism gave way to shock, and it seemed that Sergeant Spencer's breaking point was finding a dead man in his cell moments after feeding him the meal that had apparently killed him. She took her car keys from her pocket and looked at him with gentle concern. "You've turned white. Come on, let's get you home."

Chapter 14

*H*aving taken Sergeant Spencer home and made sure he was okay, leaving him with a pot of tea and the radio tuned in to his favourite night-time talk show, the two witches headed to Spellbinder Hall in Millie's Triumph.

Following the rear lights of Timothy's car along narrow country lanes, it wasn't long before the angular silhouettes of Spellbinder Hall's many chimneys broke the moonlit skyline.

"I shouldn't have left him on his own," said Judith, as the car lurched around a bend. "He didn't seem right."

"He insisted you came here," said Millie, guiding the car through the tall iron gates that marked the boundary of Spellbinder Hall's large grounds. "He wants to make sure we find out what happened to Trevor, and having both of us present for the autopsy equals two sets of eyes. Two sets of eyes that he can trust."

"You don't think he trusts Fredrick either?" asked Judith. "I know I don't. Not fully, anyway. Did you see how Fredrick looked at Dad when Timothy detected that scent on his hands? He looked at Dad like he was looking at a murderer."

Millie hadn't. She'd been watching Timothy and had seen the flicker of doubt in his eyes when he'd smelled Sergeant Spencer's hands. It wasn't just Fredrick who had displayed his scepticism at Sergeant Spencer's innocence. But who could blame either the vampire or werewolf for being taken off guard when a potential poison was detected on the policeman's hands?

Considering events as rationally as possible, Millie parked the car alongside Timothy's and turned the engine off. "You can't blame Fredrick for wondering why your father's hands smelled of the stuff that we think killed Trevor," said Millie, gently. "You have to admit — it's weird."

"Yes," said Judith. "But you and I don't think for one moment that my father is guilty. I could see on Fredrick's face that *he* did. Even if the look was fleeting."

"We wouldn't, though," said Millie, applying the handbrake. "We're —" She hesitated, struggling to find the words to convey her feelings. "We're emotionally invested in his wellbeing, I guess."

Judith gave a cold laugh, which Millie put down to heightened emotions and not intentional cruelty on her friend's behalf. "You're emotionally invested in his well-being?" she said, frowning. She looked down at the footwell, shaking her head. "Yes, you've known him for almost a year. And yes, you like him, and he likes you. But if you think you're emotionally invested in his well-being, imagine how invested I am. He's my father, Millie. I love him more than anything or anyone. I appreciate you caring for him, but you'll never know what it felt like to see Fredrick look at him like he thought he'd murdered a man. You could never know the hurt and anger I felt when I saw that look on Fredrick's face. Even if it was just for a split second. How *can* you know?"

Millie gripped the steering wheel tight, twisting it hard as she applied the steering lock. Angry at herself for keeping her secret locked up, and angry at her mother for having lied about her father for all those years, she bit her bottom lip, trapping her words inside her like angry bees imprisoned inside a glass jar. She took a deep breath and allowed three sentences to crawl out, hoping they wouldn't sting. "I *can* empathise, Judith," she said. "I'm hurt that you don't understand that. I do have feelings, you know?"

Placing her hand on Millie's forearm, Judith bridged the gap between the two seats, one half of her face in shadow, the other half illuminated softly by the moon. "I'm sorry," she said. "I never think before I speak. Of course you have feelings, and I know you care for my father. Especially because —" Judith bit off the remainder of her sentence with a quick shake of her head, her hand sliding from Millie's arm. She gave a smile. "Anyway. I'm sorry for what I said."

"What were you going to say?" asked Millie. "You know I care for your father... *especially because* what, Judith?"

Judith sighed. "It sounds so cruel to say," she answered, quietly. "But I was going to say that you care so much for my father because you have no parents of your own. It's natural to feel that way, especially as you and he have been so close over the last year. You have no mother or father of your own to love, so you project your emotions onto my father. I understand that. It's natural. Everybody wants a family."

Had anybody else uttered those words, Millie imagined she might have exploded with anger or broken down in tears, but coming from Judith the words weren't cruel. How could they be? Judith herself had lost her parents when she was a toddler. Judith had *killed* her parents, Millie reminded herself, and had been dragged from certain death out of the burning car wreck caused by the accidental magic spell she had cast.

The young policeman who had rescued Judith had eventually adopted her, and brought her up as his own, cutting all connections with the non-paranormal world and moving to Spellbinder Bay when he'd discovered that the toddler he'd adopted was a witch. Henry Pinkerton had allowed Sergeant Spencer privileged access to the paranormal world in return for the kindness he'd shown to Judith, and he and Judith had lived together ever since as father and daughter.

Millie allowed herself a forgiving smile as she looked at Judith — forgiveness for her own frail emotions, and forgiveness of Judith's words. Could there be two more messed up young women sitting in the front of a car together? Could there be two women more suited to being siblings than friends? She doubted it, and as she gazed at the pretty profile of Judith's face, she promised herself that as soon as Trevor's murder was solved, she would tell both Judith and Sergeant Spencer the truth. *Sergeant David Spencer was her father*, and she would be honoured to call Judith her sister. Those words weren't merely the truth — hopefully they would be the catalyst of a whole new beginning for her, too.

Opening her door, Millie grabbed Judith's hand and gave it a fierce squeeze. "Come on," she said. "Let's go — Timothy's waiting on the steps to the hall. We'll get to the bottom of Trevor's death in no time. And if Fredrick did even consider for a single moment that your father was capable of murder, we'll rub his face in the evidence to the contrary. Together."

Chapter 15

*M*illie gave the two granite dragons guarding the entrance door to Spellbinder Hall a cursory glance as she and Judith followed Timothy up the steps, pausing at the top as the werewolf opened the heavy wooden door, its iron embellishments worn by centuries of sea air and storms.

Stepping inside the ancient hall, Millie's eyes adjusted to the dim lighting, her nerves settling as she smelled the warm, friendly scents of old books, leather, and dust. Watched over by a full suit of armour standing in one of the dark corners, and with people immortalised in oil paint peering down at them from panelled wood walls, the three of them hurried towards the door on the far side of the entrance hall which led into the bowels of the building.

Passing through the doorway, and illuminated by

flaming torches housed in metal wall brackets, Timothy veered right, leading the way down the steep steps which led to the maze of tunnels running through the cliff below the hall, the temperature dropping by a degree or two as they descended the narrow tunnel.

The steps slippery beneath her feet, Millie remembered the last time she'd been beneath Spellbinder Hall, the time when Henry Pinkerton had shown her the gate which led to The Chaos. She shuddered as she recalled the evil which she'd seen, and sensed, on the other side of the gate, and gave a soft sigh of relief when Timothy turned right instead of left as he reached the bottom of the first flight of steps, leading them in the opposite direction to that of the chaos gate.

As they passed the entrance to another tunnel leading deeper into the cliff, Millie wondered how many steps a person would have to navigate before they reached the cave at the very base of the cliff — the cave which was home to the moonpool, the source of all the magic in Spellbinder Hall.

Much like the cauldron in the cavern below her cottage, the moonpool housed a mysterious green liquid, a liquid which shimmered and shone, and a liquid which was warm to the touch and the hiding place for strange shadows which flitted like fish below the surface. Powered by lunar beams, collected from the moon by the cliff face, the moonpool's magic coursed through the fissures of the cliff, wending its way ever upwards until it reached the old building high above, from where it was dispersed throughout the hall and across the town.

Running a hand across the wall of the tunnel as she walked, feeling smooth rock beneath her fingertips, Millie's voice bounced off the walls as she spoke. "I wasn't aware there was somebody in Spellbinder Hall qualified to do autopsies," she said.

"It's not an autopsy like you'd imagine," said Timothy, his face a warm orange as he passed one of the flaming torches attached to the wall. "It's a magical autopsy. Trevor's body won't be cut open, Edna Brockett will use magic to determine the cause of Trevor's death, and to search for further clues."

Millie's heart gave a little flutter as it did every time she heard Edna Brockett's name mentioned, or whenever she spoke to the woman. Edna Brockett had been the first person Millie had met when she'd moved to Spellbinder Bay, and during her first day in the small town, Millie had been exposed to the elderly witch's dangerous driving as she gave Millie a lift to her new home in the sand dunes.

As if Edna Brockett hadn't frightened Millie enough with her erratic driving, the witch had gone on to petrify Millie later that same day when she'd been asked to prove to Millie that magic existed. Choosing to summon a demon from another dimension, instead of merely performing a parlour trick such as levitating an object or producing a rabbit from a hat, Edna had terrified Millie and she still shuddered when she remembered the evil face the witch had conjured into existence in a fireplace.

Since that day, Edna, although stern and quite frightening, had done nothing to justify the flutter of fear which Millie experienced whenever she heard her name, but she supposed it must be true when people said that first impressions counted. The first impression she'd gained from Edna had indeed remained with her.

"Edna's an accomplished witch," said Judith, stumbling a little as the tunnel suddenly steepened. "She'll do a good job. She'll find out what happened to Trevor."

"She will indeed," agreed Timothy. He pointed at the wooden door at the end of the tunnel, its planks bound by thick strips of black iron. "We're here," he said. "Welcome to Spellbinder Hall morgue — possibly the most underused room we have."

His footsteps echoing off the walls and ceiling, Timothy hurried the last few steps and paused in front of the door. He lifted a fist and gave three quick raps of his knuckles on the thick wood.

"Who is it?" came Fredrick's muffled voice.

"It's us!" replied Timothy. "Timothy, Millie, and Judith."

The sound of the lock being turned precipitated the door swinging open, a warm glow emanating from the room beyond it. Fredrick stood aside as the three of them traipsed past him, closing the door when they were all in the high-ceilinged cave. He put a finger to his lips, indicating that they should remain quiet. "She's nearly finished," he said in a low voice, nodding towards the back of the woman who leaned over the white shrouded form on the table before her.

Both hands dancing through the air, a few inches above the sheet covered body of Trevor Giles, Edna Brockett murmured indistinguishable words under her breath, as hair-thin tendrils of brightly coloured energy sparked from her fingertips, emitting a crackling sound as they crisscrossed a route over the linen.

With her back to them, and Trevor's shrouded body in the shadows of the cave wall, it was hard to see precisely what Edna was doing — the energy spilling from her fingers not bright enough to fully illuminate her work.

Muttering more garbled sounds, Edna suddenly straightened her back as the strands of light pouring from her left hand brightened, the flash of light casting the walls and ceilings in vivid red light. "I've got it," she said, no longer murmuring. "The last of it."

Wondering what Edna had got the last of, Millie manoeuvred herself into a position which allowed her to see what she was doing. She watched in fascination as the accomplished witch formed her left hand into a claw and lifted her arm upwards, the strands of energy still flowing from her fingertips resembling the strings of a puppeteer's mannequin. Using her free hand, Edna reached for one of the small green bottles on the table next to her and popped the cork stopper out with her thumb.

As Edna lifted her left hand higher, it became apparent that the thin strands of energy flowing from her fingers had wrapped themselves around something — something that seemed to struggle. Something that glowed a bright blue — like a miniature planet, and if Millie listened carefully enough — something that seemed to hum like the wings of a bumblebee in flight.

Bringing the bottle closer to her left hand, Edna guided the small orb of blue nearer to the neck, before suddenly pushing her hand forward, forcing the captive sphere into the glassware. She replaced the stopper with a satisfied sigh and slammed the bottle on the table, before turning to face her audience. "There," she said, her knitted cardigan buttoned high up her neck, and her short greying hair as immaculate as it always was. "Everything that was in the poor man's stomach is now in one of these bottles."

"Can you tell us anything yet?" asked Judith, peering at the row of glassware on the table behind Edna. "What happened to Trevor?"

Edna looked along her nose at Judith, her thin lips set in a stern pout. "You'll have to be patient, young lady," she said. "As I was telling Fredrick before you three arrived — it's going to take some time to evaluate *exactly* what happened to Mister Giles. There's a lot going on in those bottles."

"A lot going on?" said Judith. "What does that mean?"

"It means," said Edna, "that your instincts were correct. It seems that Trevor Giles *was* killed by poison. And not just any poison — a magical poison."

"He was killed by a magical potion?" asked Millie.

Edna shook her head. "No," she said. "It may be annoying semantics, but potions are usually created to help. Poisons are created to harm. Whatever Trevor had ingested only harmed him, if it was manufactured to kill Mister Giles, then it was a magical poison, *not* a potion."

"What was that… glowing blue ball I saw you removing from him?" asked Millie. "Was that the magic?"

Picking up the bottle she'd captured the orb in, Edna peered into its depths, the blue glow of the orb dulled by the green of the glass. "Yes," she said. "This is what's left of the magic used to power the poison. It's going to take me some time to work out exactly what sort of magic it is, and then even longer — if at all, to work out who it was cast by."

"So, it was a witch who killed Trevor Giles?" said Judith. "Surely that narrows it down and puts my father in the clear! He's obviously not a witch!"

Edna glanced at Fredrick, and then licked her lips. "All will become clear in time," she said, her voice flat. "I promise."

Not liking the tone in Edna's voice, or the look she'd given Fredrick, Millie frowned. "And the other jars and bottles?" she asked, indicating the row of glassware. "Do they all contain magic, too?"

"No," said Edna, placing the bottle in her hand gently on the table. "They contain samples of everything else which was in Trevor's stomach. There was a lot — he'd certainly drank a lot of alcohol and eaten well in the past day... cakes, especially."

"Can you tell which item of food the poison was added to?" asked Judith. "We think it was in the last muffin he ate."

Edna gave a curt shake of her head. "No," she said. "Not right away, that will take time, too. You'll need to be patient."

Fredrick stepped forward, adjusting his cufflinks. His thin face danced with shadows cast by the torches which lined the walls of the cave, and his eyes reflected the flames as he spoke to the elderly witch. "Then I would ask that you get to work right away, Edna," he said. "Time is of the essence. Henry and the headmaster are due back in four days time, and I want this whole tragic situation resolved by then."

Edna gave him an enquiring look. "Is there no way at all that we can get a message to them?" she asked. "There's been a murder, Fredrick. A member of the paranormal community has been killed. I'm sure that Henry would rush back if he were made aware of what has happened in his absence."

"I'm fully aware of what has happened in his absence, Mrs Brockett," said Fredrick, his voice rumbling with menace. "And I'm sure you're equally aware that Henry and Mister Dickinson are between dimensions, on essential magical business. Even if we could summon them home, I'm not sure I would. They're meeting with the leaders of other magical communities such as ours. Leaders from all over the globe — discussing ways in which to make sure our communities stay hidden from the non-paranormal world in these times of great technological advancements. Their work is important, Mrs Brockett — if we are to remain hidden, and safe. I'd hope you would understand that."

Edna nodded. "Of course, Fredrick. These days there are cameras and satellites everywhere. The old ways won't keep us hidden forever."

"I *will* discover what happened to Trevor Giles," said Fredrick. "I can assure you of that. We don't need to concern ourselves with getting word to Henry, though. He left me in charge, and I will do what I need to do."

Edna dropped her eyes. "I know you will, Fredrick, but it's just that…" She shook her head. "No. It doesn't matter."

"But what, Mrs Brockett?" snarled Fredrick. "Finish what you were about to say."

"I was only going to ask what will happen if we find a suspect," said Edna. "Only Henry can make the stone of integrity work — how will we know if somebody is telling the truth or not without the stone of integrity verifying their answers?"

As Edna mentioned the stone of integrity, a soft

warmth erupted in Millie's palm as she recalled holding the jewel while Henry asked her questions about the murder of Albert Salmon, the old man who had been pushed to his death from his lighthouse. Millie had also observed Henry using the stone on her friend Lillieth, the mermaid, and on an elderly woman named Hilda who was possessed by a demon, who Henry had suspected of killing a metal detectorist.

Edna was making a valid point — the stone of integrity was undoubtedly a powerful way of finding out if somebody was telling the truth or not, but completely useless without Henry present to operate it.

Frederick gave a frustrated sigh. "When we *do* find the suspect," he said, pausing momentarily as his eyes shifted in Judith's direction. "Or *suspects*, then we will keep them under lock and key here at Spellbinder Hall until Henry returns and can use the stone of integrity to find out the truth." He smiled at Edna, before returning his gaze to Judith. "If, of course, the suspect is from the paranormal community. For as we all know, the stone of integrity will not work on a human."

Seeming to suddenly understand what Fredrick was insinuating, Judith glared at the vampire. "What are you trying to say? You can't think my father had anything to do with this? After everything he's done for this town!"

Fredrick put both hands up, the palms towards

Judith. "I don't think anything right now," he said. "But your father insisted that we treat him as a suspect until we can disprove his involvement." He attempted a smile, his lips curling slowly. "I hope you can understand how delicate the unfortunate situation is, in which we find ourselves, Miss Spencer."

"Well, you're barking up the wrong tree if you think my father had anything to do with Trevor Giles's death," said Judith. She pointed at the glass bottles on the table next to Trevor's shrouded body. "My father wouldn't be messing around with magic. He doesn't know the first thing about magic, even though he's been in this community for nearly thirty years and has a witch as an adopted daughter."

And a witch as a biological daughter, thought Millie, placing a calming hand on Judith's forearm. "It's okay," she said. "Nobody thinks your father did anything wrong. We have to follow procedure, though — like he wanted us to."

Judith glowered at Fredrick. "My father had nothing to do with any of this."

"And nobody has said he did," said Fredrick. "There was no need for your outburst, I didn't insinuate anything, I merely said that the stone won't work on a human."

"You were looking in my direction when you said it," replied Judith.

Fredrick frowned, his eyes half closing. "I have nothing but respect for your father, Judith," he said, lowering his hands. "And it's my respect for him which drives my decision to do as he asked me to. The circumstances surrounding Trevor's death will, of course, be fully investigated, and that includes asking Sergeant Spencer any questions which may be pertinent to the case."

Crossing her arms, Judith nodded. "In the meantime," she said, "I'll get on with trying to find out who *really* killed Trevor Giles."

"And I'd expect nothing less from you," said Fredrick. He looked at Millie. "And with Miss Thorn helping you, I'm sure you'll get to the bottom of it in no time." He turned his gaze to Edna Brockett. "Can you start work on the samples you took from Trevor immediately, Mrs Brockett?" he asked.

"I will," said Edna, a yawn escaping her lips. "First thing in the morning, Fredrick. Unlike you vampire types, us witches require at least a few hours sleep. Especially at my age."

Retrieving his pocket watch from the breast pocket of his jacket and flicking it open, Fredrick nodded. "Time has flown by. I didn't realise. The sun will be rising in an hour or two." He gave Edna a smile. "Go home, Mrs Brockett. Get some sleep." He looked around the room. "That goes for all of you. We'll begin again tomorrow." He glanced at the bulging sheet on the table and then looked at Millie and Judith in turn. "Would you two begin tomorrow by visiting the unfortunate Mrs Giles and informing her of her husband's untimely demise? I don't think visiting her at this time of the night —" He paused, glancing at Edna. "This time of the *morning*, I should say, would be fair to her or her son."

Millie nodded. "Yes," she said, not relishing the task she'd been asked to perform. "I'll inform her."

"And I'll go with her," said Judith, glowering at Fredrick.

Fredrick grunted his thanks as Millie and Judith followed Timothy towards the door, his eyes on Judith as she crossed the cave. Watching Fredrick studying her friend so intently suddenly filled Millie with unease, and it was only when the vampire put a hand to his chin and narrowed his eyes that Millie realised why. He was watching Judith with suspicion, she realised, his distrust made even more evident in the way he held his head and murmured something to himself as Judith reached the doorway.

Averting her eyes as Fredrick glanced in her direction, Millie made her decision quickly. Going against her instincts, and once again breaking a promise she'd made to herself, she concentrated hard, briefly closing her eyes as she worked on sending an invisible finger of energy from her mind to the mind of the tall vampire.

As Millie's energy brushed against that of Fredrick, he showed no sign that he was aware his mind was being probed as he crossed the room towards Edna, casting another look at Judith as she left the cave.

It was as he cast that final glance at Judith, that Millie gasped. She broke the connection between herself and Frederick as Timothy turned to see if she was all right. "What's wrong, Millie?" he asked. "Why did you make that noise?"

"Nothing's wrong," lied Millie, walking after Judith. "I yawned. That's all. I'm tired."

As she left the room she glanced over her shoulder at Fredrick, standing alongside Edna, both of them with their backs towards the door as they studied the bottles and jars on the table.

Had Fredrick *really* meant what he'd just thought? Or had it merely been one of those fleeting intrusive thoughts that all people were susceptible to? The sort of thoughts that people were ashamed of, and ushered from their minds promising never to think such a thing again?

Millie wasn't sure, but what she was certain of, was that Fredrick's thought had been a million miles away from the truth. *It had to be.* There was no way that Judith and her father had plotted together to kill Trevor Giles.

Yes — Judith was an accomplished witch, but Fredrick was disastrously incorrect if he thought that Edna Brocket was going to connect any of the magic she found in the poison which had killed Trevor, to Judith.

Very, very wrong.

Chapter 16

ypified by dirty brickwork and even dirtier windows, most of the houses in the street showed signs of neglect, but number fourteen Marigold Lane appeared more rundown than most of the other homes situated in one of the poorest areas of town.

Yellowed net curtains hung from the grimy windows, and the lopsided gate scraped along the cracked concrete garden path as Millie pushed it open. Gazing around at the rubbish strewn garden, Millie looked at Judith for support. "So, we tell her the truth?"

Judith gave a firm nod. "Yes," she said, no doubt in her voice. "We tell her exactly what happened. It's only fair and right."

Although Timothy had hinted at the fact that they hide the full truth in fear of the werewolf community turning on Sergeant Spencer, Millie agreed with her friend. When you began hiding even the smallest element of a story, then it should come as no surprise when people disbelieved everything you told them about it.

The early morning sun beginning to warm her face, Millie stifled a yawn. Yes, it was early, and yes, she'd hardly had any sleep, but she didn't want to be seen yawning by Helen Giles as she approached the house, especially as the news she brought with her was far from boring. It was devastating.

Smelling cigarette smoke as she approached the front door, Millie straightened her blouse, attempting to hide the creases which had formed during the short drive from Judith's home after she had picked her friend up.

Judith appeared as nervous as Millie felt, flicking strands of blonde hair from her face, and tucking her shirt into the black trousers she considered appropriate attire for informing a recently married woman that she was already a widow.

The muffled sound of a television coming from somewhere within the house indicated that Mrs Giles was up and about, and Millie flinched as she knocked three times on the door in quick succession. She rubbed her knuckles to ease the pain. She hadn't meant to bring her fist down so hard, in fact, she'd secretly intended to make hardly any noise at all, in the hope that Mrs Giles wouldn't be alerted to her visitors, giving Millie the chance of postponing the awful task of informing a woman of her husband's death.

All chances of postponing the visit evaporated as a woman's voice came from within the house, her shrill tone easily competing with the noise of the television. "Trevor? Is that you? Have you lost your key *again*? I'm mad at you for what you did to me yesterday! I was supposed to go to Norman's open day, not you! Where have you been all night? I know you were arrested. Norman told me exactly what happened! Did you go on another drinking binge after that bastard at the police station released you?"

Millie gave Judith a nervous glance as footsteps approached the door, and a loud clicking sound indicated the lock being turned. The door swung inwards quickly, and a short woman wearing a worn flannel dressing gown, the sleeves rolled up to the elbows, stared at her two visitors with suspicion.

She lifted her hand to her mouth, and took a puff of her cigarette, her fingertips yellowed, and her nails ragged and bitten short. "What do you two want?" she said. "I know who you are. Are you here in the capacity as Norman's teachers, or are you here in the capacity as run around lackeys for that idiot, Sergeant Spencer?" She looked at Judith, tilting her head, a smile teasing the edges of her mouth. "No offence," she said. "I'm sure your father is a perfectly nice man when he's not throwing innocent people in that cell of his."

"I'm afraid it's bad news, Mrs Giles," said Millie,

the ominous words not leaving her mouth easily. She swallowed as the colour rushed from Mrs Giles's face, making the next sentence even more difficult to speak. "Would you like to invite us in so we can all sit down?"

Tossing her cigarette through the gap between Millie and Judith, Mrs Giles rushed through the door and hurried down the garden path, looking left and right along the empty street. "It's Norman, isn't it?" she said. "Is he okay? He left early! After making his own breakfast! He told me he'd been invited to his friend's house to play computer games! What's happened to him?"

"It's not about Norman," said Millie, hurrying down the path after the frantic woman. "It's about Trevor. We should go inside and sit down."

Taking a steadying breath, Mrs Giles turned away from the garden gate to face Millie and Judith. "This is the worst type of news, isn't it?" she said, dropping her eyes. "People only tell you that you need to sit down when it's the worst type of news."

"Mrs Giles," said Judith, her voice calm. "I'm afraid it's —"

Helen Giles scrunched her eyes closed and waved both hands in front of her face, as if protecting herself from what was about to come. "Don't tell me!" she demanded. "Not out here. I think you're right — if I'm going to be hearing bad news, I want to be sitting down, with a cigarette and a cup of tea."

The small woman made her way slowly up the

footpath, her slippers making a scuffing sound as she dragged her feet. "Come in," she invited. "You'll have to excuse the mess. I haven't got around to doing any housework this week."

"Don't worry about any mess," said Millie, following Mrs Giles into the house, the stench of cigarette smoke becoming stronger as she closed the door behind her.

Mrs Giles veered right, pointing to a door on her left. "You two sit down in there, I'll fetch us some tea."

"Would you like me to make the tea?" offered Millie.

Mrs Giles shook her head. "No," she muttered. "No. I'll do it."

Millie and Judith filed into the living room as the sounds of tea being made emanated from the kitchen. Spotting the remote control amongst dirty mugs and magazines on the crowded coffee table, Millie muted the large television set in the corner, and perched on the tatty leather sofa, alongside Judith.

The room stank of smoke, and the once cream carpet showed evidence of many food and drink spillages and was home to two empty gin bottles which lay forgotten in a corner. Spotting a photograph on the mantlepiece, of a smiling Norman proudly wearing his school uniform, Millie wondered if the young boy had left so early in the morning to escape his surroundings.

"I knew Norman had it bad," whispered Judith, as

if reading Millie's mind. "But I didn't know that he lived in such poverty."

"Isn't it unusual for members of the paranormal community to be so poor?" asked Millie, her voice as low as Judith's. Aware that vampires tended to be stinking rich, due to the huge fortunes they could build up over multiple human lifespans, and conscious of the fact that witches never appeared to be poor, Millie wasn't certain about the position of werewolves on the societal scale.

"There's not *much* poverty in the paranormal community," whispered Judith, "but it exists. Especially among wolves." She looked towards the door, presumably checking the coast was clear, before lowering her voice even more. "The thing is... Trevor's never really done anything worthwhile with his life, and up until a few weeks ago when Helen married him, she'd been ostracised from the werewolf community after her first husband walked out on her. We shouldn't forget that it was probably hard for them both to get on in life, and hard for them to make much of themselves."

"That's not the only thing you shouldn't forget!" came an angry shout, startling Judith, who sat bolt upright, as if electrocuted. "You shouldn't forget that werewolves have far better hearing than you do."

Chapter 17

*M*illie shifted uncomfortably on the sofa as Helen appeared in the doorway, carrying a tray laden with three chipped mugs and a bowl of sugar. Millie looked up at her. "I'm sorry," she said. "We didn't mean to cause any offence."

"There is no combination of words in the English language which you could assemble, in any order, that would offend me," snarled Helen, slamming the tray on the coffee table, rusty brown tea spilling over the rims of the mugs. "I've lived with insults being muttered behind my back since Norman's father walked out on us. What you two think about me, Trevor, or our relationship — does not bother me in the slightest." She slumped into the worn armchair which faced the television, and took a cigarette packet from her pocket, plucking one from the box and drawing heavily on it as she lit it with a shaking hand.

She fixed Millie in a steady stare and nodded.

"I'm ready. I'm assuming you're here to tell me that Trevor has died. I've always sort of expected it — Trevor has always had the knack for getting into fights. I told him that one day it would be the end of him. I told him he'd pick on the wrong person, but he never listened. He always thought he was tougher than he actually was." She sucked on her cigarette again, tilting her chin as she blew a long stream of smoke towards the window. "Go on then... was it another werewolf that killed him? A vampire that ripped him to shreds?" She narrowed her eyes, leaning forward in her chair, her eyes on Judith. "Or a witch who cast a spell on him?"

Judith gave a little cough and added a spoonful of sugar to her tea. "We don't actually know what happened to him," she explained.

"You don't know what happened to him?" said Helen. "Then what do you know?"

"I heard what you were shouting before you opened your front door," said Millie. "So I know you're aware that Trevor was arrested yesterday?"

Helen blew out more smoke and nodded. "Yes. Francine brought Norman home after the school fête, and she and Norman told me that Trevor had been up to his old tricks again. Drinking and fighting. I was informed that he was arrested by your father, Miss Spencer, and unceremoniously carted off to a police cell."

Judith nodded. "That's right."

Helen tapped ash from her cigarette, allowing it to

flutter to the carpet. "What Trevor did to me yesterday — spiking my lemonade with gin so I fell asleep on the settee and couldn't attend Norman's school open day, made me mad. I didn't really care that he didn't come home last night. I assumed that when he'd been released from the police station, he'd gone on a drinking bender and fallen asleep in a ditch somewhere." She narrowed her eyes, staring at Judith. "Is that what happened? Did he go and get himself in more trouble after he was released by your father?"

Judith sipped her tea, only a brief flicker of an eyelid suggesting that it tasted as dire as it looked. "Trevor didn't… He wasn't…"

"Mrs Giles," said Millie, looking the werewolf directly in the eyes. "I'm afraid Trevor wasn't released from police custody last night. I'm afraid to say that Trevor died while in police custody. He died in his cell."

"He what?" demanded Helen, the colour leaving her cheeks. She filled her lungs with smoke again, and shook her head. "What?" she said. "That makes no sense! Trevor was a werewolf! Werewolves don't just die at his age — they don't get diseases or have heart attacks or strokes... I don't understand. How did he die?"

"We don't really understand what actually happened yet," said Judith. "We think —"

Helen moved quickly, propelling herself out of her seat, her pupils flashing yellow and the muscles in her forearms twisting and bulging as thick hairs burst from the backs of her hands. She emitted a guttural roar, before shaking her head and regaining control of herself, her eyes reverting to their normal colour, and the hairs retreating into her skin, her forearms frail and thin once more. She remained on her feet, staring down at the two witches. "What happened to him?" she asked. "I don't understand."

"He'd ingested something," explained Judith, her voice shaking. "Some sort of poison. We're not sure what poison, yet, but we're working on finding out exactly what happened to him."

"Poison?" said Helen. She lowered herself into her seat and shook her head. "Poison? I don't understand. How was Trevor poisoned while he was in a police cell?"

Watching Judith licking her lips nervously, her mouth opening and closing with no sound emerging, Millie spoke for her, still shaken herself by Helen's sudden rage. "We think the poison was in the food and drink which Sergeant Spencer served to Trevor, Mrs Giles," she said. "We have no idea how it got into the food, or who it was that put in there, but please rest assured that things are being done to find out. Edna Brockett is studying the poison which was found in Trevor's stomach, and Timothy Huggins is compiling a thorough list of anybody we think could be a suspect."

Her lips a thin white slash across her face, Mrs Giles lifted a hand and pointed a finger at Judith. "Her and her father should be on the top of that list," she said. "They both hated Trevor, and now you're telling me that he died after consuming a meal which Sergeant Spencer served him? They did it! They murdered my husband! Sergeant Spencer and his daughter poisoned my Trevor!"

"No – no," stammered Judith. "We didn't!"

Her eyes angry and her teeth bared, Helen stared at Judith. "You may have thought that due to the way in which Trevor treated me, I might not care that he died. I know what people say about me and Trevor, and I've heard the rumours — people saying that I only married Trevor so that I could regain my honour within the werewolf community." She took a deep breath. "Oh, there's some truth in that. There's a lot of truth in that, but let me tell you, whatever Trevor did or said to me, he was a werewolf. I'm a werewolf. There is honour amongst werewolves, and if I find out that you or your father harmed my husband…" She stopped speaking and took a long breath. "You'll find out."

Still shaken by the woman's anger, Millie spoke as calmly as she could. "I understand that you're angry," she said, "but Judith and Sergeant Spencer didn't hate your husband, Mrs Giles. You said yourself that Trevor liked drinking and fighting. Unfortunately, that way of living led to a few too many interactions with the police. There's no way that Sergeant Spencer or Judith would want to harm your husband. They both want to find the person who *did* poison Trevor."

"Oh," said Helen. "Sergeant Spencer must be

hiding behind the sofa, or behind the curtains, because I don't see him here, with you two — showing that he cares about my husband's death."

"You know how things are, Helen," said Judith, her voice edged with nervousness. "Trevor was a member of the paranormal community, my father wouldn't necessarily investigate the case, even if he could. He's human, Helen — the death of a werewolf is a matter for us paranormal types."

"Even if he could?" said Helen. "What did you mean by that? You said you father wouldn't necessarily investigate the case *even if he could*."

"It's procedure, Mrs Giles. That's all," said Millie. "Although Sergeant Spencer certainly wasn't the person who poisoned your husband, he *was* the only person present when Trevor died. It would be inappropriate for him to be investigating this case until —"

"Until his involvement has been ruled out!" said Helen, her voice rising. She stood up again and took a step towards Millie. "I wouldn't rule him out of the investigation too quickly," she said. "Not after what happened last weekend when Trevor was arrested. Sergeant Spencer had the motive required to have harmed my husband."

"Mrs Giles," said Judith, "I can assure you that —"

Helen's head turned quickly, her eyes flashing yellow as she fixed Judith in a fierce stare. "And I can assure you that Trevor told me everything that happened in that police station last Saturday night!"

she yelled. "He was ashamed that he'd hit you, Judith! It was the drink — he even managed to stay off alcohol for two days because of what he did to you. That's how ashamed he was that he'd laid a hand on a woman. I also know what you said to him, and what your father said to him afterwards.

"You told him that you'd never forgive him, and your father told him that he'd better watch his back." She sucked on her cigarette, and turned away from Judith, speaking slowly to Millie. "Sergeant Spencer had every reason to want to harm Trevor," she said. "You'd better get to the truth before certain people in my community find out what's happened. Some of them don't think much of our local police sergeant as it is, and finding out that he may have harmed Trevor would be just the excuse they need to make their feelings known."

"Mrs Giles," said Millie, giving the woman an understanding nod. "I can see why you'd *think* that Sergeant Spencer would want to harm your husband, but you must believe me when I say that he's not the sort of man who would hurt anybody. Sergeant Spencer didn't kill Trevor, but I promise that we'll find out who did. We just need a little time."

"I suggest you hurry," warned Helen. "Like I said… when *certain* werewolves find out what has happened, I know that I wouldn't like to be a *certain* sergeant."

Not wishing to let her frustration show, and wanting to diffuse some of the anger in the air, Millie nodded towards the photograph on the mantlepiece. "How will Norman take the news?" she asked, gently.

"I'm sure Norman will pretend to be sad, for my sake," said Helen. "But I don't think he'll shed a genuine tear for Trevor, and neither should he. Trevor wasn't the nicest of stepfathers."

Millie hesitated before answering. "Norman did say some nice things about him yesterday," she said, wary that she may have been crossing a line. "He said that Trevor took him fishing sometimes and played football with him."

The first real emotion she'd displayed since hearing of her husband's death slid down Helen's cheek, in the form of a single tear, which she wiped away quickly. She nodded. "When he was off the booze, Trevor was okay. He wasn't all bad."

"That's exactly what Norman said," replied Millie. She licked her lips, recalling something else the young wolf had said. "Norman also told me that you'd hinted that something bad had happened in Trevor's past… something that might have contributed to him being so… troubled."

Helen looked away as she wiped a second tear from her cheek. "Something bad happened to him when he was a child," she said. "I don't exactly know what that thing was – Trevor would never go into details, he'd only tell me that it was while he was a pupil at Spellbinder Hall. He told me that he was not welcome back at the school ever again. Don't ask me why."

"Yet he went there yesterday," noted Millie.

"He found out from Norman that Henry Pinkerton was away on some sort of business," said Helen. "And told me he wanted to visit the school for old time's sake… apparently it was Henry who had told him he was never welcome there again." She sucked on her cigarette. "I told him he couldn't, of course. I didn't want him going with me to Norman's open day. I knew he'd end up embarrassing me. He always did." She gave a small cough as she blew out smoke. "So, he spiked my lemonade with gin and went without me." She blinked, before sighing. "Anyway. That's enough. I don't want to talk about it anymore."

Millie took a deep breath, feeling awkward about what she needed to ask next, especially after Helen's reaction to the news of Trevor's death. "Mrs Giles, this is going to sound awful under the circumstances," she said. "But we think it would be for the best if the news of Trevor's death were kept quiet for the time being, just until we begin to understand what happened."

"I told you what happened," said Helen. She pointed at Judith. "Her father killed him, and it's lucky for her that my anger towards Sergeant Spencer is fuelled by honour, and not love — because if I'd truly loved Trevor, I'd be leading an angry pack of wolves towards Sergeant Spencer right at this very moment."

She closed her eyes, taking a deep breath through her nose, her chest expanding. She gave a frustrated sigh and opened her eyes. "Luckily for Sergeant Spencer, I don't agree with the old ways of the wolves — an eye for an eye, a heart for heart… a life for a life." She hesitated, her eyes on Judith. "I believe in justice, the sort of justice which Henry Pinkerton will bring down upon Sergeant Spencer when it's proven that he killed Trevor. I'm not sure how Henry will punish a human for the murder of somebody from the paranormal community, but if the punishment is anything like the punishment he would give to people like us, then I'll be happy when justice is done, without feeling the need to see Sergeant Spencer disembowelled by a pack of vengeful wolves."

A cold tingle running the length of her spine, Millie stared at the woman. Although Sergeant Spencer was obviously not responsible for Trevor's death, Millie couldn't stop the images which flooded her mind. Images of Sergeant Spencer being found guilty through some form of misplaced justice, and being given the same punishment that Henry Pinkerton had once told Millie he'd be forced to bestow upon a murderer from the paranormal community.

Being banished to the dimension known as The Chaos, an evil place inhabited by demons and all manner of evil creatures, would be a hellish punishment for a paranormal person, but Millie shuddered to think what would happen to a human if he or she were sent to that hell. She shook the awful thoughts from her head. "We'll find out what happened to Trevor," she said.

Helen gave a cold smile. "I know what happened to him," she stated.

"Mrs Giles," protested Judith, placing her mug on the tray with a little too much force. "My father wouldn't do the sort of thing you're accusing him of!"

Helen studied Judith for a few silent moments. "He's your father, you would say that." She tilted her head as she sucked on her cigarette, giving Judith a quizzical look. "Unless you had something to do with it. Maybe you helped your father. Were you there when my husband died, Miss Spencer?"

Millie put a hand on Judith's arm as her friend got to her feet in a burst of speed, her eyes flashing with anger. "Mrs Giles," she said. "I'm truly sorry for your loss, but I think we should be going now. I'll keep you informed of any developments in the case." She reached into her pocket and withdrew one of the cards that Sergeant Spencer had printed for her and Judith. She handed it to Mrs Giles. "If you need to speak to anybody, please don't hesitate before phoning me. I'll do anything I can to help you."

"I'm sure you will," said Helen, tossing the card onto the coffee table. She looked towards the doorway as a loud knocking echoed through the house. "Another visitor," she said, crossing the room. "I *am* popular today." She gestured towards the doorway. "You can say hello to whoever it is on your way out."

Keeping quiet as she followed Helen Giles towards the front door, Millie glanced at Judith. Looking nervous, her friend's face had drained of colour and her teeth were visible as she chewed on her bottom lip. A sudden rush of guilt flooded Millie's stomach, and she gave her head a quick shake. She hated intrusive thoughts, and the intrusive thought which was gnawing at the back of her mind, demanding attention, was distressingly unwelcome — and categorically untrue.

Despite what Frederick had thought, and despite what Helen Giles had said, there was no way that Sergeant Spencer or Judith were the type of people who would murder a man. As Helen Giles opened the front door, Millie gave Judith a smile. Her friend looked nervous, and Millie wasn't surprised, she'd just had terrible accusations hurled at her by an angry werewolf.

"Miss Thorn! Miss Spencer!" came an excited voice, jolting Millie back into the moment. "What are you two doing here?"

"Oh, hello Norman," said Millie, smiling at the little boy who stood on the step alongside a tall man with thick black hair which fell on his broad shoulders. "We just popped in to... urm…"

"They popped in to tell me how well you'd done during last term at school, Norman" said Mrs Giles. "They wanted me to know because I couldn't be there yesterday."

Norman looked at the floor, twisting his toe into

the redbrick doorstep. "Because Trevor came instead of you?" he said.

"Yes, love," said Helen. "Because of that."

"Is everything all right, Helen?" said the man alongside Norman. He looked at Millie and Judith, distrust emblazoned on his face. "They just came to tell you how Norman got on in school, did they?"

"Yes, Rufus," said Helen. She smiled at the big man. "Norman told me he'd be staying at your house playing computer games with Billy all morning. Is everything okay?"

Rufus nodded towards the car at the bottom of the path, in which a young boy and a woman sat. "It's Annabel's mother. She had a fall this morning. She's okay, but Annabel wanted to go over and check on her. We thought we'd drop Norman off on the way." He gave Millie and Judith another enquiring look, his tongue tracing the shape of his lips. "It's very kind of you two, giving up your Saturday morning to visit Norman's mother to let her know how her son got on in school."

"Oh!" said Norman. "Miss Spencer and Miss Thorn are lovely teachers, Mr Packston. They're always doing nice things!"

Rufus looked down at Norman. "That's nice to hear," he said.

Pushing gently past Mrs Giles, Millie stepped outside, avoiding Rufus's dark gaze. "Enjoy the rest of your time off school, Norman," she said, smiling at the young boy. "Miss Spencer and I have to go now."

"You two have a nice day," said Rufus, stepping aside to allow Judith and Millie past him. He gave Judith a strange smile. "Oh, and say hello to your father for me, won't you? He's arrested me a few times, but I suppose that's just his job."

"Yes," said Judith. "It is."

Hurrying down the path, and smiling at the woman and young boy in the car as they made their way to Millie's triumph, Millie looked back over her shoulder once more. Rufus was still watching them, and he didn't look happy. "He gave me the creeps," she said.

"He's a werewolf," said Judith. "A bit of a trouble-maker, not as bad as Trevor was, but a nuisance all the same. He and Dad have crossed paths a few times. He's alright, though."

Millie nodded, opening her car door. She looked towards the high cliff to the east of the town, her eyes finding the gleam of sunlight reflected from Spell-binder Hall's many windows. "Okay," she said. "The worst job of the day is over. We've informed Mrs Giles of her husband's death, now let's go and find out if Edna Brockett has been able to find anything out from the samples she took from Trevor." She glanced back at the house, looking away quickly as Rufus gave her a smile. "The way Helen was speaking about your father makes me think we should find out who killed Trevor as quickly as possible."

. . .

"You mean clear my father's name as quickly as possible," replied Judith, ducking her head as she clambered into the small car. "I agree. I want to be able to present the wolf community with the real killer when they eventually come knocking." She pulled the car door closed. "Which I'm sure they will when the news of Trevor's death gets out."

"I believed Helen when she said she wouldn't tell anybody," said Millie. "And I'm sure she'll tell Norman to keep it to himself, too."

"As much as she doesn't like me or my father," said Judith, fastening her seatbelt. "I believed her, too, but news has a way of travelling. Especially in a town like this."

"I'm sure everything will be okay," said Millie, aware that Rufus was still staring in their direction. She looked away from the werewolf as her phone vibrated in her pocket. A message from Timothy. "Edna has discovered something about the poison. Fredrick would like us all to meet in his study. As soon as possible."

Chapter 18

*J*udith was quiet on the trip to Spellbinder Hall, and Millie found that she welcomed the lack of conversation. Enjoying the rumble of the Triumph's engine as the sports car powered up the winding lanes toward the cliff top, she changed down to third gear and pressed gently on the throttle, the car hugging the hedge as it glided neatly around a tight bend. "Imagine how good this car would have sounded when it came off the production line in nineteen-seventy-two," she said, her voice raised. "If it sounds good now, it must have sounded like velvet back then!" Realising what a poor analogy she'd made, she smiled, and glanced at Judith. "Or a lion's roar," she said.

"I bet it was great," said Judith, turning her face away quickly and looking out of her window. "I bet it sounded amazing."

Millie applied the brake and guided the car into

one of the lay-bys — constructed to allow cars the room to pass each other if they met nose to nose on such a narrow lane. She turned the engine off and put a hand on Judith's shoulder, the trembling of her friend's body confirming that Millie hadn't imagined the tears she'd seen flooding from her eyes. "What is it?" she asked. "What's wrong?"

Still looking the other way, Judith's body rocked as she sobbed. "What if —" She sobbed again, her words cut off abruptly.

"What if…" prompted Millie, gently. "Go on."

Judith turned her head slowly, wiping tears away with the back of her hand. She opened her mouth to speak, her eyes red and the tendons in her neck stretching as she sucked in another sobbing breath. She closed her eyes and gulped, her breathing ragged. "I can't say it," she said. "I can't say it!"

Tightening her hand on Judith's shoulder, Millie nodded. "It's okay," she said. "You don't have to say anything. You can just cry. I'm here for you."

Her face crumpling, Judith gasped and opened her mouth to speak. At first, no words came out, but then a sentence tumbled from her mouth, the words tripping over one another in their hurry to be heard. "What if he did it? What if Dad did it? I can't see any other way that it could have been done! It's true what Helen said — Trevor did hit me last week! It wasn't that bad, and he didn't turn into his wolf or anything. It hurt me, but a healing potion soon got rid of the bruise. I was angry with him, I said some awful things, and Dad did, too, but..."

"Don't even think it," said Millie, trying to make her words sound like supportive advice and not the warning which she wanted to blurt out in defence of her father. "Don't even think that he had anything to do with it! He wouldn't hurt a soul. You know that."

"I know. I know," said Judith, wiping more tears from her face. "But I can't get the thought from my mind. Dad was so angry with Trevor when he hit me. I've never seen him that angry. So when he arrested him a week later... maybe he... maybe..."

"No," demanded Millie. "I won't listen to you speaking like that. You don't mean it! He wouldn't do something so terrible — for any reason. He's not the sort of man who would take violent revenge."

Taking a deep breath, Judith nodded. "I know. I do," she said. "I know he's not capable of something like that — it's just that sometimes the mind plays tricks on you, doesn't it? It makes you consider things that you don't want to consider."

"It does," agreed Millie, guilty that the weasel in her own mind had once or twice offered up conclusions about what had happened to Trevor Giles. Conclusions that had made her angry with, and ashamed of, herself. She smiled. "But you must banish thoughts like that from your mind."

Judith nodded, mascara forming dark rivulets beneath her bloodshot eyes. "It's just that I saw the way Fredrick looked at Dad. I'm sure he thinks Dad had something to do with it."

It's not just your Dad he suspects, thought Millie, recalling with clarity the vividness of Fredrick's accusatory thought. He'd considered the fact that Judith was behind the magic in the poison, and Sergeant Spencer had been the person to administer it. "It will be okay," she said, hoping her words turned out to be true.

"What's Fredrick going to think when he finds out what happened last weekend?" said Judith. "When he finds out that Trevor hit me! It's true what Helen Giles said — it is a motive for murder! Fredrick will ask why I didn't mention it earlier, but to be honest, it wasn't a big thing! There's always some drunk werewolf or rowdy human in the cells, and sometimes they play up. I just happened to be there when Trevor lost control a little. I don't think he even meant to hit me, and it hardly hurt. A little healing potion and the tiny bruise was gone. Yes, I was angry, but not angry enough to hurt Trevor, and I'm sure that Dad felt the same. I didn't really think of it until Helen mentioned it, but Fredrick might think that me and Dad were trying to hide the fact that it happened."

Using a thumb to guide a tear away from Judith's top lip, Millie smiled. "It's okay, Judith. Just tell Fredrick what happened when we get to his study."

"What if he thinks Dad did something?" begged Judith.

"Then let him think it," said Millie. "It doesn't

matter what he thinks. It doesn't matter what anybody thinks. We'll find out what happened to Trevor. I promise."

Judith's hand closed around Millie's, and some of the sparkle returned to her eyes. "Thank you," she said. "I'm sorry. I wobbled a little. I'm tired... yesterday was a long day." She sighed and shook her head. "I know Dad wouldn't hurt anybody, and I know we'll get to the truth. We always do."

Chapter 19

*F*redrick settled into the brown leather seat behind his large desk, the fading wood surface displaying scratches which time had long ago filled with grime, giving the piece of furniture the distressed look which had become fashionable in recent years.

Millie doubted very much that Fredrick's choice of desk, or any of the other furniture or fittings in his study, was based on current trends, though. In fact, the decor in Fredrick's study aptly reflected the vampire's personality; sombre, dark, and in need of some cheering up.

Glancing at the grandfather clock standing between two tall shelves lined with leather-bound books, Fredrick shook his head. "One should never trust a ghost with simple things such as timekeeping. It seems that when a person dies, their spirit loses all sense of urgency."

"Are you surprised?" asked Timothy, choosing the armchair alongside the worn wingback chair Millie was seated in. "They have all the time in the world. Why would they rush around in death, like they did in life? They are accountable to nobody."

Fredrick ran both hands through his black hair, as if applying gel. "May I remind you that Florence is a member of the Spellbinder Hall Board of Governors, and a teacher here, Timothy? She is as accountable as the rest of the staff while she continues to occupy those positions of importance."

"We can start without her, Fredrick," suggested Edna Brockett, standing stiffly alongside a drinks cabinet in the form of a globe, its lid raised to display the eclectic contents. She licked her lips as she touched a bottle of sherry propped up between two bottles of scotch, before glancing at the clock and quickly withdrawing her hand as if her fingers had been burned. "You and I are both members of the board. We can make decisions about what happens in the town. I'm sure Florence won't mind."

Fredrick sighed. "I'm sure *she* won't," he replied. Glancing at the clock once more, he relented. "Very well," he said. "Let us begin." He turned his deep-set eyes onto Millie and then Judith, who occupied an old Chesterfield sofa. "Thank you for visiting Mrs Giles this morning. How did she respond to the news of her husband's death?"

"She was angry and upset," said Judith. "Like you'd expect."

Fredrick nodded. "Of course she was," he said. "But do you think she'll keep the news of Trevor's death a secret from the rest of her community until we've got to the bottom of the poisoning mystery?"

"I think so," said Millie, shifting in her seat as a spring dug into the back of her thigh. "It was quite awkward having to ask her, though."

"It was necessary," said Fredrick. "Unless you want misinformed and angry werewolves on the hunt for Sergeant Spencer, that is."

"About that," said Judith, with a frown. "Mrs Giles is very hostile towards my father and me. She practically accused my father of killing Trevor, and she wasn't shy about insinuating that I might have had something to do with it, either."

"Her husband died whilst in your father's custody," noted Fredrick. "She's bound to jump to conclusions. Without motive or proof, though, that's all they are... wild conclusions."

Judith dropped her eyes briefly before taking a deep breath and looking in Millie's direction. Seemingly buoyed by the encouraging smile which Millie offered her, Judith continued. "It could be argued that Helen might be right in thinking that my father and I had a motive for hurting Trevor," she said. "Something happened last weekend. While Trevor was in the police station. Something I forgot to mention. Something I had almost forgotten had happened during all the chaos yesterday."

Fredrick raised an eyebrow and straightened his

back, giving his full attention to Judith. "Please inform us of what happened," he said.

"Trevor is a regular in the police cells," explained Judith. "I've lost count of how many times Dad has arrested him. Last weekend was no exception, and I just happened to be helping Dad out with some paperwork when he brought in a very drunk Trevor. He'd been fighting as usual."

"I have heard that Trevor was no stranger to police custody," remarked Fredrick. "But what was so unusual about last weekend, Miss Spencer?"

Judith sighed. "He hit me," she said. "Trevor hit me. It was more like he was lashing out and accidentally made contact with my face. There was no danger of him turning into his wolf — he was far too drunk to do that — much drunker than he was at the fete yesterday when he turned, but I was angry, and so was Dad. We might have said some things we regretted in the heat of the moment, but I can assure you that the whole incident was forgotten as soon as it had begun. Dad and I put it down to an accident and left it at that. Trevor didn't, though. It seems that he was ashamed of what he'd done. So ashamed that he told his wife about the incident."

Timothy's seat creaked in protest as he leaned forward, staring at Judith. "Helen Giles knows that her husband hit you — the daughter of the town's police sergeant? And then a week later Trevor is found dead in a police cell," he contemplated, stroking the wispy tufts of hair on his upper lip.

"That's a concerning turn of events. If the vigilante element of the werewolf community were to discover *that* information, I'd be quite afraid of what could happen. I have a feeling that fingers would be pointed very quickly indeed. Pointed in a direction that could be dangerous to you and your father."

"And neither yourself or Sergeant Spencer thought to mention this last night?" enquired Fredrick.

Judith shook her head. "We were in shock last night. I'd totally forgotten about it, Dad had too, I suppose. You saw how he acted when we came out of the police station. He was talking about going home for a party."

"He did seem out of sorts," admitted Fredrick. "He was acting very out of character. I'm not surprised that something so important may have slipped his mind."

"As long as the information stays out of earshot of the worst in my community, everything should be okay," said Timothy, offering Judith a reassuring smile. "We'll find out what happened to Trevor in no time at all, and put this whole sordid incident to rest, without awful aspersions being thrown at the good names of you or your father."

"Quite," said Fredrick, his expression unreadable. "And it seems that Edna may have discovered a clue in the poison, which could be the beginning of the trail of breadcrumbs which leads to the truth about what happened to Trevor Giles." He turned to Edna and gave a hollow smile. "The floor is yours, Mrs Brockett."

Edna stepped away from the drinks cabinet, her chin held high. She took a small green bottle from the pocket of her cardigan and held it up for all to see. "In this bottle are the remnants of the magic I retrieved from within Trevor Giles," she said, spinning the bottle slowly in her hand, the blue orb within the glass glowing softly. "I've used my own magic to reverse engineer, if you will, the magic that had been added to the poison that Trevor had ingested. Although I'm not yet sure of how the poison was administered."

Timothy cleared his throat. "May I interject?" he asked. "I've been looking into that side of things."

Edna nodded, impatience evident in her thin smile. "Please do," she said.

"I've examined the non-magical elements of the poison," explained Timothy. "My chemistry lab has all the equipment required to carry out a thorough investigation, but even after several tests, I can't be certain of how Trevor was poisoned. I can't be specific about which food item the poison was placed in, although after hearing from Sergeant Spencer regarding the speed in which Trevor died after consuming the muffin, I think we can say with some certainty that the muffin was indeed the vehicle for the poison — although I am, of course, basing that assumption on circumstantial evidence."

"Thank you," said Fredrick. "Is there anything else you'd like to add before Edna continues?"

Crossing his legs, Timothy made himself more comfortable in his seat. "As well as a lot of alcohol and food, there were a few herbs in Mister Giles's stomach, only one of which could harm a werewolf when administered in large enough doses."

"Saint John's Wort?" asked Millie, recalling what Timothy had said while smelling the air above Trevor's dead body.

"Indeed," confirmed Timothy. "Although there was not enough of it in Trevor's system to have killed him. There was barely enough to have given him a headache, which is why I think the magic Edna retrieved from Trevor must have somehow amplified the effects of the herb, causing Trevor's death."

"Where would one acquire Saint John's Wort?" asked Fredrick.

"It's a very common herb," said Timothy, "with many uses. It can be found in most health shops and even supermarkets. It's often used as a natural way to treat depression."

"So the person responsible could have sourced the herb from any number of places?" asked Fredrick. "That makes investigating that element of the case a little more difficult."

"Had it just been Saint John's Wort I found in Trevor's system, then I would have agreed," said Timothy. "However, the presence of rarer herbs in Trevor's stomach, such as kava, ginkgo leaf, and others, leads me to believe that the herbs in the poison were taken from my lab. I have a huge collection which the children use to make potions from."

Fredrick stared at Timothy for a few seconds, and then licked his lips. "So, the herbs used in the potion may have been taken from your lab," he said. "That may narrow the list of potential suspects down to the people who have easy access to your classroom."

"Not if the herbs were taken yesterday," said Timothy. "It was an open day — parents and pupils were in and out of my lab all day. In fact, I left the door open all day and didn't lock it until Judith and I had finished in there at about eight-thirty."

Frederick's eyes darted quickly to the left, falling briefly on Judith before returning to Timothy. "And what were you and Miss Spencer doing in the lab at such a late hour of the day?"

"I'd drank a lot of wine," said Judith, speaking before Timothy could. "And then Dad phoned me. He was hungry but couldn't leave the police station because Trevor was in a cell. That's when I took the cakes over. I was too drunk to drive, though, so Timothy made me a sobering potion. I went to the chemistry lab with him while he made it."

"I see," said Fredrick, studying Judith. He looked as if he was going to say something else, but chose not to at the last moment. He looked at Timothy again. "If the herbs were taken from your lab, why would such a mix of them be added to the poison? You already stated that from the list of plants you found inside Trevor, only Saint John's Wort is damaging to werewolves. Why would other harmless herbs be added to a poison designed to kill one of your species, Mister Huggins?"

"To disguise the taste?" offered Timothy. "Or maybe the other herbs became poisonous when magic was added to the mix. As you know, Fredrick, magic is a complicated business."

"Or maybe the poison wasn't designed to kill a werewolf?" offered Judith. "Maybe it wasn't meant for Trevor at all? Maybe it was meant for somebody else? Maybe the mix of herbs and magic was intended to kill somebody else, or something else."

"I find that hard to believe," said Timothy. "Werewolves are not the simplest of the paranormal species to kill. We don't die easily, and I find it hard to imagine that a poison meant for a non-werewolf would kill one of us. It seems implausible. It's my belief that the poison found inside Trevor was designed intentionally to sever the tie between Trevor and his wolf energy." He looked at Millie and Judith. "You both witnessed Trevor's wolf energy leaving his body."

"Yes," said Judith. "It wasn't a pleasant sight."

"Would you allow me to speak again, please?" said Edna, impatiently, stepping forward. "As I think I can prove that the poison *was* meant for a werewolf, and I also think I can prove that the poison was not necessarily in the muffin."

Chapter 20

The room fell silent, and then Fredrick spoke. "Then why didn't you say so before?"

"I was trying to explain when Timothy asked to interject," said Edna, scowling. "I'm too polite to interrupt." She raised an eyebrow in Timothy's direction. "Unlike some of us."

"Well, the floor is yours once again, Mrs Brockett," said Fredrick with a wave of his hand. "Please enlighten us with what it is you have discovered."

Displaying the little bottle in her hand, held upright between finger and thumb, Edna began. "As I was attempting to explain, I managed to reverse engineer the magic contained within this bottle. It was difficult, as are most things where magic is concerned, but after a couple of hours, the spells that had been used began to speak to me."

"Speak to you?" asked Timothy.

"Not literally, Mister Huggins," snapped Edna. "Metaphorically. What I mean is that I began to understand how the spells worked. I began to discover what elements had been used in the magic." She glanced at Timothy and Fredrick in turn. "For the non-witches amongst us, that simply means that we can narrow the magic down to a certain type of witch. Some witches are better at using fire or air as an element to power a spell, others enjoy using the sun."

"And which of those elements has been used in the spell contained in your little bottle?" asked Fredrick.

"None of the elements I just mentioned," said Edna, spinning the bottle and gazing at the blue light trapped within. "The magic contained in this bottle was cast using the elements of the moon and water." She placed the bottle on Fredrick's desk and pursed her lips. "And what better magic to add to a poison designed to kill a werewolf, than magic cast using a moon element? Which is why I believe the poison that Trevor ingested *was* intended to be harmful to a werewolf."

"That does make sense," said Timothy. "The moon is of great importance to werewolves. It heals us and gives us strength. Any magic that uses the moon as a source could potentially harm us."

"I agree," said Edna. "And although the moon-pool provides the catalyst for all magic in our town, it is not the same as using the power of the moon for personal spells. In fact, it can be quite difficult to harness the power of the moon directly. It takes a skilled witch, and knowing that the moon was utilised in the magic inside this bottle allows us to narrow down the list of witches who potentially cast it." She dropped her eyes and looked at Judith. "Perhaps Miss Spencer could help us with that task?"

"Why should Miss Spencer be able to help with that particular task?" asked Fredrick.

Judith spoke before Edna could. "Because I specialise in lunar and water magic," she said. "And we witches tend to swap spells with one another — mostly with other witches who utilise the same magical elements as we do." She smiled at Edna. "I'll compile a list of all the witches I know who use the moon as the main element in their spells."

"Thank you, Miss Spencer," said Fredrick.

Millie concentrated on the warmth in her chest, gaining comfort from the magical energy which resided there. She'd taken a while to understand which element it was that her magic responded to, and had finally surmised that the feelings of warmth, and the hot tingles she experienced whenever she cast a spell, meant that she drew mostly on the element of fire.

Feeling the warmth gain heat behind her breast-bone as she concentrated on the hot little ball within her, Millie watched Fredrick as he scribbled something on a piece of paper on his desk, using a long white quill as a writing implement.

His eyes fell on Judith, and Millie felt the same discomfort she'd felt when she'd seen the vampire watching her friend after Edna had performed the magical autopsy on Trevor's body.

Fredrick didn't look at Judith for long, but during the few seconds his eyes had been on her, Millie had once again seen a flash of suspicion behind those long eyelashes. She took a deep breath as she considered reading the vampire's mind for a second time. No. She wouldn't. It wasn't fair on Fredrick, and it wasn't fair on herself. Fredrick was entitled to his thoughts, whatever they were, and reading minds was a drain on Millie's energy. Energy she needed if she was to help find out who had killed Trevor, and disprove any accusatory thoughts that Fredrick may have been having about Judith.

Not really wanting to admit it to herself, through a sense of loyalty to her friend, Millie could understand why Fredrick might be having thoughts that led him to ponder Judith as a potential suspect.

If Millie hadn't known Judith as well as she did, she might have shared similar thoughts with the vampire. Trevor had hit Judith, after all, a detail which Judith had failed to mention until Helen had brought it up. Judith had taken the cakes to the police station, too, after having been in the chemistry lab with Timothy, with access to all the ingredients in the poison. Not forgetting that she possessed the magical capability to cast a spell over them using moon magic.

She gave her head a quick shake. No. She mustn't think like that. She bit her bottom lip, the pain making her wince, but having the desired effect of banishing some of the unwelcome thoughts from her mind. She bit it again, harder this time, as the most unwelcome thought refused to budge from its entrenched position in her mind — the awful thought that screamed at her, hurting her head and making her ashamed that her mind was capable of generating it.

She closed her eyes — willing it away, but with no success. She shook her head, there it was again. That thought. Harassing her. Upsetting her. It flashed bright in her mind once more. *If Judith had something to do with Trevor's death, then so did Sergeant Spencer. So did your father, Millie! You might be the daughter of a murderer, Millie!*

"Millie?" came a concerned voice from beside her. "Are you okay?"

She opened her eyes, her lip hurting, aware that everyone in the room was watching her. "Yes... yes, I'm fine," she said, offering a smile.

"Are you sure?" asked Judith. "You were murmuring to yourself, and I can see a mark on your lip. You looked as if you were biting it."

"I'm fine, honestly," said Millie, running her tongue over her bottom lip in an attempt to relieve the soreness. "I'm probably just a little tired."

"Then we shall continue," said Fredrick.

"Although I imagine that we're all tired. None of us had the luxury of much sleep last night. Miss Thorn can leave if she likes, though. Maybe she'd prefer to be tucked up in her bed than helping us get to the bottom of a murder in Spellbinder Bay?"

There it was again. The disdain which Fredrick so often showed her since she'd begun dating George. "I'm fine, thank you," retorted Millie, narrowing her eyes at the vampire.

"Very well," said Fredrick. He smiled at Edna. "Please continue, Mrs Brockett. You had enlightened us about the presence of moon and water magic within the poison, and you had eluded to the fact that the muffin may not have in fact been the vehicle for the poison." His brow furrowed as he looked at the witch. "Please explain how you reached *that* particular conclusion."

With a proud glint in her eyes, Edna grabbed the bottle from Fredrick's desk and tapped the glass with a manicured fingernail. She lifted the bottle to eye level and peered at the blue orb within. "At first I couldn't tell what it was," she said, slowly spinning the bottle. "It was a fleck of red, buried deep within the spell, almost invisible to the naked eye." She gave a smile. "But I have good eyesight. Better than some people half my age. In fact, the last time I visited an optician was in the nineties, and I was told I would never need glasses." She frowned, lowering the bottle. "That disappointed me if I'm being honest. I think a good teacher *should* wear glasses. I believe the children respond far better to a bespectacled tutor than one with naked eyes. So I bought two pairs of spectacles with non-magnified lenses — fashion spectacles, if you will. One pair with red frames, and one with silver. I never looked back. Excuse the pun."

"Edna," said Fredrick. "That's an enthralling tale you tell, but is it relevant to the task at hand?"

"Not really," replied Edna. "I simply wished to make you all aware of how keen a person's eyesight must be if they wish to discover hidden secrets within magic spells. Luckily, I have keen eyesight, so I was able to spot the almost invisible trigger buried within the spell contained inside this bottle."

"Trigger?" said Timothy. "What sort of trigger?"

"A trigger," said Edna. "A trigger which would activate the spell under certain circumstances."

"Like a delay?" said Judith.

Edna nodded. "Yes. And a spell with an inbuilt delay used in a poison would suggest that the poison was not intended to be active at the moment somebody ingested it. A poison that worked in such a simple fashion would not require a trigger — it would begin working the moment somebody swallowed it. This poison was different, it was intended to kill its victim when something triggered the spell within it."

"What sort of trigger, Mrs Brockett?" asked Fredrick. "Can you be more specific?"

"I can't," said Edna, with a shake of her head. "It could have been a word, a smell, a taste, a sight. I may never be able to tell, but what I can say is that the poison wasn't necessarily in the muffin served to Trevor by Sergeant Spencer, although that is still a possibility, of course. Especially considering how quickly Trevor died after consuming it."

"I don't think I understand," said Judith. "That would mean that as soon as Trevor had eaten the muffin, something triggered the magic in the poison and it became active, killing him?"

"Or," said Edna, a sly smile on her lips. "The muffin may have been the trigger that activated the poison. Trevor may have been poisoned hours before he died, and the muffin, or an ingredient within it, more specifically, was the catalyst that set the poison in motion, killing him instantly. I don't know exactly what happened, all I do know is that the magic in the spell contained a trigger."

"So we don't even know *when* Trevor Giles was poisoned," said Judith. "We don't know if he was poisoned in the police cell, or earlier in the day, and we're not even sure of *how* he was poisoned. Are we sure of anything?"

"Judging by the freshness of the poison, and the contents of Mister Giles's stomach," said Edna, "we can be sure that Mister Giles ingested the poison within the last twenty-four hours. We can also be sure that the poison was put inside something Trevor had eaten. Judging by some of the herbs used in the poison, I very much doubt that it was put in something Trevor drank yesterday. The taste would have been obvious to whoever took a sip, especially somebody with senses as acute as a werewolf."

"He was very drunk," said Millie. "Maybe his senses weren't operating at full capacity?"

"Considering most of the liquid in Trevor's stomach was beer," said Edna, "and considering the fact that Trevor had a strong liking for alcohol, I think it's safe to say he would have detected the poison had it been put in his drink. It is my strong belief that the poison was slipped inside something Trevor ate yesterday, and as the only morsels in his stomach were of the cake variety, I don't think we'd be too far away from the truth if we work with the assumption that Trevor Giles ate a cake containing poison yesterday."

"Okay," said Fredrick. "We have ourselves a real mystery." He stood up and smiled at Edna. "Thank you for your thoroughness, Mrs Brockett, but I fear that this is all becoming a little too complicated, and when things become complicated, I'm of the mind that simplicity is the antidote."

"Meaning what?" said Edna, pocketing the glass bottle.

Fredrick picked up a piece of paper from his desk. "We carry out some simple old-fashioned investigations, Edna," he said, brandishing the paper. "This is a list of people that may have had a reason for wishing harm upon Trevor. Timothy compiled it."

"It contains the names of everybody that Trevor upset yesterday at the school open day, and some other names of people in the werewolf community that Trevor didn't get along with," explained Timothy.

Fredrick glanced around the room. "I instructed Timothy to include the names of everybody he recalls arguing with Trevor Giles yesterday, and that of course includes my name."

"Mine too," said Timothy. "It would be unfair to compile a list of potential suspects without adding my own name — after all, everybody at the school fete witnessed Trevor and I fighting in our wolf forms." He squirmed in his seat and looked at Judith, an apology in his eyes. "Your name is on the list, and your father's name, too." He turned his gaze to Millie. "And yours. I believe you had a few altercations with Trevor yesterday?"

"Yes," said Millie. "I did."

"The fact that our names are on the list does not mean for one minute that anybody thinks it was one of us who poisoned Trevor Giles," said Fredrick. "It is purely for the sake of fairness to the other people on the list."

"A list which is incomplete," noted Timothy. "I heard talk of Trevor offending some of the parents who attended your classroom to watch the children cook, Millie. I'd appreciate it if you could add those names to the list."

"Of course," said Millie.

"I'd ask each of you to study the list," said Fredrick, passing the sheet of paper to Edna. "And add any names that you think should be on it. When we have a completed list we will solve this mystery the simple way — by asking people questions. With Henry away we can't use the stone of integrity to gauge whether people are telling the truth, or not, so we'll need to rely on our instincts."

Edna Brockett scanned the list quickly and passed it to Millie. "There's no names I can add to it," she said.

Glancing at the list, Millie took the pen which Timothy offered her. She quickly scanned the names written in Timothy's neat hand, adding the names of the parents who had been present in her classroom when Trevor had arrived. Checking the list again, Millie noted that Timothy had included the names of Cuthbert Campion and his daughter, recalling that the werewolf had informed her and Judith that he'd heard the argument in the refreshment tent between Cuthbert and Trevor.

Satisfied that she'd added all the relevant names to the growing list, Millie passed the sheet of paper to Judith who ran her eyes over it quickly. "There's one name missing," she said.

"And who would that be?" asked Fredrick.

"Mister Wurtherton," said Judith.

"Our Mister Wurtherton?" asked Fredrick. "Mister Wurtherton the History of Paranormal Events teacher?"

"Yes," said Judith. "He offered up his time yesterday, to help out at the fete. He served behind the bar in the refreshment tent."

"And had a few angry words with Trevor," added Millie.

"If I recall the conversation correctly," said Judith. "I think he told Trevor he hoped he'd choke on his drink. Or words to that effect."

"He didn't mean anything by it," said Millie. "I'm sure of that."

"As am I," said Fredrick. "However, I shall speak to him." He took the list from Judith and ran his eyes over it. "And I'd be very appreciative if Miss Thorn would speak to some of the other people on this list." He cast Millie a sideways glance. "How about you begin by speaking with Francine Jackson, Beth Taylor, and perhaps Cuthbert Campion and his daughter?"

"Of course," said Millie. "But what am I supposed to ask them? We don't even know what happened to Trevor, and we're trying to keep the news of his death a secret for the time being so as not to anger the werewolf community —"

"*Some* of the werewolf community," corrected Timothy. "Most of us are rational beings who wouldn't suspect Sergeant Spencer was capable of murder, and certainly wouldn't wish any harm upon him."

"Miss Thorn makes a valid point, though," said Edna Brockett. She turned to Fredrick. "Are you sure its worthwhile us even attempting to find out what happened to Trevor before Henry Pinkerton returns from his trip? As you've already acknowledged — we can't use the stone of integrity to discover if people are lying to us or not — so our hands are tied in that aspect. Henry could get to the bottom of the matter far faster than we possibly can. Maybe it *would* be better if we were to wait for him and the headmaster to return?"

"I think I have made it abundantly clear that we will do our very best to get to the bottom of this unfortunate situation before Henry and the headmaster return," growled Fredrick, his eyes briefly flashing vampiric black. "Henry left me in charge, and I will do everything in my power to ensure that I respect the trust he placed in me. I would be neglecting my position of trust if Henry and the headmaster were to return to a situation that I had not even attempted to resolve. I will do my upmost best to discover the truth about what happened to Trevor Giles before their return, and I'd hope that you will all give me your support."

"You have my support, naturally," said Edna. "But Miss Thorn *did* ask a pertinent question — what is it you want her to ask the people on that list of… suspects? And how should Trevor's death be kept a secret?"

Fredrick sat down again, and brushed a strand of hair from his face. "Ask simple questions. Find out if any of them hated Trevor Giles enough to have warranted their involvement in his death. Ask them any questions that you deem relevant, and as for keeping Mister Giles's death a secret, you may break the news to anybody you speak to during your investigations, Miss Thorn, and simply tell them that I have ordered them not to speak of it. I may not be Henry Pinkerton, but I am respected by many in the community. They won't go against my wishes."

"And me?" asked Judith. "What would you like me to do, Fredrick?"

Fredrick considered Judith for a few moments, the look in his eye once again suggesting to Millie that he didn't trust the witch. He gave a small, thin smile. "I hoped you would go and be with your father, Miss Spencer. Explain to him what we are doing to solve the riddle of a man dying in his custody. I'm sure he'd like to be informed, and who better to inform him than his daughter?"

Eyeing Fredrick with reciprocated suspicion, Judith finally dropped her gaze. "Okay," she said. "That makes sense. I'll go and reassure my father."

Fredrick gave a curt nod and turned to Timothy. "And if you would remain here at the hall and help Edna further investigate the poison, Mister Huggins, I would be extremely grateful. Between the two of you, I'm sure you'll be able to uncover more clues about both the magical and physical elements of the concoction."

"Of course," said Timothy. "I'll get to work right away."

"As will I," added Edna.

"Good," said Fredrick. "Then let us *all* get to work."

As Millie was about to stand, a cold chill

embraced her neck and shoulders, and a loud female voice burst from behind her seat, startling her into near frightened paralysis. "Miss Thorn, Mister Huggins, why are your classrooms home to a robed ghoul?"

Chapter 21

"*A*h, Florence," said Fredrick, staring past Millie. "I'm glad you could finally make it."

A chilly breeze blew over Millie's face as Florence glided past her and approached Fredrick's desk. "I apologise profusely for my tardiness," said the ghost, offering a curtsy, her floor length, billowing black skirt hiding the shape of her legs and hips. "I've been otherwise engaged in the pursuit of a new arrival to the hall. A terrible ghoul if ever I saw one."

"New arrival?" asked Edna. "What new arrival, Florence?"

Florence briefly flickered in and out of existence, her narrow waist becoming transparent before taking on a semi-solid form once more. She glanced at the witch, her chin held high above the climbing collar of her crisp white blouse.

She looked Edna up and down, her eyes narrowing in obvious disapproval. "I have learned over time to forgive young women such as Miss Spencer and Miss Thorn for their sins against decency, and presumably chastity, Mrs Brockett, but I will never make peace with the sight of a woman in her dotage flaunting her legs in the company of men. It's a despicable display of lustful wantonness, from a libidinous widow."

Edna's chest rose as she sucked in a deep breath and stared at the ghost. She glanced down at her pleated tartan skirt, the hem of which fell level with her stocking clad knees. "Although I have become used to your insults, Florence, they still sting on occasion," she said. "I am not in my dotage, and I am certainly not a libidinous widow, and I would ask that you show me a little more respect."

With a huff of ghostly breath, Florence looked away. "You know you're always welcome to observe me teaching my home management, manners and decorum in the presence of men, and needlework class, Mrs Brockett. You're never too old to learn something new, that's what I teach the girls who volunteered to take my class. And young Sidney of course, strange boy that he is."

"I'm afraid I'll have to turn your kind offer down," replied Edna, pulling her cardigan tight around her. "Although the last time I peeked into your classroom it was quite devoid of volunteers keen to be educated in Victorian dogma."

"Yet the three children who *do* attend will no doubt grow up to be fine specimens of womanhood and femininity," said Florence. "Although I do think that Sidney really should pursue a more masculine subject, such as mathematics or science. He *is* highly adept with a needle, though. Those little fingers and hands of his perform the most beautiful dance when he is embroidering. The lad is certainly an enigma."

"Those three children will grow into emotionally stunted adults if we allow them to be educated in the way you'd like them to be, Florence," said Edna. "You really should modernise your thinking. You may have died during a time when women were embarrassingly subservient, but these days, things are very different."

Fredrick cleared his throat, cutting Florence off as she prepared to reply. "Ladies," he said. "Must we listen to you two bickering every time you are in a room together? It's highly unprofessional." He looked at Florence. "What were you talking about, anyway? You spoke of a ghoul in Spellbinder Hall?"

"A most terrible ghoul," said Florence, hurling a final judgemental glance in Edna's direction. "Tall, robed, mysterious and anti-social."

"I saw it yesterday," said Millie. "It was in my classroom."

Florence nodded. "Yes," she said. "I'm aware that it was in the cookery classroom, and I've been trying to communicate with it, but it seems to want no contact with me. It's an extremely ill-mannered spirit - - a most grumpy and graceless fopdoodle, if you'll allow me to use such boorish language."

"Your choice of language is forgiven, Florence,"

said Fredrick. I'm certain that everybody in this room has heard worse profanities." He gave the ghost a smile. "I'm afraid that now is not the time to worry about a new ghost in the hall, Florence. We have a far larger fish to fry. A man has been murdered, hence my request for your presence in my study this morning."

"I've already apologised for my tardiness," said Florence, flustered. "But as a ghost who takes her position in Spellbinder Hall seriously, I consider it my responsibility to greet all new arrivals from the world of the spirits. Becoming a visible spirit after wandering the plains of the afterlife as an invisible entity, can sometimes prove difficult for ghosts... I like to be on hand to help them with their transition. So I have been attempting, in vain, to converse with the latest arrival all morning."

"Which is very noble of you, Florence," said Fredrick. "But a subject for another occasion. I called you here this morning to ask if you could help with the murder enquiry we find ourselves embroiled in. I realise that as a spirit you often wander the corridors unseen, and wished to ask if you'd witnessed any suspicious behaviour from, or aimed at, the unfortunate man who was murdered last night. He was present here at the open-day yesterday. His name was Trevor Giles, you might remember him from when he was a pupil at Spellbinder Hall."

"Of course I remember Trevor Giles," said Florence. "And I saw him yesterday, as did the the ghoul I've been following." Her stern face darkened and her voice took on a menacing edge. "Trevor was the most heinous of children, and he certainly wouldn't have been welcome here yesterday if Henry Pinkerton had been present. Not after what he did as a child! He should have been sent to The Chaos, not simply banished from ever returning to Spellbinder Hall!"

Fredrick gave Florence a puzzled look. "Sent to The Chaos for bullying? Don't you think that sounds a little harsh, Florence? Yes, he was a cruel child, sometimes. He was often sent to me for detention all those years ago, and he deserved the punishment that Henry finally gave him, but to suggest that he be banished to the realm of demons for a few cruel words and a black eye or two, seems overly wicked."

"That's not why Henry punished him!" snapped Florence. "I was there! I saw what happened! I saw what Trevor Giles did!"

"Just what are you saying, Florence?" said Fredrick, getting to his feet. "I know what happened. I've been a teacher here since the fifties, and I was present in nineteen-eighty-eight when the Board of Governors expelled Trevor Giles for bullying. Henry Pinkerton was livid with him, and warned him never to pass through the doors of this hall again."

Florence dropped her eyes, briefly fading from sight before becoming visible again. "I've said too much," she said. "Please forget I spoke out of turn, Fredrick."

"I don't think I can forget what was just spoken about," said the vampire. "You insinuated that Trevor had done something terrible. What was it that you think happened? What are you insinuating that Trevor did?"

Florence shook her head. "I will not say another word on the matter," she promised. "I can assure you of that, and if you wish to hear what I have to say about suspicious activity concerning Trevor Giles and the ghoul yesterday, then you shan't attempt to cajole me into saying anymore about any incident that may, or may not, have occurred in nineteen-eighty-eight. If you do attempt to make me speak, I shall simply vanish and not make myself known again until Henry Pinkerton has returned from his trip."

"She means it," warned Edna, raising an eyebrow. "She's very stubborn. A little like a mule."

Fredrick sighed and lowered himself into his seat. "Very well, Florence, but I shall be bringing the subject up with Henry when he returns." He rolled his shoulders. "Please, go ahead. Tell us about Trevor Giles. What suspicious activity did you witness?"

"I happened to be taking a stroll in the sunshine when Trevor Giles arrived yesterday," said Florence. "I was enjoying watching the tents being erected in readiness for the fete, when a taxi pulled up and Trevor climbed out. It had been many years since I'd seen him, yet I recognised him immediately. I followed him into the hall and hid myself from him as he headed up the stairs."

"On his way to my classroom," added Millie. "To watch the children's cooking display."

"Indeed," said Florence, giving Millie a smile. "And I observed in fascination as he was attacked by the ghoul I spoke of."

"Yes," said Millie. "Trevor barged into the classroom. The door slammed into the wall and frightened everybody -- even the ghost. It rushed towards the door and passed right through Trevor as it escaped."

"Good gracious, no!" said Florence. "That's not what happened at all!"

"What do you mean?" asked Millie.

Florence rose a few feet off the floor, before descending again and gliding towards the empty armchair in the corner. She settled into it, the leather visible through her torso and legs. "When a new ghost pops into this world from the invisible world of the wandering spirits, I am able to sense it. It's akin to the sensation I recall experiencing when I was alive — the sensation one gets when they comment that somebody has walked over their grave. A tingling along the spine and a cold ball in one's stomach."

"I know it," said Millie.

Florence gave a nod. "I experienced that very sensation yesterday, no sooner had Trevor Giles stepped out of the taxi. The precise second that his foot made contact with the ground, in fact."

"Are you trying to say that the ghost coincidentally moved into our dimension at the exact moment that

Trevor Giles stepped onto Spellbinder Hall property?" asked Fredrick.

"That is what I considered to have happened at the time," said Florence. "Until I followed Trevor upstairs to the cookery classroom. It was then that I understood the spirt had made itself visible because Trevor Giles had stepped onto our land."

"How could you possibly know that?" asked Judith. "If you can't even converse with the apparition."

"I sensed it," said Florence. "The spiritual energy in Miss Thorn's classroom was heavy with an emotion one doesn't often sense in the presence of ghosts. You see, when a person dies it is normal for them to be relieved of all the burdens which life had bestowed upon them... a spirit should feel only peace in death. But not the new arrival... I could sense its rage as I followed Trevor towards the classroom, and when Trevor attempted to enter the room, the spirit's anger blossomed into a anger so intense that even I was unnerved."

"The ghost attacked Trevor?" asked Millie. "Is that what you're saying?"

"Not simply attacked," said Florence. "The spirit was able to make Trevor feel its presence, such was the strength of its malice."

"Yes," said Millie, recalling Trevor swatting at the air around him. "Trevor said he'd felt it pass right through him."

"That sprit meant to hurt Trevor Giles," said

Florence. "And even after expending so much energy in that attack on Trevor, it still managed to harness enough energy to make repeated attempts throughout the day. I followed it, concealing myself from view, attempting to understand why it harboured such anger."

"And did you discover why?" asked Judith.

"I'm afraid not," Florence replied. "The spirit dripped with anger, but had expended too much of its energy to either reveal itself to the living, or to make Trevor aware of its presence. I could not tell why it felt such rage, but I was aware of a peacefulness enveloping its aura when Cuthbert Campion and his daughter were present in your classroom, Miss Thorn. It even managed to make itself visible for a few more seconds."

"Yes," said Millie. "I saw it. It left the room at the same time Cuthbert and his daughter did, but it faded before it reached the doorway."

"Indeed," said Florence. "I was alongside it, hidden from the living, wishing to observe the new arrival without bringing attention to myself, and it was only during those brief seconds in which it made itself visible again, that I became aware its anger had been replaced briefly with a gentler energy." Florence closed her eyes and sighed. "It was a beautiful energy... a tranquil energy which calmed even me." She opened her eyes suddenly. "It was short lived, though! The spirit trailed Cuthbert Campion until he happened upon Trevor Giles in the refreshment tent, and then the spirit became angry again. So angry. It tried again and again to attack Trevor, to make itself felt, but it was too weak. It was forced to remain out of sight. It followed Trevor for the remainder of the day, anger fuelling it, until Sergeant Spencer arrested and took Trevor away, at which point the spirit vanished. Even I could not locate it. It wasn't until this morning that I discovered it once more, travelling the corridors between Mister Huggins's chemistry laboratory and the cookery classroom."

Anticipation in her stomach. Millie leaned forward in her seat. "Florence, do you think it's at all possible that a ghost could have manufactured a poison in Timothy's laboratory and somehow administered it to Trevor Giles?" she asked the ghost. "If the ghost seemed to hate Trevor as much as you think it did, then maybe it hated him enough to want him dead."

Florence rested her chin on a petite hand and looked upward as she pondered the question. After a few seconds she gave a nod. "It's a possibility," she said. "We spirits are capable of extraordinary tasks if our energy is powerful enough."

"You said the ghost appeared to possess an extremely angry energy yesterday," said Fredrick. "Enough to fuel such a task as mixing a poison and administering it to a man?"

"Maybe the poison *was* given to Trevor in the police cell," said Judith. "A ghost could have easily sneaked past me and Dad and slipped into the cell with Trevor. What do you think, Florence? Could the mystery ghost be responsible for Trevor's death?"

"Yes and no," said Florence. "I would imagine its energy would have allowed it to manipulate objects quite easily. And I'm certain it *is* strong enough to mix a poison and transport said poison across town to the police station, but I'm not sure that the robed ghoul is responsible for the crime you accuse it of. After all, as I so diligently explained, I followed it yesterday and I did not witness it either mixing a poison, or pursuing Mister Giles to the police station."

"Also," said Edna. "The poison contains not just herbs, but magic, too, and as we all know, especially considering the fact that witches cannot become spirits — a ghost can't cast a spell."

"Indeed we cannot," agreed Florence. "We are capable of much, but magic is beyond the grasp of even the most powerful of spirits."

"Very well," said Fredrick, getting to his feet. "Thank you for your input, Florence. I'd be extremely grateful if you would continue your attempts at making contact with the spirit, and if you do manage to communicate with it, try and ascertain why it apparently harboured such anger towards the late Mister Giles."

"I will do my best," said Florence, floating from her seat and gliding gracefully across the room, passing from sight through the wall next to the tall bookcase.

"And I'd be extremely grateful if the rest of you would get on with the tasks at hand," said Fredrick.

"Timothy and I will head straight to the chemistry laboratory," said Edna, striding towards the door. "Between us, I'm sure we'll discover any further secrets the poison may be hiding." She paused as she reached the doorway, and stared over her shoulder. "Come along, Mister Huggins. Time is not a privilege afforded us so we may waste it."

Rolling his eyes in Millie's direction and then offering her a quick wink, Timothy clambered to his feet. "Don't fret, Edna, I'm coming."

As Timothy and Edna left the room, Judith placed the strap of her handbag around her neck. "I'll hitch a lift home with you, Millie. If you don't mind. You'll be heading that way if you're going to go and speak with some of the people on the list."

"Sure thing," said Millie, pushing herself from her seat. "Come on, let's get going."

Giving a low cough, Fredrick stepped from behind his desk. "I *was* going to ask Miss Thorn to remain behind for a few minutes," he said. "There is a personal matter I would like to speak with her about." He looked at Millie. "If you would do me the honour, of course."

"Urm, yes, that's fine," said Millie, curious, and more than a little unnerved about what it was that Fredrick wanted to speak to her about. After a year in Spellbinder Bay she could hardly recall being alone in a room with the vampire for more than a minute at a time, and certainly not long enough to have had a conversation about a personal matter. She gave Judith a shrug and offered her the small bunch of keys which she took from her pocket. "Here, wait in my car if you like."

"No," said Judith. "Do you know what? I think I'll walk home across the fields. I could do with some fresh air and I'd like some space to think. I'll catch up with you later, Millie."

"Please close the door after you, Miss Spencer," said Fredrick, as Judith walked from the room. As the door clicked shut, he indicated the seat nearest his desk. "Please sit down, Miss Thorn," he urged. "Some important things need to be said."

Chapter 22

ith nobody else in the room but herself and Fredrick, the study felt suddenly empty to Millie. Not empty of people, but empty of life. Empty of character. Devoid of even the possibility of joy or happiness.

Feeling a spring dig deep into her buttock, Millie winced with pain as she settled into the seat and gave Fredrick a smile. "How can I help you?" she asked.

Fredrick studied her for a moment or two, his gaze expressing an emotion Millie had never seen in the vampire's eyes before. Something alien to the vampire's usual demeanour. Something... warm. Something kind, maybe?

No sooner had it appeared, than it was gone, and Fredrick's eyes became cold once more. "Miss Thorn," he said. "I see the way you look at me, and I understand that you may think I have a dislike for you. I'm not blind to my own interactions with other people. I realise I can be... awkward. I completely comprehend that you may have an aversion towards me."

If Fredrick realised he often came across as awkward, Millie wondered if he was aware of how uncomfortable he was currently making her feel. She bit her lip before speaking, squirming a little in her seat. "I don't have an aversion towards you, Fredrick, but I have noticed that since George and I began dating, you appeared to have treated me differently than before."

Tilting his head, Fredrick nodded. "As you know, Miss Thorn. I had the pleasure of saving George's life on a battlefield during World War One. I was a German medic, he was a British soldier. When I saw him dying in the mud, surrounded by the bodies of both his comrades and his enemies, I saw something in him. Something that persuaded me to bite him and give him immortality. He reminded me of the son I'd once had, the son who died of old age, refusing to allow me to turn him into a vampire, afraid of the creature I had become after I was bitten by a vampire who had dragged me unconscious from a Berlin canal and saved me from death.

"Outliving one's child is an awful experience for anybody, but not ageing as your son grows old and feeble, eventually withering away to nothing, is something entirely different. Something that will cast a person into their own living hell. A hell with no means of escape."

The unimaginable horror of the experience Fredrick was describing surpassed a gentle tugging of Millie's heartstrings — instead, it tore and ripped at them, twisting them in ways that made a tear bulge at the edge of her eye. Wiping a finger across her cheek, she allowed herself to look at the vampire. To *really* look at him, for once.

Although he'd stopped ageing before he'd reached fifty, Fredrick appeared older than the age he was when he'd been bitten, in the way a child with wise eyes looks older then he really is. What was ageing Fredrick wasn't wisdom, though, it was sadness. A terrible sadness abundantly displayed for all to see — if a person wanted to see it.

The sadness swam in his eyes, it moulded the set of his mouth, it traced the furrows in his brow, and was the puppeteer of his posture as he sat looking at Millie, his shoulders tense and hunched. With a sorrowful realisation, Millie saw Fredrick for who he really was. Not a stern schoolmaster or a scary vampire, but a man. A broken man. She spoke quietly. "That sounds awful," she said.

His face crumpling, Fredrick looked away before nodding and fixing Millie in a hardened stare. "I don't expect your sympathy," he said. "I tell you these things so you may understand why George's wellbeing is of such great importance to me." He picked up a quill from his desk and studied it as he spoke, rotating it in his fingers. "We vampires are not as humans have described us over the centuries," he said.

"We are not bloodthirsty tyrants who murder innocents in the search for fresh blood. We do not, in fact, even require blood to exist. We simply require more iron than a typical human, and that can be sourced from animal meat and vegetables, or even tablets bought at the supermarket." He gave Millie a thin smile. "Would it surprise you to learn that our fangs are not intended to wound or kill, but are for the purpose of healing a person?" He shook his head. "No, not healing a person — saving a person from certain death."

"I knew vampires didn't require blood to live," explained Millie. "George has told me a lot about vampires. He also told me that there *are* vampires who *have* murdered humans for the sheer fun of it."

"Yes," said Fredrick. "There have always been rogue vampires, and I'm sure there always will be, but unfortunately, it is those vampires whom the stories are written about. The vast majority of us are not like that, and most of us have only ever bitten a human to save them from certain death — in fact, it is quite rare even to find a vampire who has turned a human into one of us. If you do meet a vampire who has bitten a human, you'll discover that they are very attached to the vampire they created, as I am to George. It's almost like being a parent to them. The bond is very strong. Stronger than any other bond a vampire will have experienced since leaving their humanity behind."

"That's why you seem so unhappy about me

dating George," said Millie. "Because you think of him as your child?" She paused and frowned. "Although if George was your child, I don't see what's so wrong with me that you'd not want a son of yours dating me." She gave a sigh. "Anyway, we've split up. We're not dating anymore."

Fredrick nodded. "I know, and George is very upset by it all, but you have misperceived my intentions," he added, replacing the quill on its stand. "I don't dislike the thought of you dating George. I believe you are good for George. George likes you, and I'm glad that you make him happy."

"Then what is it you dislike about the situation?" asked Millie, choosing not to question Fredrick about whether or not he was aware of the mystery woman who was living in George's home with him. "George told me that you even attempted to persuade him into splitting up with me when we first got together. What's so wrong with me? Is it because I'm a witch?"

"Goodness gracious, no," said Fredrick. "I'm far too long in the fang to be judging people by their intrinsic qualities. I've been a vampire for a very long time, long enough to know that beneath the skin, all human and paranormal people are motivated by the same set of values. There is little difference between the values of a witch living in Spellbinder Bay or a human trawler-man living in Canada. Both want to love and be loved, and in my experience, those are the only two ambitions, which when achieved, make anybody genuinely happy."

"Then what didn't you like about George and I dating each other?" asked Millie. "If love is so important to somebody's happiness, why did you try and prevent it from blossoming between us? Don't you want George to be happy?"

Tapping a finger on the desktop, Fredrick studied Millie with cold eyes. "I didn't want you and George to find love or happiness with one another, Miss Thorn. That much is true."

Millie narrowed her eyes, refusing to look away from the vampire's hard stare. "But why?" she demanded.

Indicating his surroundings with a wave of a bony hand, Fredrick looked away. "Take a look around my study and tell me what you see, Miss Thorn."

"What do you mean?" asked Millie, perplexed.

Fredrick raised an eyebrow. "Simply look around and tell me what you see. With regard to the furnishings and interesting pieces of decor I have on display."

If by pieces of interesting decor, Fredrick meant items such as the broken model of the galleon on an old wooden sideboard, boasting a snapped mast and rotting sails, then Millie could think of several words which might aptly describe the pieces... none of them complimentary, and none of them adjectives which would characterise them as interesting.

Her eyes fell on the dusty telephone hanging from a bracket on the wall, its earpiece dangling at the end of a worn-out cord, the drab colour matching that of the long curtains which hung limply at the tall windows. Millie frowned. "I'm not sure what you want me to say," she admitted.

Fredrick leaned back in his seat and spread his arms wide, inviting Millie to look at her surroundings once more. "It's simple. How would you describe my study, Miss Thorn?" he enquired. "Modern? Colourful? Lively? How would you describe your surroundings?"

Not sure of where the conversation was heading, and not sure she wished to offend the vampire with honesty, Millie spoke carefully. "Comfortable, I suppose, and a little... tired?"

Fredrick gave what appeared to be a nod of approval. "Tired. An astute observation. You could be describing my study, or you could be describing me, Miss Thorn." He paused, before opening a drawer in his desk. He retrieved something from inside and passed it across the desk to Millie. "Take a look at this," he offered.

Millie turned the square of card over, already guessing it was a photograph housed in an old cardboard frame.

The two faces that stared at Millie were easily recognisable, and the long sleek car parked alongside the two men helped her date the black and white image. An educated guess put the date as sometime during the nineteen-fifties, and the clothing worn by the two men helped confirm her assumption.

One of the men in the picture hadn't changed in

the slightest during the years since the photograph had been taken. Even his lacklustre hairstyle and uninspired choice of suits remained the same today as when the photograph had been taken. The other man, as handsome in the picture as he was in real life, had moved with the times. George's hair was now much shorter, and he wore regular jeans and t-shirts most of the time, but in the photograph, standing alongside Fredrick, his thick black hair stood high on his head, presumably glued in place by whatever hair product it was that young men had used back then.

The tight checked shirt George wore in the picture had sleeves which had been rolled up past the first hard curve of his biceps, and the chunky boots paired with the jeans he wore gave him the appearance of a lumberjack who might be on the way to a disco, while still dressed in his work clothes. Millie looked up from the picture and placed it on the desk, sliding it towards Fredrick. "It's a lovely picture," she said. "Judith told me that you and George travelled after you'd turned him into a vampire during the war and that you'd moved here together in the fifties."

"Yes," said Fredrick. "We came to Spellbinder Bay together, but we soon drew apart. Travelling the world together had been an adventure, but when we began to put down roots in this paranormal town, our differences became apparent. I chose the profession of teaching, and George chose to accumulate wealth and spend it frivolously on motorbikes and fast cars." He gave a low laugh. "As he still does, over sixty years later."

"As is his right," observed Millie.

"I would not suggest otherwise," said Fredrick. "What George does with his immortality is up to him. I'll always be concerned for him, of course, but I would not venture to change him or his ways. That's not the point I'm trying to convey to you, Miss Thorn."

"Then what is the point?" asked Millie.

"When I arrived in Spellbinder Bay and became a teacher here at the hall, I was given this study which we sit in today," said Fredrick. "I decorated it in the way you see it now. Everything in this room was placed here by me in my first year in the job." His eyes softened as he ran his gaze over his belongings as if experiencing nostalgia. "And look how old those things appear Miss Thorn. My belongings are old and worn, yet my body is exactly as it was when I first stepped into this room in nineteen-fifty-three. You saw the proof in the photograph I showed you. Neither George or I look a day older than the summer afternoon during which we posed for that photograph. Yet..."

"Yet..." said Millie. "Go on."

Nodding slowly, Fredrick leaned forward in his seat. "Yet George and I have been surrounded by objects which have aged. Rotted away to nothing, even." He raised an eyebrow. "And we've been surrounded by people who have aged and..."

"Rotted away to nothing," finished Millie.

"Precisely," said Fredrick. "It is an awful thing to see a loved one pacing time's cruel path as you remain static, unable to accompany or even follow them." He sighed. "The memories of watching my beautiful son grow old and die will never leave me. They will remain with me until the day I'm finally released from this immortality."

"And you don't want George to fall in love with somebody," said Millie, finally understanding Fredrick's message to her. "Somebody he will have to watch growing old and eventually dying."

"Yes," said Fredrick, softly. "I installed that lesson into George as soon as I had turned him into a vampire. He listened to me, and as he had been brought up as an orphan, he had no family to watch growing old. He was free from the awful burden of a mortal family, and he never fell in love with a woman, Miss Thorn — neither a vampire female or a fully human woman."

"George told me that it's rare for a vampire to fall in love with another vampire," said Millie.

"It is," agreed Fredrick. "It seems that spending immortality with one person is perhaps worse than falling in love with a person and losing them to old age. Both circumstances have drawbacks, it seems, and the chance of a vampire falling in love with another vampire becomes even rarer when you consider that the majority of vampires are men."

"Why is that?" asked Millie.

"Because men have traditionally taken the most hazardous jobs, such as mining or construction," said Fredrick. "And men account for the vast majority of wartime deaths, especially in times gone by. It is while doing these jobs that most men are saved from death by another vampire, as George was by me, on a battlefield."

"So there's a disproportionate amount of Male vampires compared to female vampires," said Millie. "That makes sense."

"It does," said Fredrick. "But when two vampires do manage to fall in love with one another, beautiful things can sometimes happen. If they are perfectly suited to each other. Children can be born, and happiness can thrive within their family forever."

"Yes," said Millie. "There are a few vampire children who attend this school. They seem very happy."

"It's not surprising," said Fredrick. "They have a happy life in front of them. They have never been fully human — all they've ever known is how to live as a vampire, and then, unlike people such as myself, they get to choose when they will stop ageing."

"The biting ceremony?" said Millie. "I've heard some of the children talking about it."

"The most important day in a born vampire's life," said Fredrick. "The day on which they choose to cease the ageing process and begin their immortality. Most vampires choose their twenties or thirties as the optimum age — a sensible age, in my opinion."

"Their mother bites them, doesn't she?" asked

Mille, recalling snippets of the conversations she'd heard between children.

"Yes," said Fredrick. "A celebration is arranged, and the young adult is bitten by his or her mother, stopping the ageing process. It's a beautiful thing to witness, or so I've been told." He glanced at the grandfather clock and smiled. "I've allowed myself to become distracted from what I was telling you about George," he said.

Millie smiled. "You were telling me that he's never fallen in love with either a vampire or a human," she said.

"Yes, I was," said Fredrick. "For all those years he managed to keep love at arm's length... he managed to keep the inevitable hurt which would accompany love at arm's length. He kept himself safe from heartbreak and the sort of hell I've lived in since my son's death."

"Until I came along," said Millie, quietly.

"Indeed," said Fredrick. "Until you came along, Miss Thorn."

"And you asked me to stay behind so you could warn me away from him, like an over-protective mother?" asked Millie, scornfully. She gasped. "I'm sorry. I didn't mean to sound so rude."

"No apology is necessary," said Fredrick. "However, I did not intend to portray myself as an over concerned mother when I asked you to stay behind. I asked you to stay behind so we could clear the stale air between us, Miss Thorn. I do not, as many falsely claim, enjoy conflict."

"So, you're not asking me never to date George again… if I wanted to?" asked Millie.

"No," said Fredrick. "I'm warning you that following such a path could lead to terrible heartache for both George and you, and that's not something I wish for either of you. I'm asking you to be careful, Miss Thorn, and consider the feelings of both yourself and George. Should you choose to pursue a romantic relationship with George Brown, then you have my blessing, Miss Thorn… if such a thing means anything to you."

It did mean something to her. Not the fact that Fredrick had given Millie his blessing – she would have dated George without his blessing if she so wished. It was the fact that the vampire had opened his heart to her and showed her his soft side which meant something to her. Anybody willing to display their vulnerabilities as Fredrick had, was worthy of respect in Millie's estimation. She gave the vampire a sincere smile. "It does mean something to me, Fredrick. It means a lot to me. Thank you."

Fredrick gave a dismissive wave of his hand. "Then let no more be said on the matter, and however you decipher my intentions in the future, please don't consider me hostile towards you. I'm not."

"I won't," said Millie, noticing the faint laughter

lines long ago lost in the deep frowning wrinkles around the vampire's eyes. "I promise."

"Good," said Fredrick. "And I'd also ask that you never read my thoughts again, as you did during the autopsy of Trevor Giles. It's rude to trespass in a person's thoughts without their permission."

Acting on instinct, Millie babbled. "I didn't!" she lied. "And if I had done, you couldn't possibly have known. You can't feel your thoughts being read!"

Fredrick lifted one eyebrow and stared down his nose at Millie. "Please afford me the courtesy of speaking the truth to me, Miss Thorn. I didn't *feel* you reading my mind... as you said, that would be impossible, but I know you did. Didn't you?"

Taken aback by the sudden change of direction the conversation had taken, and with guilt spiralling in her stomach, Millie's cheeks burned hot. She opened her mouth, and then closed it, before dropping her eyes to her lap. "I'm sorry," she mumbled. "Yes. I did. I read your thoughts when I saw you looking at Judith. When I saw you looking at her as if you thought she might have been guilty of poisoning Trevor. I had to know if you suspected her."

Fredrick's lips tightened. "I knew you were reading my thoughts by the way you looked at me, Miss Thorn," he said. "You thought you were hiding your actions, but they were scrawled across your face. It took a mere second and a single glance at your expression to understand what you were doing."

"I'm sorry," reiterated Millie. "But I had to know

if you suspected Judith or her father of such an awful crime."

"Of course I suspected them," said Fredrick. "The thoughts of mine which you may have read were entirely rational. Trevor died in Sergeant Spencer's cell, and Judith had been present. Yes, I suspected them, but you could have asked me, Miss Thorn, instead of encroaching on my thoughts. I would have been honest with you."

"Okay," said Millie, rising to Fredrick's challenge. "Do you still think Judith or her father had anything to do with Trevor Giles's death?"

"Are you completely certain that they are not guilty?" asked Fredrick, capturing Millie in an unwavering stare.

Millie dropped her eyes, fighting off the guilt which washed over her like a wave. She knew in her heart that neither Judith or Sergeant Spencer had poisoned Trevor, but that one little voice in her head wouldn't stop making itself heard from the sidelines. It wouldn't stop insisting that perhaps, just perhaps, it was possible that even the people you thought you knew well, were capable of things you could never imagine.

"I'd be a fool if I didn't consider them suspects," said Fredrick, choosing not to press Millie any further on the issue. "Wouldn't I? Especially now we have learned that Trevor laid his hands on Miss Spencer last week. And not forgetting that Edna Brockett has discovered lunar magic in the poison — the very magic which Miss Spencer excels at."

"Edna discovered water magic, too," Millie reminded him. "Judith doesn't practice much water magic."

"Of course," said Fredrick, diplomatically. "We should bear that in mind."

"Surely you know neither of them is capable of murder, Fredrick?" asked Millie. "Deep down, surely you know that."

"What I believe I know, and the facts laid before us, are two very different things," said Fredrick. "But if you are asking what my heart tells me, instead of the analytical conclusion my brain has reached, then I would say that of course the good sergeant and his lovely daughter didn't kill Trevor Giles, and to embellish that statement further — I don't really care if they did."

"You don't care?" asked Millie. "What exactly don't you care about?"

Fredrick stayed silent for a few moments, before relaxing in his seat. He unfastened the top button of his shirt and blew out a long breath. "It's refreshing to be able to speak so freely with somebody, Miss Thorn," he said. "You're still relatively new to the town, so you're not stifled by tradition and politics like many of the paranormal residents are. It's unusual that I feel relaxed enough in the company of others to speak so candidly, and without reservation."

More tension visibly left his body, and his mouth formed a dry smile. "I'll be honest with you. I've lived long enough to have seen hundreds of innocent people die in numerous vile ways. Wars, famines, natural disasters… I've seen a lot in my long existence, so another death – the death of Mister Giles in this instance, barely elicits an emotional response within me, especially as Mister Giles was such a nasty piece of work. When I say I do not care, I mean that I possess no urgent desire to discover who it was that administered the poison to him. I am happy to await Henry's return and allow him to take charge of the incident."

Millie frowned. "If you don't care, why are you sending us all off on errands? Why did you ask Timothy to compile a list of suspects, and why are he and Edna examining the poison? You *must* care if you're trying to find the killer," she said.

"I'm only doing what I have to do to keep up appearances," said Fredrick. "I'm certain that when you speak to some of the people on that list of suspects, you will not discover any information which will lead you to the killer – it will be a waste of your time, and I'm equally sure that Edna's examination of the poison will be in vain. We are dealing with the paranormal murder of a werewolf, not the murder of a human by another human. We require paranormal methods to solve a crime such as this – techniques that only Henry Pinkerton is capable of."

"Then why are we bothering?" asked Millie.

"Why not just wait until Henry returns? He'll be back soon enough."

Fredrick gave another smile. "Because of politics, Miss Thorn. All is not what it seems in Spellbinder Hall. I'm content in the job I perform here in the hall, I like teaching the children... it is the one joy in my existence, and I'm content with being on The Board of Governors, but to retain the positions I hold, I must keep on proving my competence. Henry left me in charge, and if I did nothing in the wake of a murder committed during his absence, other people who hold a dislike for me, or who covet my position on the Board, would speak against me, perhaps persuading Henry to remove me from my responsibilities. And I happen to enjoy my responsibilities."

"I had no idea that there are people like that here at the hall," said Millie. "There are people here who would tell tales about you? Get you removed from your job, even?"

Giving a low laugh, Fredrick nodded. "Indeed, there are," he said. "This school is ancient, and some of the people and spirits who work or live here, have been here for a very long time. Rifts between people are commonplace, and secrets are kept within cliques. You were witness to such a secret being almost accidentally revealed today, Miss Thorn."

"I was?" asked Millie.

"Yes," said Fredrick. "Florence almost revealed a secret about Trevor Giles. I've always been under the impression that Trevor was expelled from this school for bullying, but it seems that the wool has been drawn over my eyes… Trevor was expelled for another reason, and Florence almost gave that secret away today. You witnessed how she reacted when I asked her about it… she became quite angry."

"Oh yes," said Millie. "And that reminds me of something Helen Giles mentioned this morning. Her son had hinted to me that something bad had happened in Trevor's life. Something that may have contributed to the way he's acted over the years. When I asked Helen about it, she said she didn't know what had happened, but whatever it was, it had happened here at Spellbinder Hall when Trevor was a pupil. Helen said that Trevor was told he was never welcome here again because of it."

Fredrick sighed. "As far as I've always been aware, Trevor was expelled from this school because of bullying. It seems, according to Florence, that I may be misguided in that conclusion. If something else did happen which involved Trevor Giles, I have no idea what it might have been."

"Why would it be kept a secret from you?" asked Millie.

"Who knows?" said Fredrick. "Those sorts of secrets are rife amongst the staff in the school, and they cause animosity between people. They cause distrust — for instance, how do I know that I'm not the only staff member who is unaware of the real reason Trevor Giles was expelled all those years ago? Perhaps many secrets are being kept from me, perhaps I am disliked by more people than I ever imagined. That is why I will go through the motions of attempting to solve the crime committed against Trevor Giles... to prevent anybody from speaking ill of me to Henry Pinkerton. If Henry was told that I simply did nothing, and awaited his return before beginning an investigation, I'm certain that I'd be removed from my position on the Board."

"Why are you telling me all of this?" asked Millie, aware that the vampire seemed to be content in unburdening himself of many personal issues. "How do you know I'm not the sort of person to talk behind your back."

"In the same way I could tell from the flash in your eye that you were reading my mind, I can tell that you're the sort of person who can be trusted," said Fredrick. "I've become a good judge of character over the many years I've walked the earth, Miss Thorn. I know a trustworthy person when I meet one, and as for why I'm speaking to you in such a candid fashion... I wanted to clear the air between us, Miss Thorn. I hoped we could be allies and not enemies."

"I'd like that, too," said Millie. "I don't enjoy conflict."

"Then I promise no further conflict from me," said Fredrick. "Whatever you and George decide to make of your relationship."

Millie smiled. "That means a lot, Fredrick," she said.

Fredrick gave a curt nod. "Good. Now we understand each other, why don't you go and speak with some of the people on that list of suspects?"

"I'm in full agreement that I should go and speak to people," said Millie. "But I'm surprised that you still want me to — after telling me that you have no expectations of finding out who killed Trevor before Henry returns."

"My motivation in looking for clues may be selfish, Miss Thorn," said Fredrick. "I simply wish to make it appear that I'm trying to solve this crime, but I'm sure your motivations are more wholesome. I imagine you really do want to solve Trevor's murder, if not to discover who is to blame so justice may be done, then to expel that tiny part of you that still wonders whether Miss Spencer or her father may have had any part in the crime. That part of you that won't be quiet, even though you *know* it to be wrong. That part of you that all of us have inside our minds."

Millie gave the vampire a smile. "Almost," she said. "But I also want to make sure that Sergeant Spencer is in no danger from the werewolf community before the real killer is found."

"I wouldn't harbour too many concerns about that," said Fredrick. "Werewolves are apt to make grandiose threats, but even if the worse in their community did discover that Trevor had died while in police custody, I doubt that any of them would *actually* be stupid enough to do anything silly."

"I'd rather not take that risk," said Millie, remembering the anger displayed by Helen Giles when she'd been told how her husband had died. She stood up. "I'd prefer to try and get to the truth right away."

Giving Millie a thin smile, Fredrick pushed the list of names across the desk towards her "There's a lot of names on this piece of paper, Miss Thorn, maybe somebody on it *will* know something about what happened to Mister Giles. I wish you good fortune."

Chapter 23

$\mathcal{W}$inding its way uphill, into the countryside surrounding Spellbinder Bay, Briar Avenue was home to a sizeable amount of the witches who lived in the town. Large detached houses with spacious front and rear gardens lined the broad road, and colourful shrubs and plants grew in neatly mowed grass strips between the pavement and the street.

With her window wound down, Millie drove slowly, appreciating the cool breeze on her face and the sounds of children playing in the park alongside the small lake, in which ducks fought over chunks of bread thrown at them by mothers and children.

The difference between the poverty-stricken street in which Millie had been that very morning while visiting Helen Giles, and the road in which Beth Taylor resided, was stark, and as she parked on the driveway outside number twenty-four, she found herself wondering how young Norman Giles was coping with the news about the death of his stepfather.

An urgent beep from her pocket interrupted her thoughts. She unlocked her phone and read the message from Judith. The list of witches who practised moon-magic contained over two dozen names, and Millie scan read them, pausing on the name near the bottom. Beth Taylor. So, Beth Taylor utilised moon-magic in her spells.

The fact that a witch favoured the moon as an element in his or her magic, did not by any stretch of the imagination suggest that the witch was capable of murder. That much was obvious, and as Millie walked to the front door and rang the doorbell, eliciting a chorus of musical chimes from behind the blue painted door, she suddenly realised that she had no idea what she was going to ask Beth Taylor.

Yes, Trevor had offended Beth yesterday. Millie recalled the sarcastic comments he had made about the witch's weight while in the cookery classroom, but comments such as those surely hadn't incited Beth into wanting to kill Trevor?

She frowned, remembering some of the events from the day before. Beth *had* been working on the cake stall, and if the poison Trevor had taken had been placed inside a cake, as was suspected, Beth would have had every chance to put it there. She'd even helped Emma serve Norman with the cakes he'd bought for his stepfather, *and* she practised the same magic which was found in the poison. Millie bit her lip. No, that couldn't be it. Beth certainly hadn't come across as the murdering type when Millie had spoken to her the day before. She'd come across as quiet, and gentle.

The front door swung open, and a face framed by long brown hair looked up at Millie, the smile quickly being replaced by a worried frown. "Miss Thorn," said Emma. "I knew it. I knew it was too good to be true. You've come to take my TV off me, haven't you?"

"What?" said Millie. She smiled at the young witch. "No! No, of course I haven't! I wouldn't give you something on one day and then take it back the very next!"

Her face brightening, Emma smiled. "Why *are* you here then, Miss?" she asked.

"I'd like to speak with your mother," said Millie. "If she's got a few minutes to spare."

Her smile sliding again, Emma's eyes widened. "Is it because of something I did in school?" she blurted. "Because if it is, please don't tell my mum. She gets very anxious and depressed, and I don't want to add to her worries."

"No, Emma," said Millie, stepping nearer to the door and placing a hand on the teenager's shoulder. "No, Emma. You haven't done anything wrong, in fact, you've been an outstanding pupil. All the teachers speak highly of you, especially Miss Spencer

— she says she loves teaching you magic because you put so much into learning it."

Emma appeared to relax, tension leaving her shoulders, and her eyes twinkling. She stepped out of the doorway and stood aside so Millie could pass. "Come in then, Miss Thorn. Mum's in the garden with my grandmother. I think Mum will be happy that you're here. My grandmother has been nagging her all morning." She winked at Millie. "Between you and me, I think she'll be happy for an excuse to get away from her for a while."

Pulling the door closed behind herself, Millie followed Emma through the house, admiring how clean and beautifully decorated it was. Whereas Millie's cottage showed no sign that the occupier was a witch — unless a person discovered the secret cavern beneath her home, Beth Taylor's house was the complete opposite.

A bookcase loaded with spell books stood against one of the hallway's walls, and a display case housing a selection of beautifully crafted wands had been placed on top of it. Peering into the cosy living room as she passed the open door, Millie noted the broomsticks standing in one corner, and the iron cauldron standing on the fireplace, with tendrils of steam rising from it, finding their way into the chimney. "Is your mother making a spell?" she asked, spotting the pestle and mortar and the assorted herbs alongside the cauldron.

"Oh no," said Emma, following Millie's gaze.

"That's my spell!" She smiled. "Well, it's not really a spell! I'm making a potion!"

"Is it anything exciting?" asked Millie, promising herself that she really had to begin embracing the art of potion making. The potions she made were usually very boring, such as potions for curing the burns she received while cooking, or potions that helped her to get up early in the morning so she could take a run along the beach. Other witches always seemed to make far more exciting potions than she did, such as potions which would enable the user to speak with animals or see in the dark. She gave Emma an excited smile. "So? What is it? What's bubbling away in your cauldron? Something fun?"

"Not really," said Emma. "It's a potion that helps Mum get to sleep at night. She suffers from insomnia, you see. It's not really a very magical potion... most of the magic comes from the natural properties of the plants I put in it. It helps Mum, though. She gets a lot more sleep since I've been giving her a spoonful of my potion last thing at night."

It may not have been the most thrilling potion in the world, but the love which Emma evidently held for her mother was evident, and Millie experienced a blossoming of warmth in her chest as she looked at the young witch. "Your mother is lucky to have you," she said.

"No!" said Emma, shaking her head vigorously. "I'm lucky to have her!" Her voice dropping in volume and her eyes shimmering with moisture,

Emma spoke in a cracked voice. "I nearly lost her last year, Miss," she said. "She almost… She almost died."

"Oh," said Millie. "I'm sorry to hear that, Emma. I had no idea."

"It's okay, Miss," said Emma. "Nobody knew about it. Mum didn't want anyone to know about it… it's sort of a secret, so please don't tell Mum that I —"

"Hello?" said a voice from the end of the hallway, cutting off Emma's sentence. "Can I help you? Who is this lady, Emma?"

"It's my teacher, Nan," said Emma. "It's Miss Thorn, the one I told you about. My cookery teacher. She's here to see Mum."

Millie stepped forward as the slender woman with a head of soft greying curls hurried towards her, removing one of her gardening gloves as she approached and offering a hand in greeting. "How lovely to meet you," she said. "I must say, Miss Thorn, you have taught Emma well! She makes her Mum and I some beautiful cakes and scones!" Giving Millie's hand a firm shake, she smiled. "It's a pleasure to meet you. I'm Victoria. I'm Beth's mother, and Emma's grandmother." Releasing Millie's hand, she turned her back and hurried back the way she'd come. "This way, Miss Thorn, Beth is in the garden deadheading her rose bushes. You go out and find her, I was just about to make a cup of tea and fill a plate with biscuits. I do believe it's time for a break. Emma can help me. She can practice her magic. She's trying to master the magic required to make a pot of water boil, but she's not quite there yet, are you, my dear?"

Emma shook her head. "Not yet," she admitted. "I can make it nice and warm, but I can't get it to bubble."

"You'll get the hang of it soon, sweetheart," said Victoria. She led Millie into a bright kitchen and pointed through the window. "There's Beth," she said. "You go out and speak to her, Emma and I will bring some refreshments."

Millie spotted Beth Taylor standing in the shadow of an apple tree at the bottom of the long garden, moving slowly as she worked, pausing every few seconds to wipe her brow with a glove. Even from the distance Millie was observing her from, it was apparent that Beth was in dire need of a cup of tea and a break.

Exiting the kitchen through the door propped open with a metal doorstop in the shape of a rabbit, Millie followed the paved pathway winding a route past flower beds and a small pond buzzing with insect life. Watching Beth struggle to reach a high branch on the rose bush, Millie wondered if her weight and evident lack of fitness had contributed to the circumstances under which she had almost died the year before.

Angry at herself for being capable of such judgemental thoughts, Millie called out to Beth as she neared the bottom of the garden. "Beth," she said. "I wonder if I could have a few minutes of your time?"

Appearing surprised by the unexpected visitor, Beth Taylor took a few moments to recognise who it was that was in her garden. After a few seconds, the puzzled look on her face was replaced by one of recognition. "Miss Thorn!" she said, taking slow steps towards Millie. "This is unexpected. Can I help you? Is something the matter?"

"I'm sorry to arrive unannounced," said Millie. "I'd just like a few minutes of your time if you can spare them. Something happened yesterday, and I need to ask you a few questions about it."

"Something happened? What sort of something?" asked Beth, gesturing towards the circular garden table situated on a patch of gravel alongside the pond.

Settling into one of the iron garden seats, and swatting away an inquisitive wasp, Millie set her face in an expression she imagined would convey the seriousness of her visit. "It's bad news, I'm afraid," she said.

As Beth sat down opposite Millie, placing her gloves and pruning shears on the table, a flash of concern registered in her eyes. "Bad news?" she said, her voice strained. "About what?" She gave a worried gasp, and looked towards the house. "About who?"

"Don't worry," said Millie, reminding herself of Beth's anxiety issues. "Nothing has happened to anybody who's close to you. I've come to speak to you about Trevor Giles."

"Trevor Giles?" said Beth, relaxing a little. She

frowned, and her expression hardened. "What about Trevor Giles?"

"He died last night," said Millie, observing Beth's face carefully. "He was poisoned."

If Beth had indeed had anything to do with the premature demise of the werewolf, it was now that the clue would be written on her face — when the subject of Trevor's death had first been broached. A quick glance towards the floor or a twitch of an eyelid might have indicated that Beth Taylor knew something about what had happened to Trevor, but instead, to Millie's surprise, Beth smiled. "Trevor Giles is dead?" she asked.

Millie nodded. "Yes. And we don't think his death was an accident. We think he was killed by a complex poison which was purposefully administered to him. Trevor Giles was murdered, Beth."

"Murdered?" said Beth. "By who?"

"We don't know," said Millie. "That's why I'm here. I'm going to be speaking to everybody that Trevor Giles might have argued with yesterday."

"To ascertain whether or not one of them murdered him?" asked Beth. She narrowed her eyes as she looked away from Millie. "You're here to ascertain whether or not I had something to do with his death, aren't you? Because you heard him insulting me in your classroom. Well, don't worry, Miss Thorn, I can assure you that Trevor Giles didn't offend me enough yesterday to make me want to kill him. He teased me about my weight. I can handle that. I've always been teased about my weight."

Millie gave Beth a smile. "I'm not saying that I think you hurt Trevor. There are a lot of people who had an axe to grind with him. I have to speak to them all, though, as you probably understand."

Beth sighed. "Of course I understand," she said. "You're regarded as a police officer here in Spell-binder Bay, so I'll do everything I can to help you." She shifted her weight in her seat and smiled at Millie. "Ask me anything you like."

Millie nodded. "Thank you," she said. "You practice moon-magic, don't you?"

Beth nodded. "Mostly, yes. It runs in my family. I use a little water magic, too, and some fire magic when needed. Why do you ask? Has magic got something to do with Trevor's death?"

"The poison which killed Trevor contained magic," explained Millie. "It wasn't simply a mixture of toxic chemicals. It was a complicated mixture of herbs and magic, both moon-magic and some water magic."

"So you believe a witch poisoned Trevor?" said Beth.

"It seems most likely," said Millie.

"How was he poisoned?" asked Beth. "When was he poisoned? He seemed full of life when Sergeant Spencer bundled him into his police car and drove him away."

"We believe the poison was in a cake which

Trevor ate," said Millie. "But we're not sure when he ate it. Trevor Giles died in a police cell after Sergeant Spencer had served him a cake brought from the fete, but Edna Brockett has discovered a magical trigger in the poison. She's not quite sure how the trigger works yet, but it could point to the fact that Trevor was poisoned earlier in the day, and something triggered the poison while Trevor was in a police cell."

"Triggers are simple magic," said Beth. "And a trigger could be anything. A smell, a word, a time, a sight."

"Yes," said Millie, "and until Edna discovers what the trigger may have been, we're looking for other answers, like when the poison may have been put into the cake which Trevor ate yesterday."

Beth licked her lips, and then her eyes widened a fraction. "Oh my!" she said. "You think I might have poisoned Trevor because his stepson came to the cake stall and took some cakes away for his stepfather! I can assure you I didn't, and I'll happily allow Henry to use the stone of integrity on me to prove I'm not lying!"

"Henry won't be back for a couple more days," said Millie. "But when he does return, I'm sure that he'll be happy to eliminate you from any enquiries."

"Then I look forward to his return," said Beth. She closed her eyes for a moment, and then picked the pruning shears up and began fiddling with them. "I hated Trevor Giles," she said.

Millie sat straighter in her seat. "Oh?"

Beth nodded, turning the shears over in her hand. "He was always an awful bully, from the first day I had to share a classroom with him as a child he began bullying me."

"I'm sorry to hear that," said Millie, wondering if she should attempt to read Beth's thoughts. Maybe just for a few seconds, just to see whether Beth was telling the complete truth or not. No. It wasn't a good idea. Beth seemed like an astute person, and if Fredrick had discerned that she was reading his mind simply from the expression on her face, then maybe Beth would too. Anyway, the stone of integrity was a far more accurate lie detector than Millie's ability. She shook the idea from her head and smiled at Beth. "Bullying is an awful thing to have to experience."

Beth suddenly slammed the shears down onto the table, the clank of metal on metal startling a bird from a branch alongside the pond and making Millie jump. For a few seconds, the only sound in the garden was the gentle gurgling of the little fountain in the pond, until Beth let out a loud sigh. She looked at Millie sheepishly. "I'm sorry," she said. "I got a little frustrated."

"That's okay," said Mille, a little shocked at the anger which had been displayed in Beth's eyes. She leaned back in her seat. "Frustrated about what?"

"I'd always planned on confronting Trevor Giles," she said, brushing a curl from her eyes. "I'd always promised myself that one day when I'd managed to build up the courage, I'd stand in front of him and tell him how cruel he was to me as a child. I'd tell him how his bullying had affected my whole life, how his horrible words have made my whole life a misery. How he's made me afraid to leave my own home sometimes, how he's —"

Millie stood up quickly as Beth bowed her head and began making loud sobbing sounds, her whole body shaking. "Are you okay, Beth?" she asked, rushing to the woman's side and putting a hand on her broad shoulder.

Beth gave another sob, before pushing Millie's hand away and getting to her feet. She opened her mouth to say something, but let out a strangled cry of misery instead. Tears soaked her cheeks, and she wiped her face with the back of her hand before turning her back on Millie and hurrying along the garden path towards the house, her sobs still audible until she disappeared through the door.

Taken aback, Millie stood still, listening to the fountain and the buzzing of insects, and wondering what had just happened. As she began walking towards the house, Victoria rushed into the garden, her face dark with rage. "What have you done to her?" she yelled, rushing towards Millie. "What did you say to my daughter?"

Chapter 24

*M*illie took a step backwards as Victoria approached at speed, her face flushed red and her hands balled into small fists. "What did you say to her?" she demanded. "I thought it was lovely that somebody had come to visit my daughter, but I'd have never let you near her if I'd known something like this was going to happen!"

"I didn't intend to upset her," said Millie. "Is she alright?"

"No!" snapped Victoria, coming to a halt in front of Millie and relaxing her hands. Her body sagged a little as if expended of energy, and then she crossed the short distance to the table and chairs. Slowly lowering herself into a seat, she looked at Millie. "No, she's not alright. She's crying her eyes out and muttering something about Trevor Giles. Emma's taken her up to her room to try and calm her down.

That poor young girl has had to deal with so much from her mother. It's not fair on her."

"I really didn't mean to upset her," said Millie, sitting down opposite Victoria.

Victoria gave Millie an accusatory glare. "Then why on earth did you come here talking to Beth about Trevor Giles? That man ruined her life!"

Taking a deep breath, Millie studied Beth's mother. Worry lines crowded the space around her eyes, and her cheeks lacked colour. She was a concerned woman. "Okay," she said. "I'll tell you why I talked about Trevor Giles, but I'm not supposed to, and I'd ask that you keep it a secret until it's public knowledge. I was going to ask the same of Beth before she... left so abruptly."

"Keep what a secret?" asked Victoria.

"Trevor Giles is dead," said Millie. "He died last night. He was murdered. He was poisoned."

Putting a hand to her mouth, and with her eyes widening, Victoria sat motionless for a few moments, before beginning to nod slowly. "I see," she said. "But why does that news involve my daughter, and why are you requesting that it be kept a secret?"

"I'm asking that you keep it secret because a certain person might be in danger from the werewolf community if news about Trevor's murder becomes common knowledge," said Millie. "They might jump to the wrong conclusion and blame the wrong person. I want to help find the real killer before somebody is hurt."

"That answers the second part of my question," observed Victoria. "And you have my word that it will be kept a secret, but what about the first part of my question... why should the death of Trevor Giles involve my daughter?"

"Trevor Giles seemed to have enjoyed conflict," said Millie. "He was known for inviting it wherever he went, and yesterday was no different. He argued with a lot of people during the school fete, and then later that day, he died from poisoning. I'm here to ask Beth the same questions that I'm going to ask everybody who argued with Trevor Giles yesterday. I need to find out if any of them had a strong enough motive to want to hurt Trevor."

"You're here to find out if my little Liz is a murderer?" asked Victoria, her voice raised. "Of course she's not a murderer! She's a gentle person. Too gentle. I told her a long time ago that she should have stuck up for herself against people like Trevor Giles by using her magic, but she never would. She always said that magic was never intended to hurt, it was only intended to help." She sighed. "And I suppose she's right. She'd have been no better than Trevor Giles if she'd retaliated with magic."

Millie inclined her head as she looked at Victoria. "Liz?" she said, the name sounding familiar to her ears. "You just called her Liz."

"That's what I used to call her," explained Victoria. "That's the name she used to go by. It was short for Elizabeth, you see."

"And now she goes by Beth, instead," said Millie. "Why did she decide to switch from Liz to Beth?"

Victoria gave a bitter laugh. "Because of Trevor Giles," she snorted. "A bully boy managed to force a young woman to change her name because the memories attached to her old name were too painful for her to bear. Trevor Giles was horrible to Beth while they were in school. He used to call her the most awful names. Lardy Liz was his favourite, and the cruellest thing of all was that Elizabeth wasn't even very overweight when he began calling her that awful name. She carried a few extra pounds, but she began really piling on the weight after Trevor began bullying her."

Lardy Liz. That had been the name written in one of the old cookery textbooks that she'd given to the children yesterday. There had been some more insults in the books, too, but Millie couldn't recall them. She decided not to bring it to Victoria's attention. Beth's mother was already angry, and Millie didn't want her to know that she had unwittingly exposed Beth to that terrible name once more.

She imagined how hard such teasing must have been for a young girl, and remembered a time in her life when she'd been teased. Not enough to have affected her whole life, but enough to have forced her into finding a vice for a few months. Like Beth, she'd turned to food for a period, too, but she'd been able to break free from its awful grip. She gave Victoria an understanding smile. "Comfort eating," she said.

"Yes," said Victoria. "And she's never managed to gain control over it. She's never been able to break free from the cage which Trevor Giles built for her. The cage which keeps her believing that she's worthless, that she's a bad person. That way of thinking has shaped her life so far, with awful consequences. She rarely leaves the house, she has no real friends, and she even drove her husband away."

"Emma's father?" asked Millie.

"Yes," said Victoria. "He tried his best to save the relationship, but Beth took the hatred she had for herself out on him. He was forced to leave in the end. Last year."

"How sad," said Millie.

Victoria looked towards the house and then leaned across the table towards Millie. "And then she took the hatred she had for herself out on herself, instead of on somebody else," she said, in a lowered voice. "Beth tried to end her own life, and if it weren't for Emma, she would have succeeded." She dropped her eyes to the table and sighed. "That poor girl. She's been through so much for someone so young. First, her father moved abroad to work after her mother had forced him away, and then her mother tried to drown herself. No wonder she's so timid."

"I'm sorry to hear that," said Millie. "How awful."

Her expression softening, Victoria smiled at Millie. "We don't talk about it," she said. "But it actually feels refreshing to be able to speak about it for once."

"Tell me as much or as little as you want to," said

Millie. "I don't mind listening if you think it will help, and I'll understand if you want to say no more about it."

Victoria took a deep breath. "It was last year," she said. "Late at night. It was almost midnight. Emma couldn't sleep. She rarely could for a while after her father had left home. She got out of bed and went to her window to watch the moon. Emma loves the moon, as she should — we're a family of witches who use the moon's energy in our magic. It was a full moon that night, and if it hadn't have been, Emma wouldn't have seen what she did see, and she'd probably have been without a mother."

"What did she see?" asked Millie, gently.

Victoria hesitated, but then spoke with a sadness in her voice. "Her mother walking into the duck pond in the park. Emma's bedroom window has a good view of the park, but without the full moon she wouldn't have been able to see."

"How awful for her," said Millie.

"Emma panicked," said Victoria. "She ran from the house towards her mother and reached the edge of the pond just as her mother's head dipped below the surface. The poor girl was forced to jump into the water to save her mother. Luckily, when Beth felt the hand of another person on her arm, it broke the trance of despair she was in, and she allowed herself to be guided back to shore. When Beth realised it was her daughter who had jumped in to save her, she broke down. Emma phoned me, and when I arrived twenty minutes later, Emma had dried her mother off and put her in bed. She's never stopped worrying about, and looking after her mother since. She's practically her carer at this point. It's been hard for them both these last few months. I do what I can, but Emma does the most."

"I would imagine it's not been easy for you, though," said Millie.

Victoria's face folded, and she blinked as tears brimmed in her eyes. "There's nothing worse for a mother than finding out that her child no longer wants the life she blew into her," she said. "It's heart-wrenching. I'm sure your mother would agree with me. Any mother would."

"My mother died," said Millie. "When I was ten."

"Oh. It's my turn to be sorry," said Victoria. "How sad for you. I can't imagine what it must be like to lose a mother at such a young age."

"I've been luckier than most people who've lost somebody they loved," said Millie. "I... I was able to speak to her after she'd died. Because she was a witch her energy still lived on after she had passed over, and I was able to cast a spell which brought her back. Just for a few minutes."

Victoria sat upright and stared at Millie. "You brought her back here? In Spellbinder Bay?"

"Yes," confirmed Millie.

"Hmm," said Victoria. "A witch's energy always finds its way back to a magical place the witch had lived in at some time during their life. So your mother must have lived here at some point if her energy is here." She half closed her eyes as she studied Millie's face. "Now I think about it; you do look familiar."

Millie nodded. "Yes, she lived in the same cottage I did for a short period of time — Windy-dune Cottage," she said, remembering how shocked she'd been when she'd first discovered that her mother had once lived in Spellbinder Bay and that she'd managed to keep her whole existence as a witch a secret from her daughter — a secret she had died with. "Her name was Josephine Thorn."

Victoria nodded slowly. "I remember her," she said. "I never had much to do with her, but I remember her. She was nice. I'm sorry to hear that she passed over. I do seem to recall that she left town quite abruptly, though."

Victoria was right. Millie's mother *had* left town abruptly — when she'd found out that she was pregnant with Sergeant Spencer's child. Not wanting her unborn child to live a life which contained magic, she'd left town quickly, without telling Sergeant Spencer he was to be a father. She'd then spent the rest of her life hiding not only the truth about Millie's father from her but also the fact that she and her daughter were both witches. Not wanting to divulge the whole of her personal history to Victoria, Millie simply nodded. "Yes," she said. "I'm told by people who remember her that she left town abruptly."

Victoria narrowed her eyes. "And because your

mother had once lived in this magical town, her energy found its way back here when she died."

"Yes," said Millie.

"And you were able to harness her energy through the means of a spell and bring your mother back?" asked Victoria, her expression inquisitive.

Millie nodded. "Yes."

Victoria's face gave away the fact that she was deep in thought. Her eyes darted left and right, and her lips moved as she muttered something under her breath. After a few moments, she gave Millie an excited smile. "I study old magic," she said. "I have many books on the subject, as does my daughter. I know what you did! You used the spell of unspoken words. You used the power of a dead person's unheard last words to tie her to our world and bring her back, didn't you? But how? That spell requires an ingredient out of reach to most of us — a pearl of wisdom, and it requires unheard words. How did you manage to cast such a powerful spell? How did you obtain a pearl of wisdom and how on earth did you harness the unheard words of a dead person? I've read about that spell, but I've never heard of anybody using it successfully."

Millie shuddered as she remembered almost drowning as she dived deep into the ocean to retrieve a magical pearl of wisdom. She had been wearing a magical dress which had transformed her into a mermaid, but the moment she had reached out and touched one of the powerful pearls, the magic in the dress had faltered. She had sucked in water as the fin she had grown vanished and her ability to breathe underwater was taken from her. If it hadn't been for the same mermaid Millie had borrowed the dress from, dragging her to the surface, she would have died on the seabed. She shook the traumatic memory from her mind. "I had help in finding a pearl of wisdom," she said. "And my mother had left me a letter that I'd never read. Those were her unheard words."

Victoria stared at Millie. "Amazing," she said. "I'd never have thought that using written words would have worked."

"It was a risk," said Millie. "I wasn't sure the magic would work, and I had to burn the letter to cast the spell. That letter contained answers to a lot of questions I needed answers to, and burning it meant I might never have got my answers if I hadn't been able to bring my mother back."

"But the spell *did* work," said Victoria. "And you got the answers directly from your mother's mouth?"

"Yes," said Millie. "And while she was here she told me that the spell I'd cast had formed a permanent bridge between wherever it is her energy resides and this world — but she's never come back again. It's been months, and she's never returned. I'm scared that she was wrong. I'm scared that the spell was only good for one visit, and I don't have any more unheard words to burn. I can't cast that same spell again."

Victoria looked towards the bottom of the garden, her brows furrowed. "Magic is complex," she said.

"I'm certain there is a good reason for why she hasn't returned." She looked towards the house and put a finger to her lips. "No more talk of death," she said. "Emma is here."

"Of course," said Millie, sure that Emma had enough worries about her own mother without hearing about the death of somebody else's.

Victoria stood up. "How is she, my darling?" she asked, as Emma approached the table, her face downcast.

"She's asleep," said Emma. "I gave her one of the chocolate cakes I made, and she cheered up a little, and then went to sleep."

"Those cakes of yours work a treat," said Victoria, winking at her granddaughter. "All that chocolate certainly helps cheer her up." She smiled warmly at Emma. "Don't worry, sweetheart, she'll be okay. You go back inside for a moment while I say goodbye to Miss Thorn, and then we'll practice some magic together. Let's see if we can't get you boiling some water by the end of the day."

"Okay," said Emma. "I'd like that, Nan." She began walking back the way she'd come, but then hesitated and turned to face Millie. "Miss Thorn, may I ask a favour, please?"

"Of course you may," said Millie. "What is it?"

Emma gave a wide grin. "I was hoping that you'd allow me to use the cookery classroom during the school holidays. It's so much better equipped than our kitchen here at home, and the ovens are much bigger than the oven we have." She dropped her eyes to the lawn and then smiled at her teacher. "I'd also like somewhere to go, somewhere I can... somewhere I can get away to, Miss."

"You know you're always welcome at my house, Emma," said Victoria. "But I suppose when you say you want to get away somewhere, you mean to be on your own."

"Yes," said Emma. "Just for a little bit now and again." She gave Millie an enquiring look. "Can I, Miss? I'll clean up after myself, and I'll be really careful."

Being put on the spot was not something Millie relished, but if she'd wanted to refuse the young witch's request, she would have. She didn't want to, though. She imagined how hard Emma's life must be, remembering stories she'd heard about young people having to care for poorly parents. It wasn't easy for anybody to be a carer for a parent, but it must have been infinitely harder to be a teenage carer when life was tempting a person with much more exciting possibilities. Millie didn't consider the request for long. Had it been one of the less trustworthy pupils asking for access to the cookery class during the school holidays, Millie would have refused, but Emma *was* responsible. She could be trusted. When Millie added in the fact that there was always somebody present at the hall, and the fact that since the awful soufflé incident in the cookery classroom all those years ago, magical spells had been cast over the hall to prevent such a terrible accident reoccurring, it was an easy decision to make. She nodded at Emma. "Of course you can," she said.

"Thank you, thank you, thank you!" said Emma. "I'll be ever so careful! I promise!"

"I know you will, Emma," said Millie. "I'll let the other teachers at the hall know that I've given you permission."

With another excited thank-you, Emma turned away and hurried towards the house. "Hurry up, Nan," she said, glancing over her shoulder. "We're going to practice magic, remember?"

"I'll be in shortly," said Victoria. She smiled at Millie. "That was very kind of you," she said. "She loves cooking, but her mother makes it hard for her here. She watches over the girl's shoulder, fretting and worrying. It will be nice for Emma to go somewhere she can be alone while doing something she enjoys."

"I'm happy to be able to help," said Millie, walking alongside Victoria as they followed the garden path.

Stopping suddenly, Victoria turned to face Millie and fixed her with a hard stare. "I've enjoyed our talk today, and you seem like a lovely young lady, Miss Thorn, but I must insist that you never come here again and upset Beth like you did today. Any ideas you may have swimming around your head about Beth being responsible for harming Trevor Giles, are foolish in the extreme, and I'd ask that you never voice them again — unless you have real reason to suspect my daughter. It's your fault that Beth is in her bed at this time of day, and I must warn you that I won't be so friendly toward you in the future if you traumatise her again."

Looking at the older woman, Millie felt a pang of guilt. She hadn't outright accused her daughter of killing Trevor Giles, but she had suggested it as a possibility. Which it was. Victoria was doing what any good mother would do — she was protecting her child. Millie nodded. "I didn't mean to make her feel so awful," she said.

Victoria gave her a thin smile. "Well, we both know where we stand now. I hope that you find the person who killed Trevor. I really do. However awful he was, he didn't deserve to be murdered." She put a hand on Millie's back and guided her towards the house. "Come on. I'll see you out."

Chapter 25

*D*riving through the lush green countryside surrounding Spellbinder Bay, Millie discovered that it was worryingly easy to forget that less than twenty-four hours ago she'd witnessed the body of a dead man sprawled on the cold floor of a police cell. Not only had Trevor been dead, but his werewolf energy had also been leaving his body in the form of a foam which bubbled from his mouth.

It hadn't been a pleasant experience, but Millie imagined that her ability to put it from her mind so quickly was a welcome side effect of her experience with the many traumatic events she'd lived through since she'd arrived in the town.

She'd witnessed the murder of Albert Salmon on her first day in the town, she remembered, and then, on that very same day, she'd been taken to Spellbinder Hall and introduced to a vampire, a ghost, and Edna Brockett. Edna had then attempted to prove to Millie that magic was real by conjuring up an evil entity in the fireplace in Henry Pinkerton's office. It had been terrifying.

Even after accepting that she was a witch, things had become no easier for Millie. She'd discovered that her mother had also been a witch and had hidden that fact from her. Then she'd almost drowned while retrieving a magical pearl from the seabed. Not forgetting that she'd discovered Sergeant Spencer was her father, too, and she'd been attacked by a man possessed by a demon while solving another murder. Then, if those incidents weren't enough, she'd topped them off by spending the last few weeks trying to eat healthily. Hummus wasn't at the top of her list of traumas she'd experienced in the past year, but neither was it at the bottom.

When she thought things through like that, it was easy to understand why seeing Trevor Giles's body hadn't traumatised her in the way it might have some people. She supposed it was a blessing.

Glancing in her rearview mirror, Millie noticed the bright flash of sunlight on metal a few hundred metres behind her. The size of the object suggested it was a motorbike, and just before Millie returned her eyes to the road ahead, she was able to make out the rider's black leather jacket and open-faced helmet. She rolled her eyes. It was probably George — out gallivanting with his mystery woman.

When she glanced in the mirror again, there was no sign of a motorbike, and she gave a frustrated sigh.

How had she allowed a man — scratch that — a vampire, to get so deep into her mind? She'd been hurt by a boyfriend in the past and had vowed never to allow it to happen again. There she was, deep in thought about a man who refused to tell her who the woman was who was sharing his home with him.

She shook her head and opened the window a fraction as she gave the Triumph some more gas, enjoying the throaty sound of the powerful engine as she rounded a smooth bend in the road. The guttural roar of the engine had the desired effect of ridding Millie's mind of any negative thoughts, and it was with a positive attitude that she drove through Spellbinder Bay town, the bustling harbour on her left, and a row of brightly painted cafes, fish and chip shops, and ice cream parlours on her right. Tourists crowded the pavements and even the edges of the road, so Millie navigated the route carefully, enjoying the smell of hot food and sea air.

The next four names on the list of people Millie wanted to speak to all lived in the same area of the town, so she continued driving west, enjoying the sea-view.

With her window still open, the sounds of the busy town combined with the throb of the car engine to produce a soundtrack which would have lifted anybody's spirits. The call of a gull mingled with the laughter of a child, and the throbbing blast of a boat's horn announced it had returned to the harbour with a fresh haul of fish, which would be served in restaurants and fish bars later that same day. The urgent jingles of slot machines and coin pushers rolled from the open door of the amusement arcade, and the cheery voice of a busker accompanied the twang of his guitar.

Only one sound stood out as being out of place on the busy seafront, and Millie wound her window down further to make sure she hadn't been mistaken when she'd heard it. No, she hadn't. There it was again, the raised voice of an angry man. "How dare you accuse me of not paying! I'm as honest as a teabag, good sir! You, on the other hand, are as insolent as an astronaut without a refrigerator!"

Beneath the striped awning of a shop selling bric-a-brac and souvenirs, Millie saw the source of the shouting and manoeuvred her car quickly into an available parking space. She hurried along the pavement, just as Cuthbert Campion launched into another tirade. "You're a man without principles! Like a dentist without a pigeon!"

The stocky man who Cuthbert was shouting at seemed to be nearing the end of his tether, and he leaned in closer to Cuthbert's face as Millie approached, pushing past the group of spectators who'd gathered to observe the spectacle. "Just pay me what you owe me, you silly fool. Otherwise, I'll be forced to call the police," the man said in a raised voice.

"Can I help?" said Millie, placing herself between

the two men. She smiled at Cuthbert's adversary. "I'm a friend of this gentleman."

"A friend?" shouted Cuthbert. "You're no friend of mine, young lady. I've never set eyes on you in my whole life!"

The other man took a step backwards, moving away from Millie and Cuthbert. He gave his head a slow shake. "Just pay me for the fridge magnet, sir," he said. "And then we can all forget this little incident ever happened. I don't want you to get into trouble, but I won't tolerate shoplifters, whatever their age."

"Shoplifter!" spat Cuthbert, his bald head matching the colour of his angry face. "I'm no shoplifter! I'm Cuthbert Campion, teacher of English literature and Chemistry at Spellbinder Hall!"

The shopkeeper lifted his glasses and stared at Cuthbert, looking at him from several angles, before giving an enthusiastic nod of his head. "My goodness," he said. "It is you. I was a pupil at Spellbinder Hall when you taught there, Sir." He turned to Millie and spoke in a whisper, even though the crowd of spectators had moved away since the shouting had ceased. "Are you...urm. Do you know about Spellbinder Hall? Are you..." He gave a quick wink. "One of us?"

"I'm a witch," said Millie, her voice low.

"I'm Ollie," said the shopkeeper, his face relieved. He looked left and right, checking for eavesdroppers. "I'm a witch, too."

Cuthbert suddenly stumbled, and Millie grabbed

him by the arm, steadying him. He blinked a few times and then looked around. "How did I get here?" he said. "I was just about to sit down for a cup of tea with my daughter." He smiled at Millie. "Oh, hello, young lady. You're the lovely young teacher I met yesterday, at the school fete."

"Hello, Cuthbert," said Millie. "You seem to have got yourself into a spot of trouble with this shopkeeper."

Ollie shook his head. "No he hasn't," he said. "If I'd recognised Mister Campion, I'd have given him the fridge magnet for free." He gave Cuthbert an appreciative smile. "You were one of the best teachers at that school, Sir."

"Thank you for the compliment," said Cuthbert. "But what do you mean — fridge magnet? What fridge magnet are you talking about?"

Looking embarrassed, Ollie pointed at the breast pocket of Cuthbert's suit jacket. "It's in there," he said. "You picked it up and put it there and then walked out of the shop. Like I said though, Mister Campion, had I recognised you, I would never have chased you outside and confronted you."

"I'm glad you did! That's what you should have done!" said Cuthbert, slipping the fridge magnet from his pocket and studying it. "You'll never succeed in business if you don't treat everybody the same! Now, how much does this magnet cost? I like it. It captures the view of Spellbinder Bay from the clifftop very well indeed."

"It would be two-pounds-fifty," said Ollie, "but honestly, Mister Campion, I want you to have it. You might not remember me very well — I've certainly changed in the last few decades, but you helped me when I was being bullied, Sir. You taught me not to listen to the names I was being called, and I took your lesson onboard. You helped me to deal well with a hard period in my life."

Taking his wallet from his trouser pocket, Cuthbert retrieved a five-pound note and thrust it towards Ollie. "Of course I remember you, Oliver. You were a good boy and a pleasure to teach, but I insist that you take my money, and I insist that you keep the change. I always pay my way, young man."

Ollie attempted to answer, but the warning scowl that Cuthbert gave him changed his mind. He smiled and closed his hand around the money. "Thank you, Mister Campion," he said.

"Thank *you*," said Cuthbert. He put a hand to his head and frowned. "I don't feel so well," he said. "I think I should be getting home."

"My car is over there," said Millie, guiding Cuthbert gently along the pavement. "I'll take you home."

When Cuthbert saw Millie's car, he let out a delighted gasp. "Oh my," he said. "She's a beauty! They don't make them like that anymore!" He raised an eyebrow and winked at Millie. "You certainly have taste," he said.

Millie laughed as she helped Cuthbert into the little two-seater. "I've always been a fan of the old classics," she explained. "Modern cars don't seem to have any character."

As Cuthbert settled into the old leather of the passenger seat, he smiled up at Millie. "Well, you'd better get *this* old classic home before he has another funny turn and forgets where he lives."

Chapter 26

The drive to Cuthbert's home was short. He lived less than half a mile from the harbour area of town, but the solitary house in which he lived, at the end of a private lane, offered seclusion from the nearby town.

Cuthbert Campion and his daughter lived in a large seafront home, the front garden offering a similar sea-view to the one visible from Millie's cottage. That was where any similarities between Millie's home and Cuthbert Campion's ended, though. For the first time since she'd arrived in Spellbinder Bay and discovered she had access to vast wealth, built over centuries by the witches who had come before her, Millie considered spending a chunk of it on a home like the Campion's as she marvelled at the impressive building.

Set on a clifftop eroded from the hill behind it, with only a short drop to the sandy beach below, the building was an architectural delight. Huge windows spanned the front of the building, allowing uninterrupted views of the sea from every room on that side of the house, and the brilliant white walls reflected the sunlight, giving the home an even grander appearance.

Imagining how pleasant it would be to sip a cocktail on one of the balconies while watching the sunset, Millie scolded herself, reminding herself just how lucky she already was. There were plenty of people who would look at her cottage through the same envious lens that she studied Cuthbert's home through, and she was sure that Cuthbert Campion or his daughter thought likewise about other houses, too. She should count her blessings, as the saying went, and she had plenty of them to count.

After parking her car alongside a rockery planted with hardy coastal shrubs, Millie walked alongside Cuthbert as he slowly made his way towards the large front door. "It's a beautiful home," she said.

"Thank you!" said Cuthbert. "I'm lucky to own it. I was given a lot of money by the Board of Governors at Spellbinder Hall. I don't quite remember why right now. I think I had some sort of accident. My daughter will explain what happened; my memory isn't what it once was. It's a nuisance to me, and I think my memory loss makes me a nuisance to my daughter."

Not wanting Cuthbert to consider his lack of memory an even greater nuisance than he already believed it to be, Millie chose not to remind him that he and his daughter had been in her classroom the day before and that his daughter had explained everything about her father's accident. "I'm sure you're not a nuisance," she said.

As if wishing to prove Millie correct, Julia Campion suddenly swung the door open and stood in the doorway, a phone in her hand and a look of relief on her face. "Dad!" she said, the breeze sweeping a strand of hair across her face. "Oh, Dad! I've been so worried about you! I've been down onto the beach in case you'd fallen off the cliff. We must fix that low part of the fence! It terrifies me!" She showed Millie and Cuthbert the phone she was holding. "I was just about to phone the police, hop in the car, and come looking for you."

"I've been for a walk, Julia," said Cuthbert. "I wanted to pick something up from town."

Julia hurried towards her father. "What did you want to pick up from town, Dad? We don't need anything. I went shopping this morning!"

Cuthbert winked at Millie and reached for his breast pocket. "A fridge magnet, my dear," he said. "I thought it would brighten the kitchen up a little."

Julia took a gentle hold of her father's arm and sighed. "I don't think we need a fridge magnet, Dad, but at least you're home safe," she said. She looked at Millie and let out a long breath. "Thank you, Miss Thorn, but why is he with you? Did he get himself into some more bother? He always seems to be getting himself into trouble with somebody."

Before Millie had time to answer, Cuthbert turned his face towards her, his eyes pleading with her to keep a secret. Millie shook her head and smiled at Julia. "No," she said. "I was passing through town when I saw your father walking in this direction. He looked a little tired, so I stopped and offered him a lift."

Julia studied Millie's face for a second or two. Seemingly satisfied with her explanation, she smiled. "Thank you," she said. "You must come in and have a cup of tea and a bite to eat."

Glancing at the beautiful house, Millie nodded. "A cup of tea would be lovely," she said.

The interior of the house was no less beautiful than the outside, but Millie was happy to discover that beyond the modern wall hangings and clean angles of staircases and pillars, the house was lived in. The smell of baking hung in the air, and the sound of music came from somewhere in the distance, the beat of the drums sharp and urgent.

As the three of them crossed the large entrance hall, Cuthbert suddenly stopped and cocked his head to the side. He narrowed his eyes. "I can hear music," he said. "That's The Rolling Stones! They're my favourite!"

"Yes, Dad," said Julia. "You put the music on yourself. That's why I didn't hear you leaving the house."

"Did I?" said Cuthbert. He gave a broad grin. "I have got good taste!"

"You like the old classics too," said Millie, with a smile.

Cuthbert jerked his head in Millie's direction. "Who is this young lady, Julia?" he said. "Did you let her in?"

Julia mouthed an apology in Millie's direction. "This is Miss Thorn, Dad," she said. "She just very kindly brought you home in her car. You met her yesterday at Spellbinder Hall, too. She's the cookery teacher, remember?"

"Oh?" said Cuthbert, his eyes lighting up. "You're a cookery teacher? I knew a cookery teacher once! Won't you come to my study with me? I've got some photographs you might like to see!"

"Miss Thorn doesn't want to see your old school photos, Dad," said Julia.

Seeing the excitement on Cuthbert's face, Millie smiled at Julia. "I'd love to see his photographs," she said.

Cuthbert began walking toward a corridor leading off the hall. "This way, then!" he said. "Let's go!"

Julia gave a contented laugh. "Thank you," she said to Millie. "He loves going through his photographs. It helps with his memory, too. You follow Dad. I'll be along soon with some tea and cake."

Cuthbert led Millie along a long corridor and down a flight of steps to a level below the building, the heavy bass of music becoming louder with each step they took. The smell of chlorine greeted Millie's nose as they reached the bottom of the stairs, and she gazed in awe at the swimming pool beyond a set of large glass doors. Large potted plants and stylish furniture surrounded the pool and through another open door beyond the pool, she could make out gym equipment.

"Come on," said Cuthbert. "Don't dawdle! My study is just along here."

Millie smiled to herself as she walked alongside the old man. With no natural light making its way into the basement, the harsh white light cast by the ceiling lights made Cuthbert appear older than he was, and Millie felt a pang of pity for him. She couldn't begin to imagine what it must be like to suffer from an illness which affected the memory — especially from one which had been caused by a magical accident and not natural causes.

When Cuthbert reached an open door set below an archway, he smiled at Millie. "Here we are," he said, speaking with enough volume to make himself heard over the powerful sound of Mick Jagger's voice. "My study!" He hurried inside, making his way towards the stereo system perched on a shelf. He pressed a button, and the music stopped. He smiled at Millie. "It's quite amazing," he said, "this system is connected to the internet, and I can listen to any music I like for as long as I like without turning a record over or changing a CD. I miss some things about the old days, but having to keep turning records over is not one of them."

"It's a lovely room," said Millie, admiring the book-laden shelves, the antique desk, and the seascapes hanging on the walls.

"It's where I feel most at peace," said Cuthbert, taking a thick leather-bound book from a shelf. "My photographs," he explained, placing the album on the low coffee table situated in front of a small sofa. Sitting down, he gestured at Millie to take a seat, too. "That's one thing I do miss about the old days," he said, opening the photograph album. "Having real memories. Memories you can pick up and touch. Not like these days when everybody has thousands of photographs stored in those little phones they carry everywhere. It's too easy to take pictures these days, so people have too many of them — I don't think they mean as much to people as they used to."

"There is something special about a photograph album," agreed Millie, studying the fading photographs on the first page of the book. She pointed to one of them and smiled. "Is that Edna Brockett?" she asked.

"It certainly is," said Cuthbert. "This is my album of school photographs. I had a habit of taking my Polaroid camera everywhere with me in those days, including to work. I remember the very day I took that picture of Edna. She'd just had her hair done, that's why she looks so proud."

"She looks very different than she does these days," said Millie.

"That's what age does to a person, young lady,"

said Cuthbert. "Wait until you see a photograph of me back then! I was quite different, I can tell you! There aren't many pictures of me in this album, as I was always behind the lens, but we'll come across one soon."

"I'd love to see one of you," said Millie as Cuthbert flipped to the next page.

After that page he flipped to the next and then the next, smiling as he pointed at people, some of who Millie knew and some who were complete strangers. It was when Cuthbert flipped to a page in the last third of the book that the atmosphere in the room changed.

Noticing that Cuthbert had gone rigid next to her, and his hand trembled as it hovered over a group photograph in the book, Millie turned to look at the old man. "Are you okay?" she asked.

Cuthbert licked his lips and nodded. "This is a photograph of all the pupils and teachers in one of the years I taught. I lined us all up in the gym and had another teacher take the photograph." His finger shook as he placed it below a man with a head of thick curly hair. His hair grew wildly in all directions and gave him the appearance of a man who didn't have the time to focus on the trivial things in life; such as haircuts. Cuthbert cleared his throat. "That's me," he said.

"Never!" said Millie, widening her eyes at the bald man sitting next to her. "I would never have guessed!"

Cuthbert nodded slowly, his mood darkening by

the moment. "Age has certainly changed me," he said. "The kids used to call me Mister Mop back then... on account of my huge mop of hair."

"Mister Mop," murmured Millie. "I've heard that somewhere." Half closing her eyes as she wracked her mind, she nodded as the answer came to her. "It was written in one of the old textbooks in my cookery class. One of the children read it out. There was more to it... I think it said something like *Miss Everest loves Mister Mop*."

Cuthbert made a strangled sound in his throat and moved his finger left on the photograph, indicating an impressively tall woman who towered over everyone else in the picture. "The kids called her Miss Everest," said Cuthbert, his voice faltering. "Because of her height. The children loved her... they used to ask her silly questions, like — how's the weather up there? Those sort of things. It was innocent fun. She was my best friend at school, on account of us both being halflings, but the kids read more into it. They teased us about being in love, although I was happily married to my lovely wife. Miss Timkins was just a friend. A very good friend. A friend I miss dearly."

A coldness suddenly brushed Millie's skin, as if she were looking at a ghost on the page before her. "Miss Timkins the cookery teacher?" she asked. "Miss Timkins who was..."

Cuthbert gave a slow nod. "Miss Timkins who found herself in the oven. She was teaching the children how to make soufflé. Her favourite dish at the

time, and one of mine, too. Cream of tartar and eggs
— who'd have thought that such different ingredients
would go together so well? I can still remember her
showing me how to make a soufflé during a lunch
break. I used to spend most lunchtimes in the cookery
classroom with Miss Timkins, eating something she'd
prepared and looking out of the window at the view
over the cliffs and sea. They were wonderful times.
People say that a man and a woman can't have a
platonic relationship, but Charlotte and I did. We
were the best of friends... until that day. Until —"

Millie put a hand on Cuthbert's wrist, steadying
his shaking hand. "Are you okay?" she asked.

His demeanour changing from friendly and affable, Cuthbert stared at Millie, his sunken eyes glinting
with anger. He slid a finger across the photograph,
stopping as the tip of his nail sat below the smiling
face of a young boy, his tie loose and his hair ruffled.
"There he is," snarled Cuthbert. "Evil thing! Like a
fox which has learned mathematics, like a goose
which dislikes the gander! Like a... like a —"

"Cuthbert?" said Millie, concerned. "Are you
alright?"

Cuthbert's voice rose in volume, and he span
angrily in his seat to face Millie, his eyes now burning
with rage. "Who are you, young lady? You look like a
farmer who has forgotten how to read, like a sailor
who has stitched his last yarn! What are you looking
at?"

Edging away from Cuthbert, Millie reminded

herself that his anger was just a symptom of his so-called metaphorettes. Telling herself that didn't make Cuthbert's sudden anger any less unnerving, though, and Millie felt a flood of relief as Julia's voice came from the doorway. "Dad! What's wrong? What's happened to set you off?"

"We were just looking at photos," said Millie. "He was fine, and then..." She sighed. "I'm sorry, maybe I shouldn't have agreed to look at photographs with him."

"Nonsense!" said Julia, setting down a tray of steaming mugs and slices of cake on Cuthbert's desk. "It does him good to remember the old days. It's nothing you've done; something always sets him off. A photo sometimes, music at other times... sometimes he can just be sitting still, and he'll zone out into an episode." She stood in front of her father with her hands on her hips. "I heard the way you spoke to Miss Thorn, Dad," she said. "I think you owe her an apology!"

Cuthbert frowned, and then looked at Millie, offering her a conspiratorial wink. "This is my daughter," he said. "She can be a real live wire sometimes. Please excuse her rude interruption. Now, where were we? You were telling me something about Trevor Giles, weren't you? What's he done now? He's a naughty young fellow!"

"No," said Millie, sitting straighter as she stared at Cuthbert Campion. "I never mentioned Trevor Giles. Why did you mention Trevor Giles?"

"Goodness me," said Cuthbert. "You two ladies do like to talk, don't you? You're like a pair of sheep without rules. Like squirrels which have forgotten a birthday."

"Dad," said Julia, rolling her eyes at Millie. "Please don't be rude."

Millie gave Julia an enquiring look. "That name," she said. "Trevor Giles... does it mean anything to you?"

Julia smiled. "It's one of many names he rants about sometimes. It doesn't mean anything to me." She studied Millie's face. "Why? Should it? You look concerned."

"Do you remember the man your father argued with at the school yesterday?" said Millie. "The man in the doorway of my classroom —"

"The same horrible man who was in the refreshment tent," said Julia. "Yes, I remember him. He was very rude indeed. He was horrible to my father."

"That man was Trevor Giles," said Millie. "And something happened to him last night. He was —"

"Did you say Trevor Giles?" roared Cuthbert. "An evil child. An awful boy!"

"You called him evil yesterday, too," said Millie, "but why do you keep calling him a boy?"

Cuthbert pressed his finger hard onto the photograph, pointing out the same boy he'd been indicating a few minutes ago. "There!" he said. "Trevor Giles! The awful boy! I'll never forgive him!"

"Forgive him for what?" asked Millie, staring at

the young boy in the picture, and recognising a little of the adult Trevor Giles in him. "What did he do?"

"He... he." Cuthbert looked at his daughter. "What did he do, Julia? I can't quite recall."

"I don't know, Dad," said Julia. She smiled at Millie. "I doubt he's done anything. Dad's probably just angry that he was rude to him yesterday."

Staring at Cuthbert, and then at Julia, Millie stood up. She gestured at Julia to follow her towards the desk, and under the pretence of helping herself to a slice of cake, spoke quietly. "Julia," she said. "Trevor Giles died last night. He was murdered."

Putting a hand to her mouth, Julia gasped. "What?" she said. "He was murdered?"

Millie nodded. "Yes," she said, recalling the bag of cakes which Julia had brought into the refreshments tent. The same bag which Trevor had stolen a cake from. A cake he had eaten. "He was poisoned," she continued. "And we believe that the poison may have been put into a cake he'd eaten at some point during the day yesterday."

Julia's face remained expressionless for a few moments, but it was easy to see that she was thinking. Her lips drew together, and her body language took on a defensive stance, her arms closing across her chest and her shoulders tense. "Are you trying to suggest something, Miss Thorn?" she asked carefully. "Because I remember that Trevor Giles ate one of the cakes which I brought into that musty tent yesterday, and I also recall my father placing his hand in the bag, but if you think that either myself or my father had anything to do with that man being poisoned, then you're very much mistaken. Neither of us had any reason to want to hurt him, and even if we did — we're just not like that. Neither of us would hurt anybody, let alone kill somebody!"

"I'm not saying that," said Millie. "I was just wondering if —"

"What *are* you two gossiping about?" asked Cuthbert, getting to his feet and ambling towards the desk. "Oh, I see, you brought cake and tea without telling me, Julia. Well, I'd very much like a slice and a cup."

"I brought it in right in front of you, Dad," said Julia. "You'd... drifted off again into one of your..."

"Funny turns?" said Cuthbert. "You can say it, my dear. Funnily enough, I was beginning to explain to Miss Thorn why the Board of Governors gave me all that money. Enough money to allow me to build this house after my wife died and live a life without financial strain. I know it was something to do with an accident, Julia. It was something to do with what causes me to have my funny turns, wasn't it?"

Still eyeing Millie with suspicion, Julia nodded. "Yes, Dad. You had an accident involving a potion you'd made to help ease headaches. It seems that some of your halfling witch magic may have leaked into the potion, and when you took it, it did something inside your brain. You'd been teaching an English lesson not long before you took that potion. You were teaching metaphors and similes, and after taking the potion, something happened which made you begin shouting out metaphors that don't make much sense."

"Oh yes!" said Cuthbert, taking a mug of tea from the tray. "You quite comically call it my metaphorettes, don't you, my dear?"

"Yes, Dad," said Julia. "And it affected your memory, too. That's why you can't remember a lot of what happened on that day, or a lot of what's happened since."

"Ah, yes," said Cuthbert. "And that's why Henry Pinkerton made sure I was financially secure... because I'd had an accident while teaching at Spellbinder Hall! It's all coming back now!"

"Yes," said Julia. "That's why they gave you the money. They were very kind to you."

Cuthbert picked up a slice of cake and took a small bite. "I'll show you some more photographs after our impromptu tea break, Miss Thorn," he said.

"No, Dad," said Julia, placing an arm on Millie's back and guiding her towards the door. "Miss Thorn must be leaving now. She has other things to be doing."

"She does? What do you have planned for the rest of the day that is more important than looking at my old photographs?" said Cuthbert, with a teasing wink.

"Miss Thorn must find out who has done something bad," said Julia. "So that innocent people don't get blamed." She looked at Millie. "Isn't that right, Miss Thorn?"

"Yes," said Millie. "That's right."

"Well, you'd best be hurrying off then, Miss Thorn," said Cuthbert. He waved a hand in his daughter's direction. "See our guest out then, Julia. She's got places to be."

Chapter 27

*A*s Millie followed the road towards Spellbinder Hall, she pondered over what had happened in the last two hours. She'd discovered that Beth Taylor had harboured a dislike for Trevor Giles, stemming all the way back to her school days. While not proof that Beth had poisoned Trevor Giles, Beth had also been in the position, while serving on the cake stall, to have tampered with the cakes which she and her daughter had sold to Norman. Beth was undoubtedly capable of being able to cast the magic spell which had been in the poison, too. Her house had been full of magical literature and pieces of interest, and she was a witch who practised moon magic.

Millie turned left almost half a mile past the harbour, taking the steep lane which led to the cliffs on which Spellbinder Hall was built. As she flicked the indicator off and glanced in her rearview mirror, she spotted the gleam of chrome. She looked in the side mirror and smiled. She'd know the shape of the rider's upper body anywhere, and the open-faced helmet was a dead giveaway, too. There was no doubt that the motorcyclist attempting to keep a respectable distance from Millie's car, was George. But why was he following her? She looked at the road in front of the car again and concentrated. She had more important things to focus on than a vampire following her on a motorbike.

She thought about what she was going to say to Fredrick when she got to the hall. She was going to explain what she'd learned at Beth's house, and then she was going to relive the strange conversation she'd had with Cuthbert Campion. Cuthbert had seemed very angry at Trevor Giles for some unknown reason, and *he'd* also been around cakes which Trevor Giles had eaten, as had his daughter.

Millie had concluded that perhaps it *was* better to wait until Henry Pinkerton returned to Spellbinder Bay before pursuing the murder case any further. After all, the first person on the list of potential suspects she'd interviewed had turned out to have motive and opportunity, and then on the way to talk to more people on the list, she'd happened upon Cuthbert Campion, who also appeared to hold a grievance against the murdered man. Perhaps it would just be better to wait until Henry could utilise the stone of integrity before speaking to any further suspects. It seemed that suspects were stacking up fast. Too fast to continue an investigation without being able to clear people's names along the way. Henry could do just that with the stone, and Millie hoped Fredrick would agree — she'd begun to realise just how difficult finding the killer would be without magical intervention.

As her car rolled out of a swerving bend to the right, Millie glanced in the mirror again. There was George. He was closer this time, and when he appeared to realise how much space he'd made up on Millie's car while hidden from her in the bend, he slammed on his brakes, causing his front wheel to push out from beneath the bike. The bike wobbled, and Millie gritted her teeth, certain she was going to witness George losing control of his machine. Luckily for him, the front wheel responded to his input on the handlebars, and the bike remained upright, travelling in a straight line once more.

Millie breathed a sigh of relief. Although George was a vampire, and vampires wouldn't be hurt by a simple fall from a speeding motorcycle, she didn't want him to crash. If he wasn't injured, his bike would have sustained damage, and she knew just how much he cherished his motorcycle.

When she lost sight of George in the next bend, Millie gave the Triumph a burst of fuel. The car surged forward, putting space between herself and her pursuer. When she'd rounded the next bend, she guided the car to the side of the road and leapt out. She heard the deep roar of George's motorbike approaching, and stepped out into the road, lifting her hand in traffic cop fashion.

When George saw her, he applied the brakes and slowed the bike, coming to a stop a foot away from where she stood. He put his feet down and wagged a finger at Millie. "You'll get yourself killed!" he shouted over the sound of the engine. "Standing in the road like that."

Millie raised both eyebrows and stepped forward, enjoying the smell of the bike's engine fumes. She reached over the small plastic screen which afforded the bike rider some protection from the wind and twisted the key in the ignition. When the engine had spluttered into silence, and George's grin had grown wide enough to risk pushing his helmet from his head, Millie gave a thin smile. "And you'll get yourself killed by braking too hard in a tight bend when you realise you've got a little too close to the car you were following."

George's grin grew even wider, and his eyes twinkled with mirth. He lifted both hands in mock surrender. "Okay. You got me. I was following you."

"May I ask why?" said Millie.

The vampire's face took on a serious expression. "It's time I told you," he said. "About her. About Emily. It's time I told you who she is. Emily agrees with me, too. I thought I'd follow you, and speak to you in person rather than over the phone."

So that was her name. Emily. The woman who had been a regular pillion passenger on George's bike while wearing mini-skirts and tight tops, was named Emily. The woman who had moved into George's home with him, and had been the focus of all his attention for the last few months, was named Emily. Millie bit her lip as she looked at George, preventing herself from saying something she might regret. She had to seem as disinterested as she could manage. "That's a nice name," she said. "Emily. I was expecting her name to be something a little more... I don't know... less innocent. I didn't expect a mini-skirt wearing floozy to have such a dainty name."

"Please don't speak about her like that," said George. "She means a lot to me. You'll understand why, soon enough."

"Oh, I guessed she means a lot to you, George," said Millie. "I mean, you did let her move in with you, and you did neglect our relationship to concentrate on her. I think the fact that she means a lot to you goes without saying."

"It's not what you think," said George, fiddling with his helmet strap. "I've promised you that much."

"And I said I believed you," said Millie, still a little ashamed that she'd read his mind to verify he'd been telling the truth. "It's not who she is that matters so much, George. It's how you totally dropped me to concentrate on her that matters."

Leaning over the motorbike's handlebars, George smiled up at Millie, his brown eyes swimming with sincerity. "I had to do what I did," he said. "How about I take you out somewhere nice for dinner so I can tell you the full story about Emily? How about tonight?"

Frustration and inquisitiveness vied for control over Millie's emotions. On one hand — one huge hand, she was frustrated with the vampire. Angry, even. On the other hand, she was very curious about the woman who had been at the centre of George's life for so long. She gave a neutral smile. "Maybe," she said. "But not tonight. I'm in the middle of something very important."

"Something important?" asked George. He leaned further over the handlebars and gave Millie his nicest smile — the one which lifted his lips higher on the right than it did on the left. "Such as?"

Seeing the glint of intrigue in George's eyes, Millie gave a casual shrug of her shoulders. "It's nothing to concern you," she said. "In fact, it's a secret. I can't tell you, I'm afraid."

"Oh, it is, is it?" said George, his voice playful. "I see."

Millie nodded, reaching for her pocket as her phone vibrated against her thigh. "It is, George," she said, giving him a wink. She glanced at her phone. The number displayed on the screen was not familiar, but she answered it anyway. "Hello?" she said.

"This is Helen Giles," came the answer. "I decided to use the phone number on the card you left me, but only after a few minutes of consideration. I might be too late."

"Too late for what?" asked Millie, alarm building in her chest.

"Too late to warn you," said Helen. "About Rufus... the werewolf who brought Norman home when you were here this morning."

"What about him, Helen?" said Millie, her mouth drying.

"I told you that werewolves have good hearing," said Helen, speaking quickly. "Rufus overheard what you were saying to Sergeant Spencer's daughter while you stood watching him from next to your car, outside my house. I heard too, and it's a good job I got Norman indoors, or he might have heard. Luckily he didn't, and I got to break the news about his stepfather's death to him in a more acceptable manner. Not that it mattered. I don't think he's very upset."

"What about Rufus?" asked Millie. "What's happened, Helen?"

"I'm not sure anything has happened yet," said Helen. "You might still have time. After you'd driven off this morning, Rufus was livid. He kept his temper under control because Norman and his own son and wife were there, but he was angry. Very angry. He'd heard you speaking about Trevor's death, and he heard you talking about clearing Sergeant Spencer's name. I told him everything that you and Miss Spencer had told me, and he was furious. I talked him down, though. I made him promise that he wouldn't do anything rash, and I trusted his word."

"So, what's happened?" said Millie, panic gripping her. "Tell me, Helen."

"I got a phone call from one of my friends about five minutes ago," said Helen. "It seems that Rufus has built himself some sort of posse, and my friend's husband is part of it. A pack of enraged werewolves is headed for the police station. They're after Sergeant Spencer, Miss Thorn, and not to ask him questions. They think he killed Trevor. The sergeant is in grave danger."

Chapter 28

"I need your help," said Millie, pocketing her phone and staring at George. "We need to move fast. Sergeant Spencer is in danger!"

"What sort of danger?" asked George, twisting the key in the bike's ignition.

"It's a long story," said Millie, her stomach flipping as she realised it wasn't only her father who was in danger. Helen Giles had told her that the werewolves were heading for the police station. They'd soon realise that the building was locked up and nobody was there. Then they'd go straight to Sergeant Spencer's home. His address was no secret — Spellbinder Bay was a small town.

When the wolves arrived at Sergeant Spencer's home, they'd find someone else there with him. She turned her back on George and hurried for her car. "Judith is in danger, too," she said. "We've got to get to their house. Quickly."

"Wait!" yelled George. "We'll get there faster if you jump on the back of my bike."

He was right. Without thinking, Millie turned on the spot and hurried to the rear of George's bike. She ripped open one of the panniers and removed the spare helmet which she knew George stored in there. Ignoring the long blonde hairs that had snagged in the soft inner lining of the helmet, and the smell of a strange perfume, she pulled the helmet on and swung a leg over the seat as George pressed the start button, and the engine burst into life. She tapped George on the shoulder and wrapped her arms around his waist. "Go!"

George wasted no time. With a heavy roar from the engine and a rattle of gravel on expensive chrome, the bike lurched forward. "What's Sergeant Spencer in danger from?" he yelled, turning his head slightly so Millie could hear him.

"Werewolves!" shouted Millie. "A few of them. They think Sergeant Spencer killed one of their own."

Skilfully guiding the bike around a bend as if it was on a rail, George's body tensed, and the bike gathered speed. "Hold on!" he warned.

Gripping the leather of George's jacket tighter in her hands, Millie pressed herself harder against the vampire's back and forced her feet against the pegs. Wind noise gathered in her ears and hedges blurred past on both sides as the engine screamed and the front wheel of the bike lifted for a moment as the machine accelerated.

Leaning with George as he dropped the bike into a corner, the rider's foot-pegs screeching as they dragged along the road surface, Millie forced herself to be calm. She couldn't waste much-needed adrenaline on being worried about a motorbike crash — she required it in bucket loads to help her through the potential fight which lay ahead.

As the narrow lanes widened into urban streets, George slowed the bike, flicking it left and right as he dodged cars and navigated tight turns. Within five minutes of Millie sliding a leg over the seat of the bike, George took a final right turn into the road in which Sergeant Spencer and Judith lived together.

Millie's heart dropped as she spotted a red pickup truck outside the cheerily painted house at the far end of the street. "They're already here!" she warned. "Hurry, George!"

Waving a man out of the way as he walked into the street, George gave the bike a final burst of fuel and covered the short distance in seconds.

Before the bike had even come to a halt, Millie leapt off, managing to keep her balance as her feet slammed into hard tarmac. As she ripped the helmet from her head, fear grabbed her in a steel grip. The sounds coming from her father's house could have been coming from a horror movie soundtrack being played through a powerful sound system, but the truth was far more terrifying.

The savage, guttural roars were the sounds made by real-life werewolves, and the screams and shouts for help were being made by the two people the werewolves were attacking.

Drawn by the awful sounds, a crowd of people had gathered outside the house, and more residents stepped out of their homes as the sounds grew in intensity. Some of them held phones to their ears, and others appeared shaken and scared, their faces white as they stared in horror at the house from which the awful sounds emanated.

As George hurriedly placed the bike on its stand and tossed his helmet aside, some of the people turned their attention away from the disturbance unfolding in Sergeant Spencer's house and onto the new arrivals. One of the onlookers, a young woman with short blue hair, stared at George for a second or two and then let out an ear piercing scream. She raised an arm and pointed, screaming again, and then turned her back and began running along the pavement. "He changed into something!" she yelled as she ran. "His eyes turned black, and he grew fangs! I saw it!"

As more people turned to look at George, he looked down at Millie, his eyes coal black and his long fangs menacing. "Don't worry about them," he said. "The concealment spell will sort it out later."

"Oh, I don't care who sees what!" said Millie, running towards the garden gate which hung limply from its smashed hinges. "I only care about what's going on inside that house."

"I'm going in first," said George, leaping into action. Using the strength and agility his vampire form afforded him, he bounded along the pathway, easily overtaking Millie, and disappeared through the splintered front door. A loud crashing sound came from Millie's right, and she instinctively ducked as one of the bay windows situated at the front of the house was obliterated by what she recognised as a surge of magical energy. That was a good sign. At least Judith was using her magic to fight back. At least Judith was alive.

Hearing onlookers in the street scream as another flash of magical energy flew from the smashed window and soared skywards, Millie quickened her pace as another animalistic roar vibrated in the air.

Reaching the door, she heard a shout from George, and to her relief, another from Sergeant Spencer. The knowledge that her father was still alive, yet required her help, pushed her forward, her magic growing hotter and angrier behind her breast bone.

Entering the house, Millie held out a hand before her, charging it with magical energy which coursed through her arm. She moved quickly through the hall-way, passing pictures that lay smashed on the floor, and noticing with horror the deep gouges in the walls. Only the sharp claws of a werewolf could have done such damage, and Millie prayed that the same claws had not yet made contact with either Judith or her father.

The sight which greeted her when she burst into the open plan living and dining area, confused her for a moment. A wall of fur formed a semi-circle around a corner, and claws swung viciously through the air, accompanied by guttural growls and savage roars of rage.

Understanding that the wall of fur was created by the backs of four muscular wolves, and that George, Sergeant Spencer, and Judith were on the other side, fighting to keep the monsters at bay, Millie gritted her teeth and concentrated on her magic.

Almost tripping on an overturned coffee table, she moved closer to the wolves. The muscles in her forearms trembling, she gave an angry shout and released a spell from her fingertips.

Responding to her shout, two of the wolves span to face her, their teeth slick with saliva and their eyes an angry yellow. Their heads brushing the ceiling, they both took a step towards Millie just as her spell thudded into the chest of the largest of them. Spittle flying from its mouth, it gave a roar which reverberated in the small room and brought its clawed paws to its throat as the spell Millie had cast took form.

Thick bands of magical energy twisted around the creature's throat and its cries became panicked as the magic tightened, threatening to choke the beast to death. As the wolf dropped to its knees, it suddenly transformed, and wriggling on the floor, begging for help, was a tubby naked man, his eyes wide with fear as he struggled to breathe.

While Millie had been concentrating her magic on one wolf, the other wolf which had turned to face her had almost reached her, and swiped a massive paw through the air, the razor-sharp claws barely missing Millie's face.

Stepping backwards, she lifted one arm in instinctive defence while releasing a spell from the other hand. The spell flew from her fingers, smashed into the wolf's torso, and spread quickly across its muscular body, daubing the creature in a purple glow. The wolf stopped moving, frozen in magical stasis, and fell with a thud to the floor where it remained paralysed by magic.

As Millie turned her attention to the last two wolves, she shrieked with horror. It seemed that the wolves had gained the upper hand. Judith lay on her back, unmoving, and with blood flowing from a deep gash on her head. George wrestled with one of the wolves, the two creatures an equal match for one other, and both of them snarling and roaring as vampiric fangs met fur, and wolf claws shredded hard flesh. Not too worried about George, knowing he would heal quickly, Millie concentrated on the last wolf, which was bent double as it opened its jaws wide and prepared to deliver a bite to Sergeant Spencer. A bite which would surely kill him.

Bleeding profusely from the head and neck, Sergeant Spencer lay on his back, using both hands in an attempt to fight off his attacker. Even as the wolf's teeth neared the policeman's throat, his eyes swimming with terror, Sergeant Spencer was only focused on one thing. One person. "Judith!" he shouted, delivering an ineffectual punch to the wolf's snout. "What have they done to you?"

Knowing she had only moments to act before the wolf delivered a killing bite, Millie focused. She ignored the rancid stench of werewolf breath and the blood which had splattered the walls and continued to flow from both Judith and her father, and she ignored the vicious fight which George was locked in. Instead, she focused only on the build-up of angry magic which throbbed in her chest, begging to be released. Anger controlling her, Millie clamped her teeth together in a grimace of rage and thrust her hand towards the beast attacking her father, releasing her magic in a burst of magic so powerful it rocked her backwards on her feet.

The flash of bright orange which accompanied the burst of energy lit the room in a brilliant light, and the wolf her magic was aimed at paused momentarily before the magic hit it with overwhelming force.

Never sure of what form any of her spells would take, Millie knew this one was different. This spell wasn't going to form tendrils which held her enemy in bonds of magic, neither was it going to paralyse her opponent. The spell she'd just cast was meant to hurt. It had been delivered with a rage Millie had never before experienced, and she didn't care if the wolf lived or died. She only cared about the man sprawled on the floor. *Her father*.

Moving at speed, the spell slammed into the muscular flank of the wolf, causing it to emit a howl so loud that the air in the room throbbed. Standing suddenly upright, the wolf howled again as smoke rose from its thigh, and hot fingers of flame licked at its fur.

The wolf trembled in pain and screeched as fire spread across its body, the stench of burning hair filling the room. Moving away from Sergeant Spencer, the creature lowered itself to its knees, and in an instant had transformed into a human. With flames still hot on his flesh, the man, who Millie recognised as Rufus, screamed in agony. "Stop it!" he begged.

"Call your friend off first!" yelled Millie, pointing at the wolf still locked in vicious combat with George. Contemplating the use of another spell, but not wanting to hit George accidentally, she shouted again. "Call it off, or I won't stop the burning!"

"Jason, stop!" yelled Rufus, slapping at the flames which enveloped his arms. "It's over! Stop!"

As George delivered a hammer-blow punch to the big wolf's chest, the creature took a step away from the vampire and quickly transformed into a tall, thin man. He put his hands up in surrender as George approached him with his fangs bared in an angry snarl. "Stop!" he said. "You know it's against the rules. You can't attack me while I'm in human form and you're in vampire form!"

With a rumbling growl, originating deep in his throat, George put his face inches from the man's. "Rules?" he said. "You seem to have thrown all the rules out of the window today. You've attacked a witch and a human, and you've attracted attention from the non-paranormal population. You have no right to talk about rules!"

After casting a quick spell in Rufus's direction, which immediately quenched the flames which had spread further across his body, Millie got to her knees beside Judith. With her fingers on the unconscious witch's throat, she smiled with relief at Sergeant Spencer as he scrambled towards his daughter, blood still dripping from his neck and head. "She's alive," she said. "But we need to get her to the moon-pool. It will help her." She'd witnessed the moon-pool below Spellbinder Hall heal an unconscious mermaid in the past, but Millie was aware that the pool would be of no help to Sergeant Spencer. The pool only helped paranormal folk, not humans. She looked at him with concern. "But you need a hospital. You're badly cut. Too badly cut for a healing potion to fix."

Placing his hand on Judith's arm, Sergeant Spencer shook his head. "No," he said. "I want to make sure Judith is okay first. I'll be fine." He looked towards Rufus, who moaned in pain as he inspected burnt patches on his skin. "You'll pay for this," he said.

"Like Trevor paid for hitting your daughter last week?" spat Rufus. "Are you going to poison me, too,

Sergeant Spencer? What about my friends? Are you going to poison all four of us? If they're still alive, that is."

Millie turned her attention to the other two wolves. Both were still and silent. The one in wolf form remained paralysed by magic, and Millie cast a simple spell which released him. As he transformed into a man, his claws sliding into his hands and feet, and his coarse body hair retreating into his skin, Millie released the other man, too. He coughed and spluttered as the magical tendril of energy slid from around his throat and evaporated in a spiral of black smoke. He stared at Millie with wide eyes, fear scrawled on his face.

Standing up, Millie took her phone from her pocket. "I'll phone Fredrick," she said. "We need to get Judith to the moon-pool as quickly as possible."

"And we need to get these wolves to the dungeons," said George, in his human form once again. "I'm sure Henry will have something to say to them when he gets back."

"And I'll have something to say to him," said Rufus, nursing a burn on his hand. "I'll be telling him that it was Sergeant Spencer who killed Trevor Giles." He looked at Millie. "Helen Giles told me everything you said to her. She told me that Sergeant Spencer gave Trevor the meal that killed him, and she told me that Trevor had hit his daughter last weekend. From where I'm standing, it looks like an open and shut case, and I'm sure that Henry Pinkerton will agree.

We wolves simply doled out the punishment that was coming the sergeant's way. Unluckily for us, you and your pet vampire stopped us before we could extract the full price, although... I have to say, young Judith doesn't look too good. I'm not sure that the moon-pool will be able to save her." He gave Sergeant Spencer a toothy smile. "If she doesn't make it, we'll call it quits. An eye for an eye and all that."

Ignoring the blood that still dripped from his wounds, Sergeant Spencer launched himself from his kneeling position next to Judith. He crossed the room quickly, but not fast enough to outpace George who grabbed him from behind in a bear hug. "No!" he said. "It's not worth it, Sergeant." He gave Rufus a withering stare. "He's not worth it."

"You'd better hope Judith survives, Rufus," warned Sergeant Spencer, shrugging George's arms from him. "I promise you that."

George looked at Millie. "Phone Fredrick quickly," he urged. "We need transport to Spellbinder Bay, and then we need to work out what to do with all those people outside who witnessed what went on here today. I think it's too big of a problem for a simple concealment spell to deal with. If something isn't done soon, news will get out, and the world's press will be on our doorstep. And we don't want that. And then maybe somebody could tell me what the hell has been going on around here?"

Chapter 29

*A*s Fredrick turned the heavy key in the last of the dungeon doors, ignoring the shouts of protest from the werewolf on the other side, he shook his head. "I can't ever remember a time when four of the dungeons were used simultaneously," he said, sliding the key into his pocket and turning to face Millie and George, his face bathed in the glow from a flaming wall torch. "And it just *had* to happen when Henry left me in charge."

"I can't believe *any* of this has happened," said George. "We've been in this town since the fifties, Fredrick, and I don't remember anything happening that's even remotely as violent as what occurred today."

Millie sighed. "It will be over soon," she said. "When Henry gets back he'll find the killer."

George looked at the floor, and then at Millie.

"I've known Sergeant Spencer since he arrived in Spellbinder Bay, and I respect him… but."

"But what?" said Millie, the small hairs on the nape of her neck bristling.

George frowned. "Just from hearing what you two and Timothy have told me, and piecing things together for myself… don't you think that there's an outside chance that Sergeant Spencer, or Judith, may have had something to do with Trevor's death? I mean, Trevor did die in that cell a few moments after he'd eaten that muffin which Sergeant Spencer gave him, and Timothy is adamant that the sergeant's hands smelled of the same poison found in the cake. You told me that Edna discovered moon-magic in the poison, too, and —"

"Judith practices moon magic," finished Millie. She scowled at George, wishing she could ram a fist into that hard jawbone of his. "Don't you dare suggest anything like that again, George. Sergeant Spencer is a good man! He's one of the best men in the town, and I won't hear you talk about him like that! He's my—" She bit off her sentence, and gave George a hard stare. "He's my friend, alright? And so is Judith. I'm sure there's a perfectly reasonable explanation for everything that has happened since yesterday, but I think we should wait until Henry returns before investigating any further."

"I agree, Miss Thorn," said Fredrick. "Things have taken a turn for the unexpected. I think it's best for everyone if we press the pause button until Henry returns." He turned his back and began walking along the narrow tunnel, his long shadow trailing behind him. "Let's go and check on Miss Spencer. She's been in the moon-pool for an hour. She'll have started to heal by now. And then we should focus our attention on increasing the power of the concealment spell. Too many non-paranormal people witnessed too much of our business today. That needs fixing. Quickly. I'll get one of the witches on it right away."

The tunnels which led to the moon-pool cavern became steeper, narrower, and lower as they burrowed deeper into the cliff, and it was with relief that Millie stepped out of the dim torchlight of the tunnels and into the soothing green glow of the cave.

At the very base of the cliff, the floor of the cavern was soft sand and crushed seashells, and a gentle salty breeze blew along the narrow passage that led onto the golden beach just a few metres away.

The concealment spell protected the entrance to the passageway on the beach, emitting magic which persuaded non-paranormal people who ventured too near the fissure in the cliff face to turn around. Millie wondered what a non-paranormal person would make of the cavern if they inadvertently found their way inside it. They'd probably be shocked and mesmerised, in the same way she'd been when she'd first entered the magical place.

Although she was no longer shocked by it, it was hard not to be mesmerised by the moon-pool. The pool, surrounded by a wall of rocks and stone, was made up from the same green liquid which filled the cauldron in the cavern beneath Millie's cottage. Not as thin as water, or as thick as oil, the liquid was somewhere in-between the two, and the glow it gave off shimmered in a wide range of greens, its light reflected off the cavern walls as it illuminated beautiful stalactites and stalagmites, giving the cave a calming magical quality.

Millie had learned that the cauldron in her cavern was connected to the moon-pool via ley-lines which crisscrossed Spellbinder Bay, the most prominent intersection of the lines being directly beneath Spellbinder Hall, where the pool was situated.

The cauldron beneath Millie's cottage worked not only as a vessel to produce potions and spells in, but also as a means of gathering some of the magical energy which flowed through Millie's veins — the same magical energy which had coursed through the veins of all the witches with whom she'd shared a bloodline — the only bloodline of witches permitted to reside in Windy-dune cottage — the only witches who the secret cavern beneath the cottage would reveal itself to.

The magic which the cauldron collected from Millie would be sent along invisible lines of energy, to the moon-pool itself, and then released into the cliff below Spellbinder Hall where it would work its way upwards until it reached the hall and was put to work.

Whereas the bulk of the magic collected by the moon-pool was captured from moonlight which fell on the cliff face, and used to power such necessities as the concealment spell, Millie's magic was used for a different purpose.

It had taken Millie a while to accept that her presence in Windy-dune Cottage was the reason that the gate to Chaos— a portal which led from the world Millie inhabited to a world of evil and demons, remained locked. Although some evil managed to cross between worlds on rare occasions, it was Millie's innate magic which prevented armies of demons and monsters from entering the world she lived in and cherished.

It was an unnerving responsibility, but Millie had become used to it, and barely thought about it anymore.

Approaching the edge of the moon-pool, Millie put a hand on Sergeant Spencer's shoulder. "How is she," she asked.

"She's getting better," said the policeman, the wounds on his head and neck covered by bandages, and judging by the scent of antiseptic and herbs which rose from him, a healing potion, too. "Her wounds have closed, but Edna says that Judith needs to recharge her magic. She tried so hard to repel those werewolves, but there were too many of them. Her magic wasn't strong enough."

"She'll be right as rain soon enough," commented Edna Brockett, standing at the opposite edge of the pool, alongside Fredrick and George, her face dancing with green light. "She's a strong young witch."

"I agree," said Fredrick. "During my time here in Spellbinder Bay, I've seen the moon-pool perform miracles. Young Miss Spencer will be perfectly healthy again very soon."

Millie got to her knees beside Sergeant Spencer and gazed at Judith. Floating in the pool, her hair a fan of gold which swayed with the movement of the liquid, she looked at peace. Mysterious shadows flitted below the surface, their form occasionally becoming tantalisingly recognisable, and their movements creating currents in the liquid which made Judith rise and drop gently as the magic healed her.

Millie turned to look at her father, concerned that even in the glow of the pool, his face was a pasty white. "How are *you?*" she asked. "You took some nasty injuries."

Sergeant Spencer placed a hand on Millie's shoulder, making her long to embrace him in a hug and tell him that she loved him. He smiled at her and removed his hand. "Without you and George arriving when you did," he said, "I think Judith and I would both be dead. You're a powerful witch, Millie. That much is obvious by the way you handled those wolves. I'll forever owe you my life."

Millie swallowed a sob which rose unexpectedly in her throat. He owed her his life? No, he didn't! He'd gifted her the life she was living! It was because of him that she'd been born. His blood flowed through her body along with that of her mother. He owed her nothing. She reached for the big man's hand, the warmth of his skin a welcome sensation. "I'd do anything for you," she said. "For you and Judith. You don't owe me your life. I'm just relieved that you're both alive."

Squeezing Millie's hand, Sergeant Spencer closed his eyes for a moment and gave a soft sigh. "Me too," he said, lifting his free hand to his forehead and massaging his temple.

Noticing more colour leaving his face, Millie looked at the sergeant with concern. "What is it?" she asked. "You don't look well."

Looking as if he were about to smile, but gritting his teeth instead, Sergeant Spencer's face contorted as if he was in pain. "It's just a headache," he murmured. "I'll be okay soon."

The click of heels on stone filled the cavern, and Millie looked away from the policeman as Timothy appeared in the darkness of the tunnel mouth leading from the hall. He looked around the cave and smiled. "Our problem with the witnesses will be fixed very shortly," he announced. "Mrs Herbert has managed to adjust the power of the concealment spell. The memories of any paranormal incidents will be completely wiped from the minds of any non-para-normal person who witnessed them. Mrs Herbert has informed me that the spell may inflict headaches on those affected by it, but the intensity of the memories that were created by what occurred today at Sergeant Spencer's home required aggressive methods to wipe them."

"I'll personally thank Mrs Herbert myself," said Fredrick. "She's a gifted witch. I've often said that her insistence on teaching mathematics wastes her talents."

"I did offer my assistance," said Edna, crossing her arms. "I could have done everything that Mrs Herbert did, Fredrick. I could quite easily have adjusted the power of the concealment spell myself. Probably a little quicker than Mrs Herbert managed."

"Your vast knowledge of magic was required down here in the moon-pool cavern," said Fredrick, diplomatically. "You had the important task of ensuring Miss Spencer began her healing process." He gave Edna a knowing smile. "You had the most difficult of the two tasks. I thought I'd made the correct decision in which job I allocated which person."

Uncrossing her arms, Edna shifted her weight from foot to foot and nodded. "Yes, yes," she said. "You did, Fredrick. I'm not sure that Mrs Herbert would have coped with the urgency of the situation involving Miss Spencer's health emergency. You did the right thing by giving me the most difficult task."

"Good," said Fredrick. He let out a long breath. "It seems that between us we've managed to prevent some dire situations from becoming irreparable."

Suddenly, Sergeant Spencer gave a strangled cry, and Millie turned to face him, letting out a gasp of shock as the big man's face crumpled in pain and he slid to the floor, holding his head in both hands and moaning. "Help," he mumbled. "There's something wrong with my head."

Quickly leaning over the stricken man, Millie placed a hand on his chest and looked into his eyes, worried that they had become so bloodshot. "What is it?' she asked. "What's wrong?"

"I don't know," moaned Sergeant Spencer. "I've never felt pain like it."

"I think I might know what's wrong," said Edna, rushing around the pool and kneeling beside the policeman. "And it's not good!"

"What is it?" demanded Millie, as Sergeant Spencer moaned again, his eyes rolling in his head. "What's wrong with him?"

"It's the concealment spell," said Edna. "It's been changed, and without Henry here to ensure the magic doesn't affect Sergeant Spencer, all his memories are being wiped. He's in so much pain because the magic has thirty years of memories to erase. It's not the same as erasing a few memories from the people who witnessed what happened today. The concealment spell works on those people daily — it's always in the background, making sure they're unaware of the paranormal world around them.

"Sergeant Spencer is different, though. His mind is brimming with long-held memories. Memories which form his identity." She looked at Millie, horror on her face. "I'm afraid that the spell is going to erase everything that Sergeant Spencer knows about the paranormal world, and when I say everything, I mean everything. He won't even remember Judith is his daughter if we don't do something. Judith is a witch. She's a paranormal person — the spell will remove every trace of her from his mind. Sergeant Spencer will not be the man any of us know when the spell has finished with him. We'll all be strangers to him, and the spell will never allow him to form new memories of any paranormal person. He'll be lost to us all." She sniffed as she wiped a tear from below her eye. "His poor daughter!"

"What can we do to stop it?" demanded Millie, a sickness rising in her throat. "What can we do, Edna?"

"Nothing," said Edna. "Only Henry Pinkerton can stop it. He's not only the human face of the magic within Spellbinder Hall, but he's also the conscience. He makes the decisions that magic simply can't make. Without Henry guiding the concealment spell, Sergeant Spencer would never have been allowed to get close to Judith and all the paranormal people he calls friends. Henry guided the magic, but now the magic has changed. Mrs Herbert has altered it, and without Henry here to steer the spell, the magic will treat all non-paranormal people in the same way. It will make no exceptions for Sergeant Spencer."

"How long does he have?" asked Fredrick.

"A day at the most," said Edna. "If the spell isn't controlled before then, Sergeant Spencer will be lost to us. It's possible that Henry would be capable of reversing the magic at any point before that time, and be able to return the sergeant's memories to him, but if the spell is allowed to finish its job, then his memories are lost forever."

"But Henry isn't due back for another two days!" said Millie.

"And there's no way of reaching him," said Fredrick. "He's between dimensions, in a place we can't access. The headmaster is only with him because Henry has the ability to take one other person with him as he travels. Nobody else may travel his routes, and there is no possibility of getting a message to him." He shook his head slowly. "I don't know what to suggest."

"Can Mrs Herbert undo what she did?" asked Millie, desperation in her voice. "Can she return the spell to the way it was before she adjusted it?"

"No," said Edna, a hand on Sergeant Spencer's forehead. "When she adjusted it, the spell was reset. In terms that may make more sense to you, Miss Thorn, it's as if a computer has been wiped of a program, and Henry Pinkerton is the only person who can reinstall it."

"So we have to reach Henry," said Millie. "There must be some way of getting a message to him!"

Edna dropped her eyes and sighed. "No, Miss Thorn," she said, softly. "I'm afraid there's not. I'm afraid we cannot do anything."

Chapter 30

*C*omprehending what Edna Brockett had said, Millie kneeled motionless on the sand next to Sergeant Spencer, a tear warming her cheek. The man whose memories were being erased, and who was moaning in discomfort on the floor of a magical cavern, his deep breathing suggesting he was not fully conscious, was her father. She repeated those words to herself as if it were only now that they made any real sense to her. As if she'd only just understood that the words were true. *Sergeant David Spencer was her father*, and within a day he would not even remember who Judith was, let alone her — the daughter he'd never known he was a father to.

Regret crowded her mind, and she let out a sob. She'd had months in which she could have told him he was her father. Months in which she could have forged some sort of relationship with him. Now it was too late. Her father would soon be like her mother was to her — lost.

Whereas her mother was lost to her in a place she'd promised Millie she'd return from again, yet never had, her father would be lost to her while being right there in plain sight. Able to speak to her, but never knowing who she was. Another horrifying thought struck her, and she looked at Edna. "What will happen to a person who has thirty years of memories taken from them?" she asked.

Edna was silent for a moment, and then she gave a sigh. "I'm not sure," she admitted. "But I can't imagine anything good can come from it. I don't want to imagine what such a thing could do to a human mind."

Another tear running the length of her cheek, Millie took Sergeant Spencer's hand in hers. "It will be alright," she said. "Everything will be alright."

His hand tightening on her fingers, Sergeant Spencer gave a groan and opened his eyes slowly. He gazed up at Millie. "I'm not sure that it will," he said.

"You can hear us," said Millie, gripping his hand tighter.

"Yes," said Sergeant Spencer, his face showing the pain he was experiencing. "I can hear you. I heard everything that's been said."

"We need to move the sergeant immediately," said Edna, getting to her feet and beckoning Timothy and George to her side. "Take him to the school infirmary," she commanded. "There are things that can be done to ease his pain."

"No," moaned Sergeant Spencer. "I have to stay here. With Judith."

"Sergeant Spencer," said Edna. "If you've heard everything that's been said, then you'll understand that you don't have much time until you won't remember anything about the past three decades. The only person who can help you is Henry Pinkerton. By moving you to the infirmary, I may be able to prolong the time it takes for the spell to work on you. I might be able to save just enough of your memories so that Henry may return you to normal."

Millie leapt to her feet. "Come on then," she said. "Let's go. Timothy, George, carry him carefully."

"No," said Sergeant Spencer. "Stay here, Millie. Please. Stay with Judith until she's taken from the pool. I have to know that she'll wake up with somebody she cares for next to her. She thinks the world of you, Millie."

"But I want to make sure you're going to be okay," said Millie.

Sergeant Spencer closed his eyes and gave a groan of pain. He rubbed his head and spoke slowly. "Please stay with her, Millie. And when she wakes up, please support her when she finds out what's happening to me. She's going to need you. I'm her father. I'm the only family she has. She's not going to cope very well. If I'm going to forget who she is, I have to know that she's going to be okay. Promise me, please."

"Okay," said Millie. "I'll wait here with Judith until she's ready to leave the pool. And I promise I'll be here for her. Always."

"Thank you," said Sergeant Spencer as George and Timothy lifted him to his feet, and propped him up between them.

As the vampire and werewolf helped Sergeant Spencer from the cavern, Millie put a hand on Judith's face. "How much longer does she need in here?" she enquired.

"Not much longer," said Edna. "Half an hour at the most."

"And when she wakes up, Miss Thorn," said Fredrick. "You'll have the unenviable task of explaining what's happening to her father. It's going to be very hard for Miss Spencer when Sergeant Spencer leaves Spellbinder Bay. She'll require support for a long time to come."

"When he leaves Spellbinder Bay?" said Millie. "Why would he leave Spellbinder Bay? His home is here! Everything he knows is here!"

"Everything he *knew* is here," said Fredrick. "The unfortunate man will not remember a single thing about this town when his memories have been erased. His whole existence here has been as part of the paranormal community. He's been a good friend to us and was accepted into our midst, but that fact will work against him. The concealment spell will undoubtedly discover paranormal elements to every single one of the memories he made since moving to our town.

When his memories have gone, Sergeant Spencer will have to go, too, I'm afraid."

"That sounds horrible," said Millie. "You sound horrible — speaking about him like that."

"I didn't intend to sound horrible," said Fredrick. "When I said the sergeant must go, I said it only for his sake, not ours. This place will no longer feel like a home to him, it will be a place he doesn't recognise. He won't know how he got here, and that will terrify him. It would be better for the poor man if he were taken back to the place he lived before he became embroiled in the paranormal world. I'm certain that our community will see to it that he'll be financially sound and have a home. We'll ensure he receives all the medical support he requires, too. This whole affair may have lasting traumatic implications for him. He will, after all, be losing thirty years of his life."

Suddenly, like a train bearing down on her, everything that was happening became too real. She'd never have a relationship with her father, her mother seemed unable to cross once again into Millie's world, and both Sergeant Spencer's and Judith's lives would be ruined. Hers too, of course.

Closing her eyes as dizziness overcame her, Millie took deep breaths. As if the cavern was closing in on her and the oxygen was being sucked from the air, she stumbled backwards, her throat tightening and a sickness rising within her. Her vision blurred as she stepped away from the pool, and her heart thumped hard in her chest.

Then came peace, and Millie welcomed the soft embrace of the sand as her legs went from beneath her and she fell to the ground.

Sounding like voices from a dream, Millie tried to focus on the concerned words of Edna and Fredrick, but then they were gone, too, lost to the blackness which she willingly gave herself to.

SHE AWOKE TO WETNESS ON HER FOREHEAD AND opened her eyes to see Edna standing over her. The older witch used the flannel in her hand to wipe Millie's head once more and gave her a reassuring smile. "You're okay," she said. "You're in the infirmary. Everything seemed to have got on top of you, you fainted, but you'll be fine after a nice cup of tea."

"Judith?" said Millie.

"She's in another room in the infirmary. She's fine now. She's having a sleep," said Edna.

"Does she know?" asked Millie. "About her father?"

Edna shook her head. "No," she said. "We thought you should tell her before she sees him. She trusts you far more than she does any of us."

"How long have I been here?" asked Millie, her mouth dry.

"Not long," said Edna. "Less than an hour. It wasn't the faint that kept you here, you recovered from that quite quickly, but you were exhausted.

You've been asleep. You needed it, so I didn't wake you up."

Gazing around the room, Millie's eyes fell on the rows of potion pots which lined the shelves on the walls, and the trolley in the corner laden with a heaped plate of sandwiches and a large teapot paired with a smaller coffee pot.

Following Millie's gaze, Edna smiled. "Hungry?" she asked.

Millie nodded. She was hungry. Famished, in fact, and she needed her strength for what she was planning on doing next.

Selecting a few sandwiches, Edna prepared a plate for Millie and poured her a cup of tea, adding three heaped teaspoons of sugar.

Not wishing to offend Edna by explaining that she preferred coffee and drank it black with no sugar, Millie accepted the hot drink and took a long sip, pleasantly surprised at just how much better the sweet liquid made her feel. She took a bite of a ham and mustard sandwich and only then realised just how hungry she really was.

Edna watched on in approval as Millie devoured the light meal, and when she was finished, took the plate from her and placed it back on the trolley. "I have some news relating to Trevor Giles," she said, withdrawing a small bottle from her pocket. The bottle which contained the poison Edna had retrieved from Trevor's stomach. "I've discovered what the trigger in the magic was designed to be activated by, and I've also discovered another ingredient. A puzzling ingredient."

Millie stared at Edna. "You're wasting time on that when you could be trying to find a way to stop a man's memories from being obliterated?"

"Nobody is wasting time," said Edna. "It just so happens that lots of people are working on a way to save Sergeant Spencer. We all care for him, as I'm sure you are aware." She gave Millie a stern stare. "And anyway, I discovered this before the awful werewolf attack. I've not had the time to mention it until now. I thought you might be interested as you seemed invested in finding out who had killed Mister Giles."

"I'm sorry. I am interested, Edna," said Millie, the food and sweet tea beginning to return some of her strength. She propped herself up on one elbow, giving Edna a tiny portion of her attention, the rest reserved for composing the speech she was going to deliver just as soon as her legs felt solid again. "What is it? What have you discovered?"

Holding the small bottle at arm's length and spinning it in the light flooding through the tall window, Edna narrowed her eyes and spoke. "I think we can safely say that the poison was meant for a werewolf," she said. "The trigger which activated it was moonlight. A cruel way to activate a poison intended to kill a person who thrived on the moon, but since when have murderers been anything but cruel?"

"Moonlight?" said Millie, affording Edna a little more attention. "It was moonlight that triggered the poison? But Trevor was in a police cell when the poison killed him. How did moonlight trigger it, and was the poison in the muffin Sergeant Spencer had given him or in something he'd eaten earlier in the day?"

"We don't know yet," said Edna. "Timothy is looking into it. He's the expert on werewolves and moonlight, but the other ingredient I found in the poison is more puzzling."

"Why?" said Millie. "What is it?"

"Love," said Edna, studying the bottle in her hand. "Not purposely added. Love never is, but love sometimes finds its way into potions made by witches for their loved ones."

"Somebody who loved Trevor Giles made the poison which killed him?" said Millie, swinging her legs over the side of the low bed. "A witch who loved him?"

Edna pocketed the potion and reached for Millie's arm, helping her to her feet. "It's a mystery," she said. "Which will be solved eventually, but until then, as you rightly pointed out — there are more pressing matters to be getting on with, so if you're feeling better, I shall leave you and go and check on Miss Spencer."

"Yes," said Millie, testing her legs for strength. "I feel a lot better." She looked towards the door. "Where's Sergeant Spencer? I'd like to see him."

"He's in the room at the end of the corridor," said Edna.

"If you're looking after me and Judith, who's looking after him?" asked Millie. "He's not on his own, is he?"

"No, of course not," replied Edna. "Timothy sat with him for a while and now George is with him. He'll be happy to see you, I'm sure. He was very concerned when we told him you'd had a funny turn."

Would he be happy to see her, Millie wondered. How would a man react to the news that he had a second daughter? To the news of a second child whose mother had kept her daughter's existence a secret from him? Millie suspected he'd be shocked. Angry as well, but maybe happy, too, she hoped.

One thing was for sure, though, she was going to tell him right away, whatever his reaction might be. While she'd been asleep her mind had been busy, and she'd woken with absolute clarity. It didn't matter how much time she'd wasted by not telling him before, what mattered was that she told him now, before his memories were wiped. She walked determinedly towards the door. "Thank you for looking after me," she said.

"You're welcome," said Edna. "Tell Sergeant Spencer we're working hard to find a way to help him, and tell him I'll bring Judith along to see him as soon as she's awake. I expect he'll want to spend as much time with her as possible."

"I'll tell him," promised Millie, leaving the room. She lowered her voice to a whisper as she made her way towards the room at the end of the corridor. "And then I'll tell him that he's my father, and that I love him."

Chapter 31

*H*earing voices as she approached the room at the end of the corridor, Millie prepared herself for what she was about to do. *What she was about to say.* She'd look Sergeant Spencer straight in his kind eyes, take a deep breath, and simply say three little words. You're my father.

The voices grew in volume as Millie neared the open doorway, and she became able to make out the words which were being spoken. She listened as George spoke. "I may as well tell you my secret," he said.

"If I'm not going to be able to remember it by tomorrow?" replied Sergeant Spencer, managing to keep his sense of humour.

George laughed. "You're the perfect person to unload secrets on," he said.

Pausing a few steps away from the door, Millie leaned against the wall and kept quiet.

"I'm honoured," said Sergeant Spencer. "I think."

"You should be," said George. "I haven't told anybody else yet."

"Well now I am intrigued," said Sergeant Spencer. "Go on then, spill the beans."

Nobody spoke for a few seconds, and then George let out a long sigh. "There are certain people I wish I'd been able to tell a long time ago, but it wasn't only my decision, there was someone else to think about."

"Your mystery woman?" asked Sergeant Spencer.

"You know about her?" said George.

"This is a small town, George. Everybody knows about her," replied the policeman, his voice taking on a serious note. "Especially Millie. She spoke to me about her when she first appeared on the scene. She was quite upset."

Millie closed her eyes as she remembered the occasion Sergeant Spencer was speaking about. She'd had a conversation with him at the kitchen table in Windy-dune Cottage. When she'd explained that she thought George was cheating on her, Sergeant Spencer had been there for her, listening, and then explaining why he didn't believe that her assumption was correct. She hadn't known at the time that he was her father, but she'd felt remarkably close to him as he'd given her his advice.

Shifting her weight from one foot to the other as her calf muscle began to ache, Millie listened carefully as George gave his response. "I know," he said. "I know it was wrong of me not to tell her, but I couldn't. Emily didn't want me to, and I had to respect her wishes."

"Emily?" said Sergeant Spencer. "So that's the name of the young lady I've seen on the back of your bike as you zip around the countryside." He paused and gave a low laugh. "Not always obeying the speed limits. I might add."

"I've got a heavy throttle hand," said George. "What can I say? It's a curse."

"Well, get on with it then," said Sergeant Spencer. "Tell me your secret. This pain killing spell which Edna cast over me will only last so long, and then my concentration will slip again."

"Okay," said George. "I've known you since you moved to this town all those years ago with Judith, and in all those years you've never known me to have a personal relationship with anybody, have you?"

"No," said Sergeant Spencer. "You've had friends, of course, but no personal relationships that I can recall. Until Millie."

"Until Millie," repeated George. "So imagine my surprise when not long after I'd developed a relationship with her, another woman came into my life. Somebody very important. Somebody I hadn't seen for seventy years. Somebody I created. Somebody who has my blood running in her veins."

"Emily is your daughter?" asked Sergeant Spencer.

"Not quite," answered George. "But in the vampire world, she's just as precious. Emily's mine,

Sergeant. She was twenty-five when I delivered the bite to her throat which saved her life and transformed her into a vampire, and now that she's turned up in Spellbinder Bay, she's my responsibility. I take that responsibility very seriously. Very seriously indeed."

"I understand that," said Sergeant Spencer. "I know how much vampires care for their creations. I know how much Fredrick cares for you, George."

"He does," said George. "And as well as saving my life on that battlefield, he's been a wonderful mentor to me ever since. I hope I can provide Emily with the same guidance that Fredrick provided me with."

"You said you hadn't seen her for seventy years, George," observed Sergeant Spencer. "How did that happen? Why haven't you seen her in all that time?"

Millie heard George take a long breath before he spoke. "When Fredrick saved me from death, I was grateful," he said. "But I was ready to die. I was used to seeing death all around me every single day of my miserable existence during that war. It was awful. Watching friends dying daily and hearing the screams of men around the clock. It was almost a relief when that German bayonet disembowelled me. I realised I was going to escape the horror of war."

"I can't imagine how terrible that must have been for you," said Sergeant Spencer.

"It wasn't pleasant," said George. "But luckily for me, Fredrick was there. He was a medic for the German army. He should have been my enemy, but as

I lay dying in no man's land, he found me and saw something in me. I reminded him of his son, he told me, so he chose to bite and save me. He turned me into who I am today, and I've been grateful to him ever since."

"I can imagine how grateful you feel," said Sergeant Spencer. "And I imagine Emily feels the same gratitude towards you?"

"It's complicated," said George. "She wasn't as grateful to me for saving her as I was to Fredrick when he saved my life. And because of that, she's been hiding away for the last seven decades. She became what we in the vampire world refer to as a shadow dweller. She's spent the best part of seventy years hiding away from humans and vampires. She's existed rather than lived. Until now."

"Why?" asked Sergeant Spencer.

George sighed. "Because I saved her life after she'd tried to take it," he said. "Fredrick and I lived together in America at the time. In New York. It was late at night on July the twentieth nineteen forty-eight, when it happened. I'd been enjoying a night-time motorcycle ride to New Jersey, and I had to cross the George Washington Bridge to get home. That's when I saw Emily. On the other side of the railings, staring down at the river."

"About to jump," said Sergeant Spencer.

"Yes," said George. "It was obvious, so I stopped my bike and approached her. She told me to stay back, and I realised from her accent that she was an

English girl. That was good — we had something in common, so she opened up to me. She told me that she'd met and fallen in love with an American soldier stationed in Britain during the war. Unfortunately, he was injured during the D-day landings in nineteen forty-four and was evacuated to Britain. He'd lost a leg, suffered an awful head injury, and lost the sight in one eye, but within six months he was well enough to travel home to New York. Emily went with him, and they married."

"But things didn't go to plan?" asked Sergeant Spencer.

"No. Emily told me everything was going well," said George. "Her husband had been getting better and better, and after four years of recovery, was using a false leg and had become accustomed to having only one eye. They planned to have children, and then one night, her husband died in his sleep. Just like that — as a consequence of the head injury he'd received. A blood clot, Emily told me. The day I found her on the bridge was the day of her husband's funeral, and I knew from the tone in her voice and the look in her eye that she was going to jump. Nothing I could have said would have prevented it, so I approached her slowly. Even in my vampire form, I couldn't have reached her in time. All she had to do was take one step into the dark, and she would be lost. And that's what she did. She thanked me for listening to her story, gave me a final smile and stepped into the night without making a sound."

"How sad," said Sergeant Spencer. "The poor girl."

"It was sad," said George. "So that's why I did what I did. Saving a person's life is a very special thing for a vampire. It's not something we take lightly, and many vampires never do it. It's in our nature not to save lives, as there are just too many people to save. It would be impossible, and it would become a burden. Sometimes, though, the right opportunity presents itself. I was Fredrick's opportunity, and Emily was mine. Something happened inside me, something forced me to act, and before I knew what I was doing, I was in vampire form, and I'd leapt over the side of the bridge. The water was cold and the night was dark, but such things don't hinder a vampire. I dived beneath the surface and found her quickly. Bones were broken, and her lungs were full of water, but there was a weak pulse — all that is required for a vampire's bite to work."

"You saved her," said Sergeant Spencer.

"Yes," said George. "I dragged her to the surface and bit her immediately. She was reborn as a vampire right there, in the cold waters of the Hudson River. As soon as she opened her eyes, she knew what I'd done to her. I should have let her die. That's what she wanted. She stared at me with such hatred as we were taken downstream by the river. She screamed at me, already aware of what she was, and aware that she was immortal. Then she stopped screaming and asked me one single question."

"What was it?" said Sergeant Spencer.

"She asked me my name, and when I told her, she turned her back on me and swam to shore. I left her alone but searched for her the next day, and the next, and the next. I searched for her for a month, but she had taken to the shadows. I never saw her again, until a few months ago when she arrived in Spellbinder Bay looking for me. She turned up on my doorstep, her hair how it had been in the forties, and her clothes very old-fashioned. It was like looking at her on the day she'd jumped from the bridge."

"That must have been a shock," said Sergeant Spencer, his voice betraying signs of pain again.

Resisting the urge to burst into the room to see if her father was okay, Millie continued listening.

"It was," said George. "She'd used my name to find me, and when she arrived, she was scared. She'd been in the shadows for so long. Society had changed since she'd gone into hiding, and she didn't know how to cope with it. She needed help to fit in, and she made me promise not to tell anybody who she was. She was ashamed of what had happened to her. Of what she was. She insisted on pretending she was human, and she wanted to fit into society as a human and not a vampire — so I found her a job as a nursing assistant at the nursing home. She fitted in, and soon she was dressing like the rest of the young women who worked there."

"And began taking motorbike rides with you," said Sergeant Spencer.

George laughed. "Yes," he said. "She found it amusing that I was riding a motorbike on the day I found her on the bridge, and here I am, seventy years later, still riding a motorbike."

"And would she mind you telling me about her, George?" asked Sergeant Spencer. "Even though I'm going to forget all about it quite soon."

"No," said George. "She won't mind. She's permitted me to tell people who she is. Since she arrived, she's been watching how the paranormal people in Spellbinder Bay conduct themselves. She's no longer ashamed of being a vampire. She's accepted who she is and she's ready to fit in. In fact, I was talking to Millie about her before we heard that you were in danger of being ripped apart by werewolves."

"I'm thankful that you and Millie came for us," said Sergeant Spencer. "My life as I know it may be coming to an end, but not Judith's. You and Millie saved her life. You're a good man, George, and Emily is lucky to have you as her mentor."

"I'll do the best I can for her, but It was quite a shock," said George. "When she turned up on my doorstep. Imagine having it happen to you."

"I don't think that there's any chance of a vampire turning up on my doorstep and telling me that I created them," said Sergeant Spencer. "But I can imagine somebody turning up and telling me I was their father. I'm not sure what I'd do. I think the shock might kill me. One daughter is enough, thank you very much."

Millie slumped against the wall, Sergeant Spencer's words ringing in her ears, and stabbing at her heart. Blood rushed to her head, and she steadied herself as dizziness threatened to take her again. Hearing a chair scraping on the floor, and the soft squeak of George's leather jacket, Millie moved slowly away from the door.

"You're leaving are you, George?" asked Sergeant Spencer.

"Yes," came George's reply. "I'll find Edna and get her to come and see you. Your face is showing signs of pain. I think you might need another of her painkilling spells."

"Check on Judith for me as well, would you, George?" asked Sergeant Spencer. "I don't care what happens to me, but I have to know Judith is alright. She's all I have. She's all I need. She's my life."

Chapter 32

By the time George left the room and entered the corridor, Millie had retreated far enough so that when she turned around and began walking towards Sergeant Spencer's room, George would have no idea that she'd been standing outside the room and eavesdropping.

The vampire gave Millie a smile of concern as he approached her and glanced back over his shoulder before speaking in a lowered voice. "He's doing alright," he said. "Edna cast a spell over him which helps with the pain. It also reduces his anxiety about the situation he's in, but Edna didn't tell him that. If he seems a little unconcerned about what's happening to him, it's just the spell doing its job."

"I understand," said Millie.

"Is Judith awake yet?" asked George. "He's asking about her."

"She's still asleep," replied Millie. "Edna will wake her up soon."

"What about you?" said George, his brow furrowed. "Do you feel better? Edna said you had a funny turn."

"That makes me sound like I'm sixty years older than I actually am," said Millie. "I didn't have a funny turn. I fainted, due to stress, and probably not having eaten enough over the last twenty-four hours."

Looking as if he wanted to reach out and touch her, George nodded. "You should look after yourself," he said.

"I know," said Millie, finding herself gazing into George's eyes. As deep and mysterious as ever, they stared back at her with compassion, her image reflected at her in hazel.

Biting her lip, she stopped herself from saying what she wanted to say. She wanted to tell him that she'd heard everything he'd told Sergeant Spencer about Emily. She wanted to tell him how sad Emily's story was, and how she thought George had done the right thing by rescuing her from death. She wanted to tell him that he'd acted in Emily's best interests when she showed up in Spellbinder Bay after seventy years of life in the shadows, and she wanted to tell him that he was a kind man.

She wanted to tell him all of those things, but she couldn't. She didn't want George to know that she'd been skulking in the corridor, listening to a private conversation, but mostly, and with a sinking feeling of regret, she realised that she didn't want to have that conversation with him at all.

It was a conversation that would lead to him expecting her understanding, and maybe forgiveness. It was also a conversation which George would consider a route back to a romantic relationship with her. It was with a sickening realisation that Millie understood that a romantic relationship wasn't what she wanted anymore. Her life only had room for growing one relationship with a man, and the man she wanted to cultivate a relationship with was not George, it was her father. She smiled at him. "I'd better check on Sergeant Spencer," she said.

George stepped aside. "Of course," he said. He reached out and took Millie's hand, holding it gently. "I know how much he means to you, and I know it doesn't seem as if much is being done to help him, but believe me, some of the best brains in Spellbinder Bay are working on a way to halt his deterioration, and to get a message to Henry Pinkerton. There's still hope for him, Millie."

"I know," said Millie, walking away, George's fingers trailing across her palm as her hand slipped from his. "But I hope somebody finds an answer soon."

Not looking back, she hurried to the room Sergeant Spencer was in and gave a polite knock before peering through the doorway. The room felt warm and was well equipped with medical equipment, both conventional and magical. In one corner, alongside the window, stood a machine designed to monitor a patient's heartbeat, while magic potions stood in neat lines behind the glass front of a cabinet placed alongside a bookcase brimming with spell books.

His condition being purely magical in nature, Sergeant Spencer was not surrounded by beeping machines or fitted with a cannula through which medicine could be administered. Free of such medical equipment, the policeman lay on a large bed with plump pillows to support his head and a colourful patchwork quilt beneath him. With his eyes closed and his chest rising and falling regularly, he looked peaceful as he rested, and Millie kept sound to a minimum as she settled into the seat meant for visitors.

Watching him as he rested, Millie suddenly felt as if she were trespassing, as if she were violating his privacy. She expelled such thoughts, sure that Sergeant Spencer would prefer to have company than be alone as he lay in a hospital bed.

Watching him as he blew out regular slow breaths, Millie smiled as she recognised parts of her own face in his. She lifted a hand to her chin and ran a finger across the shallow cleft, her eyes tracing the same shape on her father's chin.

Suddenly, and without warning, a sob burst from her mouth, and her eyes spilt tears. Her vision misty, she watched the man in the bed. His memories were being taken from him even as he slept, and Millie could hardly bear the fact that none of those memories involved a father and daughter relationship between the two of them. The irony came to her uninvited, yet accurate — while she had only recently discovered that Sergeant Spencer was her father, and had been planning for the day she could begin making memories with him, his memories were being stolen from him, and with them, his whole identity.

As Millie wiped tears from her face with the back of her hand, something soft brushed her cheek causing her to lash out instinctively. Her hand made contact with something light but solid, and she winced as a high pitched squawk rattled her eardrum. "Ow!" screeched Reuben. "It's me! I landed on you! Don't hit me! Birds have very fragile bones! One swipe of that meaty arm of yours could mean curtains for me!"

"I'm sorry," said Millie. "You could have warned me that you were here instead of just landing on my shoulder. This place is full of ghosts, and you know how I feel about ghosts. They make me nervous."

"I *would* have announced my arrival," said Reuben, "but I had something in my beak which prevented me from speaking. It's on the floor, now. Those chunky sausage fingers of yours saw to that. You could have maimed me, you know."

"I said I was sorry," said Millie.

"Never mind about me," replied Reuben. "How is the sergeant? Timothy has filled me in on everything that's happened. It's him you can thank for the fact that I'm not administering a stern dressing down to you. You missed twelve of my feeding times, Millie. I've been quite distressed, but thanks to Timothy calming me down, you're off the hook. You know, Timothy really is a nice chap. I wish you could see past his macho exterior and into his squidgy insides. You and he would make a fine couple."

Ignoring half of Reuben's speech, Millie frowned. "Twelve feeding times? It's not even been a day since I last fed you, and I always leave emergency seeds in your bowl."

"Yes, twelve," confirmed Reuben. "You might not recognise them as valid, but I certainly do, and as for emergency seeds — it would have to be an emergency stemming from a cataclysmic event of the sort the world has not yet witnessed, before I dined on seeds." He shook out his feathers, his wingtip brushing Millie's face. "Anyway, Victoria fed me. She made me a cheese and pickle sandwich. I told her that you wouldn't mind her rummaging through the kitchen."

"Victoria?" said Millie. "Beth's mother? What was she doing at the cottage?"

"I don't know who she is," said Reuben. "And I stopped caring when she agreed to put cheese between bread slices for me. She told me you'd spoken with her earlier today. She had a message for you, but when I told her you weren't home, she wrote it down. She insisted on using one of your envelopes, too. I have a feeling she didn't want me to read it. I told her that anything she wanted to say to you, she could tell me, but she disagreed.

"Anyway, I used that special link we share as a witch and familiar to find you. I hope you're appreciative of my efforts. I had a belly full of cheese and a good film to watch, but I chose instead to become your personal mailman. You'll find your mail on the floor, where it landed when you smashed it from my beak." He fluttered the short distance to the bed and landed gently next to Sergeant Spencer. "Poor fellow," he said, quietly. "Is there nothing anybody can do to help him?"

"People are working hard to come up with a way to help him," said Millie, reaching for the small white envelope next to her foot. "I have faith in them."

"How long has he been asleep?" asked Reuben.

"Not long," said Millie, using a fingernail to open the letter. "I'm going to wake him up soon. I'm going to tell him, Reuben."

Despite what she'd heard Sergeant Spencer say to George, she was still going to tell him. Even if he did respond negatively. A negative response was still a better outcome than one of the alternatives. The idea of watching Sergeant Spencer's memories being taken from him while knowing that he'd never — not even for a minute — known that Millie was his daughter, was tragic. That chain of events was not something she would accept. Even if the only memory of Sergeant Spencer as her father was of him telling Millie he didn't want her as a daughter, that memory was still infinitely better than having not a single memory of him as her father.

"Good," said the cockatiel. "I'm glad. You'd regret it if you didn't."

Unfolding the letter she slipped from the envelope, Millie began reading, her mind spinning as she made sense of the words before her.

Dear Millie,

Firstly, I should apologise for the way I treated you when you came to visit Beth. I was very abrasive and rude towards you, and I am truly sorry. I was reacting as a mother protecting her daughter, but I understand you meant Beth no harm; you just wanted answers to your questions.

Although I can be of no help with your murder enquiry, I do believe I can be of some help in the matter of your mother and her failure to revisit this world.

After you had left, I consulted some books on the matter. Although not apparent in the way it is written, I believe I understand why your mother has not yet returned as she promised she would.

The problem lies with the permanent bridge between her world and yours, which you told me your mother had spoken of. Your mother would have genuinely believed that a permanent bridge had been formed until she attempted to use it once more.

The bridge, of course, is metaphorical in construction. It is more likely to be a simple barrier of energy, a gate if you will, between the place your mother's energy resides, and our world. Having scoured the old texts, and performed a few translations, I think I understand why your mother hasn't revisited you. The bridge she spoke of is only permanent when used by occupants from both worlds the bridge reaches between. When the spell that you cast formed the bridge, it would have felt permanent to your mother. The mistake she made in telling you so was a simple one to make, but in reality, the bridge will only remain permanent when you have used it to cross to her world in the same way she did to yours.

Having given you that information, I'm sorry that I cannot provide you with a suggestion as to how you can use the bridge. I will continue to study the books in search of an answer, but I'm not sure that I will discover one.

I hope this note helps you understand why your mother has not yet returned, and please know that my door is always open to you.

With regards,
Victoria

P.S. I'm sorry about the mess in your kitchen. Your familiar forced me to prepare cheese sandwiches for him. He flew onto the roof of your cottage with my car keys and refused to come down until I had fed him.

He possesses quite a rude vocabulary, doesn't he?

Folding the note, Millie sighed.

"What did she say?" asked Reuben, cocking his head. "Did she say anything about me? If she did, it's probably slander and lies."

"No," said Millie, giving her familiar a smile. "She didn't say anything about you, Reuben.

Victoria thinks she knows why my mother hasn't revisited."

Reuben gave Millie an inquisitive look, his head laid on his shoulder. "You don't look very happy about that revelation, if I may say so. We've both been working hard to try and find out why your mother hasn't returned. I'd have thought you'd have been relieved, at least."

"I am," said Millie. "But at the moment I have bigger priorities."

"Of course," replied the bird, turning his gaze to the man in the bed next to him. "Sergeant Spencer. Your father."

"I've already lost my mother," said Millie. "I had a long time to get used to the fact that she was dead. When she returned, it was amazing, beautiful, miraculous — all of those things, but now she's gone again, I'm sort of used to it. I've had almost fifteen years of practice." She stood up and approached the bed, placing a hand gently on her father's chest as it rose and fell. "But not him. He's different. I've only recently discovered that he's my father, and it seems that I'm going to lose him before I even get to know him. My mother is gone, Reuben. My father is here, but he's going to be gone soon." Tears ran a warm course down her face. "I don't think I can bear it," she wept. "I'm not strong enough, Reuben."

"You are, Millie," said Reuben. "You are strong! You're the strongest person I know. I won't hear you speaking in that way about yourself! Not after what you've overcome in your life." With a brisk flapping of wings, he flew from the bed and landed on Millie's shoulder. He placed his beak tenderly against his witch's ear and spoke in a whisper. "Wake him up, Millie. Right now. Wake Sergeant Spencer up and tell him he's the father to a courageous, beautiful, intelligent, kind, and amazing daughter."

"Thank you, Reuben," sobbed Millie. "Those words meant a lot to me." Taking a deep breath and wiping as many tears from her face as she could, she moved her hand to her father's shoulder. She looked into the sleeping man's face. "You're my father," she whispered.

"Louder, Millie," urged Reuben. "Shake that man awake and tell him."

Applying pressure to his shoulder, Millie leaned closer to Sergeant Spencer's face. "Wake up," she said, shaking him gently. "Wake up."

"He's in a deep sleep," said Reuben when the policeman failed to respond. "Shake him harder."

Raising her voice and shaking him with more intent, Millie stared into his face. "Wake up!" she commanded. When Sergeant Spencer gave no indication he was about to wake up, Millie moved her hand to his face. Maybe he required a gentle pat on the cheek to raise him from his slumber. As her fingers made contact with his cheek, Millie gasped. "There's something wrong!" she said. "He's freezing! He's so cold I can barely touch! Go and get Edna, Reuben."

As if responding to Millie's voice, footsteps echoed in the corridor and the concerned voice of Edna Brockett drifted into the room. "Hurry, Fredrick! This is serious, we may be too late!"

As Millie attempted to wake Sergeant Spencer again, Edna Brockett burst into the room, accompanied by Fredrick. She pushed Millie aside and leaned over Sergeant Spencer, her hand on his face. "It's as I thought. We're too late!" she said. "The concealment spell has accelerated. He has little time left until his memories are gone!"

"What is it?" said Millie. "What's happened, Edna?"

"It's the werewolves in the dungeons," said Fredrick, from behind her. "They've been yelling their protest about being locked up. They've also been making it quite apparent that they believe Sergeant Spencer is responsible for killing Trevor Giles. The passion behind those accusations has not gone unnoticed by the magic within Spellbinder Hall. The extreme emotions of the four werewolves have affected the concealment spell. The werewolves are paranormal. Sergeant Spencer is human. The spell is acting to protect the paranormal community against what it believes to be an attack from a non-paranormal person. The spell senses an emergency. It believes, as much as a non-sentient stream of energy can believe, that Sergeant Spencer attacked our community."

"And the speed in which the spell is working has

increased dramatically," added Edna. "The spell has placed the poor sergeant in stasis so he cannot attack any more members of our community. His memories are being erased at an alarming rate. I'm afraid I cannot see a way out. I'm afraid that Sergeant Spencer, as we know and love him, is lost to us."

Chapter 33

"No!" said Millie, her hands trembling as she stepped away from the bed. "No! That can't be right!"

"I'm afraid it is," said Edna, moving a hand towards Millie, who backed away, shaking her head. "We must be strong, though. We need to think about Judith. She's going to be awake soon, and when she learns about what's happening to her father, she's going to be devastated. She'll need our strength to help her through the hard times which lay ahead."

Still shaking her head, Millie screwed her eyes shut. She wanted to scream. She wanted to hit something. *Somebody*. She wanted to collapse to the floor and curl into a ball. She wanted somebody to take her in their arms and tell her that everything was going to be alright. She wanted her mother. She wanted her father.

Pushing Fredrick aside as she made for the door,

Millie allowed her tears to flow. She bumped into somebody as she pushed through the doorway, not caring about who it was, and increased her speed until she was running. She followed corridors, not thinking about where she was going or what she was going to do when she got there. She wanted to put space between her and her problems, and running seemed the most appropriate way to do so.

Taking three steps at a time she made quick work of two flights of stairs, and it was only as she ran along another dark corridor and smelled the sweetness of warm cinnamon and chocolate, that she realised she'd instinctively made for the nearest place she considered safe; her classroom.

Through hot streaming tears and the sound of her loud weeping, she still discovered herself wondering why she could smell baking emanating from her classroom. It was the school holidays. Nobody should be there.

She sighed. Emma Taylor. Of course, she'd allowed her to use the classroom during the holidays. It appeared that it hadn't taken the young witch very long at all to make good use of the permission.

Deciding that entering the classroom and speaking to Emma might help her to calm down, Millie began taking back control of her emotions. She sucked in four deep breaths and used the sleeve of her shirt to wipe her face clear of tears. She imagined her eyes were still puffy and bloodshot, but that didn't matter, Emma was a teenager, she'd seen people cry before. She wouldn't judge her or ask questions.

Taking one last deep breath, Millie put a smile on her face, and pushed the door open, the scent of baking becoming stronger as the door creaked on its old hinges. She looked towards the line of ovens as she entered the room, and froze, a scream stuck in her throat.

The figure which had been bent double in front of an oven, its hooded head level with the glass door as it peered inside, stood up straight and turned its attention towards Millie.

An eerie silence seemed to fill the classroom, an oven fan providing the sparse sound that there was. The door closed behind her with a soft thump, and she jumped, the soles of her trainers squeaking on the floor. She stared at the ghost, her mouth dry and her heart galloping. "Hello?" she offered.

The towering apparition remained silent, the shadows formed by its hood offering no clue as to what lurked beneath the black robes. It shimmered for a moment, and then moved toward Millie, gliding silently as it approached her.

"Stay back!" warned Millie, raising both hands. "Please stay back!"

The ghost stopped abruptly, its hood moving slowly from left to right, giving the impression that it was studying Millie. It lifted an unhurried hand and extended one of its gloved fingers, pointing to a spot over Millie's right shoulder.

Moving cautiously, Millie turned her head. "The blackboard?" she said. "You're pointing at the blackboard?"

The ghost gave a slow nod.

"You want to write on it?" asked Millie, the tremble in her voice betraying her fear.

The ghost nodded once more.

Moving backwards towards the door, Millie gave a nod of her own. "Okay," she said. "Go on. Use the blackboard."

Moving with elegance, the apparition floated a few inches above the floor as it approached the blackboard. Seemingly aware of Millie's fear, it gave her space, choosing to skirt the edge of the room.

Millie steadied her breathing. The ghost meant her no harm. That much was obvious. She watched in fascination as the ghost attempted to take a piece of white chalk from the shelf at the base of the blackboard. Its fingers passing straight through the chalk and the board, the ghost paused for a moment, its form flickering. It waited for a few seconds as if gathering strength and then tried again. This time it managed to take the chalk between finger and thumb, and slowly lifted it to the board. Making careful marks on the surface, the ghost began writing.

As the first sentence was formed, Millie nodded. "Of course," she said, remembering the group photograph she'd seen in Cuthbert Campion's home. Miss Timkins had towered over everyone else in the picture, and here she was in Millie's classroom, towering over her.

She reread the sentence. '*I'm Miss Timkins,*' it said, in a childlike scrawl. Millie took a step towards the ghost as it wrote another three words, this time the writing a little neater. '*Don't be scared.*'

"I'm not," said Millie, moving closer to the ghost. "Not anymore."

Miss Timkins gave a slow nod and put chalk to board once more. '*I wear the robes to hide the scars. Something terrible happened to me.*'

"I know," said Millie. "I've been told about your accident."

Miss Timkins shook her head slowly, her hood drooping over whatever terrible injuries it hid. She touched the chalk to the board, white dust falling as she wrote. '*It was no accident.*'

"What do you mean?" asked Millie. "Did someone put you in the oven on purpose?"

Miss Timkins nodded, her robes suddenly flickering and the chalk dropping to the floor as she vanished. Almost immediately, she reappeared and took another piece of chalk from the tray. She lifted it to the board and wrote slowly, her handwriting barely comprehensible. '*Strength fading*' she wrote, the chalk wobbling in her grasp. '*What happened to me was no accident. I was put in the oven by a pupil. It was Trevor Giles, he —*'

Miss Timkins flickered and Millie jumped as a

loud squawk came from behind her. "Open the door! Quickly! It's important!"

"Don't go," said Millie, as Miss Timkins faded from sight. "It's only my familiar."

The chalk the ghost had been holding clattered to the floor, snapping as it landed, and instinctively, Millie knew the spirit would not be returning. Not for a while, anyway.

"Millie!" squawked Reuben from the corridor. "Open this door!"

"What is it?" asked Millie, swinging the door open. "I think I was just about to witness a murder confession from a ghost."

Reuben flew quickly into the classroom. "As intriguing as that sounds, and as eager as I am to ask you what you're talking about, what I have to tell you is far more important!"

"So tell me," said Millie.

"We might be able to save Sergeant Spencer," said the bird. "We might have found a way to save your father, but it's dangerous, Millie, for both of us." He landed on Millie's shoulder. "But I'm willing to take the risk if you are. Get back to Sergeant Spencer immediately. There's someone with him who has an idea." He lifted his beak and jerked his head towards the ovens. "Is that chocolate soufflé I can smell?" he asked. "Are you making soufflé?"

"No," said Millie, hurrying across the room and switching the oven off. "It wasn't me who made it."

Chapter 34

$\mathcal{H}$urrying along corridors and down flights of stairs, Millie winced with pain as Reuben kept his balance on her shoulder with sharp claws that hurt. "He came bearing good news, and you winded him when you ran out of the infirmary room," said the bird. "You barged into him and just left him there, gasping for breath."

Millie rounded a corner at speed, almost knocking over the suit of armour which guarded the empty corridor in complete silence and indifference. "I know I banged into somebody, Reuben," she said. "But who was it, and what's the good news?"

"It was one of the ASSHAT fellows," said Reuben. "The one who wasn't all there to begin with. The one whose brains were like jelly."

"Really?" said Millie, slowing as she navigated another corner. "I haven't seen either of them around here much. They stay locked away in The Chaos gate room."

The two scientists, who were given the job of examining the magical gateway to The Chaos, had been employed in Spellbinder Hall ever since their accidental involvement in a murder case. They'd been dragged into the case while studying a skeleton which they had believed was the remains of an extraterrestrial being. The skeleton had not been an alien, though — it had been the still living bones of a demon, but the two men from The Alien Search Syndicate and Hazard Awareness Team, or ASSHAT for short, hadn't known that.

When the junior member of ASSHAT had found himself possessed by the demon, people had almost been hurt, but using magic, Millie had subdued the possessed man, and the demon had been sent back into The Chaos. The man who had been possessed — Peter Simmons, had suffered from damage caused by a brain injury before the creature had taken control of his body, but when the demon had been cast from him, his brain injury had healed, and the two scientists had been offered a job at Spellbinder Hall. Using scientific methods, instead of magical ones, it was hoped that they might be able to help prevent more evil entities from passing through the gate.

"It's lucky for you that they have kept themselves hidden away in The Chaos gate room," said Reuben, as Millie turned into the final corridor and hurried towards the room at the end, the room in which her father lay. "Because if they hadn't, they might not have come up with a way to contact Henry Pinkerton."

"They know how to contact Henry?" said Millie. "So have they done it? Have they sent him a message?"

"It's not that easy," said Reuben, launching himself from Millie's shoulder and entering the room before her. "It's not that easy at all."

Hearing excited chatter coming from the room, Millie followed her familiar inside and stared at the faces peering back at her. George and Timothy were there, as were Fredrick and Edna, and they were all gathered around the tall, thin man wearing a white lab coat and holding a clipboard.

Sitting in the seat next to the bed, paying no attention to anybody but the man in the bed, was Judith, her face white and her eyes red from crying.

"Tell her, Peter," said Timothy.

"I don't think it's a good idea at all," said George. "Not if I can't go with her. If anything happened to her, I'd never forgive myself. None of us would ever forgive ourselves."

"It's Millie's decision," said Fredrick, giving Millie a brief look of concern.

"What's my decision?" asked Millie.

"Tell her, Mister Simmons," said Edna, standing alongside Sergeant Spencer, her fingers on his wrist. "But hurry. His pulse is weakening by the second. The magic is working quickly. If Henry doesn't intervene soon, I'm not sure we'll be able to help him."

As Edna spoke, Judith's upper body shook, and she wiped away tears as she sobbed. "Dad," she said, her words strangled. "Please hold on. Please fight. Millie might be able to help you."

Moving to the seat in which Judith sat, Millie put a hand on her friend's shoulder and squeezed it gently. "I'll do whatever I can to help him," she said. "If somebody would just tell me what it is I'm expected to do."

Peter Simmons cleared his throat. "It's simple in theory," he said, peering down his long nose at Millie. "But *possibly* a little dangerous in practice." He paused. "Actually it's *probably* a little dangerous. Or perhaps *certainly* very dangerous indeed."

"What is?" asked Millie. "What can I do to help? I don't care how dangerous it is, I just want to help."

Peter Simmons gave Millie a thin smile. "The problem as I see it, is that somebody needs to get a message to Mister Henry Pinkerton," he said. "So Henry can help Sergeant Spencer, but the problem with that seemingly simple task lies in the fact that Henry Pinkerton is currently between dimensions, in a place only he can travel to and he's not due back in time to save our unfortunate friend from total memory loss. That's the predicament we find ourselves in, is it not?"

"Yes, Mister Simmons," snapped Edna, her words laced with impatience. "That's the predicament we find ourselves in, but please, won't you just tell the girl what you and that other mad scientist have discovered? This is no time for long-winded speeches, Mister Simmons!"

Clearing his throat, Peter Simmons nodded, his cheeks a bright red. "Yes, of course," he said. He smiled at Millie. "Myself and Mister Spalding heard news of what was happening to poor Sergeant Spencer, and we both instinctively knew that we might have found an answer to your problem. We've been studying the gate to The Chaos very carefully since we were lucky enough to be given jobs here at the hall, and it very soon became apparent to us, through the use of speciality equipment, that the gate is not only an entrance to the dimension you know as The Chaos. It is, in fact, an entrance to more than one dimension. We believe that the dimension which you know as The Chaos is just the first destination on the other side of the gate. We believe, through evidence gathered from repeatable experiments, that when in The Chaos, a person may travel to neighbouring dimensions, if they possess a particular type of energy."

"What energy?" said Millie, already assuming she knew how he would answer.

"Your magic, Miss Thorn," said Peter. "There is a reason why yourself and other witches from your bloodline have been able to keep the gateway closed to invaders from The Chaos. Mister Spalding and I believe that your magic acts as a key, and we believe that anybody with a key can travel freely through dimensions. We think that you can step safely through the gate."

"We know that people can step through the gate," said Millie. "Henry has banished paranormal criminals to The Chaos in the past. Why would my magic make me anymore different than them?"

"Because you can come back, Miss Thorn," said Peter. "Those other poor souls can never come back. I think that your magic not only keeps the gate locked to intruders but also allows you to travel through it. Both ways."

"You're telling me that you want me to go into The Chaos?" asked Millie, recalling how terrifying even a glimpse into the dimension had been. "How will that help Sergeant Spencer?"

"Because I believe you'll be able to find Henry Pinkerton," said Peter Simmons. "I believe that when Henry travels along the beams of energy he speaks of, he's actually travelling through dimensions. When he travels from one side of the world to the other in the blink of an eye, I believe he's using dimensional routes."

Reuben flew to Millie's shoulder. "Peter thinks that the meeting Henry and the headmaster are having, with other representatives of the paranormal world, is being held in a place that you can reach by travelling into The Chaos," he said.

"That's right," said Peter. "And I believe the place will be easy for you to discover if you don't..." He looked at his shoes and gave a polite cough. "If you make it there in one piece, Miss Thorn."

"If a demon doesn't get you," said Reuben. "That's what he's trying to say, but as I told everybody here before I came to find you, I'm going with you if you decide you want to risk it. I'll protect you with my life."

"Of course I'm going," said Millie. "I'll do anything to save Sergeant Spencer's memories. But, no, Reuben, I won't allow you to come with me. You used to live in The Chaos. You told me how awful it was. I would never ask you to return."

"Yes," said Reuben. "I once lived there. I was what people in this world would have called a demon. I wasn't evil, though, and it was the most wonderful day when Esmeralda dragged my energy from that awful dimension into this one and placed me in the body of this bird. I have her to thank for saving me from an eternity in that hell, and I will do anything to help a member of her bloodline. And even if you weren't of her bloodline, I'd still do anything to help you, Millie."

"Reuben can travel freely between dimensions, too, Miss Thorn," said Peter Simmons. "Because Esmeralda brought him into this world to be her familiar, he is imbued with her magic — the magic of your bloodline, Miss Thorn. He may travel with you, but the body he uses now will be left in this world, waiting for him to return to it."

Millie turned her head to the right and stared at her familiar. "So you'll..."

Reuben answered her question before she could finish it. "Yes, Millie. When I pass through the gate, my energy will find the body I was born in again. The body of a monster."

Chapter 35

*F*ar below Spellbinder Hall, the gate room occupied a cave in the cliff, the entrance sealed with a thick metal door. The last time Millie had stepped inside the room, it had been so that Henry could show her the gateway to chaos. She shuddered as she recalled the fear she'd felt as she'd ran from the room after staring into the gate and witnessing a demon attempting to break through. The same fear filled her mind as Peter Simmons prepared to open the door.

As Peter pushed it open, Millie realised the room was a very different place than when she'd been there last. A little of her trepidation left her when she smelled coffee brewing and saw the plate of custard slices on a sideboard decorated with a small vase containing a posy of wildflowers.

It seemed that Peter Simmons and Graham Spalding had done what lots of people around the world did in their place of work. They'd made it their own, adding the creature comforts which would help tedious hours tick by.

Graham Spalding glanced up as the procession of people entered the room, his blue eyes bright against the crisp white of his lab coat. He reached for the small stereo on the desk next to him and turned it off. As the music that had been playing was silenced, Millie became aware of a humming sound emanating from behind a wooden screen on wheels which stood in the centre of the room. The screen hadn't been there to hide the gate when she'd last visited, but she remembered the sound the gate had made — the soft hum which had reminded her of wind passing through the branches of trees.

Graham stood up and smiled. "Hello," he said. "I'm assuming that since you're all here, a decision has been made?" He looked directly at Millie. "You're going to step through the gate, Miss Thorn?"

Millie took a deep breath. There was no time for small talk. Time was of the essence. She gave a firm nod. "Yes," she said. "Both Reuben and I are ready to go. Can we get on with it?"

"Of course," said Graham, hurrying to the screen and dragging it across the room on squeaky wheels. "I'm eager to see you step into it, not only so that the sergeant might be helped, but so that we can tell for sure that our hypothesis is correct. Although I'm quite certain that you and Reuben will be able to pass safely back into this dimension, it will be a relief to see it happen."

"How sure are you that you're correct?" asked George, concern on his face.

"I'm eighty per cent certain," said Graham Spalding. "Those are good odds."

"Those are odds that Millie has to decide for herself whether to take or not," said George. He approached Millie, gazing into her eyes. "You don't have to do this," he said. "You or Reuben. I know it will be awful if Sergeant Spencer loses his memories and is forced to move away, but at least he won't be lost to another dimension, or... dead.

"Judith is still up there in that room with him, holding his hand, she's stronger than some people think. She'll survive his loss, Millie. As harsh as that sounds, it's true, and she would never forgive herself if her father lost his memories and something terrible happened to you, too." He smiled at the little bird perched on Millie's shoulder. "You too, Reuben. We've had our differences, but you're brave, and I'm honoured to know you."

"I'm not dead yet, bloodsucker," snapped Reuben. He dropped his head and shuffled his feet on Millie's shoulder. "But thank you, George."

George smiled and turned his attention back to Millie. "You too," he said. "You're brave, but that doesn't mean you have to put your life on the line like this."

She wanted to tell him. She wanted to tell everybody assembled in the room that Sergeant Spencer was her father, and that she'd do anything to help him, but she wouldn't. She couldn't. Not until she'd told Sergeant Spencer himself. For the time being it was only her, Henry Pinkerton, and Reuben that knew, and soon, all three of them would be in a different dimension than her father. She smiled at George. "I know the risks," she said. "And I'm happy to take them."

Presumably aware of the determination that Millie felt in the way she held her head and stood firm on her feet, the vampire nodded. "Okay," he said. "We'll be willing you on, and we'll be waiting for you here when you get back. Both of you."

"George," said Millie. "I need you to get a message to Florence for me. If I don't make it back."

"You'll be back," said George, firmly.

"Please," said Millie. "Just humour me."

"Okay," said George, with a concerned frown. "What is it?"

"Tell her that I know who the new ghost is," said Millie. "And tell her that the ghost had a reason to want to kill Trevor Giles. Tell Florence that I know she said the ghost hadn't left her sight during the school fete, but I'm not so sure. The ghost had real motive. Florence is the best person to deal with it. She'll know what to do."

"I'll tell her," said George. "But you'll be able to tell her yourself. As soon as you're back."

"There's no need," came a soft voice from Millie's

right. "I watched the events unfold in your classroom, Miss Thorn. I know who the ghost is, and I understand the motive. Please be assured that I will investigate thoroughly." She moved alongside George and gave a curtsy. "May I also say how courageous I consider both yourself and your familiar to be. I wish you success on your journey."

"Thank you, Florence," said Millie.

"May I offer you my best wishes, too?" asked Timothy, approaching Millie. "I'm ashamed that it's members of my community who have put Sergeant Spencer in the position he's in. If those blasted wolves hadn't done what they did, then you and Reuben wouldn't be about to embark on such a dangerous quest."

"It's not really a quest," said Millie. "But thank you, Timothy."

"Not a quest?" said Timothy, incredulous. "You're about to search a dimension fraught with danger, for someone who might be able to save somebody we all love. You'll be facing heinous demons which have the ability to rip you apart, and you're armed only with the magic you have within you. I'd say that was a quest, and I wish you godspeed!"

Reuben moved his beak close to Millie's ear. "I'm not sure that I trust him anymore," he whispered. "I'm not sure that I want you to pursue him romantically, as I've advised in the past. He seems devious. George is far nicer, especially after how he just spoke about me. I'm touched."

"Reuben," said Timothy, tapping one of his ears with a podgy finger. "Whispering doesn't work around a werewolf."

"I think we should be going, Millie," said Reuben. "I'm sensing hostility."

"We should be going," agreed Millie, turning slowly to face the circle of white light contained within a vertical ring of stones. "We can't waste any more time."

"When you step through," said Graham Spalding, "you're looking for other gates similar to this one. The gates should not be too far from where you arrive in the next dimension."

"I don't recall being aware of other gates," said Reuben. "I lived on the other side of this gate for an age, and I only remember seeing this gate. The gate to this world."

"The other gates would have been hidden to you," said Peter Simmons. "This gate would have been visible because it had already been breached by demons from your world. The others will be visible to you now you have the same magic as Millie within you."

"Each gate will take you to another dimension," said Graham. "But you won't need to travel to each one to find Henry." He handed Millie a leather pouch. "This is the jewel which Henry calls The Stone of Integrity. It's tied to Henry by strong bonds of energy, and it will lead you to him."

"You're sure?" asked Millie, taking the pouch and pocketing it.

"Peter and I have tested it," replied Graham. "We're certain. We passed it through the gate on a rod, and the stone began vibrating almost immediately. We think the stone's vibrations will increase in intensity the closer it gets to Mister Pinkerton. Think of it as a homing device."

Millie nodded and stared into the ring of light. "What do I do if I come across a demon?" she asked.

"You do nothing if we come across a demon," said Reuben. "You leave it to me. That's what you do. I'll deal with any demons. I'll be a little bigger than this cockatiel when I take on my true form again."

"Okay," said Millie, stepping onto the stone plinth, her eyes squinting against the bright light cast by the gate. "Let's go, Reuben."

"Good luck," said Edna, as Millie stepped onto the flat slab of rock the gate sat upon.

"Yes," said Fredrick. "Good luck. It is a brave thing you're both choosing to do."

Concentrating only on the task at hand, Millie approached the glowing circle. A little taller than an average man, the gate was large enough to walk right into without needing to duck, and as she neared the wall of light, she closed her eyes tighter to shield them from the brightness.

A soft breeze blew from the circle, making her hair dance on the peripherals of her face, and the humming grew louder with each step she took.

Remaining on her shoulder, Reuben dug his claws deeper into her as the breeze became stronger.

When she was close enough to put out her hand and touch the light, she turned her head to look at her familiar. "After three?" she asked.

"I'd prefer five," answered the cockatiel. "But three is fine, too."

Millie smiled. "Okay, on the count of three, I'll walk into it. Hold on."

"No, I'd better not hold on," answered Reuben. "I'll leap into the light. The body of the cockatiel will remain here in this world, and I will occupy the body I was born into, and you wouldn't want me sitting on your shoulder in my true form, believe me."

Readying herself to walk into danger, and preparing herself to see her familiar in his true form, whatever that might be, Millie took a deep breath through her nose, blew it out through pursed lips and counted slowly. "One. Two. Three."

Forcing herself into the circle of light, aware that Reuben had left his perching place on her shoulder, her breath left her in a gasp as the glow enveloped her and the ground fell away beneath her.

Screaming as she tumbled, and blinded by the light, Millie called for Reuben but received no answer. Then suddenly, emerging from the light at high speed she saw solid ground. Knowing if she hit it at the rate she was travelling, she would be smashed to pieces, she closed her eyes and awaited the bone breaking impact, a scream forming in her throat.

Chapter 36

*H*er arms outstretched before her in an instinctive attempt to break her fall, the scream left Millie's mouth. Against the backdrop of wind noise rushing past her, she could hardly hear the sound she made, but her throat hurt as she expelled fear from her body.

And then, suddenly, it was over. Rather than hitting the ground with a body breaking thump, she found herself stepping gently across the threshold of a gate just like the one she'd stepped into in Spellbinder Hall.

That was the last of any similarities between the world she'd left behind and the world she was in now, though. In place of wildflowers in a vase and plates of custard slices on a sideboard, was gloominess, cold, and an awful stench which made her want to gag.

The smell which burned her nostrils and turned her stomach had a mustiness to it which made Millie think of death and decay, and she screwed her nose up in a futile attempt to form a barrier against it.

Still standing on the stone plinth she'd stepped onto, the circle of light behind her illuminated the area in a shimmering brightness.

Noting that she was in a cave with rough walls formed from rock, Millie scanned her surroundings, fear bubbling in her stomach. Scanning the uneven floor, she gasped as the light reflected off something long and thick. Something white. It wasn't alone, she realised, as she ran her eyes across the floor. The bones were everywhere — some small and some large, and some lying in piles, including the occasional skull of an unrecognisable creature staring back at her from the darkness.

Cold fear gripped her body, and Millie took a step backwards as the unmistakable sound of shuffling footsteps emerged from the darkness to her right.

As the footsteps grew louder, fear gripped her in a tighter grasp as light was reflected by two red orbs which approached her slowly. Understanding that the circles were eyes, Millie realised that her fear had pinned her to the spot on which she was standing, unwilling to allow her a step in either direction — not further into the room, nor backwards into the safety of the gate.

The large eyes peered at her from the gloom, and the sound of heavy breathing became apparent as something approached her, the shape of an elongated head beginning to form as it stepped into the light.

Attempting to swallow her fear, Millie searched for her magic, discovering it in the place it should be — in her chest, alongside the ball of terror which had taken up residence within her. As the creature loomed close, its eyes deep red and its breathing laboured, Millie prepared to defend herself, allowing magic to trickle along her arms and into her outstretched fingers.

As a spell quivered at her fingertips, ready to be released, more of the creature became illuminated by light, and Millie stared in horror as a mouth at the end of a bulbous snout began to open, revealing rows of pointed teeth which glinted viciously under the white glow of the gate.

Her forearms throbbing with magical energy, Millie prepared to cast her spell, but as the first sparks crackled at the ends of her fingers, the creature spoke, its voice broken at first but then becoming familiar. "Millie, don't you dare cast that spell, it's me, Reuben!"

"Reuben?" said Millie, unable to comprehend that the huge beast approaching her had only very recently been a tiny creature capable of flight.

Resembling a crude version of an upright hippopotamus, Reuben lumbered from the shadows on two stumpy legs. He emerged into the light, his thick grey hide wrinkled, and short hairs protruding from his long face. Nostrils flared as he took deep breaths, and his bright red eyes, sunken in folds of flesh, peered along his snout as he stared down at

Millie. "Speak to me," he said. "Say something! Or am I so ugly that you can't bring yourself to talk with me? I knew it! I knew you'd never accept me in my true form! You can't judge a book by its cover, they say in your world, yet look at you — you have judgement written all over your face! You think I'm ugly, don't you?"

Millie swallowed as she stared up at her familiar. "I'm not judging you," she said, running her eyes down his body, noting the sharp claws on the little hands at the ends of short arms. "I'm getting used to you, Reuben. It's hard to believe it's you — that's all. There's nothing ugly about you, though, I promise."

Reuben moved even closer to Millie, bringing with him a smell similar to the aroma given off by the fortnight old cooked cabbage that she'd once found in a hidden Tupperware pot at the back of her fridge.

He gazed down at her, his eyes unblinking, trapping her in an intense red stare. "Kiss me, Millie," he said, bending slowly at his thick waist. "Kiss me on the top of my head and tell me I'm a good boy, like you do when I'm a cute little cockatiel. After all, according to another of the sayings in your world, beauty is only skin deep. I know you can see my inner beauty, so kiss me and show me you accept me as I am." He looked at her with large, pleading eyes, before bowing his head. "Please."

Studying the bulging drops of an unknown brown substance which oozed from deep skin pores on Reuben's giant head, Millie bit her lip. The smell emanating from her familiar invaded her nostrils, and she was confident she could taste it on her lips as she moistened them with her tongue.

"Go on," murmured Reuben. "Kiss me on my head and ask me who's a pretty boy."

Wanting to show her familiar that of course it was what dwelled within him that mattered to her, and wanting to show him that her love for him was not based on a cute feathery face with bright red cheeks, Millie took a deep breath and then held it. She moved her face closer to the rubbery flesh of Reuben's broad head, which still oozed with viscous trickles of brown liquid, and pursed her lips in readiness to show him that her love transcended his appearance.

When her lips were centimetres from his head, and her eyes watered from the stench she was sure was rising from the brown oozing sludge, Reuben suddenly drew backwards and straightened his back, staring down at her as he let out a booming laugh. "Psych!" he said. "I got you! I got you! Oh, gosh, look at your face! That was so funny!"

"What are you doing?" asked Millie.

"I didn't expect you to kiss me," said Reuben. "I'm fully aware of what I look and smell like! I got you though, didn't I? I tricked you!"

"Reuben, this is not the time for fun and games," said Millie. "We're here to help my father, remember? Every minute we waste is precious."

"I was just trying to lighten the mood," said Reuben, his eyes wide and staring. "I saw how scared you looked when you stepped through the gate. I wanted to make you feel better. That's all."

Millie smiled. "It was funny," she relented. "And just so you know, if it weren't for that foul liquid oozing from your skin, I'd kiss you all day long."

"That foul liquid, as you call it," said Reuben. "Is what may save our lives. It won't hurt you, but it's highly toxic to some of the most terrible demons which live here. Even the smell will keep the worse of them at arm's length. Stay close to me, and it will only be the smallest of demons who will pose a risk to you, but I'll be able to fight them off. It's no coincidence that I managed to stay alive in this place for so very, very long. It was thanks to the poison my body produces."

"That's good to know," said Millie, looking away from Reuben's intense glare. "But do me a favour, would you? Blink for heaven's sake. You haven't stopped staring at me. I feel like you're looking into my soul."

"It's another evolutionary trait," said Reuben, with a hint of pride in his voice. "Like the poison. I have no eyelids, you see. I can't blink, but I'm very well adapted to seeing in the dark. I'll spot danger before it spots us, don't you worry."

Gazing into the dark at the end of the cone of light produced by the glowing gate, Millie shuddered. "You'd better put those eyes to good use then," she said. "We need to find gates which lead to other dimensions." She took the leather pouch from her pocket, feeling the vibrations of the stone before she tipped it out into her palm. As the orb made contact with her skin, it vibrated with more intensity and gave off a soft blue glow which cut into the darkness.

"That makes a fine torch," noted Reuben, stepping off the stone plinth with a heavy thump of big feet on earth. He pointed into the dark. "The exit from the cave we're in is that way. Follow me. When we get outside, the stone will tell us which way to go." He began walking, a loud cracking sound filling the cave as he took a long stride and stood on a bone, breaking it in two.

Walking alongside Reuben, Millie placed her feet carefully as she crossed the bone-strewn floor, holding the stone before her. The light offered by the stone extended a few feet into the darkness, and Millie gave a startled shriek as a dark shape crossed her path in the dim cone of light, scurrying close to the floor as it passed from left to right.

"It's okay," said Reuben. "It won't hurt you. Most creatures in this dimension won't hurt you. We're all collectively known as demons, but the majority of us don't wish to cause harm to anybody or anything."

They walked for less than a minute, dodging bones and spotting shadowy forms skulking at the edges of the cone of light the stone gave off. Then the ground ahead of them became a little less dark, and a breeze blew across Millie's face, ridding her nostrils of the awful stench she was becoming accustomed to. "I smell fresh air," she said. "And I see light."

"The cave entrance is just ahead," said Reuben, pointing a clawed finger.

Her eyes adjusting to the slight change in light, Millie could just about make out the difference between the inside of the cave and the dark world beyond. "It's night-time," she said in a low voice.

"It's always night time in this world," answered Reuben.

Stepping through the crack in the cave wall, and into a warm breeze, Millie stared into the distance, her eyes beginning to pick out details. As Reuben shuffled alongside her, she stared at the undulating terrain ahead of them. Gentle slopes rose and fell as they vanished at the horizon, and the remains of trees pointed at the sky with dead branches and broken trunks. "There was light here once?" suggested Millie, finding the sharp outline of a dead forest on a hill.

"It was before I was born into this place," said Reuben. "But yes, there was light once, or so the stories go."

Taking a few steps forward, Millie turned and looked at the cave they'd exited. She gasped as her eyes followed a wall of rock into the sky where it continued to rise until she could no longer see it in the gloom. As she looked left and right, she understood what it was. "A wall of rock?" she said.

Reuben nodded. "Yes. With no top and no ends. There is no way over it and no way around it." He looked left and right, his eyes reflecting the crimson hue which seemed to tinge the dark skies. "Which way?" he asked.

"I don't know, Reuben," said Millie. "This is your world."

"You have the stone, Millie," answered Reuben. "We're looking for gates to other dimensions which I couldn't see before coming to your world. I'm as lost as you. The stone will lead us to Henry."

Millie nodded. Holding the stone before her, she moved it left and right, focusing on the strength of the vibrations on her palm. As she moved it to the left for the third time, she began walking. "This way," she said. "The vibrations are stronger."

Hearing the heavy footsteps of Reuben following close behind, she walked alongside the sheer cliff which rose on her left, staring into shadows as she passed them, and concentrating on the instructions the magical jewel imparted through vibrations.

Suddenly, a sound which made Millie's blood run cold, echoed across the dead desert's sandy surface, bouncing off the wall of rock and reverberating in the air. She stopped in her tracks, staring into the distance as the sound rose on the air once more — a screech so terrifying it reached deep inside her and spread cold fear throughout her body. "What was that?" she whispered, turning to face Reuben.

"That is a thing that populates the nightmares of people in your world," answered her familiar, his large nostrils sniffing the air. He lifted a short arm and pointed a claw. "Look," he said.

Millie looked. Then she gasped. From a dead forest which tore at the sky with spindly fingers of broken wood, poured shadows which moved swiftly across the landscape, dust rising as they manoeuvred in unison like a herd of stampeding cattle. "They're coming this way!" she said. "What do we do?"

"We concern ourselves with the thing that is chasing them," said Reuben. "Those creatures you can see are its prey, and all they want to do is escape. They are no danger to us." He began walking, his strides longer than they had been previously. "Quickly, Millie. Use the stone. Graham and Peter assured us that other gates wouldn't be far from the gate we passed through."

Matching Reuben's speed, Millie moved quickly, vibrations not only growing stronger in her palm, but in her feet, too. "I can feel those creatures as they run," she said. "The ground is shaking."

"Just keep going," urged Reuben. "What is the stone telling you?"

Closing her hand on the stone, Millie concentrated on the series of powerful vibrations which ran through her hand. "The vibrations are becoming stronger with every step we take," she said. "We're going the right way."

Another screeching scream sounded from her right, and Millie stared in horror at the horizon. The horde of galloping creatures was still running, but had veered away from the wall of rock and was heading away from Millie and Reuben, dust rising high above the ground behind them. It was not the shadows of the prey animals which gave her the most significant cause for concern, though — it was the colossal shadow which stalked the horizon. Striding on at least a dozen arachnid legs, its circular body high above the ground, the creature screeched once more, before pausing and shifting direction quickly. "What is it?" said Millie, terror rising in her throat.

"A creature like that has no name," said Reuben. "It does not need a name. Those creatures are rare, Millie. I didn't expect to encounter one. I wouldn't have risked this journey had I known one would find us."

"It's not chasing those other creatures anymore," said Millie, as the huge beast appeared to sniff the air, its silhouette a living nightmare against the dark crimson sky. Her stomach sank as the creature turned slowly, facing the wall of rock and lifting its head to the sky as it emitted a blood-curdling screech. "Why isn't it chasing those creatures anymore, Reuben?"

"It never was," said Reuben, placing sharp claws on Millie's back as he urged her forward. "It sensed us when we passed through the gate. It's coming for us, Millie. Find those other gates, quickly, we don't have time to get back to the gate into our world. Hurry!"

Chapter 37

The ground shook violently beneath her feet, pebbles and dust bouncing with each heavy step the creature took. Sprinting alongside the towering wall of rock, Millie risked looking over her shoulder, wishing she hadn't when she saw the beast as it looked when not silhouetted in black shadow against the horizon. Not a spider, and incomparable to anything Millie had ever seen, the creature stalked the two of them on long legs which creaked as they bent.

The head which protruded from the vast, bulbous body, was placed at the end of a long, thin, multi-jointed neck. Its rows of multiple eyes were large enough to be visible at a distance, and like Reuben's, they appeared unable or unwilling to blink.

Taking gasping breaths which made her lungs sting, Millie forced her legs to work harder. "It's getting closer!" she yelled, the stone of integrity vibrating excitedly in her hand.

"Concentrate on finding the gates," ordered Reuben. "I'll be able to keep it at bay for a short while with my poison."

The ground rocked once more as the creature drew closer, and Millie almost lost her footing, regaining her balance as Reuben urged her on. "Run!" he shouted from behind her. "And don't worry about me! Just find those gates and get out of this dimension!"

She *was* running. She was running as fast as she could. She was running so fast that she could hardly breathe anymore, let alone answer Reuben. But she wasn't running to leave Reuben behind, alone with the awful creature. She was running just far enough ahead so she could pause and take control of herself once more. With control came correct use of her magic, and with correct use of her magic, she had a chance of defeating a beast even as large as the one which wanted to kill them.

Hearing the creature screeching again, Millie stopped running and turned to face it. Her heart boomed inside her chest as she saw it up close, towering over Reuben, its body quivering with muscles and its large mouth drooling thick saliva from the rubbery lips it peeled back to reveal teeth as long as Millie's arm. Slamming huge beetle-like feet into the ground surrounding Reuben, causing dust to rise in clouds, the demon made repeated attempts at getting its mouth within biting distance of her familiar, who stood helplessly below it with only the pungent stench of his toxic brown liquid to repel it, and the almost insignificant threat of the teeth he bared in warning.

Glancing in Millie's direction, and seeing she'd stopped running, Reuben shouted. "Run, Millie. If I sacrifice myself here today, I want to know it was for a good reason. Find those gates and then find Henry!"

As the creature let out another screech, like metal gears grinding under strain, Millie shook her head. "No!" she yelled, watching in horror as the creature lunged once more at Reuben, backing away as it neared the smaller demon's head and was repelled by the warning stench. "I've got this! I've got my magic!"

"Run, Millie," begged Reuben. "Please! Magic won't stop it. It's too powerful."

Ignoring her familiar, Millie forced magic from her chest, preparing herself for battle as it ran the length of her arms and tingled in her hands.

It was only then that she noticed something had changed. The jewel clenched in her fist wasn't vibrating as powerfully as it had been less than a minute ago. She stared at the orb, and then she stared around at her immediate surroundings. There was only a massive wall of rock to her right and a lifeless dark desert to her left. She gazed at the ground and saw the dust inside her footprints bouncing and rising in clouds as the creature slammed feet into the ground.

Walking slowly, Millie retraced her footsteps, hoping she was right. One metre. Then two metres. Then five, and ten, and then the orb began vibrating vigorously.

Almost standing close enough to Reuben to reach out and touch him, she screamed as the attacking demon noticed her and lifted a foot high in the air. Aiming it at her, it forced it toward the ground with a creaking of the hard shell that covered its leg, screeching once more as it attacked. As the foot travelled towards her at speed, Millie dived to the right, hoping again that she was right. She launched herself into the long-dead dry wood of the brambles which had once grown up the rock wall, but now covered its base like a rusty barbed wire fence.

Thorns cut her skin and grabbed at her clothes, but she felt no resistance from the wall of rock she should have slammed into face first.

Instead, she landed with a gentle thump in soft sand and found herself bathed in white light, which flooded from a semi-circle of dimension gates standing in the centre of the high cave.

Scrambling out of the cave again and into the brambles, Millie screamed at Reuben. "This way! There's a cave! The entrance is too small for it to fit through. Come on!"

Turning his eyes in Millie's direction, Reuben gave a cry of pain as one of his attacker's powerful limbs grazed his arm. Struggling to remain on his feet, he limped towards the bramble bushes, dark blood trickling from his wound.

"Hurry!" warned Millie, as the creature aimed a bite at Reuben, its long teeth closing with a vicious snap in the place Reuben's head had been just a second before.

Grunting in pain, and with his blood flowing faster, Reuben struggled towards the brambles, and just as Millie was beginning to think her familiar wasn't going to make it, he threw himself at the thorny stalks.

With brambles grasping at his arms and legs, Reuben lumbered through the dead plants, and then, with a final push, he was through. "You found the gates," he said staring around the cavern. "You found them."

"Get further inside the cave!" Millie yelled as Reuben stood hunched over in the low entrance, his back towards the leg which Millie spotted approaching at speed, scything through brambles, and aimed with the intent of mortally injuring or killing its target.

As Reuben took another step towards safety, a sickening crack rose above the snapping of bramble stalks, and Reuben stumbled forward, the brightness in his wide eyes fading and his mouth contorted as he cried with pain.

Thrusting the stone of integrity into her pocket, Millie grabbed her familiar's clawed hand as he fell to the ground, and pulled hard. Reuben was far too heavy for her to be able to drag, though, and as the creature slammed another leg into the brambles, its heavy foot landing a short distance away from Reuben, Millie called on her magic.

Sending a surge of energy along her arm, she closed her hand tight on Reuben's clawed hand. As another leg sped through the cave entrance, this time its trajectory suggesting it would find Reuben's exposed back, Millie pulled hard.

Her magic worked, and as if he weighed no more than a feather blowing on a breeze, Reuben rose gracefully into the air, his blood a steady stream as it fell to the sandy floor. As a leg thudded into the ground where the shape of Reuben's body made a large indentation in the sand, and a pool of blood darkened the floor, Millie dragged him to safety.

Unable to reach far enough into the cavern to hurt its prey, the creature bellowed its anger as it slammed feet into the sand, as if attempting to dig its way in.

Dropping Reuben gently to the floor, his wounds illuminated by the white glow of the dimension gates, Millie put a hand on his face, his skin thick and rubbery beneath her fingers. "Reuben," she said softly. "Reuben, can you hear me?"

A soft groan was the only response Reuben gave, and Millie became more aware that the red of his eyes was fading. As the demon at the cave entrance made another attempt to break through the small opening, Millie gathered herself internally and focused on using magic to heal her familiar. As competent as she might have been at making healing potions, she knew she was not accomplished enough to heal wounds with only her magic — especially wounds as severe as the gash that laid one side of Reuben's torso wide open, and the smaller incision which had parted the flesh of his arm.

Ignoring the thick legs which probed the cave entrance, and the snorting huffs of frustration the creature gave as it attempted to reach its prey, Millie gathered her magic. Concentrating as hard as she could on what she considered to be healing intentions, she allowed energy to trickle from her fingertips as she ran a hand over the ragged edges of Reuben's severest injury. Not responding to the treatment, the wound oozed more blood, and her familiar gave another soft groan, his voice weak.

She tried again, forcing more energy from her fingertips, and concentrating hard on knitting flesh and muscle. Encouraged, as the very edges of the wound appeared to move inward, growing healthy tissue as they attempted to close the gash in Reuben's body, Millie forced more magic into her hands.

She gave a panicked cry of frustration as the wound ceased to respond to her magic, the rift between healthy flesh widening again as the torn edges retreated. "No!" she said, trying again.

As she bent over Reuben, urging him to stay awake as she worked, she paused as she heard something. Was it a voice? She gazed around the cavern.

The creature at the entrance seemed to be giving up, its legs no longer inside the cave and its snorts and grunts becoming less frequent. The dimension gates hummed quietly as they glowed, but there was nobody else there. She shook her head. Of course she was imagining voices. She was in a high-stress situation — her familiar, no — her friend, was dying and she could do nothing to stop it.

She shouted in angry exasperation, forcing more magic into Reuben's wound, terrified when there was no response from the flesh. Then she heard it again. This time a little clearer. "Millie," came the garbled voice, as if its owner was calling to her from beneath a sheet of water. "Millie! Come to me!"

Flicking her head left and right, Millie stared around the cave. It was empty. The lights from the gates illuminated every crevice, and as far as she could see, there was nowhere else to hide. Then she studied the gates. Eight of them. In a semi-circle, and each one on a stone slab, just like the gate in Spellbinder Hall.

Each gate glowed softly, but each gate looked as normal as an entrance to another dimension *could* look. And then she saw it. A brief movement from the gate closest to her, a shadow passing across the light, a shadow in the shape of a hand. A shadow which stopped moving and spread its long fingers, pressing them against the gate like a hand pushing on a glass pane in a window.

The voice came again, this time recognisable as a

female, but no less distant. "Bring Reuben through the gate, Millie, we can save him."

Staring into the light, Millie approached the gate, beyond the hand she could make out the form of a slim female, the shape suggesting she wore a long floor scraping dress. She stepped onto the stone slab, squinting her eyes. It was like trying to see through a snowstorm. The shadowy figure refused to come into focus, moving slowly as Millie watched it. Then it spoke again, its voice still far away. "Bring him through, Millie."

Now only inches from the gate, Millie reached for the glowing circle of sparkling light and touched it gently with a single finger.

As if her finger was a pebble being dropped into a pond, ripples of light spread across the surface of the gate in response to her touch, and it was in the gap between two of those ripples that she saw into the other dimension. She stared at the woman, who smiled back at her, her brown hair long and the slight bend in her nose as pretty as ever. Through a sob which exploded from her mouth, Millie spoke quietly, as if speaking too loudly would break the spell she felt as if she were under. "Mum," she said, tears burning her eyes. "Mum. Is it really you?"

Chapter 38

The woman on the other side of the gate nodded, her voice muffled as it reached Millie. "Yes, darling. It's me. Bring Reuben through, quickly. We can help him."

"Yes, of course!" said Millie, stepping backwards off the stone slab, confusion and emotion crowding her thoughts. Her mother had said *we*. Who was the person or people with her mother, and why was she standing on the other side of a dimension gate?

Assuming from the lack of screeches and legs floundering in the entrance of the cavern, that the creature had given up and left, Millie charged her arm and hand with magic and grasped Reuben's hand in hers.

Her familiar made no sound, and his body was still, but Millie could feel the soft thump of his heart in his hand as she sent magic coursing through his body and lifted him, weightless, into the air.

Guiding him onto the stone slab, Millie moved quickly. The initial shock of seeing her mother, replaced by urgent concern for Reuben's health, she stepped quickly through the gate, closing her eyes as she tumbled through wind and noise, holding Reuben's hand tightly in hers.

When she felt firm ground beneath the soles of her trainers, she opened her eyes and blinked. She was standing in a lush green forest. If the delicate bluebells which carpeted the forest floor, and the ancient oak trees were anything to go by, she suspected she was in an English forest.

The chirping song of familiar birds cemented that notion in her mind, as did the quaint architecture of the numerous thatched roof cottages which rose from clearings in the trees.

"Quick, Millie," came a voice from her right. "Bring him here. He doesn't have much time!"

Her back to Millie, her mother hurried towards one of the cottages. The white dress she wore was made more vivid by the glorious colours of the flower garden that grew behind the white picket fence surrounding the small cottage.

Her magic still keeping Reuben floating behind her, Millie hurried after her mother. "How?" she said, as her mother opened the garden gate and beckoned Millie through.

"This is where I live now, Millie," said her mother, rushing along the pathway towards the open door. "But there's no time for that now. Esmeralda is waiting inside. She's the only witch who can save Reuben."

Esmeralda. The dead witch who Millie had heard so much about, but never imagined she would meet. Esmeralda had been the magical occupant of Windy-dune Cottage when she'd died, and Millie had moved in only a few days after her death.

She was also the witch who had first taken Reuben from The Chaos and placed him in the body of a cockatiel. It made sense that she might be able to save his life.

"This way," said her mother, entering the cottage.

Smelling herbs and the aroma of baking, Millie followed her mother, being careful not to bang Reuben into walls or doorways as she floated his large body behind her.

Leading Millie into a spacious kitchen, complete with an open fire that had a cauldron suspended above it, her mother pointed at the huge table with an elderly woman standing next to it. "Put him on there," she said. "Esmeralda will help."

Esmeralda smiled at Millie from beneath snow white hair, her wrinkles softened by the amber glow of the fire. "Don't worry," she said, as Millie allowed Reuben's body to descend gently. "He'll be alright. I can save him."

As Reuben's weight settled on the table, Millie noticed with terrible fear that he was no longer bleeding from his wounds. "The bleeding," she said. "It's stopped. Is he still alive?"

Her face calm, Esmeralda kept a reassuring smile on her lips as she placed a hand on Reuben's broad chest. She looked at Millie through electric blue eyes. "He's fine," she said. "He's strong. He just needs a little help."

As Esmeralda began muttering under her breath, her eyes closed and a blue haze surrounding the hand which lay on Reuben, Millie felt her mother's hand on hers. "You need to go, darling," she said. "You have to find Henry. Your father's memories are fading fast."

"You know about that?" asked Millie.

"Of course I know," said her mother. "I've been watching you from the shadows ever since I came back here after my last visit, and discovered I couldn't get back to you."

Millie pulled her mother gently towards her and held her in a soft hug, the smell of her hair the same as she remembered it being when she was a little girl. "You couldn't get back to me because I needed to cross into your dimension before the bridge between our worlds was built," she said, hoping the information in Victoria's letter had been accurate.

"I know," whispered her mother. "And here you are, Millie, you've crossed into the dimension in which deceased witches live. From today on, I can cross between worlds and visit you whenever I like." She pulled away from the hug and placed her hands on her daughter's shoulders. She stared into Millie's eyes. "But now you must go. Your father needs you more than I do. You'll find Henry by passing through one of the other gates in the cavern you just left behind. The stone in your pocket will lead you to him."

"Please look after Reuben," said Millie, stepping away from her mother. "He's very important to me."

"We will," said her mother. "Now go. And be careful."

With a nod, Millie turned her back and ran from the cottage. She hurried along the garden path, enveloped in the sweet fragrance of flower pollen, and sprinted towards the dimension gate which was guarded by two old oak trees, one on either side.

Bounding up the single step and onto the stone slab, Millie didn't hesitate as she leapt into the circle of light, no longer afraid of crossing between dimensions.

FINDING HERSELF BACK IN THE CAVERN, REUBEN'S blood gleaming in the sand below her, Millie took the stone of integrity from her pocket and held it before her, feeling the vibrations running the length of her arm.

She moved it towards the four gates on her left, and the vibrations decreased, when she moved it to the right, the stone danced in her palm. "This way," she said out loud as she leapt from the slab of rock.

She passed the first two gates with no noticeable increase in vibrations, but as she reached the final gate, the stone throbbed as it was drawn to its owner's magic.

Without hesitation, she pocketed the stone and hopped onto the stone slab, stepping into the glowing circle of the gate.

Keeping her eyes open, she gritted her teeth as wind rushed past her and bright light flooded her vision. And then she was through the gate, in yet another dimension. This one was warm and sunny, and the unmistakable sound of waves crashing on a beach came from somewhere to her right.

With the stone vibrating in her jean's pocket, Millie hurried towards the sound of the sea, following a narrow path, flanked on each side by thick jungle and palm trees.

The squawk of a bird came from somewhere in the trees, and Millie thought of Reuben, promising herself that if her familiar survived and made it back to the body of the cockatiel waiting for him in Spellbinder Hall, she would never threaten him with seeds again.

Sunlight peeped through the gap in the trees above her, warming her arms as she ran, and the sound of the sea became louder as the stone of integrity bounced against her thigh.

Then the path widened, and Millie was greeted by a sweeping turquoise view of the sea, birthing white-topped waves which broke gracefully on a beach formed by golden sand.

She stopped running as the stepped onto the

beach, a warm breeze stirring her hair and seabirds gliding high above the ocean. Looking left and right, Millie used a hand to shield her eyes from the sun, searching the vastness of the long beach for signs of human life.

Knowing only that Henry was in the same dimension she was in, Millie pondered her next move. Henry could be nearby, or many miles away. Reminding herself that Henry required no gate to travel across dimensions, and supposing the people he had gone there to meet, did not either, she realised that the gate was not a landmark that suggested Henry was near.

With only the vibrations of the stone in her pocket guiding her, Millie chose left over right, and began walking. The sand soft beneath her feet, making every step harder than it should be, she walked alongside the wall of trees that marked the boundary between jungle and beach, glad of the cooling shade the trees afforded her.

After what seemed like an hour, her clothes drenched with sweat, and the shade from the trees retreating into the jungle as the sun moved across the sky, she happened upon a stream trickling from the jungle and onto the beach.

Kneeling beside it, thankful for the rest, she cupped her hands and splashed handfuls of the refreshing liquid over her face, closing her eyes and licking droplets from her lips.

Ready to drink, she opened her eyes and lowered

her mouth to the surface, her tongue dry and her throat sore. It was then that she saw it, its reflection growing large in the water as it approached her from behind, a bony hand reaching for her.

Not able to prevent it from leaving her mouth, she let out a scream and flipped herself over, her legs scrambling for purchase in the wet sand as she pushed herself backwards through water. "Get away from me!" she warned, drawing magic from her chest.

The creature paused and gazed down at her, its pinched nose too high above its lipless mouth, and the grey skin which shaped its skeletal face stretched tight across high cheekbones.

It stared at her with soulless black eyes, the rest of its tall, thin frame hidden beneath a black robe, the hem of which swirled in the gentle current of the stream.

Her hand outstretched, Millie continued to push herself backwards, suddenly aware that she'd seen a face like that before, on two different occasions. Once in the fireplace of Henry Pinkerton's study, when Edna Brockett had conjured it into existence, and the second time when she had first peered into the Chaos Gate when Henry had introduced her to it.

Her eyes locking with horror onto the flap of dead flesh which peeled from the monster's hairless scalp, Millie attempted to get to her feet, her hand throbbing with magical energy as she prepared to fight off the heinous monster.

The creature shifted its head slowly from left to

right, its dark eyes never leaving Millie's face, and just as Millie was about to launch a spell in its direction, it spoke. Its clipped voice surprised Millie. It spoke confidently, in the sort of voice that Millie would have expected to hear from a student studying at Oxford University, and not emerging from the dead mouth of a denizen of hell. "Are you here for the meeting, Madam?" it said. "Because if you are, you're late. Quite late, I'm afraid. The meeting began almost five full moons ago. It will be coming to an end shortly."

Scrambling to her feet, Millie nodded, putting all fear aside. She was there to help her father, and she was in a hurry. Anyway, anything or anybody who spoke with such an educated accent surely didn't mean her harm. "I'm here to find Henry Pinkerton," she said. "It's an emergency! I need his help!"

"Ah, Mister Pinkerton, the delegate from Spellbinder Bay," said the creature, nodding its rotting head slowly. "A wonderful man. I'll take you to him; I'm sure he'll want to know about an emergency." He lifted a bony arm and pointed inland. "That way, Madam. Follow the stream. I'll be right behind you."

Reluctantly turning her back on the creature, Millie splashed through the stream, climbing from it as a path emerged on the bank-side. The sound of footsteps crunched in dry grass behind her, and her skin crawled as she imagined the creature's eyes on her back.

"I'm not bad, you know?" came a low voice from behind her.

"Pardon?" said Millie, risking a glance over her shoulder.

The creature's mouth spread wider, displaying blackened teeth and a rotting tongue. *Was it smiling*? "I said, I'm not bad, you know?" it said, as Millie faced her front again and hurried along the pathway. "I realise I look quite different from people in the dimension you call home, but I was rescued from the dimension you would know as The Chaos. I was rescued and brought here by people such as Henry Pinkerton. I work for them, now — welcoming guests such as yourself to this dimension. Do you have a name, Madam? I have a name. I was given a name when I was brought here. I was never given a name in the other dimension, but now, I am named Terrence. Do you like my name, Madam?"

"I do," said Millie. "It suits you. I'm Millie, Terrence. It's a pleasure to meet you."

"You, too, Millie," said Terrence. "You'll see a fork in the pathway just up ahead, turn left there, and we'll be at our destination in a minute or two."

Millie hurried, moving even faster when she saw the fork in the path, she turned left, away from the stream, and was happy to find herself walking on a paved trail with neatly planted flowerbeds on either side.

"The Meeting Pyramid is just ahead," said Terrence, now walking alongside Millie. "I'll announce your arrival."

"I'm not sure I need my arrival announced," said

Millie, feeling the stone vibrating harder in her pocket. "I just need to speak to Henry Pinkerton as quickly as possible."

"It will be necessary," said Terrence. "The delegates follow strict protocols. It helps them deal with the important issues of your world in as orderly a manner as possible."

"Okay," said Millie. "But I need to find Henry quickly, Terrence. Somebody I love is in grave danger."

"Turn right here, Millie," said Terrence, indicating a pathway leading into tall trees. "We've reached the Meeting Pyramid."

As Millie turned right and cleared the tall trees which had been shielding her view, she stopped walking and gasped, her eyes following the pyramid into the heavens.

"Are you alright, Millie?" asked Terrence, stopping alongside her.

"Yes," said Millie, gazing at the huge structure which rose from the jungle. The huge white stones it was constructed from sparkling in the sun, the pyramid climbed high into the sky, its peak lost in a heat haze. "It's amazing, Terrence. I've never seen anything so spectacular."

"Haven't you?" asked Terrence. "I was led to believe by the people who visit from your world there are many of these structures in your dimension. I'm told that none are in use any longer and some have crumbled, but they are widespread, especially in a region now known in your world as Egypt."

"Really?" murmured Millie.

"Pardon?" answered Terrence.

"Nothing," said Millie. "I was talking to myself."

"If you're in such a hurry, Millie," said Terrance. "You would be well advised to stop staring at the Meeting Pyramid in such a peculiar fashion, and to begin walking again." He pointed towards the tall wooden door at the base of the pyramid, its surface painted with hieroglyphics and colourful portraits of animals. "That way, please, Millie," he said. "It is through that door that you'll find Mister Pinkerton."

Chapter 39

$\mathcal{T}$errence gave the metal chain alongside the doors a firm tug, and with a loud creak, the huge doors began to open inwards, their hinges creaking under the vast weight they supported.

The corridor beyond the door was dimly lit, with only wall torches to guide the way with flame, but the sunlight which crept in as the doors opened illuminated the walls, allowing Millie to make out more hieroglyphics carved into the massive stone blocks.

Terrence began walking into the pyramid. "This way, Millie," he said.

As Millie followed him into the gloom, the hinges creaked again as the doors closed behind her, extinguishing the sunlight. Following Terrence along the corridor, Millie smelled the air. Not musty, as she might have expected, the air carried the fragrance of burning oils and herbs, reminding her of a perfume shop.

Soon, Terrence turned right and paused when he reached another large door. He looked at Millie with black eyes, the flap of skin on his scalp threatening to peel away completely as he tilted his head. "We're here," he said. "When the door opens, I'll announce you and then call you in."

Millie nodded. "I understand."

"Good," said Terrence. "The people behind this door are good people, but they have aeons of traditions to uphold. They may appear aloof and uncaring, but they mean well."

With that, Terrence pulled on a chain next to the door and adjusted his robe as the doors swung open. Giving Millie what she assumed was a smile, he strode out of the gloom of the corridor and into the vastness of the huge, well-lit hall, which Millie could see beyond.

"Ladies and Gentlemen," he shouted, looking left and right at areas of the hall hidden from Millie's view. "It is with pleasure that I announce the arrival of a visitor. A young lady named Millie. She seeks an audience with the delegate from the town she resides in — Mister Henry Pinkerton of Spellbinder Bay! Mister Pinkerton's urgent attention is required involving an incident in the other world. Millie is here to make that request." He turned to look at Millie and beckoned her with a bony hand. "Come on," he hissed.

With her mouth dry, Millie walked into the hall, immediately aware of just how much bigger it was than it had appeared from the other side of the doorway. Gazing upwards it seemed as if there was no ceiling, only the point high up where the four outside walls formed the pinnacle of the pyramid.

The smell of burning oils was stronger in the hall, and wisps of black smoke rose from tall metal stands, each with a flame burning below a concave plate, which Millie guessed were used to heat the fragrant oils.

The hall was silent, but the sort of silence which Millie associated with a library. Not completely silent, and somehow apparent that the silence was forced — as if it would be willingly broken at any moment if given a chance.

And then Millie's eyes adjusted enough to the light, and she was able to make out the sloping sides of the hall. She spun on the spot, both terrified and amazed at the sight that greeted her.

The four internal walls had been built at an angle opposite to the outside walls of the pyramid. A steep slope rose on each side of the hall, affording a surface on which to build seats. Rows and rows of people climbed high into the pyramid, until the wall changed direction again.

An empty row at the base of the wall in front of her told her that the seats were hewn from stone, and stairs wound their way between them, steep in their construction and running in diagonal lines which turned back on themselves, creating stairways that resembled the winding mountain pathways that sherpas would lead mules along.

Surprisingly relieved to find herself feeling safe next to Terrence, Millie stopped walking and stared at the faces which gazed down at her. There was no way of estimating how many sets of eyes studied her, and she decided she'd rather not know.

Suddenly, a male voice rang out, breaking the silence and bouncing off the walls. The man stood apart from the main crowd, standing beneath a canopy made from palm fronds. Wearing a white robe and carrying a staff which gave off a metallic glint, his face was hidden by a gold mask which resembled one of the Egyptian gods which Millie had learned about in school. "State your purpose, Millie of Spellbinder Bay. So we may make a decision," he shouted.

A murmur of agreement spread throughout the hall, sounding like a passing breeze, and then it was quiet again, the breeze blown out. Millie shifted her weight from one foot to the other, discomfort gnawing at her stomach. She looked at Terrence, one small part of her mind trying to recall which Egyptian god was portrayed by a dog. "What's happening? Where's Henry?" she asked.

"Up there somewhere," said Terrence. "Who knows where? The delegates change seats often so that they may speak with as many people from your world as possible. That is how they keep the paranormal population in your world safe from oppression and victimisation."

"But I just want to speak to Henry," whispered Millie, aware her voice was rising in the hall and being amplified by the shape of the room.

"You can't just speak with him," said Terrence. "You require permission, which can only be given after a vote. This is an important meeting, Millie. Every paranormal town or city in your world has sent two delegates here to represent it. In the case of your town, those people are Mister Henry Pinkerton and Mister Dickinson."

"That's right," said Millie, avoiding the million estimated eyes which gazed down at her.

"What seems to be the problem?" came the voice of the man in the dog mask again.

Anubis. That was it.

"Millie requires a moment to gather her thoughts," shouted Terrence, his voice ringing out with perfect clarity across the hall. He looked down at Millie and lowered his voice. "A meeting like this hasn't happened for four centuries, Millie. You will need to present a good reason in order for them to allow Henry to leave."

"I do have a good reason," argued Millie. "I could lose somebody I love if Henry doesn't come back with me."

"And every paranormal town and city in your world could be wiped out by humans if valuable lessons are lost by cancelling this meeting," said Terrence. He put a hand on Millie's shoulder, his skeletal fingers feeling strangely reassuring. "Go on, Millie, explain your case to them before they become tired of waiting for you to speak and ask you to leave."

If she'd thought speaking to a few parents in her classroom had been hard, talking to the acres of faces staring down at her would be a Herculean task. She made fists out of her hands and then relaxed them, and concentrated on breathing as she moistened her lips. She lifted her chin like she'd seen politicians do to make their voices go further, and took a deep breath. "Hello," she began.

"Please raise your voice!" shouted the man with the golden mask. "There are some in this hall whose ears have long ago ceased to function as intended."

His comment was met with a chorus of laughter, and Millie pressed the toe of her trainer into the hard stone floor. She took a long smell of the essential oils which moistened the air, and then spoke again. Louder, this time. "Hello! I stand here before you to ask for your permission to speak with Henry Pinkerton. Something awful has happened in the town I live in, and only Henry can prevent it from becoming worse."

"What is the awful occurrence you speak of?" asked the man.

Millie swallowed and then spoke. She began at the start, explaining about the death of Trevor Giles, telling the crowd about the false accusations the werewolves had levelled at Sergeant Spencer, and finishing with a description of what was happening to Sergeant Spencer's memories.

After a brief pause, she looked directly at the man with the staff. "That is why I need Henry to come back with me. Only he can reverse the damage that is being done to Sergeant Spencer," she said.

The man stared at her for a long moment, the mask he wore disguising his emotions. Then he gave his head a long, drawn-out shake. "I'm not convinced that your problem is serious enough to necessitate the conclusion of this meeting," he said. "I will put it to the vote, but will advise the delegates to vote against it."

Millie scanned the crowd, desperately searching for the friendly round face of Henry Pinkerton, or the tall, thin body of the headmaster. She could see neither of them, though, and wondered why not one of them had spoken up yet. "Please," she begged, sensing with dread that the man she was speaking to was not the sort of man accustomed to changing his mind. "Please don't let this happen to Sergeant Spencer. He doesn't deserve it!"

"Terrible things happen every day to people who don't deserve it," replied the man. "Why should this sergeant be any different? If this meeting is cancelled, something awful could happen to a lot more than one person. This meeting is a way for us paranormal people, from every corner and continent of the world, to swap ideas and to make sure the human population never discovers us. For if they did, we would be wiped out. Humans are vicious. They destroy things they do not understand!"

"No!" yelled Millie. "No! They do not! Not all of them! Most of them are kind, caring, and most of all, loving! Sergeant Spencer is one of those people. He gave up everything he had after rescuing a young witch from certain death! He gave up his normal life with humans to live in a paranormal town! He adopted that young witch and brought her up as his daughter! He is a wonderful man!"

"And I am regretful about the situation he is in," said the man. "And I am regretful that he will lose his memories and a girl will lose her father. But that is still only one father and one daughter whose lives will be altered. Cancelling this meeting could result in many more lives being altered. I do not consider your request to hold any merit, and I will advise that it is ignored."

Millie straightened her back and took a step forward, shrugging Terrence's hand from her shoulder as he attempted to calm her. "No!" she shouted. "It's not one daughter and a father! It's two daughters and a father! Sergeant Spencer is my father, too, but he doesn't know that. If he loses his memories he'll never be permitted to know — the concealment spell won't allow him. If you don't allow Henry to come back to Spellbinder Bay, you're preventing a daughter from ever getting to know her father, and you're preventing two daughters from becoming sisters! You'll prevent any children either of us may have from having a grandfather, and you're preventing my father from being that grandfather!" She took another step forward. "You *must* let Henry come back with me."

The man lifted his staff slowly. Then he brought it down hard, slamming it into the ground, the sound reverberating around the hall. "You do not tell me what I must or must not do," he said, his voice angry. "You made an impassioned plea, but nothing you have said will make me change my mind." He took a step forward, and stared around the hall, turning slowly to look at the people behind him. He lifted the staff again. "You all heard the young woman's request. When my staff comes down, you will vote with a show of hands. I will ask who is for and who is against the meeting being drawn to a premature ending so that Mister Pinkerton may leave. For as you all know, we are as one. We cannot continue our meeting with even one person not in attendance. It will be a long time before another meeting such as this one is arranged, and it is with that thought that I ask you to vote against the motion."

"No!" said Millie.

The man turned and stared at her, and then lifted his staff higher. Just as he was about to slam it to the ground, a voice rose from behind Millie. "Wait! I wish to speak!"

The man lowered his staff slowly. "And what would you say, Terrence? This is highly unorthodox!"

Terrence took a few steps and stood beside Millie, his hand finding her shoulder. He stared up at the man in the mask. "You are wrong, Ammon," he said. "You should allow Henry Pinkerton to return with Millie."

"Oh? I should, should I?" shouted Ammon. "You would do well to remember your place, Terrence!"

"I am well aware of my place," said Terrence. "I am aware of who I am and where I came from. I came from The Chaos, rescued by you, Ammon. You saved my life when people like me were being murdered by the evilest of demons. Three demons were killed when my life was saved, and I was brought here, almost dead. You knew that the demons would seek their revenge on my people. You knew that by saving me, others would die!"

"I would not have left you there to be killed in such a savage manner," said Ammon. "It is not my way!"

"Yet you will allow this girl's father's life to be destroyed. While only harbouring speculation that by cancelling this meeting, harm might come to you and your people. It is doubtful that such things will happen, but it is guaranteed that lives will be destroyed if Henry Pinkerton is not allowed to return to his home. You saved my life in the knowledge that others would die because of your actions, yet you refuse to help a man with only speculation that perhaps one day, others might die."

Terrance span slowly on the spot, looking at everybody in the room. "You all heard of the sacrifices Millie told us her father had made. He sacrificed the life he knew to help a young witch. To help one of you. I would ask that you vote to allow this man to be saved. I would ask that you vote to allow this man to have a relationship with his family, but most of all, I would ask that you vote to save this man because it is the right thing to do."

"Enough!" yelled Ammon, the sharp crack of metal bouncing off the walls as he slammed his staff into the ground. "Now we will vote. Those who are against Henry Pinkerton being permitted to leave, raise your hand."

In total silence, everybody in the room remained motionless, and Millie's heart skipped a beat. Only one person raised an arm, and that woman was one of the officials seated next to Ammon.

Ammon slammed his staff to the ground once more. "I will ask again!" he shouted. "But remember my advice — you would all do well to take it! Raise your hand if you are against Henry Pinkerton being allowed to return to his home."

The only sound in the vast hall was a distant cough, and Ammon became visibly irritated, passing his staff from hand to hand. He waited for half a minute and then spoke in a defeated tone. "Those of you who wish to allow Henry permission to leave, raise your arm."

The hall erupted with the sound of rustling clothing and the jangle of jewellery, as arms were thrust above heads.

Sinking into his seat, Ammon raised his staff.

"The vote has been taken. Henry Pinkerton may leave. This meeting is over."

Millie turned to Terrence and gripped him in a fierce hug. "Thank you," she said.

Remaining limp in her arms, Terrence made a low sound in his throat. "Thank *you*," he said. "Nobody has hugged me in a very long time." His hands finding Millie's back, he squeezed her gently. "It was not only the words I spoke which swayed the opinion of the crowd," he said, in a low voice. "Nobody respects Ammon. They used to, but he has become authoritarian in his outlook. This meeting, for instance, is deemed a waste of time by the majority of the community. The delegates will be happy it is cancelled. They just required a push in the right direction."

"Thank you for giving them that push, Terrence," said Millie, pulling away from the hug, aware that the hum of excited conversation had replaced the silence in the hall.

"It was my pleasure, Millie," he said. He lifted a hand and pointed a long finger. "Mister Pinkerton is here."

Millie gave an enormous sigh of relief as she turned to face Henry, smiling at the short man as he hurried across the stone floor towards her, his round spectacles threatening to slip off his nose as he ran. "Henry!" she said. "I'm so happy to see you!"

"I'm sorry to hear what has happened at home," said Henry, taking Millie's hand. "And I'm sorry I couldn't come down here as soon as you entered the hall, but the rules forbade it."

"You're here now," said Millie. "That's all that matters. Will you go back to Spellbinder Hall and help Sergeant Spencer?"

"Of course I will," said Henry, smiling at her. "And we will get to the bottom of the murder you spoke of, but I have a question for you first, Millie. Do you remember when I first came to visit you in that squalid flat of yours in London, and I used magic to open the gate which had rusted closed?"

"Of course I remember," said Millie. "I had no idea how you'd done it."

"Well now it's my turn to ask you how you managed to pass through a gate, Millie," said Henry. "How did you get here?"

"Graham and Peter discovered that if I stepped into The Chaos, I would be able to step back through the gate safely because of my magic," explained Millie. "They surmised that I'd be able to find you by passing through other gates when I got to the chaos. They were right." She reached into her pocket and withdrew the stone of integrity and its pouch. She handed the vibrating jewel to Henry. "This helped, too. It showed me the way."

Taking the stone and placing it in the pouch, Henry looked Millie up and down. "Forgive me for saying this, Miss Thorn, but you look like you've been in the wars. Your clothes are wet and torn, and I suspect the patch of red on your shirt is blood. Are you alright?"

"I'm okay," said Millie. "The blood is not mine. It's Reuben's. He came with me and was injured by a demon. He's being taken care of, though. By my mother and Esmeralda."

"By your mother and Esmeralda?" said Henry. "How can that be poss —" He stopped speaking, and shook his head. "No. That can wait. There are more important things to focus on." He offered Millie an arm. "Take hold of my sleeve. We'll be back at Spellbinder Hall in a jiffy."

"You can take me with you?" asked Millie. "What about the headmaster? Shouldn't you be taking him back with you? I can travel through dimension gates."

"Of course I can take you with me," said Henry. "I've told Mister Dickinson he's to wait here. I can only take one person at a time, so I will come back for him when I've helped Sergeant Spencer. I won't hear of you placing another foot in The Chaos, in order to travel home through gates, Miss Thorn. It's dangerous."

"Yes," said Millie. "It is."

As she grasped a piece of Henry's red suit jacket, the small man gave her a warm smile. "I was proud to hear you announce to this hall full of people that Sergeant Spencer is your father, Millie. Am I to suppose that everybody back in Spellbinder Bay knows, too, or is it still a secret which I should not mention?"

"It's still a secret," Millie said. "But as soon as you've helped Sergeant Spencer, I'm going to tell him, and then I'm going to tell everyone else."

"Then we should hurry," said Henry. "I've been looking forward to the day on which you gave him the news, and it seems that day is almost here!" He nodded his head at Terrence. "That was a heart-warming speech you gave. Thank you."

"You're welcome," said Trevor, a glint in his black eyes indicating a hint of pride. "You're both welcome."

Henry nodded. He took his glasses off and slipped them into his pocket. "Hold on, Millie. The journey will be brief and disorienting."

Grasping Henry's sleeve a little tighter, Millie smiled at Terrence. "I'm ready," she said.

Chapter 40

*A*lmost as soon as Henry had instructed her to hold on, Millie felt her feet leave solid ground. A huge pressure built in her chest, and just as the pressure turned to pain, her feet were on solid ground again, and her chest felt normal.

"My word!" came a voice from her left. "You did frighten me! I wish you would give me a warning when you're going to pop into existence like that! It's no good for my heart!"

"Your heart is in splendid health, Mrs Brockett," said Henry. "Which is more than I can say for poor Sergeant Spencer. He doesn't appear to be at all well."

"He's not," said Edna. She took Millie's hand in hers, giving it an affectionate squeeze. "I am glad to see you back, Millie," she said. "We thought perhaps the worst had happened to you. Since you've been gone, though, the poor sergeant has worsened, and

Judith is in an awful state. I've given her something that will help her sleep, but I must say, I'm ever so relieved that you have both returned." She smiled at Henry. "Please save him. I want everything to get back to normal as soon as possible."

Henry took his glasses from his pocket and placed them on his face. "I'll see what I can do, Mrs Brockett. Millie has thoroughly explained the events which led up to this moment. It seems that the concealment spell has been allowed to run havoc in the poor man's mind."

"You can help him, though?" said Millie.

"I'll do my best," said Henry, approaching the bed. "But I'm going to need some peace and quiet. You two are more than welcome to stay, but please lock the door, Mrs Brockett. I don't want any disturbances. The work I have to do requires concentration."

"The others are busy," said Edna. "Timothy is sitting with Judith, and Fredrick and George are still waiting for you at the gate, Millie. We didn't expect you to come back with Henry."

"I've left the headmaster behind," said Henry, rolling up his sleeves and sitting on the edge of the bed. "I'll return for him at a later date."

"Reuben is still in there, Edna," said Millie. "He's injured, but somebody is caring for him. I'm glad that Fredrick and George are waiting at the gate. I wouldn't want Reuben to return with only the scientists there to greet him. He's been through a lot."

"I'm sure Reuben will be fine, my dear," said Edna. "He's a fighter."

"You have no idea," said Millie. "He was willing to sacrifice himself for me. He's a hero."

"Then he'll be treated as such when he returns," said Edna, striding purposefully to the door, pulling it closed, and turning the key in the lock. "Nobody can get in, Henry. You can begin."

Still sitting on the bed, Henry took one of Sergeant Spencer's large hands in his. He closed his eyes and began speaking quietly, as if reciting a prayer in a language Millie couldn't understand.

As Henry spoke, Sergeant Spencer's body suddenly jolted, as if Henry's hand was a conductor of electricity. Henry spoke louder, and the policeman jolted again, this time more violently, his back arching and his hands making trembling fists.

"Is he okay?" asked Millie, stepping towards the bed.

Edna pulled her back with a gentle hand on her shoulder. "Let Henry work," she said. "The spell has wormed its way deep into the sergeant's mind. Henry must follow it."

Sergeant Spencer's back arched again, and he made a groaning sound as his legs kicked upward.

Releasing the sergeant's hand, which dropped limply to the quilt, Henry stood up. He bent over the policeman and put his hand on his forehead, murmuring more strange words under his breath.

Then, with a gasp and a shake of his head, the

policeman woke up. He opened his eyes and stared around the room.

Millie rushed to the bed and put a hand on his arm, relief rushing through her like a drug. "Are you okay? How do you feel?"

Sergeant Spencer gazed around the room, his salt and pepper fringe slick with perspiration. "Judith!" he shouted. "Where's Judith?"

"How much do you remember of what has happened, Sergeant Spencer?" asked Henry.

"Everything," said the policeman. "I think." He tried to prop himself up on his elbows but fell back to the bed. "Where's Judith? Is she alright?"

"Yes," said Edna. "She was resting after the moon-pool had healed her wounds, and during that time, the concealment spell put you into magical stasis. Judith became very concerned, so we thought it best that she rest a little longer. I gave her a little something to help her relax."

"I want to see her," said Sergeant Spencer. He blinked a few times and lifted a hand to his head, rubbing it. His lips visibly dry, he gave a thin smile. "Millie," he said. "Are you alright? You saved us from the wolves. You and George saved us. Thank you."

"You don't need to say thank you," said Millie, her hand still on his arm.

Sergeant Spencer smiled and looked past Millie. "Henry, you're here. Have I been asleep for that long? The last I remember, you weren't due back for a couple of days."

"Millie and Reuben ventured through the chaos gate," said Edna. "They crossed dimensions to find Henry and bring him back."

"You did?" said Sergeant Spencer, gazing at Millie through eyes filled with pain. "Thank you." Suddenly, he gave a shout, startling Millie. He lifted both hands to his head and held them against his face. "My head," he mumbled. "It hurts."

Pulling Millie aside, Henry put his hand on the policeman and closed his eyes for a few seconds. "This is not good," he said.

"What's wrong?" asked Millie. "What's wrong with him, Henry?"

"The concealment spell is simple, yet complicated," said Henry. "The job it does — keeping our community hidden from the outside world, is simple, how it achieves that task, is complicated. What's happening to the sergeant is one of those complications."

"What is it that's happening to me?" moaned Sergeant Spencer. "It hurts."

Henry waved a hand across the policeman's face and muttered a few words. Almost instantly, Sergeant Spencer dropped his hands from his head. "Thank you, Henry. The pain has stopped."

"Unfortunately, that's all that has happened," said Henry. "I cast a pain relieving spell on you, Sergeant Spencer. It is powerful and will last, but complicated things are happening in your mind that I can't stop.

Not until I can prove that you didn't kill Trevor Giles."

"But he didn't kill Trevor Giles," said Millie.

"Of course he didn't," replied Henry. "I know that. I don't think he killed Trevor Giles or knows anything about what happened to him. Most people in Spellbinder Bay would agree with me, but those werewolves which Fredrick locked away in the dungeons disagree. They've made their thoughts known to the magic which powers the concealment spell. The magic is doing what it's supposed to do — protect the paranormal community from humans. The magic is not conscious in the way we understand that word, it works on instinct, and instinct is forcing it to treat Sergeant Spencer as if he's guilty of a crime against us as a community. We must prove his innocence in order to save him."

"But you're the human face of the magic in Spellbinder Hall!" said Millie. "You're the living embodiment of the magic, its conscience. You are the magic, that's how it's been explained to me! Why can't you stop the concealment spell working on him?"

"I'm a part of the magic, yes," said Henry. "But I have as much control over the magic as you have over your body, Millie."

"Total control!" said Millie. "So do something to stop it."

"If I ask you to move an arm, or jump on the spot, or hold your breath, you'll do it," said Henry. "You have that control over your body. If I ask you to stop your heart beating, you won't be able to, and for a good reason. That's the control I have over the magic, Millie. I can affect certain things, but even I can't get to the heart of the matter. I can't do anything to change the way the heart of the magic beats. We must give it what it wants — proof that Sergeant Spencer is not a threat to us."

"How do we do that?" asked Millie. "You can't use the stone of integrity on him to prove his innocence; he's a human."

"No," said Henry. "I can't, but I can use it on paranormal people. When you told your story to Ammon and the assembled delegates, you mentioned suspects from the paranormal world. Bring them to me, and I will use the stone on them. If one of them is guilty, Sergeant Spencer will become innocent by proxy, and all of our problems will be solved."

"That might be tricky," said Millie. "Before I passed through the chaos gate, I made contact with a ghost who is new to this school," she said. "I've found out who she is and I believe she was about to confess to murdering Trevor Giles before she was startled by Reuben, and left in a hurry. I'm not sure how to find her again, and I'm not sure if she'll allow you to use the stone on her. Or if it will even work on a ghost."

"Oh, it will work," said Henry. "But a ghost committing murder? I'm not sure I've ever heard of such an accusation being made. Who is this ghost, Miss Thorn, and how do you suppose she killed Trevor Giles? You said he was poisoned."

"Florence said she saw the ghost flitting between the chemistry lab and my cookery classroom," said Millie. "Herbs found in Timothy's lab were found in the poison, and as for the magic which Edna found in the poison, the ghost was a halfling when she was alive. She had a little magic which she might have been able to use."

"Half witch and half werewolf?" said Henry. "They are rare. Who is this ghost, Miss Thorn?"

"It's the ghost of Miss Timkins," said Millie.

"Miss Timkins the cookery teacher?" said Henry. "The poor soul who turned herself into a soufflé and was accidentally placed in an oven?"

"Yes," said Millie. "But before I went into the chaos, she wrote something on the blackboard. She told me that Trevor Giles had put her in the oven, and that it hadn't been an accident. She had a reason for wanting Trevor dead, Henry."

"Of course it was an accident," said Henry. "Mister Dickinson witnessed it. He was quite clear as to what had happened. Trevor Giles had no idea that the soufflé he was putting in the oven happened to be his teacher."

Suddenly, the temperature in the room dropped, and the hairs on Millie's arms stood on end. A voice spoke from behind her, and she turned quickly, stepping backwards as a tall robed figure stared down at her. "It was no accident," it said. "But I did not kill Trevor Giles."

Chapter 41

"You can speak?" said Millie.

The ghost nodded. "My abilities as a ghost fully developed not long after I had communicated with you in your classroom. Now I'm complete, and I have connected with an old friend."

Millie stepped back even further as another ghost stepped through the wall and stood alongside Miss Timkins. "I told you that the robed ghost had not killed Mister Giles," said Florence. "I informed you that I had not taken my eyes off the ghost for the entirety of the school fete. She made no poisons in the chemistry laboratory or tampered with any food, and she did not follow Sergeant Spencer to the police station after he had arrested Mister Giles."

"Then we must be certain of that," said Henry. "Sergeant Spencer's very existence is at risk if we do not solve Trevor Giles's murder quickly." He approached the robed figure and removed the stone of integrity from his pocket. "Would you mind holding out your hand, Miss Timkins? As your abilities are fully formed, I assume you have the power to interact with solid objects."

"No," said Miss Timkins. "I won't. Not until you've heard my story. The story of what happened to me thirty years ago."

"Which I can verify," said Florence. "You won't need the stone to prove she is speaking the truth."

"How can you verify her story, Florence?" asked Millie. "You weren't even aware of who the ghost was until now."

"Robes protect a ghosts identity from other ghosts, too," said Florence. "But now that Miss Timkins has approached me and made her identity known, I can verify her story, because I was there when it happened," she said. "I was watching as she was put in the oven, but for reasons which will soon become apparent, I was never able to speak of what I saw. I will speak today, though."

Henry pocketed the stone and nodded. "Then tell us your story, Miss Timkins," he said. "And do not mistake my haste for discourtesy. I am relieved to see you after all these years, but discovering the truth about Trevor's murder is the most important task at hand if I am to save Sergeant Spencer's memories."

"I understand," said Miss Timkins, her hood hanging low. "I'll tell it with urgency." She rose a few inches above the ground, and her robes flickered briefly as she glided across the room and took up a position next to the window. Then she began talking. "It was a normal day," she said. "I was a little excited because it was the day before the big announcement."

"I remember," said Henry. "I was about to announce who was to be the new headteacher after the old one had left. It was between yourself and Mister Dickinson, and if it's any consolation, I was going to name you as headmistress, Miss Timkins."

"I know," said Miss Timkins. "Most people knew. I had more experience, and the general feeling throughout the school was that I would be given the position. I was very excited. I was to be on the Board of Governors!"

"Yes," said Henry. "Poor Mister Dickinson was quite distraught after what happened to you. He always said it was you who had deserved the job. He promised to always uphold your values of fairness and kindness in all of his dealings with the pupils. I think he's done that well, Miss Timkins. I think he's honoured your memory."

"Yet his first job as headmaster was to close down the cookery classroom," said Miss Timkins.

"A terrible tragedy had occurred in there," said Henry. "It was the right thing to do."

"The truth is that he wanted my memory wiped from Spellbinder Hall," said Miss Timkins.

"Pardon?" said Henry. "What do you mean by that?"

"As I was saying," said the tall ghost. "It was a normal day. I was excited about possibly becoming the new headteacher, and the sun was shining outside. I was happy. I was teaching the children how to make soufflés when there was a knock on the door. It was Mister Dickinson."

"Go on," said Henry, as Miss Timkins paused.

"I called him in, and he told me that he'd like a word with me. He said he'd wait until I'd finished what I was doing, and then it happened," said Miss Timkins.

"What happened?" asked Edna.

"One moment I was explaining how to pour a soufflé mix into a baking dish," said Miss Timkins. "And the next moment I felt a terrible pain, and I was that soufflé mix."

"Yes," said Henry. "You'd been suffering from witch dementia, had you not? I believe it's quite prevalent in the halfling community. All that suppressed magic can sometimes cause problems. You accidentally cast the spell which transformed you into a soufflé mix."

"No," said Miss Timkins. "That's not what happened. Yes, I had some problems with my magic. All halflings do. The wolf and the witch both wish to be released, and sometimes one manages to make itself known, but that is not what happened on that day. It was Mister Dickinson. He cast the spell which turned me into that soufflé."

Edna gasped, and Millie put a hand to her mouth.

"Mister Dickinson?" said Henry, his face white.

He removed his glasses and rubbed his eyes. "Are you sure? Why would he do such a thing?"

"It seems that being headmaster was very important to him," said Miss Timkins. "So important that he would commit the most terrible crimes to guarantee himself the position."

"He wanted the position that badly?" said Henry.

"Yes, and after he cast the spell, I could still see and hear," said Miss Timkins. "It was the most awful experience. My vision was blurred, and my hearing was muffled, but I saw him cast another spell, this time over the children, and then he spoke to Trevor Giles. He chose Trevor because he was easily manipulated, it wouldn't take much magic to persuade him to place me in the oven. And he did it. He laughed while he did it. He seemed to enjoy doing it, but I know he was under a spell. And then, as the heat began to hurt and I knew my days were ended, I saw Florence appear. I heard her shout, and then I became aware that Mister Dickinson had cast another spell."

"He prevented me from moving or making a sound," said Florence. "It was quite awful. I was forced to watch as he used magic to manipulate the children's minds. Telling them that they would remember the incident as an accident, that they would never quite be able to remember exactly what had happened, but that they would have recollections that it had been Trevor who had put Miss Timkins in the oven."

"And then," said Miss Timkins. "As the pain

became too great to bear, and I was about to let myself go, the classroom door opened, and there was my most dearest of friends, Cuthbert Campion. The children called him Mister Mop because of the mass of curls on his head, and they teased us about being in love with one another, but we weren't. Not in that way. He was married, and I loved him as a friend. He was the only fellow halfling I had ever met, so we had much in common, and a solid bond between us. So strong was the bond, that as the pain grew, my energy reached out to him — like an identical twin reaches out to a sibling. As the witch part of me died, my energy left my body, and found Cuthbert, telling him what was happening to me. My last memory is of Cuthbert storming into the classroom, and the last sound I heard was him shouting. 'She's burning! Get her out!' And then, everything went black."

"My goodness," said Henry, lowering himself onto the bed, next to Sergeant Spencer. "My goodness."

"Then he ruined another life," said Florence. "The children were still under the influence of magic, and I was immobilised. Mister Dickinson appeared shocked when Cuthbert stormed into the classroom, and cast a hasty spell at him. It only took a few seconds before Cuthbert stopped shouting, looked a little confused, and sat down. He asked Mister Dickinson what was happening, and Mister Dickinson simply told him to go back to his classroom and forget everything he'd seen. Cuthbert did as he was told. It was two weeks later before the spell finished its work, and Cuthbert was left with muddled memories and no job."

"But Cuthbert had an accident," said Henry. "With a headache potion, he'd made. It affected us deeply, especially after what had recently happened to Miss Timkins. Mister Dickinson suggested we took his job from him for the safety of the children and that we compensated him handsomely, so he would never be without. Which we did."

"That is what Mister Dickinson told you," said Florence. "He made up the story about the headache potion. It was true that he'd made a potion, but that wasn't the cause of his confusion. It was the short-circuiting of his mind, which Mister Dickinson's evil spell had caused."

"The awful man!" said Henry, his face reddening. "But what about you, Florence? Why did you never speak of this? Why has this remained a secret for all these years?"

"Mister Dickinson was always very powerful," said Florence. "Very powerful indeed, was he not?"

"Yes," said Henry. "He is a formidable man."

"And it was with little effort that he was able to prevent me speaking about what I had witnessed," said Florence. "After Cuthbert had vacated the class-room, in a daze, Mister Dickinson cast a spell which secured my silence. If I were ever to utter a word to anybody about what had happened, I would be dragged from this world and back to the darkness of the world of wandering spirits. I did, of course, consider sacrificing myself so that I might have brought Mister Dickinson to justice, but that seemed foolish. He had done what he'd done, I couldn't change that, and I knew that one day his spell over me would weaken, and he would be exposed. That day has come. His spell is weak."

"It's weakened because he's no longer in this dimension," said Millie.

"Yes," said Florence. "And it will remain weak until he returns."

"If what you have told me is true," said Henry. "He will not be returning. He cannot travel here without my help, and I will not help him. I will contact Ammon and ask that Mister Dickinson be kept a prisoner. He will stand trial in time."

"Why now, Miss Timkins?" asked Millie. "Why did you wait all these years until you came back as a ghost, and then only when Trevor Giles arrived at the school?"

"I've been trying, Miss Thorn," said Miss Timkins. "Oh, I've been trying. As you know, witches cannot become ghosts, their energy leaves them and resides in a different dimension, but they are not ghosts."

"Yes," said Millie. "I know."

"Because I am a halfling," said Miss Timkins. "I believe that Mister Dickinson was under the impression that the same rules applied to me. I think he believed that I could never return as a ghost. But he was wrong. It took a long time. So long, in fact, that when I became aware of a consciousness again, and was able to peer from the shadows, the school had changed drastically. Teachers who weren't vampires had aged, and none of the children I remembered remained. It was a strange experience, like being in a dream, but with time I was able to bring myself closer to this world again, as if I was pushing through a barrier, but unable to break through. And then, just the other day as I watched you preparing to speak to the parents at the school open day, Millie, it happened."

"You were there the whole time?" asked Millie.

"I've been present since you began teaching here at Spellbinder Hall, Millie," said Miss Timkins. "I've enjoyed watching you. I was never able to make myself known to you, though. However hard I tried."

"Then why on the day of the fete?" asked Millie. "What was different?"

"I was so close to being able to make myself known," said Miss Timkins. "But I could never quite find the energy to do so, and then, during your presentation to the parents, I glanced out of the window and saw him climbing out of a taxi cab -- Trevor Giles. Much older of course, but unmistakable in his appearance. Seeing him after all that time, shocked me, and suddenly, I knew I could make myself seen. It was as if the shock was the fuel I'd required to make that last push. I stood quietly in that room watching you all as you watched me. I didn't know what to do. I was as scared as you were."

"And then you tried to attack Trevor," said Millie. "When he barged into the classroom."

"No," said Miss Timkins. "I was angry when I saw him. Very angry, but I had long accepted that Trevor Giles had put me into the oven while under the influence of magic. But when that door slammed open, and he barged into the room, it was like being in the oven again with the door being pushed shut, trapping me, with Trevor's laughing face on the other side of the glass. I panicked and rushed for the doorway. Trevor was in my path, and I felt him as I pushed through him. I felt his pain, and I felt his misery, and I felt his sorrow, and then I was gone. I didn't kill Trevor Giles. I wanted no revenge for what he had done, and anyway, the feelings of his which I experienced when I passed through his body, make me think his life was ruined by what Mister Dickinson had made him do. All those children will have muddled memories about what happened, but imagine what Trevor's memories would have consisted of? The knowledge that he'd put me into that oven."

"I'm so sorry," said Henry. "I'm so, so sorry. I never knew."

"You couldn't have known," said Florence. "And then Mister Dickinson got rid of the last chink in his armour. He persuaded you to expel Trevor for what he'd done to Miss Timkins, even though you had accepted Trevor's explanation that is was an accident, that he didn't know what he was doing."

"Yes," said Henry. "I expelled him with a heavy

heart, but I insisted he was not expelled for what I thought had been an accident. I instead, insisted he was expelled for the bullying he'd always been guilty of. He'd always had a nasty streak, and to be completely honest, a child like him shouldn't have been a pupil here at the hall. So yes, I expelled him and warned him never to step foot on Spellbinder Hall grounds again."

"An instruction he followed until he knew you were away on business," said Edna.

Henry frowned. "And look where the decision to visit the school got him. He's dead."

"Yes," said Millie, "and we need to find out who killed him." She looked at Sergeant Spencer and gave him a reassuring smile. "Before somebody else's life is ruined."

"Then go and bring me some suspects, Miss Thorn," said Henry. "The stone of integrity will demand the truth from them, and then maybe we will be able to prove Sergeant Spencer's innocence."

"Wait!" said Sergeant Spencer. He propped himself up in the bed and stared at Millie. "You can read minds."

"Yes," she said, "but the stone of integrity is far more accurate. Sometimes it's hard to see what people are thinking."

"No!" said Sergeant Spencer. "That's not what I mean. I mean you could read my mind. You could ask me if I killed Trevor, then read my mind, and then Henry could use the stone on you. He can ask you if my answer is true or not. If the stone says you're telling the truth, then perhaps the concealment spell will accept my innocence?"

"Yes!" said Henry. "That may work! We may have found a way of saving Sergeant Spencer!"

"Please excuse me," said Miss Timkins. "I'll leave you to your important work. I have something equally important to do. I hope you won't mind me using your classroom, Miss Thorn. I need to make a soufflé."

Millie smiled as she shook her head. "Of course I don't mind," she said. "You already made one soufflé, though. I left it in the classroom. I turned the oven off to stop it from burning."

"That soufflé won't do the job," said Miss Timkins. "That was a practice recipe. My halfling magic was still weak after becoming a ghost, but since telling you all my story, I feel invigorated. I feel as if I have enough magic within me to be able to add enough to the soufflé. The soufflé which will cure Cuthbert."

"Cure Cuthbert?" asked Millie, sure that the shadow beneath Miss Timkins's hood was beginning to glow. "You can do that?"

"Of course," said Miss Timkins. "We are both halflings. When I saw him with you and his daughter in your classroom, Miss Thorn, my heart broke. Not only had he aged, and his wonderful head of hair been lost to time, but hearing him speak in such confused terms broke my heart. Cuthbert was a clever, articulate man — not a man who struggled to make himself understood. I am certain that if I donate some of my magic to Cuthbert, his mind will heal. And what better way to deliver the medicine which will help him, than by placing it in what was once his favourite food."

"What a wonderful idea," said Millie, now absolutely sure that something was happening beneath Miss Timkins's hood.

"I must give credit for the idea to one of the young ladies in your class," said Miss Timkins. "Emma Taylor. I've been watching you teach your class for a long time, and young Emma always adds her mother's medicine to the cakes she bakes for her. I hear her talking to herself as she does it, happy that it will help mend her mother's mind. I want to do the same for Cuthbert."

"Medicine?" said Millie. "What medicine does Emma add to the cakes she cooks?"

Miss Timkins didn't answer, though, and Millie stepped away from her as a flash of light erupted from beneath her hood. "What's happening?" she said, raising an arm to shield her eyes.

"A transformation," said Florence. "She's unburdened herself of the awful tale of her death, so now she may appear as she was before she died."

A breeze swept through the room, ruffling papers on a shelf and making the leaves of a potted plant dance. And then, the robe Miss Timkins wore dropped to her feet and dissolved in a cloud of black smoke and soot.

"The poor woman," said Millie, staring in horror at the scars which covered every centimetre of her tall, slender frame.

"Don't be sad for her," said Florence. "Watch."

As Millie watched, the burned skin which stretched over Miss Timkins's hairless head began to shift, and tiny blonde hairs grew slowly, erupting suddenly into a waterfall of gold which flowed over her shoulders and framed the pretty face which formed, as scars fell away like the scales of a fish beneath a fishmonger's knife.

More scars fell, and as they did, the black robe she'd been wearing was replaced by a bright flowery dress, covered by an apron emblazoned with the Spellbinder Hall coat of arms. And then, the transformation was complete, and Miss Timkins stood proudly tall, her elegant neck long, and her eyes a bright seascape blue.

"Miss Timkins," said Millie. "You're beautiful."

Miss Timkins's shapely lips formed a smile, and she gazed happily at Millie. "Call me Charlotte, please. Now, if you'll excuse me, I have a soufflé to prepare."

With that, she strode gracefully past Edna and Henry, and straight through the door, leaving a small cloud of what Millie suspected was flour hanging in the air behind her.

Chapter 42

"Are you ready, Millie?" asked Henry, the stone of integrity in his hand.

Millie nodded, and smiled at Sergeant Spencer. "Don't worry," she said. "It won't hurt."

"I'm sure it won't," he replied, sitting up on the bed and swinging his legs over the side.

"You should remain lying down," said Edna, placing her hand on his arm.

"No," said the policeman. "I want to be in this position so that when my innocence is proved, I can stand up, run from this room, and find Judith."

"We should begin," said Henry. "The concealment spell is working quickly. If this doesn't work we still have to use the stone on the suspects you spoke about, Millie." He looked at Sergeant Spencer. "Are you ready?"

The policeman nodded.

"Good," said Henry. He cleared his throat. "Sergeant Spencer, did you or did you not murder Trevor Giles, and if you did not, do you know who did?"

Sergeant Spencer spoke loudly and clearly. "No. I did not murder Trevor Giles, and I do not know who did."

"Thank you," said Henry. He smiled at Millie. "Go on. Read his mind, you only need to verify the truthfulness of his answer, and then I can use the stone on you."

Millie stood directly in front of Sergeant Spencer and gathered her energy. Reading people's minds was always an unnerving prospect, but the idea of rummaging through the mind of the man who was her father, filled her with anxiety.

She loved him. She supposed she loved him like any girl would love her father, the difference being that her love for him was unreciprocated. It could be no other way — he didn't know he was Millie's father.

Closing her eyes, Millie concentrated, waiting for the familiar fuzziness which clouded her mind whenever she used her ability. When the fuzziness came, she imagined a spiral of energy wending its way through the space between herself and her father, the spiral twisting and turning as it wormed its way towards her father's head, and more importantly, what was contained within it.

She knew Sergeant Spencer would feel nothing, the person whose mind she was reading never did, but Millie waited with trepidation for the electric pulse of energy which always shocked her brain at the moment her mind connected with somebody else's.

Willing the finger of energy to cross the gap between her mind and Sergeant Spencer's, Millie gave a low gasp as her energy brushed the energy of her father. Electric pain forced her to screw her eyes tighter closed, and she formed fists of her hands, her long fingernails hurting her palms.

Something was different, Millie realised, as pain spread across her forehead, raking her whole head with icy fingers. A pressure built within her skull which made her wince, and her breathing became shallower. Not wanting to show her discomfort, she concentrated on taming the pain, willing her mind's eye to ignore it — to focus instead on what was on the other end of the strand of energy, the mind of her father.

She forced more energy along the invisible conduit, but the pain blossomed in her head, making her gasp. She lifted a hand to her head and looked at Henry. "I can't," she said. "I can't do it. It's as if there's a barrier between us."

Henry frowned, and then a strange expression spread across his face. He turned to Edna. "Go and check on Judith, please," he said.

"But I might be needed here," Edna protested.

"Edna, please go and check on Judith," Henry repeated. "And Florence, perhaps you could go and check on your new friend?"

Dropping into a shallow curtsy, Florence nodded.

"Of course," she said. "You need not ask me twice, like Edna forced you to. Perhaps you could remember that when you're choosing the new headteacher. I'm assuming there will be a new one; now Mister Dickinson has been exposed."

"I've already made a decision about that," said Henry. "And I've decided it's going to be the person who should have been given the job three decades ago. Now, would you two ladies be kind enough to leave, please?"

"Of course," said Edna, a scowl on her face. She kept her chin high as she walked to the door, then unlocked it and slammed it behind her as she left.

Simply turning away from Henry, Florence glided slowly across the room and vanished through the wall adorned with oil portraits of people Millie didn't know.

"Is everything alright?" asked Sergeant Spencer. "Why can't you read my mind, Millie?" He looked at Henry. "It's the spell, isn't it? It's done too much damage to my mind. Is that why you asked the others to leave — so you could break the news to me?"

"No," said Henry. "I asked them to leave because I think Millie needs some privacy to be able to do her work. I'll be leaving too, Sergeant. You two need some time alone." He gave Millie a look which bored into her soul. "You know why you can't read his mind, Miss Thorn. There is a barrier between you two that only you can bring down. I'm sure you understand me." He put the stone of integrity in his pocket. "Come for me when you're ready, Miss Thorn."

When the door closed behind Henry, Sergeant Spencer stared at Millie, his eyes concerned. "What is it, Millie?" he asked.

Closing her eyes momentarily, Millie took a deep breath and looked into Sergeant Spencer's face, painfully aware that her face was lit up with emotion.

She dropped her eyes as Sergeant Spencer stared back at her, her heart pounding against her chest wall, drumming out an urgent beat which added to the rising fear which clawed at her insides. She knew what Henry had said was right. Her mind wouldn't connect with Sergeant Spencer's until he knew the secret which acted as an impenetrable wall between them. She'd known her power had its limitations, and now she was confronted with the largest of them.

She couldn't read Sergeant Spencer's mind unless he knew she was his daughter. Maybe it was because she was being so dishonest with him, or perhaps it was Millie herself jeopardising her own ability, forcing herself into having to tell him the truth. Whatever the reason, be it magical or personal, Millie knew that the only key that fitted the lock of the door which kept Sergeant Spencer's thoughts safe, was honesty. She took a deep breath, her legs like jelly, and then she opened her mouth to speak, but no words came.

The policeman rose quickly from the edge of the bed, a fierce look of concern on his face. "What's wrong?" he said. "I've never seen you look like that!

You didn't even look that scared on the night I picked you up when you were running away from Spellbinder Hall. Are you okay? Do you need to sit down?"

Millie vividly remembered the night he was talking about. She'd just discovered she was a witch, and the way the news had been broken had terrified her. She'd burst from Henry's study and ran from the hall as fast and as far as she could, until Sergeant Spencer had found her in a country lane and made her feel safe again.

That night had been scary, but the feelings of fear she'd known all those months ago paled into insignificance when compared to how she felt right now.

She shook her head, the words catching in her throat as she spoke, her chest muscles tight. "No," she said. "I don't need to sit down, but I'd like you to sit down again."

"Millie," said Sergeant Spencer, still standing. "What is it? What's wrong? Tell me. Did something happen when you tried to read my mind? Were you lying when you said that you couldn't read my thoughts?" He tapped his head with a big finger. "Did you find something bad? Something awful in my head? A thought that scared you? Is that what happened?"

Her legs unsteady below her, Millie gripped the hem of her shirt. "No," she said. "I was telling the truth — I couldn't read your mind. There was a wall between us, a wall that my powers couldn't penetrate."

Sitting down and leaning forward on the edge of the bed, Sergeant Spencer gave Millie a kind smile. "Is that what you're scared of?" he asked, "the fact that you couldn't read my mind? Are you scared because you think you're losing your mind-reading powers? Are you scared that you're losing your ability?"

"No, that's not it," said Millie. She gulped, the very atoms that held her body together feeling as if they were coming apart, giving her the uneasy sensation of floating above her own body. She took a deep breath through her nose and gripped her hem tighter. She looked at the man on the bed. *Her father*. She repeated it in her mind. *Her father*. A tear bulged in her eye before winding a warm route down her cheek, quickly followed by another, and then another.

"Millie!" said Sergeant Spencer, springing to his feet. "Are you okay? What is it? Please tell me."

Millie took a stumbling step backwards, her breath leaving her in ragged gasps as she sobbed. "I didn't think it would be this hard!" she said. "I thought it would be easy to tell you! I even began to think you'd be happy, but then I heard what you told George, and I couldn't tell you. Then you were put into stasis by the spell, and I promised myself that I'd tell you as soon as you woke up, but I can't! I don't know what words to say!"

"Millie," said Sergeant Spencer. "Let me help you. Tell me what's wrong!"

Not used to losing control, Millie took another

step backwards as Sergeant Spencer stood up and approached her. She put a hand up. "No," she said. "Please don't come any closer. Please sit down again."

Sergeant Spencer gave a deep sigh and stepped away from Millie. He lowered himself onto the bed, his face a muddled mix of bewilderment and deep concern. "What is it?" he said, his voice almost a whisper. "Please tell me. What is it you want to tell me? What did I say to George? Tell me, Millie — please."

Millie wiped the back of a hand across her face, smearing tears across her lips. She tasted salt, and then she sobbed again. She felt degraded, as if she had no control, as if she was one of the weak women portrayed in films — the type of woman who couldn't control her emotions. She knew nothing could be further from the truth, but she couldn't prevent herself from emitting another long, ragged gasp as fresh tears replaced the ones she'd wiped away.

Through blurred vision, she looked at the man on the bed, and then she understood why she had no control over herself. Sergeant Spencer was sitting right there, and yet, he was absent. He was there as the man who'd been nothing but kind to her since she'd arrived in Spellbinder Bay, but he wasn't there as her father, and Millie was as sure as she could be, that when she told him the news, he would no longer be there as either.

It would be just like he'd explained to George. Of course he wouldn't be able to deal with the news that he had another daughter! He already had a daughter! A daughter who may have been adopted, but meant as much as any daughter born of blood would mean to him. When Millie told him that she was his real daughter, his immediate thoughts were going to be with Judith — the person he'd known for three decades, and how she would cope with the news — not with the feelings of a woman he'd known for less than a year.

Millie had gone her whole life without a father — who was she to come barging into the life of a man and his daughter, disrupting their relationship, and expecting Sergeant Spencer to be as happy as she'd been when she discovered there was a man in the world that one day might walk her down the aisle. Of course he wasn't going to be as happy.

"Millie," said Sergeant Spencer, his eyes as kind as ever. "Tell me what you have to say. I can help you. Nothing is ever as bad as you imagine it's going to be."

Covering her eyes with a shaking hand, Millie nodded. She turned on the spot slowly, until she was facing the wall lined with oil portraits of people she didn't know, instead of facing the man she wished she'd known for her whole life. "I can't look at you when I tell you," she said.

Sergeant Spencer's voice sounded kind as he answered, and Millie wondered if he'd sound so kind when she dropped her bombshell. "That's fine," he said. "Just tell me what you need to say."

Pondering the portrait of an elderly woman dressed in Victorian clothing, staring back at her from the wall, Millie licked tears from her lips. The woman's expression was stern, but kind, and the artist had captured a fierce determination in her eyes which seemed to cross the centuries, urging Millie on. *Tell him*, Millie imagined the woman saying. *Be courageous. Tell him.*

Millie gave the portrait a smile and a curt nod. She closed her eyes so tight that she forced a flood of hot tears from them. "You're…" she began, her hands held by her sides in tight fists, her nails digging into her palms. "I'm your…"

"What?" whispered Sergeant Spencer. "I'm what? You're my what?"

Picturing her mother's smiling face, Millie put her chin on her chest and took three slow breaths. She spoke slowly, her voice monotone and low. "You're my father," she said, the words alien to her. Words she'd never spoken before. Words she'd never had the opportunity to speak before. "You're my father, and I'm your daughter."

She sobbed, the total silence behind her verifying her fears. He didn't care. She didn't think she could force herself to turn around and face the disappointment and fear which would be scrawled across Sergeant Spencer's face. Her father's face. "I didn't know how to tell —"

The hand which fell on Millie's shoulder shocked her, and as it applied pressure to her, spinning her on the spot, the big fingers hurt her flesh. But as her father pulled her into his broad chest, his arms enveloping her and his smell filling her nostrils, all the pain left her, and her tears spilt onto the blood-stained, white police shirt he wore.

She let her emotions go, releasing everything she'd stored up so tightly for so long. Wrapping her arms around her father, she cried louder when she felt his lips on her head, kissing her.

"I see it now," said her father, his voice spiked with emotion. "I understand everything. It all makes sense… why you look so much like her. Why she left Spellbinder Bay all those years ago without even a goodbye. You're Josephine's daughter. You're mine and Josephine's daughter." His body suddenly tensing, her father gave a low sigh. "Oh no. Your mother's dead. That means Josephine's dead."

Tilting her head, Millie gazed up at her father. "I can explain why she left without telling you. I was given a letter by Henry… from my mother. It was written on her death bed, it —"

Not allowing her to finish, her father hugged her tighter. "No. I don't want that conversation right now. We can talk about your mother later," he said. "If you don't mind."

Millie shook her head, smiling up at her father, both sad and happy that he was crying with her. "I don't mind," she said,

"Good," he said. "This moment is meant for just

the two of us. Father and daughter. We've been apart for so long, Millie."

"Yes," said Millie, closing her eyes. "We have."

As Millie settled into her father's warm hug, she heard a gentle voice from beside her. "Millie, David, do you mind if I interrupt?"

Opening her eyes to see the smiling face of her mother, Millie placed a calming hand on her father's chest as he jumped in fright and stared in shock at the woman who stood beside Millie, smiling at him. "It's okay," Millie said. "Mum can travel between worlds, now."

"Josephine," said Millie's dad, a tear on his cheek and a shaky hand reaching for the mother of his daughter. His hand passed straight through her form-less wrist, and he sighed. "I'm sorry you died so young."

"And I'm sorry I never told you about Millie," answered Millie's mother. "I'm so very sorry, David. I had my reasons."

"Please don't," said Millie. "Please save this conversation for when I'm not around. This is the first time I've ever been in a room with both of my parents, and I don't want it to be about regrets. I want it to be about hope."

"Of course," said her mother. "I understand. I came here with good news, though, Millie. Reuben is back. He's perfectly well and is back in the body of the cockatiel. He's with George, they seem to get on really well together."

"Reuben is nothing if not fickle," smiled Millie. She looked up at her father. "I'd better do it," she said. "I'd better read your mind and report to Henry. We still need to save your memories."

"And I need to find Judith," said her father. "I need to explain what's happened." He put out a hand and cupped Millie's face. "Everything that's happened."

"I can help you, David," said Josephine. "If you like. I can tell her why I kept Millie a secret from you."

"Yes," said Millie's father. "That might be a good idea."

"Are you ready, Sergeant —" began Millie. She returned her father's smile. "Are you ready, Dad?"

Her dad smiled. "Yes," he said. "Read my mind."

Chapter 43

*A*s Millie answered Henry's question, the orb vibrated in her hand. "I read David Spencer's mind, and I can verify that he is telling the truth when he says he did not kill Trevor Giles," she stated, confidently.

As the orb glowed blue, Henry smiled. "That's it, Millie," he said. "Now we wait for a moment or two. I'll feel it if it's worked."

A moment or two seemed like an hour, and Millie gnawed the inside of her cheek as she studied Henry's face. Then Henry smiled, and then he lifted his hand, offering a high five. He automatically dropped it, his face flushed, and reached for the pocket watch on the end of the chain tucked into his breast pocket. "Never tell anybody I did that, Miss Thorn," he said. "I was relieved that Sergeant Spencer was saved. I have a soft spot for the man."

Millie crossed her heart. "I promise I won't say a word," she said.

"And how did it go?" asked Henry. "I would imagine he was overjoyed to find out that he's the father of such a wonderful young lady?"

Managing to fight back tears, Millie smiled at the kindly old man. "It's early days yet, Henry. I had to rush off soon after telling him, so that you could perform the stone of integrity test on me."

"Then I imagine you'll want to get back to him," said Henry. "Why don't you go and tell him that it worked. Tell him his memories are saved." He gave Millie a smile. "Both the memories he's already made, and the wonderful ones he's going to create."

"No," said Millie. "He's explaining things to Judith. You tell him, Henry. I don't want to interfere. It's going to be a shock for Judith. I think they'll need some time without me around them."

"You're a thoughtful young lady," said Henry. "And, anyway, we still have work to do. Trevor Giles's murderer is still on the loose. Why don't you take Timothy or George and bring me the suspects you named. The stone of integrity will discover the killer if he or she is among them."

"I don't think the killer is among them," said Millie. "But I think I know who the killer is, and if I'm right, it's all been an awful tragedy."

"Then go, Millie," said Henry. "Your hunches have already proved correct twice since you've lived among us. If you're correct again, you'll have solved three murders in one year, Miss Thorn."

ACCEPTING A LIFT FROM TIMOTHY, MILLIE FOUND HER car where she'd left it at the side of the road, when she'd leapt on the back of George's motorbike.

As Timothy prepared to drive away, Millie gestured at him to roll down his window. "Remember everything I told you," she said.

"Yes, yes," said Timothy. "I'll go to the police station and carry out the test. And if you telephone me and tell me your suspicions are correct, I'll tell Fredrick and Edna what you've discovered, and then arrange a meeting with Henry."

"Yes," said Millie. "Because if I'm correct, some difficult decisions will have to be made."

As the sound of Timothy's car faded into the distance, Millie climbed into her Triumph and turned the key in the ignition. The engine roared into life, and as she drove, she prepared to ask some difficult questions.

She ran over what Charlotte Timkins had told her once more in her mind, and when she arrived at number twenty-four Briar Avenue, she took a deep breath before walking slowly along the driveway and ringing the doorbell.

Victoria answered, and gave Millie a warm smile. "Hello, Miss Thorn. I hope you got my note? I'm not sure that I should have trusted your familiar to deliver it to you."

"Yes," Millie said. "I got the note, and you were right, I needed to cross to my mother's dimension to enable her to travel here again. It worked."

"My, my," said Victoria. "You didn't waste any time! How on earth did you figure out how to travel to the realm of dead witches? I must admit, I thought it would be an impossibility."

"It's a long story," said Millie.

"Is that why you're here?" asked Victoria. "To tell me about it?"

"No," said Millie. "I'm afraid not, Victoria. Can I come in, please? I need to speak with you about Trevor Giles's death."

WHEN MILLIE LEFT THE HOUSE HALF AN HOUR LATER, Victoria remained on the doorstep as Millie drove away, her eyes so red that Millie could still tell she'd been crying as she gave her a wave from the bottom of the driveway.

When Victoria closed the door behind her, Millie dialled Timothy's number, and when he answered, she spoke with regret. "I was right," she said. "Tell Edna and Fredrick, and tell Henry we need to speak to him. Urgently."

As Millie, Edna, Timothy and Fredrick each took a seat in front of the large, polished desk, Henry peered at them over the rims of his round spectacles. "You have the answers?" he said. "To the mystery of what happened to Trevor Giles?"

"Miss Thorn discovered the answer," said Fredrick. "She's a credit to the school and a credit to the paranormal community in general."

"Indeed," added Edna. "I've known a lot of witches in my time. Miss Thorn is one of the best."

"Quite," said Henry. "Miss Thorn has done a lot for our community since she arrived in this little town, and if she's solved yet another murder, this will make it her third." He gave Millie a warm smile. "Your father will be very proud of you," he said.

Taken aback, Millie nodded slowly. It was the first time her relationship with her father had been spoken about so candidly, and the hairs on her arms stood on end as she reminded herself yet again that she had a family. She belonged. "I hope so," was all she could think to say.

"Oh, he will be," said Henry, pushing his glasses higher up his nose. "Sergeant Spencer is a lucky man to have you as his daughter. Now, if you'll begin, Miss Thorn. Please fill me in on what has happened. Who murdered Trevor Giles, and why?"

"Wait one moment," said Timothy, turning in his seat to look at Millie. "Sergeant Spencer is your father?"

"Later, Timothy," said Henry. "I'm sure you'll all

be made aware of Millie's wonderful news in due course. For now, we focus on Trevor's murder."

"For a start, it wasn't murder," said Millie. "It was an accident stemming from an act of love."

"Hence the reason I found traces of love in the poison," said Edna.

Timothy cleared his throat. "Choose your words carefully, Edna," he said. "We now know it wasn't poison at all."

"Not poison?" said Henry.

"No," said Millie. "It was a potion, made by a young witch. A young witch who was desperate to make sure nothing terrible happened to her mother."

"And what a sad tale it is," said Fredrick, solemnly. "For Trevor Giles, and the young witch and her mother."

"Who is the young witch?" asked Henry.

Mille took a slow breath. "It's Emma," she said. "Emma Taylor."

Henry took a few seconds to process the information, and then he sat back in his seat, took his glasses off, and began rubbing the lenses on the sleeve of his jacket. "I see," he said. "So when you said the witch was young, you meant young. Have you spoken to her? How did you find out it was her?"

"Yes," said Millie, "I've spoken with her. It was something that Charlotte Timkins told me which made me think. She told me that she's been watching my class from the shadows. She saw Emma do something which triggered my suspicions."

"And Emma has confessed to it?" asked Henry.

"I haven't told Emma what has happened," said Millie. "I asked her some questions without revealing why I was asking them, and it's apparent that it was a potion which she made that killed Trevor. At the moment, she doesn't know her potion killed a man, and I'm hoping we can keep it that way. Her grandmother knows, and that's the way I'd like to keep it."

Henry stared at Millie, and then nodded. "We will make a decision when we've heard the story. So, tell me, Miss Thorn, what happened? How did a potion made by one of our pupils kill Trevor Giles?"

"It's so simple that it made Trevor's death seem complicated," explained Millie. "Last year, Emma's mother attempted to do something unfortunate. She attempted to take her own life. She tried to drown herself in the duck pond opposite the house she lives in."

"She did?" said Henry, sorrow in his eyes. "The poor woman. I had no idea."

"None of us did," said Edna. "She never spoke to anybody outside her family about how she was feeling."

"She could have approached me," said Henry. "I would have listened."

"No," said Millie. "No, she couldn't have spoken to anybody here at the school. It was because of school that she began feeling depressed."

"Why?" asked Henry, gently.

"Because she was bullied here as a child," said

Millie. "By Trevor Giles. The things he said to her when she was a young girl shaped the rest of her life. She's never really recovered. She became anxious and depressed. Her whole life was affected by it."

"I'm sorry to hear that," said Henry. "The poor woman."

"And then last year it came to a head," continued Millie. "Her marriage had split up, and things must have just become too hard for her to bear, so she walked into the duck pond. At night-time. Beneath a full moon."

"What happened?" asked Henry. "Did she change her mind? Did somebody see her and save her life?"

"Emma saw her," said Millie, flatly. "From her bedroom window. She couldn't sleep, so was watching the moon. She practices moon-magic, you see, and enjoyed studying the night sky."

Henry nodded. "I see."

"Thanks to the brightness of the moon," said Millie, "Emma was able to see her mother stepping into the pond. She ran across the road and was able to save her mother's life. She jumped into the water and guided her mother back to the shore."

"What an awful thing for a girl so young to have to experience," said Henry.

"And she never wanted to experience it again," said Millie. "So she began researching ways to help her mother's anxiety and depression."

"Go on," said Henry.

"She began making potions," said Millie. "Simple

potions, using herbs with properties known to treat symptoms of depression and anxiety. Herbs she took from Timothy's chemistry laboratory."

"Valerian root. Lavender. Herbs such as those," added Timothy. "I never noticed they were going missing."

"Emma made potions which she added to the food her mother ate," continued Millie. "But she didn't just use herbs. She used magic, too."

"The potions the young girl made were simple," said Edna. "Yet remarkably well thought out."

"In what way?" asked Henry.

"Emma added a trigger to them," explained Millie. "The ingredients would work without the trigger, the herbs lifting Emma's mother's spirits a little, but it was when her mother was exposed to moonlight that the magic really happened. Emma had surmised that should her mother attempt to take her life again, she would do it at night-time when everybody else was asleep, and probably using the same method she'd already attempted — drowning herself in the pond."

"I see," said Henry. "So young Emma added a trigger which moonlight would activate."

Millie nodded. "If her mother stepped out of the house at night, even the faintest glimmer of moonlight would trigger the potion's full potential, cheering her up, and hopefully saving her life."

"Emma added another backup, too," said Edna. "She used a little water magic which would boost the potion further."

"In case her mother made it as far as the pond," said Henry, placing his glasses back on his face.

"A clever young witch," said Edna.

"And it was a potion such as this which killed Trevor Giles?" Henry asked.

"Yes," said Millie. "It was a complete accident. A series of events occurred which nobody could have foreseen."

"Beginning with what?" said Henry.

"Beginning with my class baking cakes to sell on a stall at the school fete," said Millie. "They baked them the day before, and unknown to me, Emma made a special batch of muffins containing a little of a potion she'd made. Charlotte Timkins told me she'd observed similar behaviour from Emma throughout the term, so it wasn't the first time. Being an honest young lady, Emma didn't take them home with her that night, she waited until the next day, offered to help run the cake stall at the fete, and paid for the special batch of muffins she'd made. She put them in a box and separated them from the cakes for sale, ready to take them home with her."

"Yet somehow, one of these cakes found their way into Trevor Giles's mouth?" asked Henry.

"Yes," said Millie. "The other two girls who offered to help Emma on the cake stall got bored, so Emma's mother offered to help her. When Norman Giles arrived to buy some cakes for his stepfather, Beth Taylor insisted that Emma sold him the fresh muffins from the box behind the counter, instead of the cakes which were going hard under the sun. Beth didn't want Norman getting into any trouble with his stepfather — she'd already seen how nasty he'd been to Norman earlier that day. She insisted that Norman took the cakes that Emma had put aside for her."

"Beth Taylor would have had no idea the cakes contained a potion," added Edna.

"No. She was used to Emma making her cakes," said Millie. "It was how Emma got her mother to take the medicine she'd been making. And Emma wouldn't have been concerned about somebody apart from the intended recipient eating them," she continued. "She knew they wouldn't have harmed anybody — they'd only have made the person who ate them feel a little happier."

"Or a lot happier if exposed to moonlight," added Timothy.

"As was the case with Sergeant Spencer," said Fredrick. "When we left the police station after removing Trevor Giles's body from the cell, Sergeant Spencer acted very out of character. He appeared very chirpy for a man blaming himself for the death of a prisoner in his custody. We thought he was in shock."

"But it was the moon activating the trigger in a potion," said Millie. "Emma had told me earlier that day she'd given Sergeant —" She paused, her cheeks warming. "Given Dad two cakes from the box meant for her mother after he'd helped her pick up a box full of coins she'd dropped at the cake stall. She gave him them to thank him for his help, and even commented on how much he'd enjoyed them. Emma was amused, and proud, that he'd enjoyed them so much he'd licked his fingers clean of any traces of melted chocolate."

"Which is why I smelled what we thought was poison on the Sergeant's hands," said Timothy. "His fingers were covered in traces of the potion, which wouldn't have been removed by simply washing his hands."

"So why did this harmless potion prove fatal to Trevor Giles?" asked Henry. "Was it more powerful than Emma anticipated? Did Trevor consume too much of it?"

"No," said Timothy. "It was because Trevor was a werewolf. A werewolf weakened by alcohol and the fact that he'd changed into a wolf earlier in the day, and had been involved in a fight with me at the school fete."

"Yes," said Henry, with a frown. "I was disappointed to hear that you'd fought in front of children, Timothy, but I realise it was for a valid reason. I'm told that Trevor changed first and was threatening violence."

"Timothy subdued Trevor," explained Fredrick. "Trevor was drunk and argumentative. He transformed into his wolf to attack me. Timothy intervened."

"The fight was understandable then," said Henry, offering Timothy a smile. "You were protecting people. I'd have expected nothing less from you, Mister Huggins."

Timothy bowed his head. "I was just doing my duty, but the fight left Trevor in a weakened state, and combined with the alcohol in his system he was very vulnerable."

"Vulnerable to a supposedly harmless potion?" asked Henry.

"There was one ingredient in the potion that can prove a problem to werewolves when taken in large enough doses," said Timothy. "Saint Johns's Wort."

"But it doesn't kill them," said Henry. "It simply makes werewolves feel a little unwell for a short period of time, doesn't it? I'd never have allowed it to be stored in your laboratory if I thought it was a hazard to werewolf children."

"Normally it would be of no great danger to a wolf," said Timothy. "But what happened to Trevor was different. He was weak from his transformation and fight with me when Sergeant Spencer arrested him, and the alcohol prevented him from regaining his strength as quickly as he should have. That wasn't the only problem, though. A wolf requires moonlight to recharge his or her powers fully, and Trevor was locked in a cell with only a small window constructed from thick security glass."

"So Trevor was exposed to no moonlight which would begin his healing process," said Henry.

"That's right," said Timothy. "Until just past nine o'clock, when the moon was at the correct angle in the sky to allow a tiny sliver of light through the window and into the cell. I went back to the cell earlier, at Millie's request, and did some calculations. Trevor Giles had died on the very spot that would have been in the path of the smallest amount of moonlight. Trevor was killed by the very thing that should have helped him."

"How?" asked Henry.

"When the moonlight touched his skin, the trigger in the potion was activated," said Timothy. "Trevor had eaten the cakes which Norman had bought for him from the stall earlier that day, so there was plenty of the potion in his system. The Saint John's Wort within the potion was imbued with magic and began making Trevor unwell. The potion only required the tiniest amount of moonlight to activate it, but unfortunately for Trevor, instead of cheering him up, it killed him.

"Had the window been made of thinner glass, or had he been outside, he would have survived, but the minimal moonlight making it into the cell was not enough to begin the wolf healing process. It was too late for him — the Saint John's Wort had worked faster than the moonlight could work to heal him. His wolf energy sensed he was dying and left his body, and then it was over. He died within seconds."

"And Sergeant Spencer wrongly thought he'd caused his death by feeding him a poisoned meal," said Fredrick.

"Yes," said Millie. "He served Trevor his meal at

almost precisely the same time that the moon had risen enough to allow a sliver of light into the cell. When he closed the door and Trevor began choking, and then died, he thought it was poison in the meal he'd served him, but really it was a potion already inside Trevor which had just been activated."

"And then when Sergeant Spencer opened the cell door, Trevor was dead on the floor with his wolf energy leaving his mouth in the form of a blue foam," said Timothy.

"And before the potion had activated, Trevor was able to swallow the bite sized muffin that Dad had served him," said Millie.

"It's understandable, then, why he blamed himself," said Henry. "He opened the cell door to find a man foaming at the mouth after eating a muffin he had served him."

"Yes," said Millie. "It seemed obvious to him that it had been his fault."

"And unfortunately for him, a few bad apples from the werewolf community found out that he was somehow implicated in the so-called murder of Trevor Giles," observed Henry. "Leading to the almost catastrophic chain of events which could quite easily have led to two young witches losing their father, and our town losing a good man."

"Yes," said Millie, quietly.

Henry sighed. "You all did marvellously well in my absence," he said. He turned his face to Millie and removed his glasses. "And you, young lady, showed remarkably bravery, along with your familiar, when you stepped through the gateway into The Chaos. You should be proud of yourself."

"No," said Millie. "I did what anyone would have done. I was trying to save my father." She smiled at Henry. "Family is everything. Family comes first."

"Yes," said Henry. "It is, Millie, and I have no appetite for destroying any family. I suggest that Emma Taylor is never told of the devastating effects her potion had on another person. She would never forgive herself. She must be warned about adding potions to people's food, though. That is a dangerous practice. If her mother requires medical help, then we will reach out to her and offer her the support she needs. Emma should not be burdened with such worries at such a young age."

"Of course," said Millie. "I'll speak with Emma."

"And I'll speak with Helen Giles," said Timothy. "She'll need to be informed of what happened to her husband. I'm quite sure she won't want Emma punished, though. She's a good woman at heart."

"And, Fredrick, make sure she is financially compensated," said Henry. "Money won't make up for the loss of her husband, but it will enable her to bring Norman up in a better way than he's been accustomed to so far in his young life."

"I will," said Fredrick.

Henry nodded. "You did well in my absence, Fredrick," he said. "You dealt with very challenging circumstances and did the best you could. Thank you.

If Miss Timkins ever gets fed up of the job she was supposed to begin thirty years ago, then it shall be yours."

"I appreciate the kind words," said Fredrick.

"What about the werewolves in the dungeons?" asked Timothy. "What shall I tell their families?"

"And Mister Dickinson," added Edna. "What will happen to that awful man?"

"Mister Dickinson will not be bothering us again," said Henry. "He is under lock and key, and Ammon plans to put him on trial very soon. If he's found guilty, he'll be sent to The Chaos. A man with his powers will survive in such a harsh world, but it will not be an easy, or pleasant, existence."

"And the werewolves?" said Millie.

"They are already regretting their actions," said Henry. "I'm sure that a period of time in the dungeons will remind them that violence is not acceptable in a civilised community. It is lucky for them that they did not kill anybody, or they would have found themselves sharing a harsh world with Mister Dickinson."

Edna let out a long sigh. "Phew," she said. "So life is back to normal?"

"Yes, Mrs Brockett," Henry said with a smile. "Life is back to normal." He looked at Millie. "But not for you, Miss Thorn. For you, life is going to be very different."

Chapter 44

*M*illie peered through the glass pane in the classroom door. Emma was busy at the far end of the room, tidying up spilt raisins and chocolate chips. A liberal dusting of flour covered the front of her apron and her face, and a welcoming aroma of baking cakes seeped past the door and into the corridor.

Millie smiled. The young witch looked content.

A soft breeze blew across Millie's face, and the hairs on her forearms stood on end as the temperature around her dropped suddenly. Still not as comfortable as she would like to be around ghosts, she turned her head slowly to the right, aware of a presence next to her. The tall woman gave her a reassuring smile. "You don't like ghosts?" she asked. "Do you?"

"It's not that I don't like ghosts," protested Millie. "It's just that I don't like being surprised — and having an apparition suddenly appearing in front of you, is the essence of surprise."

Charlotte gave a soft laugh. "I was the same once," she admitted, her eyes on Emma as she washed a mixing bowl at the sink. "I was scared of ghosts. Spellbinder Hall used to terrify me. Cuthbert used to laugh at me; he used to tell me that one day I'd be a ghost, too." She gave a deep sigh, and the air in the corridor became colder. "I never thought I'd be such a young ghost, though. I thought I'd live a long life, but it wasn't to be."

Moving slowly, Millie reached for Miss Timkins's hand, her fingers passing straight through the ghost's elegant wrist. "I'm sorry," she said. "I'm sorry about what happened to you, and I'm sorry about suggesting that you might have had anything to do with what happened to Trevor Giles."

"There's no need for you to be sorry," said Miss Timkins. "I understand why you may have thought I was responsible for his death, and as for what happened to me, well, I'm here again, aren't I? Doing what I always loved to do — watching enthusiastic children learn how to cook. Especially one like Emma who comes into school during the holidays to cook. It makes me so happy to watch them learn."

Looking up at the tall woman, Millie frowned. "I've had a thought, Charlotte. Why don't you teach cookery again?"

Charlotte's narrow face broke into a shy grin, and her eyes twinkled as she took in what Millie had said.

"Really?" she asked. "That would be wonderful. I could be an assistant to you! I'd love nothing more!"

"Actually," said Millie. "I thought it would be the other way round. I'm only a part-time teacher, anyway, and I'm sure you're a far better cookery teacher than I'll ever be. Perhaps you should become the full-time cookery teacher here at the hall, and if you ever need any help, I'll be your assistant. It's your decision, of course — you are the headmistress."

"I'd like nothing more, Millie!" beamed Charlotte. "Thank you!"

As footsteps bounced off the walls of the corridor, Charlotte turned to face the approaching man. "He's going to be so excited when I tell him I'm the cookery teacher," she said. "He'll like nothing more than eating his lunch as we look out of the classroom window together."

"How is he doing?" asked Millie, in a low voice.

"It's been over a week since he ate the soufflé," said Charlotte. "And it was only yesterday that he fully recovered. But he's fine. It worked."

"Ah! Miss Thorn," said Cuthbert, as he approached. "It's wonderful to see you now I can remember your name! I do believe an apology is in order, though — my daughter has informed me that I've been most rude to you on occasion."

Millie smiled. "No apology is necessary, Cuthbert," she said. "And I'm over the moon for you. It must be such a relief to be rid of that metaphorettes."

"Oh, goodness gracious, yes!" said Cuthbert. "I feel like a mouse who's gained a new hat!"

"Pardon?" said Millie, giving Charlotte a sideways glance.

Cuthbert broke into a bellowing laugh. "I'm joking, young lady! My brain is fully operational again, thanks to Charlotte's wonderful soufflé."

"I'm glad to hear that," said Millie.

The classroom door swung open, and Emma smiled up at them, a paper bag in her hand. "I've cleaned up after myself, Miss Thorn and Miss Timkins." She gazed at Cuthbert. "And Mister..."

"Mister Cuthbert Campion," replied Cuthbert. "I was once an English and Chemistry teacher here at Spellbinder Hall. A long time ago."

"Are you ready, Emma?" asked Millie.

"Yes, Miss," said Emma. "And thank you for offering me a lift home, although I don't mind walking."

"It's my pleasure," said Millie. She held the classroom door open for Charlotte and Cuthbert and said her goodbyes, before putting a hand on Emma's shoulder as she walked alongside her. "And what we spoke about?" said Millie.

Emma lifted the paper bag. "Only chocolate, Miss. No potions. It's like you said — it's not nice to trick people into eating things they might not want to. I'll never do it again. Anyway, chocolate cheers Mum up without needing to add a potion!"

"Good," said Millie. "And your mother? How is she?"

"She's doing great!" said Emma. "It's only been a week since Nan made her speak to somebody who could help her, and she's much better already. She's taking me to the cinema tonight! It's the first time we've been in years, but Mum wants to get out more."

"That's wonderful!" said Millie.

"What about you, Miss?" asked Emma. "It's Friday today. Have you got plans for tonight?"

"Yes," said Millie. "I have. I'm going out for a meal. With my father and my sister."

GEORGE'S MOTORBIKE WAS PARKED OUTSIDE HER cottage when she got home, and as she opened the red front door, the sound of laughing voices greeted her.

"No way!" said George.

"Way!" replied Reuben. "He was as tall as ten houses and had at least fifty-four legs! He posed no problem for me, though. He'd threatened my witch! Nobody threatens my witch. I lost the plot, George! I lost my temper and battered that demon all over the chaos!"

"You're the man, Reuben!" said George, tossing the cockatiel a peanut, before lobbing one in the air and catching it in his mouth. "It's a shame you fell over and injured yourself, after you'd found the secret cave with the gates in, and dragged Millie to safety, though."

"Yeah, but I'm fine, man. I'm fine," said Reuben.

"Hello boys," said Millie, closing the door behind her. "Having fun? I heard you telling George the story of your epic adventure, Reuben. You made it sound... amazing."

Reuben hopped along the back of the sofa, dodging George's hand and pistachio nut shells. He launched himself into the air and landed on Millie's shoulder. "Please don't tell him the truth," he whispered. "He's so cool."

"The truth is," said Millie. "That you're a hero, Reuben, and you can tell that tale anyway you like." She pointed at George's legs. "Feet off the sofa, George. Please."

"Sorry," said George, adjusting his seating position. "I hope you don't mind me being here. I came to ask you something, and Reuben invited me in for a while. We've had fun."

Scanning the mess of nut shells and chocolate bar wrappers covering the sofa, Millie nodded. "I can see that," she said.

"I'll clean that up," said George, scrambling to his feet.

"No, leave it," said Millie. "It's fine. What is it you wanted to ask me, George?"

George looked at Reuben. "Would you give us a minute?"

"Of course," said Reuben, flying from Millie's

shoulder, and out of the open roof window. "You two sort things out, you make the perfect couple."

Millie rolled her eyes at Reuben's feathery back, and smiled at George. "So, what is it?"

"I need to talk to you, Millie," said George, approaching her. "I want to tell you about Emily. I want to tell you who she is, and where she came from, and I want to ask you if we still have a future together... you and me. I thought you could meet Emily. Tonight, at The Embarrassed Lobster. I've booked a table. It's steak night."

As light poured from the roof window and landed on George's face, highlighting his good looks, Millie sighed. George was impossibly good looking, funny, and even clever on occasions. He'd lied to her though, or at least hidden the truth, and Millie wouldn't stand for that, however good the reason George had to keep the truth from her was.

Then there was what Fredrick had told her. Of course it wouldn't work. Of course it would end in heartache. Millie would age and George wouldn't, how could that be a good thing?

She shook her head. "I'm sorry," she said. "I don't think we have a future, George, not romantically, anyway. And as for Emily, I know who she is. I heard you telling my father about her. I was in the corridor, and I heard it all. I think it's a sad story, George, and I think what you did for her was the right thing, and I'm glad she came to find you after all this time. You're a good man, and Emily is lucky to have you to guide her, but as for you and me?" She shook her head again. "I'm sorry."

George closed his eyes for a moment. "I understand," he said. "I've lived long enough to know when somebody has made up their mind." His face broke into a wide grin. "And I'll live for a lot longer yet, so when you've grown old and lonely, and live alone with fourteen cats and a herb garden, don't come looking for me. This cool cat will still be zipping around the countryside on his motorbike, with no time for rude old women!"

Millie laughed. She laughed hard, and when she'd finished laughing, she lifted herself onto tiptoes and kissed the vampire.

Blushing, George smiled. "What about the meal tonight? The table is booked. How about you meet Emily anyway?"

"I'm sorry," said Millie. "Dad and Judith are taking me out for a meal."

"Oh," said George. "Anywhere nice?"

Millie shrugged. "I don't know. They haven't told me yet."

Chapter 45

The Embarrassed Lobster throbbed with life. The orange glow in the windows acted as a welcoming invitation to passers-by, and upbeat music rolled from the open door, riding on the malty fumes of locally brewed beer.

Friendly voices rose from the beer garden alongside the pub, which offered an expansive view of the sea, its calm surface reflecting the moon, and Millie's nose twitched as she caught a whiff of the star of the night — juicy steak and battered onion rings.

As Millie entered the pub, she was almost knocked off her feet by Timothy as he exited, wiping his mouth with the back of his hand and appearing as if he was about to let out a mighty belch.

He gulped as he banged into Millie, swallowing any burp that may have been about to escape. "I'm sorry," he said.

"It was my fault," said Millie. "I wasn't looking where I was going."

Timothy shook his head. "No," he said. "You misunderstand me. I'm sorry, but you're two weeks late for our date. I invited you to steak night on the day of the school fete. I'm afraid I'm no longer interested."

"Timothy," said Millie. "You were so polite and respectable during the time you helped me solve Trevor's murder. Why have you reverted to this old Timothy? Why are you so brash again?"

Timothy smiled, and then gave a loud laugh. "This is who I am!" he said. "I'm Timothy Huggins! Biggest wolf in town, and if you'd please step out of my way, I have to be going. The night is young, and I've got a belly full of meat. Somewhere in Spell-binder Bay is a young lady craving the attention of a man like me, and I'm going to find her!"

"Okay," said Millie, stepping aside as Timothy passed. "Good luck to you, and good luck to the woman you're hunting."

Timothy nodded and hurried into the night, and then, just as Millie was stepping over the threshold of the pub, she heard her name being called. "Millie, wait!" said Timothy.

"What is it?" she said.

Timothy dragged his feet as he approached her, and then he looked at the floor. "I'm not going around the pubs looking for a woman," he said. "I wouldn't know what to do if I found one. I'm going home to play video games online. I'm not brash, Millie. Not really."

"Really?" said Millie.

Timothy nodded. "Really," he said. "I put an act on when I'm around women."

"Why?" asked Millie. "It won't work, it will push women away from you, not attract them."

"Then it is working," said Timothy.

Millie frowned. "Please explain that, Timothy."

"I want to push women away," said Timothy. "They intimidate me, and I know what I look like. I'm twenty-six, but I look like a teenager. I still get asked for identification in pubs. I'm overweight, and I have spots. What woman is ever going to want me? I became used to women rejecting me when I got close to them, so I decided never to let a woman get close to me." He gave a long sigh. "I make women hate me, Millie. On purpose."

"Timothy," said Millie. "That's the quickest route to never being happy. Those things you said about yourself are —"

"I know," said Timothy. "And I don't want your advice. I don't mean that disrespectfully, Millie, but I'll sort my own issues out eventually. I wanted you to know it's an act because I respect you. I don't want you to think badly of me. I think very highly of you."

Millie smiled at the werewolf, but as she was about to tell him that she respected him, too, he turned his back and hurried away. "I'll see you around!" he shouted.

"Next week?" shouted Millie. "Steak night?"

"Maybe!" yelled Timothy, bathed in a soft glow as he hurried beneath a streetlamp. "I'll need to check my diary!"

Shaking her head, a smile on her lips, Millie strolled into the pub. Seated near the window was a woman with her back to the door. With long blonde hair and painted nails which clicked on the wine glass she held, she laughed as George made a joke.

When George spotted Millie, he waved at her. "Millie," he said. "Can I get you a drink?"

"No, thank you," said Millie. "Dad and Judith are waiting for me in the restaurant."

Standing up, George put his pint glass down and gestured at Emily to turn around. "Emily," he said, as she turned in her seat, her face happy. "This is Millie." He smiled at Millie. "Millie, this is Emily, she knows that you're aware of her story."

Ambushed, Millie shrugged and approached the table, taking the hand which Emily extended in greeting. "Hello, Emily," she said.

"Millie," said Emily, her words spoken delicately. "How wonderful to finally meet you. I've heard so much about you."

"And I've heard a lot about you," said Millie.

"I'm so sorry I stepped on your toes when I arrived in Spellbinder Bay," said Emily. "I was confused and unhappy. I needed sanctuary, and George gave it to me. He kept me away from people, like I'd asked him to. I realise that perhaps I was selfish. I had no right to come between you two."

Unable to hold any malice toward a woman who'd been through so much, Millie gave her a reassuring smile. "No," she said. "You don't need to apologise, Emily. I can only imagine how hard things were for you. You needed George. You needed a family."

"Yes," said Emily, her eyes a soft brown beneath emerald eyeshadow. "We all need family, and George told me you'd found yours too. That's so wonderful!"

"Thank you," said Millie. "And I must be going. They're waiting for me."

"Enjoy your evening," said Emily.

"You, too," said Millie. She smiled at George. "And you."

As she walked away from the table, she took a deep breath. It was still proving to be nerve-wracking when she intruded on her father and Judith, but it was becoming more natural, and anyway, Judith had accepted her as the sister she'd always wanted, never once showing any jealousy or animosity towards her.

The restaurant door creaked as she stepped from the bar, and into the room which smelled delicious. A waiter rushed past her with a tray heavy with meat, and a family laughed as they joked together.

And then Millie saw her family seated at a circular table in a corner, both of them smiling at her, and her sister waving.

"Millie," said her father, getting to his feet, his smile wide and happy. "You look beautiful!"

"Thank you," said Millie, settling into the hug her father offered.

Lowering herself into the seat her father pulled out for her, Millie smiled at Judith as she filled a glass with red wine.

"Dad chose the wine," said Judith, a fake grimace on her face. "So don't blame me."

Millie lifted the glass to her nose. She took a long theatrical sniff, and screwed up her nostrils. "I'm getting vinegar and old socks," she laughed.

"Oi, you two," said her dad, his eyes twinkling. "Don't gang up on your father! And there's nothing wrong with the wine. It's the house special."

"I'm sure it will taste just fine," said Millie. "After three glasses."

"If you don't want it, don't drink it," laughed the big man. "It means more for me."

Millie sipped her drink and smiled. "It tastes, fine, Dad."

"That still sounds weird," said Judith. "You calling him Dad, but it sounds so right, too."

Their father smiled. "And it feels nice," he said. He lifted his glass and held it toward the centre of the table. "A toast," he said. "To the two most wonderful girls in the world. The girls who I'm honoured to call my daughters, and the girls who I will do anything for. I love you both, and I want you both to know that I'm here for you, at any time, and for anything." He lifted his glass higher. "To family."

"To family," said Millie, blinking away tears as she clinked glasses and sipped her wine.

"Are you okay, sis?" said Judith, taking Millie's hand in hers. "Don't cry. You'll get red eyes."

"That doesn't matter," said Sergeant Spencer, taking an envelope from his inside pocket. "I have something for you two that will get rid of puffiness under your eyes." He placed the envelope on the table. "I won them at the raffle. Two tickets for a day of pampering at the Golden Sands Spa and Restaurant. I thought it was the perfect place for two sisters to go for their first day out together as siblings."

As more tears filled Millie's eyes, and she squeezed Judith's hand, she glanced to her right as movement in a dark corner caught her eye. She smiled at the woman with long brown hair and a slight bend in her nose, and she let out a sob as her mother's voice reached her, only perceptible to her ears. "I love you, Millie, and I'm so proud of you."

Millie nodded, sobbing with happiness as her father wiped a tear from below her eye with a thumb. "I'm sorry," she said. "I'm trying not to cry."

Her father shook his head. "You cry for as long as you like, and when you've finished, we'll be here for you when you want to cry again. We'll always be here for you. We're family."

The End

About the Author

Sam Short loves witches, goats, and narrowboats. He really enjoys writing fiction that makes him laugh — in the hope it will make others laugh, too!
You can find him at the places listed below — he'd love to see you there!

www.samshortauthor.com
email — sam@samshortauthor.com

Also by Sam Short

The Water Witch Cozy Mystery Series - listed in reading order below.

Under Lock And Key

Four And Twenty Blackbirds

An Eye For An Eye

A Meeting Of Minds

The Spellbinder Bay Series - listed in reading order below.

Witch Way to Spellbinder Bay

Broomsticks and Bones

Spells And Cells